THE
SCROLLS
OF SIN

THE
SCROLLS
OF SIN

A COLLECTION OF TALES

DAVID ROSE

RELATED WORKS

Amden Bog: A Novel in Stories

CONTENTS

BLACK MAGIC SUMMER

"My neck had been killing me all bleak buzzard day. Wet
feet, my hands filthy, my ring mail pushed my boots down
further, further into hot, loose mud. There in a high window
I saw a pretty girl. How she waved and blew her kisses.
Watched as we marched off. Off to war. To die under the
foul Ordrid's blades and a black banner. Cut and hacked,
sliced to gobs, like thieves having spread open watched-upon
doors, rather than the legs of her; lithe, cool and welcome."

—Testimony of a peasant, one who lived

"You!" Umbort Ouvarnia spat in the face of his interrogator.
"Ordrid scum! Gods curse the world—twins, no less. You two look
like the frogs that jump around in my fountain." The nobleman
twisted helplessly in the ropes that hung him upside down. "How
many gardens do you have," he said, summoning his strength.
"*Hmm?* In this foul coffin of a keep?"

Having been bitten, punched, and flung down a flight of
unforgiving stairs, Umbort Ouvarnia's head now throbbed as if
his skull had been swapped out with the hatching egg of a dragon.
He fought the pain, twisting his wrists under the ropes that con-
stricted his bare chest and arms. After his suggestion that he be

used for ransom, the only thought that had prevailed in the early hours of his capture was his escape. To see his little ones again, their honey-dew eyes, plump jowls parting, giving smiles to make envious the sun. But that had all withered away. Dying like a man now, a noble ambassador of his House's iron pride. He worked his ankles futilely in their ropes, and then gave up, letting his head hang.

"Coffin," Edimor Ordrid said, amused, wiping his face. Twin Ordrids were indeed in this foul room, deep in their keep in the city of Nilghorde. With them, dangling from a rafter, was this prized prisoner. Edimor picked up his knife from the worktable. "You work in money, no? Counting and stacking all your precious coins. We do the same work, you and I." The young necromancer hissed, "I just delight in one, unique addition. Your beads: I must find mine. In the air. In the seas and in the mind. In the polluted heart of clever men. Once skewered onto the cosmic abacus, then and there do we learn...*magic*. Learn what fire ignites the leaping frog who jumps and cheats the death who pursues him—invented a way? Invented a way to manipulate death, you ask? Dear me, Umbort Ouvarnia—you mean discovered *the* way."

At the snap of a finger, the other twin, Edomax, stopped ruining a perfect stack of cordwood to prance over and knock senseless Umbort with a choice log.

Now in the quiet once more, Edimor could focus on their work. There would come a moment where his brother Edomax would make fire. Until the imbecile managed to balance the arrangement of the logs with a remembrance that his bald head sat on his neck, their task would have to be illumined only by the cruel sun staring at Edimor through embrasures in the thick wall. Edimor wiped his sleeve across his sweating, hairless brow.

It was true that Edimor and Edomax were twins—though, by the sight of them, or any other working sense, the two couldn't be further unalike. When Edimor failed to memorize a string of runes, he beat his head against the wall. His brother did so for recreation. The one time they were tasked with patching up an undead servant, Edimor strained nights on end to learn how his grandfather so seamlessly charged life in the dead. Edomax played with the creature's balls. One would study the contents of a brazier, the other would get his head stuck in it. One toiled. One played. One burned white-hot with hawk-eyed ambition, the other dallied, entranced by the trite and perverse.

Edimor focused on a brown loaf, cutting the bread into slices. He then used his teeth to pry free a stubborn cork, sticking his knife inside the jar, whipping around the blade and pulling it out coated with butter. He spread the butter onto a slice, chomping down on his meal, for what he and his half-wit brother were doing was hungry work.

Edimor poked the Ouvarnia in the ribs with his blade. "Nope," Edimor said. "Still out."

"That's good, Eddie," Edomax said. "Just give me the word, I'll club 'im again. Nice and swift for you."

Edimor checked the purple mush sticking to his mortar and pestle. "We don't want to kill him. Not yet." Crushed Ghorlaxium needed to sit, but it had been long enough.

Brewing a broth that made its drinker spill truth was not the hardest potion to render. The components were trim. Verbal? No. Somatics? Never. Alignment of certain planets, current phase of the moon, summoning entities of the shadow realm? How the magistrates would have lusted to learn all that was needed were a few key materials and a lucid imagination.

Edimor watched as his brother finished stacking the cord-wood under the cauldron. Two spells needed to be cast this day. A Ghorlaxium truth-serum was not as hard as shooting one's soul into a waiting corpse—but the damn broth better be perfect!

Prior to Umbort's last knock on the head, according to the fair-haired worm, Ordrid magic had gotten out of control. Yes,

Edimor conceded, there were the abductions and, yes, there were the flying things infecting the once-quiet air. But the whole Orisulan peninsula roused to a stir? Melodrama. Farmers, merchants—all fleeing, pushing south to the city of Oxghorde, where cobbled streets bloated to new records with the passing of each moon. This economic strain prompted the House of Ouvarnia—"at last," the noble Umbort cried—into armoring their horses and taking paths of wagon trains, right into the city of Nilghorde.

Edimor watched Edomax cup his hands around the flame of a tallow candle. When Edomax burns himself, Edimor mused—which he likely would—he could hardly feel a greater heat than the summer furnace that had oppressed the battlefield, so recently suffered. The uncontested mammoth, Nilghorde still towered grey, bulking black against the western sea. In it trafficked no Ouvarnian hordes. Nor were they slinking up alleyways. Once officially challenged, the proud, twisted, ever-vengeful House of Ordrid sundered forth. They met the Ouvarnias first in the sprawl between the House's home cities. The countryside was soon an ebb and flow, staining the grounds red, be it untilled fields or the cobbled steps of Pelliul's westernmost gate.

Edomax had been deemed too demented and queer, at least while the combat was young and no dire signs had yet to call for more sworders. Thus, the demented and queer and imbecilic of the two had been stuck in the keep during the last battle, withering and tricking until called upon by his brother.

Edimor had been injured. The Ouvarnias and their deputized underlings circled him and his conscripts, hacking and swinging until no Ouvarnia lived and Edimor's left arm hung lifeless. Now in a sling, the injury made spellcraft damn near impossible. A dimwit with two working hands would have to do.

Ghorlaxium proper was for those from the shadow realm. Ghosts, the fleeing peasants would have said. A diluter existed for controlling, in a sense, those whose hearts still naturally pounded.

Edimor used his good hand to sprinkle the cutting agent. Leaves of Luka, included at the age-old five-to-one ratio, never failed. Using a pestle almost the size of the club that had broken his arm, he mashed the compound into a gooey purple paste.

Satisfied, Edimor took in the full sight of hanging, mouth-open Umbort. He had been captured right as Edimor had been helped into a casualty wagon. They'd long deprived dashing Umbort of his effects: his clothes, his stars and bars, his decorative crosses. And dignity, too.

This prisoner of war did not impress the elders. Sent to fall, striking branch after consecutively lower branch, most of Edimor's uncles varied in their hatred but all stood classically firm in one observation: the Ouvarnia's dismal use. Umbort had been cast down to finally greet Edimor and Edomax, like a divitch ball coach putting his worst players in only after a game was victoriously certain. But in this game, Edimor sneered, a war between two great Houses, victory was far from guaranteed. This looming cloud had struck fire in Edimor; he was pleased his father and uncles allowed him now the wiles of his "puny spells."

Edimor needed to learn Umbort's deepest, darkest secrets. In order to provide his House with vital layouts of the Ouvarnian keep? Yes. Provide insights into that House's vulnerable troves? That too. Or, grinning, shoot his soul into his dead body. One of the most difficult of necromantic arts, but—if he could just do it—if Edomax could follow the simplest of instructions—using Umbort's body, *Edimor* would ride to the city of Pelliul, suffer the hugs and kisses, suffer the tales told of wandering, wait, assassinate their top leadership, then trot back home the sung hero.

It was not easy, being an inmate in a House where one failed spell meant no dessert as children and no honor as men. Some nights, gazing up at the moon, Edimor—to his shame—furtively wished to live the life of ease peasants seemed to wallow in. They never had to contend with a twin who was attached to his reputation like a malignant tumor. But even for those few unfortunate farmers and tradesmen who did, they surely did not live under the shadow of an older brother like Maecidion.

Maecidion, the Great Maecidion, the up-and-comer who was spoken of like the thrice coming of Prince Basofial. Yes, the great Maecidion, hair long and black streaming in the battle wind; he had yet to fail a single spell, mumble incorrectly a lone incantation…and he had never dared shoot his soul into enemy dead, either.

Edimor watched Edomax point toward the cauldron and began reading from the scroll he'd prepared. Edimor focused his mind. He visualized the necessary sequence of images: crystalline skies, crystalline skies being penetrated by a lone flying star—unimpeded by cloud or rain, the crystalline skies—

Edomax said the transmutations, lowering his finger at the dry kindling, then, with an audible pop, Edomax turned around, his head and shoulders covered in snow.

"You blundering idiot!"

"Sorry, Eddie," Edomax said, shivering. "Give me another chance, I—"

"You'll get it right or else! How else will I—we achieve any semblance of glory if you can't tell the difference between a pyre uncial and a simple hoarfrost?"

Edimor watched, huffing. Edomax reread the scroll and pointed his finger. This time the logs lit up, licking the cauldron's base with a greening flame.

Edimor shut his eyes, listening to the crackles, smelling the smoke. He began again: Crystalline skies, then crystalline skies being penetrated by a lone flying star—unimpeded by cloud or rain, then the crystalline skies being penetrated by a lone flying star that falls, cutting through to the center of the world, ending in a perfect, according solitude:

The truth.

Edimor opened his eyes. The water would be boiling soon. Until then, his only charge was keeping his brother at bay, away from Umbort, who he prowled and circled as lustfully as a hyena. Other than learning what "more important" Ordrids had already poked free; that this prisoner of theirs was but a mild financier, Edimor had gotten little out of Lord Stitched-lips—a metaphor he and Edomax had attempted to turn into flailing reality until the wretched Ouvarnia could no longer stomach the sight of an approaching needle. Edimor picked up his knife again, this time slicing open Umbort's thigh. Now, swinging and writhing, upside down as a bleeding bat, Umbort was no longer spared the indignity of his screams.

"Oh," Edomax cooed, having defied his brother's request the moment their plaything came to. "Pain, that's all you feel. You want to feel good, yes?"

"Max," Edimor said, wiggling a corked empty vial. Edimor handed it off to Edomax, who then went skipping back to the cauldron. Turning to Umbort: "Fresh water right before boiling point," Edimor said. "First bubble—scoop up and put a cork on the vial. All else in the cauldron: useless as you."

Edimor walked over, joining his brother. He now held the vial, filled and sealed by Edomax as directed. He pulled out the cork, putting the glass rim to his lips. He sucked free the faintest taste, mixing the potion with its last ingredient. *Perfect, according solitude—the truth*, he thought, spitting the fluid back into the vial and sealing it firmly.

"Now," he said. "We are ready."

Umbort's eyes grew wide. He wiggled, shouting, "Do your worst! My family will lay this dungeon to a rightful waste. Turn me into a toad. Burn me with warts. Turn me to tatters. My name shall be bronzed with full honor in my family's halls. Can either of you utter such things?"

"Max," Edimor said, trying to feign lack of interest in the

man's screed. "Make sure our creature's mouth remains open, please."

He should have known better. Any of the torture tools lying about would have lived up to the challenge. Yet, Umbort Ouvarnia was being steadily sent to his grave while enduring a molestation of tickles.

"Open," Edomax said.

"*Mm-mm*," Umbort protested from sealed lips. Edimor said nothing.

"Ooh-pen." Edomax crept his hand up the rope, gripping the man's most sensitive pulp.

"Stop!" Edimor said. "Stop that, you abnormality." But the fondling opened Umbort's mouth quicker than hot iron. Edimor seized the opportunity and shoved the potion down his throat. Edomax took a knee, using his hands now to clasp around the man's head, slapping four fingers over his mouth as the potion sprayed from Umbort's nostrils.

Umbort Ouvarnia gagged and choked, he seethed and he snotted, and then he swallowed.

Edimor's scroll was almost full. "Let's see," he said, taking one eye off the parchment to gauge the state of Edomax's boredom. "We have the names of your children, the colors of your horse, the *name* of your horse, the names of the sots who empty its trough. Ah yes." Edimor rattled off the very last of them, then shook out his wrist.

Once sauntering through the jasmine streets of Pelliul, that city would take him to this man's home, his family, his over-with life. No detail was too small, too insignificant. He had to impersonate this—looking again to his hastily written notes— this confirmed bore to perfection. The House of Ouvarnia dealt not in magic, but their suspicions had grown understandably in recent days. Anyone suspected of Ordrid contamination was disarmed and promptly quarantined.

Edomax sat on the top of the staircase. "Can we *please* get on with it?"

Ignoring his brother, even when he threw and shattered a cupel, Edimor looked at the docile face of his captive. "One last question, Umbort. What is the worst way to die?"

As he had with all the other questions, without hesitation, Umbort languidly replied: "To suffocate."

Edimor shrugged, tossing a log that still burned at one end. Edimor had even prepared a bucket of oil that would've ignited like summer. Not the whole body, of course. Just a leg. An arm too, maybe. Perfect wound by warfare for the shiny Ouvarnian banquets. "Very well then," he said. This was perfect, actually. "Oh, Edomax."

Edomax placed a thick rag over Umbort's face until his inverted lungs burst. With his good hand, Edimor applied a reconstructive lather usually meant for undead slaves. That gash in the thigh he'd made required attention. Edimor wanted to look good for "Umbort's" return.

"How happy they will be," he said to Edomax, still pinching the dead man's nose between his thumb and finger. "Maecidion never dared *this*. How they're going to greet me. A warrior home. They'll squawk and they'll sit and they'll drink and sleep and then, one by one, I'll slice their vile throats."

✳

"Every single crack?" Edomax asked from outside the coffin, paintbrush dripping with glue.

Edimor laid lordly in his temporary bed. The coffin was lined with straw. A superfluous comfort no doubt, but he wasn't dead yet. He stank of the oils Edomax had bathed him in. They would prevent his flesh from decaying while he was away. Yet, in this deeper realm of the keep, there were other villains scurrying about. Wrapped in the vestments of the tomb, Edimor lifted his head. "Yes!" he said, eyeing Edomax from over the lid. "Every crack. Make it so no vermin can squirm through. When I return, when I reenter, well, I'd like be un-gnawed on."

"And you want me to nail down the lid?"

"Raped by a snake! Yes!"

Edomax concentrated on his brushing. "What do I say if Father or an uncle asks where you are?"

"They won't," Edimor said, thinking of the limp, lifeless, naked body lying just a few feet away. "They don't care. But, if we'd be so lucky, just take them down here and pry the lid. I shouldn't be gone long."

"I will count the minutes."

"Don't get smart—and when I'm gone, stay the hell out of my bevy."

"Ah, yes." Edomax snickered. "The bevy." It was well known Ordrids practiced their craft on slaves. Living, undead, no matter; the stock Edimor had compiled only attested to his trial-by-failure ambition. That they remained locked away for future experiments incited his dear brother to occasional outbursts. It was unfair, Edimor was so often told, that only *he* be granted a flock of flesh. Though they shared a room, they shared little else. And their father, tired of Edomax's pleas, cast aside the complaint by flippantly declaring he could have his brother's bevy if, and only if, there was no one who wished to claim it. "It will remain untouched, dear brother."

With the coffin planks sealed, Edimor was ready—ready to weave the great spell, the spell long white faces at the long table had said only the elders had the faculties to muster. The torches burned from their designated sconces. From their middle, sitting up in the coffin, Edimor cast his good arm skyward. Edomax stood near; holding a torch in one hand and a thick scroll in the other.

Through the torchlight Edimor fixed his eyes on the wan outline of Umbort, sprawled and twisted on the stone floor.

Edimor began the rites. Edomax held steady the scroll, unspooling it as the long incantation required. As if guided by the hands of a demon, Edimor's head whipped down, then cocked up to gaze at the ceilinged blackness with eyes glossing a full and loathsome white.

Out of the supine, oiled body Edimor flew. What were flickering flames burned with the violence of stars. Shadow itself congealed, becoming a tube, one which Edimor still trafficked.

Detached from all corpus, his mind—*he* was free. Free to relive instant visions he could not shake nor change.

Unhinged cruelty had always been his flaw. Now there was nowhere to hide. Nodding meek yesses to those positioned above one moment, harboring every grudge, then stamping up or down stairs to lash out on a convenient slave or his slow demented brother the next. Most Ordrids were cruel, but few had failed to master their contempt with the same abysmal floundering as he.

If that weren't enough, another imp hounded him—and not the good kind—*those* perched on the mantles all over the keep. It was established the twins were homely, yes. A type of dreadful beauty flowed abundantly from most Ordrid loins, but Edimor and Edomax were afflicted with a mild woe that periodically sprouted from their bloodline like heads of laughable cabbage. Some never grew hair, a mark on aesthetics that usually bore no concern to the males who draped themselves in dark garments to call upon the moon. Edomax, for one, could care less, but a bald head on an insignificant frame had always driven the afflicted Edimor barreling mad. Sure, he laid with his father's harem as regular as the rest, but none of the laced voluptuaries put him in the warmth of their eyes, as they so eagerly did for, of course, the black-maned Maecidion.

Alien black became shadow. Shadow became the walls and

ceiling of the crypt once more. And Umbort Ouvarnia opened his eyes, seized by the throbbing in his wounded thigh, listening to Edomax Ordrid chortle and jig as he slowly rose from the cold, barren floor.

✳

"Make sure that lid is shut." Never had the fair voice of an Ouvarnia commanded the catacombs.

"Yes, Eddie," Edomax snickered, chasing him up the stairs. "Bevy, bevy, soon be mine."

As they emerged triumphantly into the workroom, the sun was setting through the embrasures and the cauldron was cold. Umbort put back on his clothes.

"All I need now is his horse," Umbort said. "Thank the gods we keep all their stallions."

"Yes, yes, and then off you will be."

Focused on his work like the wolf on its kill, drunk with the soul-shooter having worked, Umbort didn't even realize until his rear end met the stairs that his ascent from the workroom had been halted.

"Out of my way," he ordered, dusting himself off, eyeing a wandering batch of his family's hulking conscripts. He had no reason to fear their swords. Part of the plan was Edomax's escort. Demented or not, his brother could validate their brilliant scheme.

While the Ordrids worked in the supernatural and, equally useful, the superstitions and fears of men, the latter could also be their undoing. The House of Ouvarnia dealt in land, commerce, politics, allowing for the galvanization of even the lowest serf. In what privy scholars call the "Black Magic Summer," the two Houses fought viciously between the waning nettielium and the first yellow of the maple.

Armored farmers and tradesmen lied to by the promise of land; they would lay the grand assault.

Dead Ordrids' clothes were incinerated, their jewels crushed to dust. Regardless of its state, an Ordrid corpse would be nailed to a stake above well-tended flames. The remains would then be collected, brought back to Pelliul, and then added to wet waiting mortar; used, once solid, to strengthen their great home's western wall. The wall that faced Nilghorde and the distant Ordrid keep. For years after, even skeptics were unable to shake the sight of the passing fungi that had burst hideously from the unsealed cracks.

Outnumbered, the senior Ordrids soon offered what Edimor would have called a sinister posture of peace.

Although peace resumed, and ever after the Houses skirted about the other, it was whispered, still whispered, that the Ouvarnias now cremate their own, guarding their remains day and night, fearing the vilest of retribution.

But all such war and all such peace Edimor would not know.

"He escaped!" Edomax cried to the conscripts. "He escaped from the room just below!"

Umbort swung around. "Max?"

"He is an Ouvarnia," his brother sneered. "Sworn enemy of our glorious House. Owner of bevvies that belong to I."

Umbort spit out every credential of Edimor Ordrid to deaf ears. Edomax clapped and gleamed and he licked his lips as the stairwell slung red. Edimor looked through enemy eyes, he screamed through a lacerated throat that was not his own. He cried out his own name through enemy lungs as the mailed barbarians, allies under the black banner, laughed and hacked him merrily to pieces.

THE LEAF OF THE PALM

"To the palms!
For their leaf alone,
Of all the god's tall,
Select who to walk,
Who better to crawl.
Coming a leader,
Corruptible dread,
Turn the skies a bruised blackness,
Turn the white sands to red."
—*Ullumon the Lathairboni's Chant to the Wind*

"I want to go home!"

Conabitt Lotgard's nanny peeled away from her looking glass. The crone was old, draped in the regalia of his family's immense staff. "But young master, you *are* home," she sighed, as tired of the brat as he was her repulsive odor. The young boy crossed his arms, bettering his defiance, continuing to stare out at the night through the golden square of the carriage window. "Come now, we mustn't always be so glum. Your sisters have taken quite a liking to the place."

"I hate Suela."

South of the mighty Orisulan peninsula, Suela, the land of black-skinned men, teemed with dust, danger, and the wide dripping forests this boy was not allowed to play in. That there were cats the size of hounds, moving castles called elephants, all would have enchanted normal boys, and Conabitt Lotgard, if anything, playing out his fantastic adventures with a fleeting attentiveness was very much a normal boy. Stiff rules of the colony, however, forbade any venturing out beyond their continuously refortified walls.

A great sea divided these lands, Orisula and Suela—and now, the young boy from the happiness he'd once clutched like bird eggs.

The grim old nanny was still squawking. "Your father arranged the day's amusements in the hopes of, well, amusing you."

"People dancing like monkeys and painted like clowns," the boy snarled, "beating on drums. It's boring. Boring, boring, boring." The carriage rocked onto an uphill. The soldiers who accompanied them—six, Conabitt had counted—all rode war horses. Their metal shoes clicked and clacked, confirming they'd reached the cobbled path hewn from the jungle that weaved back to the bright lanterns of the colonial gate.

Conabitt's mood lightened as he listened to their muffled bellows. Out in the wild Suelan night the mailed and bearded men trotted, spear tips pointing towards the heavens, shields polished, free. He wondered what such men talked about on these nights, and if being assigned babysitting duties made such warriors resent the skinny boy, tucked away like one of his sisters' diaries.

An old hand, thin like vellum, brushed back the golden hair seemingly determined to conceal his pout. This was not out of affection, as his mother's rare caress would have been. The nanny's insolent grooming was one of the many ways the crone asserted the young noblemen was in all ways ignoble. "We shall be home soon. We shall have to put you straight in the bath, you—"

"*Shh.*"

He'd been short with her lately. This he was aware, and he was not proud. But she could suck rocks.

He sat up and peered out the window. After a moment, she seemed to notice too; the soldiers had stopped talking. The carriage still moved, the horse shoes clinked and clanked as they had, but—no, there were voices, now.

Conabitt disobeyed another rule. Dark trees passed his head. Carriage lanterns caught in their bobbling the heavy back end of a mounted horse. Its rider, clad in the chainmail and sash of an Orisulan uniform, sat still and serious as a statue. Except the large man was looking this way and that, behind him, not seeing Conabitt's sprouted head, then whispering to someone on the other side.

When the wood *thunked*, it splintered under Conabitt's chin. His first thought was someone had thrown fruit, as his mates had back in the Morgeltine District. Then came the hoots, the yells. Then he saw the spear. He reached out and touched its tip, buried deep in the rosewood.

"Formation!"

He could not see the rest. The carriage shook, jostled by giants, or worse than, the men bursting out of the jungle hooting insanely. A face appeared, glistening demonic in the window, sending the boy scrambling into his nanny's arms where they together screamed. Soldiers galloped and hacked and soon screamed, too. The carriage shook, then again, then shook and stopped. There was another awful scream then the doors creaked and swung open.

"Savages!" the woman cried, clutching an ornamental blade better for no more than opening a sealed letter. "Away with you!"

"Looki, looki," one round, sweating head turned to the other and said. The Suelan bit down on a wet, bone-handled knife and then leapt inside. Outside the doors, to the rear of the carriage, tall heads had gathered in a row. They shined, bald under the light of the moon as this crawling demon, eyes glowing white, whiter than anything the boy had ever seen, steadily advanced.

Muscles like rope twitched, with every grunt, with every forward placement of an unhurried hand.

The Suelan grabbed onto an ankle. Desperate not to be dragged out and eaten, the nanny clung to a curtain, bringing it down as she plunged her letter opener into dark, resilient flesh.

Moon rippled on a slimy back. He became an explosion of jolts, crawling back out into the hot night with his captive and his cohorts waiting.

The young boy could not move. Couldn't breathe. Couldn't think. He stared at his nanny. A blur of arms and shoulders engulfed her.

"He?"

"*He*," moaned the man smiling at: "da boy."

The young boy, just shy of eleven, saw again the wet, bone-handled knife. He looked into those big white, unblinking eyes and felt as if he'd slip off of them, right off the edge of the world. He screamed, he was sure of it, a pitched girlish wail, breaking the ambushers into coarse rounds of laughter.

Far in the distance, the lanterns of his father's colony burned along the walls and above the high, proud gate. Unseen by any sentry, far down on the red-cobbled path, the young boy is pulled out of the carriage and his ankles and wrists bound with vines.

The soldiers in his games *died*. The soldiers in the books read to him, they *die*. The sliced and clubbed soldiers being dropped beside him, they too now—face down in the dirt. His cry earned a prompt gagging.

What terror struck him no one can tell, for a child so full of wonder, without yet the jaded faculties of adulthood, only dimly contemplated the primal fear of soon not being. He was scared of the pain.

The dray horse that had once pulled the carriage had been especially targeted. What horses hadn't been slain the black men now collected, handing the reins to one dressed in the spotted hides of a great cat.

Chainmail jingled as pockets were pilfered and belts cut free. The sounds of bare feet shuffling in and out of the carriage went on long enough that young Conabitt slowly began to think less and less about spears.

Arching his back and pinning his chest, he found that if he strained his neck he could lift his head and see. The poor old woman was being carried to someplace behind him. Her garments now torn and darkened, she no longer screamed. Terror renewed when she was flopped onto the litter beside him, staring at him in the full display of fresh death.

The Suelans continued their collecting. Of the six, not one Orisulan soldier had survived. The newest blood-flinging corpse revealed they'd taken a cruel Suelan with them. As the poles and vine of the litter squeaked under its burden, the ambushers, a crowd now showing close to ten, gathered around Conabitt.

He laid his chin hopelessly in the dirt and stared at someone's gnarled, potato-like toe. One of them was talking in a deep, authoritative way. Someone else was responding, in the *boos* and *ohs* of their native tongue, in a tone that sounded like a question.

"Me!" was the response. The big toe and its accompanying foot vanished, replaced by others, some widening in their stance as the men argued.

Compliments of decades of occupation, many Suelans now spoke broken Orisulan. Daring to see who, Conabitt watched as the cat-hide man pointed to another the boy could not see. The cat-hide man continued: "No-ting change! I take boy. Make demand on da whites."

With absolute delicacy, Conabitt rolled onto his side.

"Boy, I poke out you eyes, you lookit me."

He tried to look away, but that was the worst thing one could ever tell a boy. Conabitt squirmed and wriggled and slammed his eyes, only to crack them open upon the foulest man in the lot. The ambushers now seemed split into parties, like his preferred board game where two pieces ruled smaller ones to a plethora of strategic dooms. One such piece was clearly the man in spotted hides. The other, the Suelan whom Conabitt was supposed to not be looking at, was bleeding from a fresh wound. His hair, twisted like vines, sprouted from the top of his head like a horse mane. "Hole hostage, yes," this second man was saying. "Demands—no. For gold. Not else."

There was grumbling. "Da boy be da white rulah's seed," the cat man pleaded. "Now our chance. Now!"

They were back in their voweled tongue, stomping and spitting. All debate ended when one out in the periphery revealed they'd found coins, turning the gathering into a grabbing frenzy.

The men were evil, and the men laughed. They laughed so as the trees themselves seemed to leer down at Conabitt. Working his wrists to mitigate the vines, Conabitt suddenly stopped. He thought he heard a chuckle, out from somewhere deep in the night, a laughter that was somehow…different. What manner of Suelan hid in the shadows may have enjoyed being born right out of a nightmare. When a second, fouler laugh rang out, every man turned and faced the black.

"We go now," the cat man said, his voice bereft its confidence. The captured horses, whose reins were still in his hand, stomped and snorted uneasily.

The ring of Suelans was being encircled by snickers and giggles, hideous, sounding like no group of men the boy had heard. Horsemane slapped the killing side of his club, moving squarely over the boy, planting one leg on each side. Bushes rustled as things shouldered through.

The next thing Conabitt heard was a collective cry. Every horse bolted onto the cobblestones. Hyenas were everywhere, running and snickering and tearing away flesh from their screaming hosts.

Stricken by a new, more ghastly fear, the pain of being eaten propelled Conabitt into squirms. Somehow he managed to get his hands out in front. Spears stuck into the sides of demoniac dogs, spears and knives dropped by Suelans before succumbing to the loud, bloody, ball-like maulings around him. Blades to cut the vines binding him were everywhere. But he could not move.

No farther away than the bedside candle he'd light after suffering a lucid nightmare, a dark, capable muzzle blew steam onto his mouth. Fangs were the only thing left in the world, yellow, so close and still. The hyena's eyes: into them the boy stared, frozen, as a lifeless glimmer shifted.

The beast leapt, knocking Conabitt so hard he didn't feel the dead Suelan's knee that crashed into the back of his head. Right beyond the boy, Horse-mane wrestled with those same fangs, slaying the beast with a knife's upward plunge.

"You," Horse-mane looked at Conabitt, tossing aside the dying animal. "You not die by bite. You die by Suelan." The knife was already over his head, smeared in blackness of the blood and moon. "You die!"

Conabitt flailed and cried, caught in the man's free hand and hoisted to his knees. Two more hyenas sent the boy back down. What few stars he could see spun and swam. The moon blinked, an indifferent eye. Horse-mane was the last to die, taking one of his two killers with him.

The hyenas laughed. Some panted, wounded. A favorite game the boy and his mates used to put each other through had been the time-honored tradition of choking one another and then roaring with mirth as their victim stumblishly came to. He felt that sensation, those moments before blipping out of the world. But he was awake. He was still alive. And alive in the night, he could see a man—a shape, black, withered, and deep as though a bottomless crack in the earth had stood upright to leer at him, the voice, cooing the beasts who rubbed on him their muzzles, cool and coy as a snake's slither.

The boy's head fell and rested on a gnawed-on knee.

✳

A grinning coconut hung over him. It looked shiny, happy even.

Hyenas made their noises somewhere nearby.

"Silence, you wooly devils," the coconut demanded.

"Where am I?" Conabitt whispered.

The coconut pulled back, becoming the sweating face of an old man. "In my hut. I saved you from da rebels."

Old eyes went over the boy's bruised, scraped skin. Conabitt felt an impulse to touch his wounds, but doing so, he found them lathered and dressed. The old black man, by contrast, hadn't so much as a cut or bump on the head.

Hyenas tromped and snickered outside the door.

"How you feeling?" the old man said.

"I want to go home."

"Yes, don't we all."

Conabitt looked around. "You're not home?"

"Not since my exile," the old man said merrily before getting serious. "Giving leaders good, blood-shedding broths, turns out, dear boy, is no good for quarrels."

"Can you take me home?" He sat up in a cot made of hides, pulled drum-tight by strands of hair. He was in a single, sizable room chopped by partitions of beams and the skin of a gargantuan lizard.

"Why you want to go back?" the man said, pushing him flat. "A young boy, in dee jungle? Some would call dat paradise." Conabitt didn't like the feel of the old man's hand, which lingered on his bare chest like the dry tongues of cats.

When his rescuer's hand lifted, so did the man's eyes. He and Conabitt looked about the room, the old man seemingly pleased to point out and identify the various gourds and cupels. Strewn about them, sooty braziers burned.

Since arriving on the north shore, this strange land had been presented to the boy through copper-clasped books and an array of tutors. One such academic had partially indoctrinated him in local lore. Only a wizard—though the blacks called them something different—would decorate their hut in (casting his eyes to the barked rafters) nailed-up bats, nailed-in ears, and a beheaded monkey that hung from a hook.

"Are you a," the boy fumbled, rising, "a latta, ladair—"

"Indeed, dear boy." The man's face creased to a wide grin, exposing yellow teeth and spaces between them. "Da Lathairboni, enchanters of da wild. We do God's work," quickly adding, "just lookit theez dressings. You took nastier fall dan you know." It hadn't seemed *that* nasty, though the boy kept his thoughts to himself. "I am Ullumon," the old man said, running his spidery fingers over the scalp of his bald, ashen head. "Ullumon da Lathairboni."

The Suelan seemed to be waiting for something, displeased when the young white showed no sign of recognition. "I am Conabitt L—"

"Yes." The old man let him slip off the bed and wander toward a corner. "Da whole continent know who you are. Seed of da rulah—but you be eefin more special dan dat."

"For gold? Where's my nanny?"

"Gold!" the man spit. "Gold be nuttin'—gold be for doze spear-chuckas back dare. Oh, and dee old woman, had to leave her body. Poor ting."

That pulled him back to reality. "Thank you for saving me." And the boy meant it, his fate at the hands of those men now only beginning to bubble to a grim surface. Distracting himself from another thought on the matter, he fixated on something sad yet wholly magnificent: a dead cat. Conabitt bent down to gaze upon a leopard that had been put in a curled position underneath a cluttered table.

"Oh, my pleasure." Ullumon said. "My pleasure, dear boy. But we must do some-ting about your name."

"Did the hyenas kill this, too?"

"I dink I call you…Diamond."

Conabitt bent down further, running his hands through the black and yellow fur. A sudden roar sent him toppling over backwards, sparing the removal of his head by way of a lightning-fast paw.

Ullumon laughed. "That is Leebu."

The boy gaped, seeing above those flashing teeth that the living cat had only one eye. That keen yellow orb glared at him, its owner growling less as the boy backed away.

"It's—it's alive."

"Dat he be. Dat be he—at least for a little while longah. He be as old as I, as da cat year's leap. Do not mind Leebu. In fact, he will be one of you greatest teachers."

"He will?"

"Most certainly."

"And the hyenas?"

"Friends!" Ullumon cheered, rising to his feet and reaching for his staff. "We all friends here."

"Why *Diamond*?"

"'Cuz," Ullumon said as if he'd been waiting. "'Cuz, dear boy, you be special and small and white as a Suelan lily. And," he hobbled just beyond a partition, "I dink you be hard. Harder one day, like hammered steel. With," flinging the partition aside, Ullumon exposed a bubbling cauldron, "a little tutelage."

The Lathairboni took hold of a hollowed horn and dipped it into the pea-green broth. "I will teach you, Diamond, da fruits and joys of power."

"But why me?"

"Other than you land in dis old man's lap? Told you, you special, dear boy—now, yes, da fruits of power. Wouldn't you want such tings when given da spear one day to rule you own whites?"

Replacing his father in some stuffy throne seemed to the ten-year-old as the cloudiest of yet-to-comes. "I suppose," he said, prodded by a moment's want to correct the kind old man that his father only ruled a colony. "And you'll take me home after?"

"Of course."

There was another answer as to *why him*, one Ullumon refrained from delivering when he poured the broth back into the vat and gave the abomination a good stir. Because the magician was a degenerate, and imaginative, getting old, and running out of nights to corrupt much more than the beasts he tasked with his wiles.

"We will make you heavenly and mighty." Ullumon handed the boy the horn, gesturing him to dip into the vat. After a moment's hesitation the boy sipped, sipped then drank. He began to swish, almost immediately. "Sleep now. We start tomorrow."

✳

A captain swung open the door to the governor's office, exchanging the hellish heat of the Suelan morning for the hellfire being lobbed inside. The meeting already in full swing, the career-ending accusations had already rolled downhill, wheeling across the polished floor and onto the toe of his forward-most boot.

"Are you the man who was in charge of last night's convoy?" Conabus Lotgard had said it cold. Worse, he had to say it twice. A decorated man, ghastly pale, eyed the helmet the governor pawed then answered him on behalf of the captain: "He is, my lord."

Before explanations could be attempted, before pardons begged or pallid final salutes given, the young officer was dragged screaming from the office, out of the mansion and onto the colony's gallows where his neck was summarily broken.

"Now," Governor Lord Conabus Lotgard said, cooling further and slicking back an escaped flume of hair that had been hanging like a blond root in his grave. "Turn this fetid land upside down if you must. Find my son."

The colonel, reunited with his feather-crest helmet, commanded and barked and ordered his staff back out into the day. A pair of perched hornbills took flight, egressing from the rock the colonel threw at the horses who'd returned to the gate riderless.

"You heard Lord Lotgard." The colonel eyed each of his five remaining captains. "Scorch the earth. Kill every savage if you have to, man, woman, monkey-eyed nit—find that boy's precious hide or lose your own. Dismissed!"

When he awoke, Conabitt didn't sit up in his blue silken sheets. The young boy, groggy but getting better, gazed upon the Suelan room, now brightened by the rays of a late morning. The door was open, leaving in place of the night's darkened wood a solid block of sun.

Conabitt sprang onto his knees, pinning his back against the wall's dried, armor-like mud. No hyenas entered. After careful moments he determined that none lounged or panted beyond the threshold either. Calm now, slipping out of bed, he tiptoed to the doorway.

Gobbles and drawn-out screeches—he'd thought he'd heard such, and he was right. Odd, but it sounded like the old man was talking to who or whatever was carrying on. Outside, the dry earth was beaten by wide, menacing prints. Not just hyena, though they'd made many, but cats. Not just that old leopard's. There were other things, too, not quite man's, perhaps a largish type of monkey. Something told the boy that all the animal crap that was absent may be stinking nearby in the jungle, a wall-thick green that leaned in on all sides as if to learn the secrets of the lonesome hut.

Two hideous birds sat out on a low branch. Conabitt imagined if a dragon and a rooster had a baby, the result would be these winged things, with their open beaks, swinging and shuttering. Ullumon stood below, feeding them. "Oh?" He laughed. "Dank you, hornbill. Dank you. Excellent work. Good morning, Diamond. You sleep like Leebu. Careful, watch you step now."

Conabitt looked down to see he was stepping into a snare. A more careful glance revealed a high number of insidious traps, some swinging with their new captives.

His mother had told him that when his father was overworked, excusing his behavior was the best thing to do. Stress, she'd say. Then maybe it was the stress from the brushes with death playing with the boy, or so he wagered. Brushes that poor, old wretched woman and six warriors had been unable to escape. His heart didn't hurt for them as he felt guiltily it should, but rather, he wondered how the old black man could look so different in the light of day.

Conabitt had once put a drop of his father's Saffreen oil in his sister's lemon water, rendering her giddy until she had to be excused from the table. Maybe there had been something in that drink?

Ullumon looked little different than a burned version of his mother's father. Tall and without hair, gangly, long arms that ended in fingers always fiddling about in jars, or pouches, or feeding strange birds that he still spoke to. But nothing, what—*eerie?*—whatever he'd seen a night ago.

"We ready for our first lesson?"

The boy dithered. "What do I have to do?"

"Come. Come, dear boy." Back into the glow of the hut's stuffy warmth they went, up to a new cauldron bubbling. One pop farted out a smell so noxious the boy thought he was going to fall over.

"Please," the boy looked up, "don't make me dri—"

"Drink, yes. It's not so bad going down." Ullumon dipped in a horn, sucking out its ooze nectar so not a drop remained. "Diamond, you must know, once you drink," the old man paused and rubbed his chin. "Do you know how da first day of fall be better dan da rest? Da otha days we all call fall? How dee cool winds feel da coolest da first time? Or, I know, dear boy, I know, how opening one of your daddy's gifts, how da surprise be only once—this, this be like da Uulgunii."

The Uulgunii, or God's Broth, was what waited for Conabitt. Explained in terms a boy would understand, Conabitt learned that once imbibed, God's Broth packed a magical punch. Though servings would be plenty, the first cup, or the first dirty cattle-ash horn, bestowed fantastic gifts. So much so, habitual drinkers of the God's Broth teemed with envy at the sight of a drinker's first dive into animal wonder.

"Wid a few more odds an ends," the Lathairboni said, gesturing to random charms that hung about the rafters, "we show you what no white boy ever has seen. Special be the soup of da Lathairboni, but it last only a few day." Ullumon handed him the loaded horn. "You drink when you ready."

At this, the old man left the boy to start a tirade against the one-eyed leopard. Leebu had wandered in from some morning outing to lie down upon exposed, half-empty sacks. What composition made up their bulk the boy could not say, but as he dared another sniff at the fetid broth, he aptly guessed that they were not to be laid on.

Ullumon yelled nonsense and grumbled low. The feline retaliated with drawn-out, articulate snarls. It amused the boy; the two seemed to be genuinely arguing with the other, chock-full of the pauses and talk-overs one would expect in a parlor room debate.

Something like taking a dare to jump off a low bridge onto the roof of a moving carriage, or how his mates had once convinced him gulping down live frogs was an inestimable rite of passage, Conabitt put the rim to his lips. He drank slowly, watching the old, black, crazy man stomp and wiggle bony fingers at Leebu.

"I told you, Leebu," Ullumon said, clear as day. Clearer.

"Rooibos and wormwood are one thing, but one cat hair in Goonu powder and the whole thing is ruined, damn you."

"Shut that toothless mouth," Leebu said. Conabitt felt as if he'd been put in a sack and hurled in the air. Or it was like he'd walked neck-deep out in a river, sinking below, and in doing so discovered he now gazed upon a new world with the open eyes of a fish. Leebu continued, snapping back at whatever threat Ullumon had made while the boy's revelation had blocked all hearing: "Contagion? You haven't cast a contagion spell since I sucked on my mother's teat. I'll lay where I wish."

"I put a spell on you," Ullumon raged, "and another is coming! Keep it up!"

"It can talk?" Conabitt heard himself say, in growlish vernacular.

"Ah," Ullumon exclaimed, also in cat language, clapping his hands. "Look who joins the conversation!" His strange take on Orisulan words was now absent. The old man spoke fluent and clear. "Leebu, you want to ask Diamond here if my magic is any good?"

Leebu snorted, curling himself into a ball.

"How long will it be like this?" The boy felt like he was going to float away.

"Oh," Ullumon smiled up at the rafters, "two days, dear boy. Maybe three."

"Then I won't be able to talk to animals?"

Leebu looked up without stirring. "By then, you'll wish you couldn't."

"Shut," Ullumon kicked at the leopard, turning his would-be nest into a burst of powders, "up!"

After Ullumon shooed the cat from the sacks and tightened them to his satisfaction, the leopard and old man gazed upon their new pupil. The still, clear stare of a cat with fangs like dinner knives shook the young boy. "Hello," he quivered, furthering his fortitude until he straightened his back and tried again. "Hello, Leebu."

"Hello, *Diamond*," said the cat.

"Leebu, you should have a moment with the boy," Ullumon pilfered through a cupboard, "while I prepare for our great, grand adventure."

Leebu was also old. That, the boy could see. Exactly how much grey had encroached on the cat's proud spots was a bit harder to tell, for light inside the place sparkled with flitters of dust caught in the lens of a washed-out red. But no doubt the proud cat's former yellow had withered from a kingly hue down to its flaxen frown. His black held up well, mostly, nowhere better than the scar running across his face that had taken with it an eye. The other side, the good side, the one with the eye, cocked up at Ullumon. "Not this time. I've helped with enough of your experiments."

"You will and that's the end of it!" Ullumon slammed shut the cupboard and ushered the cat out and the boy along with it.

Only a couple strides took them out of the cleared grounds that surrounded the hut and into the dense, moist wall of the jungle. The boy followed, parting vines and sniffing the tart forest floor that made smells when he stepped on herbs undetected. The cat's yellow backside disappeared between the flamboyant green of banana leaves, reappearing when Conabitt almost tripped.

"Quiet," Leebu growled.

Conabitt whispered, "What are we looking for?" Game, surely. Marvelous game. The leopard was likely to—

"For a place where I can sleep and you not bother me."

"…Oh."

After a while, they came to a natural tent made by fallen trees. Monkeys, alerted by the presence of the lumbering cat, hooted and hollered amongst the canopy. "Cat—cat—cat! Big cat—cat—cat!"

"They won't bother you?"

Leebu growled, "No," saying nothing until he had kneaded the grass into the right position and plopped down. "I mean bothered with the questions, boy. Your new master would have you pelting me."

The boy sat down. "He's not my—you two aren't friends, are you?"

"You hear them? Up in the trees?" The boy nodded. "Weak. The lot of them. The lot of *you*. Freedom, that precious running meat, she is only had one way. In the jaws she squeals. Under the paw she submits, only and if you're alone." The cat's golden eye flashed. "The problem with you social animals…" Leebu laughed, in the dry, sinister smirk that is a cat's laugh. "Too many to count on all your plump little fingers. You rely on others. Rather than seek yourself, you become each other's excuse, the other's hooting face of falling, failing hopes. Blame the other." The cat looked up. "They see me, astride below, and they fear, but did you know they also pity? Pity me. They know not the untethered bliss. A life of solitude. The scent whiffed eternal of perfect, centered oneness."

"…I don't think I understand."

"That's your lesson from me, boy. Oneness. Seek it. I've spent most of my life in service to that foul man. Plucked from wilder days."

"My lesson?"

Teeth were out before he could blink. "Be of service to no one, Diamond."

⁕

"Ah, dee friends are back!" Ullumon stood outside his door, draped in satchels. He pointed his staff at Leebu, switching back to cat speak. "Did he teach you? Show you things of the jungle?" The boy looked over at Leebu.

"Yes. Quite."

"Good. Then we are ready to get started."

Perhaps a boy is normal; he who trots off into a great wilderness. Perhaps so, but his remarkable zest and light-footedness may have come, at least partly, from the God's Broth coursing through his veins.

Ullumon told Conabitt the three of them were to walk to a glade. There, further instructions would be given. Getting into a "glade"—something Conabitt imagined as a small sort of opening—would once again require parting the jungle wall. Inside, it puzzled the boy that the throaty sound of frogs and insect trills remained as he'd always heard them. Those monkeys had spoken, more or less. Leebu orated better than his father's most versed house servant. Conabitt turned to ask the old man of this, but the sight of him prompted Conabitt to wait.

"Do you need a hand?" Conabitt said. The old man focused intently on the ground, already huffing and grunting over fallen, spore-ridden trees. Leebu lagged behind, his long tail leisurely flicking as the Lathairboni struggled.

This was the way of it, long through mazes of green, up a small hill where the Suelan sky peeked down eternal blue, down a slope and into bush that began giving way.

The boy couldn't help but wonder how the old man had managed the night before. "Did he ride a hyena back to the hut?" the boy would have asked Leebu, imagining the cat would have chuckled that dry, sinister smirk again. "Are you unwell?" he spoke aloud.

"Time be not kind, dear boy." Ullumon hacked and coughed, then leaned on his staff. "Right through dare."

Tall bush ahead glowed yellow at its lining. Behind them, the afternoon sizzled on a bustling lawn.

The glade, adorned only with the sporadic up-shoot of dark shrubs, clanked and rippled with the colliding horns of some strange sort of deer.

"What are they?" Conabitt asked Ullumon.

"Impala," said Leebu, licking his lips.

Ullumon took note, banishing the cat up into a tree.

Ullumon and Conabitt advanced, watching the herd. "Day are all male," Ullumon said, digging into a satchel before turning jovial, "like you, me, and dat awful cat back dare." The boy gazed in wonder at the deer's black and white and tan brown, their weird, wood-like spiraling horns. The whole lot seemed preparing from some great battle, gaining speed to crash into one another or preening their weapons on a nearby shrub. Nearest the boy, two young males locked horns and wrestled one another through a kicked-up dust.

After the clash, once a winner was vaguely established, Ullumon startled the boy with a guttural call. The boy instantly perceived the sound as the language of the beasts. Ullumon summoned over the loser, who wasted not a moment to trot up.

"Tell us," Ullumon said, "dear impala, why do you tussle so?"

"Me mom used to giver stillborns to the baboons. When I'm king of me own herd there'll be no stillborns." The beast blew hot air from his snout and stood tall. "I'm prime and virile and strong."

"Is that true?" Conabitt said in Orisulan. He knew of baboons, and the thought of some demonic monkey gnawing on a dead deer baby sickened him.

"Oh, yes," Ullumon said. "Payment to da baboons for watching over dem. Remember dat, dear boy, da power of alliance."

Before rejoining the others, the impala enchanted the boy with talks of training to fight, honing what is given to us, and to the victor goes "the woman, the women, the woman, the women." The boy uncontrollably wished that he could be one of these, just for a day. His mates had wrestled and played with oaken swords, but nothing so fun as this. He expressed such feelings to Ullumon, going on and on as the Lathairboni was pulling his fist out of his satchel.

A fine golden powder rained down on Conabitt. The Lathairboni said something but this time the boy could not understand. Nothing existed for the boy but pain. An all-encompassing throb that contorted the boy's hands and knees, sending him down onto them. It felt as if his head was growing away from his shoulders, a head that now burst. This would account for the sudden, freak change in vision, but nothing could explain the sense that he was no longer *he*.

"Like what you see?" Ullumon was holding the looking glass that had belonged to the boy's nanny. The boy walked, perhaps crawled, swiftly. Unable to see well directly in front now, the boy turned his head to the side. The glass was cracked, and behind the shards was the face of a young impala.

"But—" the boy said in the guttural tongue.

"Is the pain gone?"

"But how?"

The Lathairboni leaned onto his staff, eyeing the horizon beyond the ruckus. "It seems to me, dear boy, you should have other questions on your mind now." Conabitt the impala turned and faced his bachelor herd, instantly struck with a prompting of his own instincts. "Now go and win."

Conabitt trotted on his hoofs, nervous beyond measure at what the others may say. But in him there sparked something else.

"Have a go?" one said, not entirely pleasant.

He needed no instruction. They paced out, turning as duelists and colliding headfirst into the other. They went one way, then another. Digs in the dirt were and were not avoided. In the distance, seemingly on the far side of the world, Ullumon cheered. There was nothing else now, only force. Little by little it seemed the other waned, boosting the boy's heart until at last dazzling in joy itself as his opponent trotted off to find another.

"I did it, I did it!" Conabitt bloomed, galloping back to Ullumon. The Lathairboni coated him in a pinkish powder.

"Victory!"

Whirling back to a sweating, dust-matted boy: "I actually did it."

They departed, rustling Leebu from a nap and beginning their return journey. The boy relived his encounter in his head, in his heart, with his hands and his mouth until every bird and snake within the vicinity of a well-fired arrow finally knew of his feat. Once back on the summit of the jungle hill, they stopped to stare at distant plumes of smoke.

Leebu sniffed the air. "Looks like your human villages are burning."

"Come," Ullumon said. "The night draws near."

"Where's all that coming from?" the boy asked.

Ignoring the question, Ullumon turned. His eyes bore a faint menace. "Da elephant has seven rows of molars. Remember dis. After da seventh iz gone da elephant starve. Remember dis lesson, Diamond. We only have so much time. Reap what iz yours while fit to."

✳

"This one?" Conabitt saw only a pile of dirty rags. Uprooting his face from a swelling bag, the old man gave a nod. The boy grabbed the travel cloak and handed it over.

"We must leave," Ullumon said. "Tonight." He confiscated the candles the boy was packing. "Leebu knows the hidden trails."

The evening had come and with it the stars, before the storms rolled in. Now the night beyond the hut echoed with the chorus of frogs in a calm vacuum, the world wet and gleaming. Whatever had burned and caused long spires of black smoke in the afternoon had to have been extinguished by the gusts that ended an hour ago. Initially caught in the first wave, the soaked and soggy trio had filed in with no intent to find cloaks or put back candles. The humans were exhausted and may have settled in for a quiet night around a brazier's fire, if it hadn't been for the hornbills.

"They are coming, they are coming," squawked the birds. The moment the rain ended, the two had returned to pitch a fit. With his satchels still wet and dripping and slung about him, the old man had limped outside. Behind him went the boy. "They are coming! The white—"

Ullumon silenced the male with a gesture. Turning to Conabitt, "Fetch a sip of water for da old man."

When Conabitt returned, the hornbills stared down uneasily. Back out under the tree, Ullumon shook in his hand what any Orisulan would have called a potion. "Time for another, Diamond."

The boy uncorked the crude vial and drank down its contents without thought. Burning, emboldening, this liquid was thick, brown, and sick. And at its bottom the dear boy's realization: the man loved him. More so maybe than his own scowling, governing father did. This sensation persisted in him as Ullumon looked up at the birds.

"Continue, hornbill."

"They are coming, coming. The whites. Burning villages, they are."

The female interjected in a lighter lark: "Herders. Told on you."

Both flapped and spoke together: "Told them you may have the white boy."

"Day all wanting me gone!" Ullumon erupted. "And dis be how day mean to do it."

"No one spared," the male seemed to have said after.

"Does dis bother you, Diamond?" The old man was looking at him. The Lathairboni knew that while God's Broth dissipated slow, the charmer, the potent Goonu powder dissolved in hyena blood, would wear off quickly. Wasting no time, he said, "You don't wish to be found by da whites."

"I hate Suela," the boy said. "Well, I thought I did. I want to go back to the Morgeltine."

"Why?"

The boy seemed to provide his answer as if coughing up a lump. "My—my father."

"Ah." The Lathairboni put a hand on his shoulder. "He was a calma, fairer man? Back dare? Back den?" The boy thought about it and nodded. "Maybe, dear boy, you were too young back den to see him for who he was. Who he iz."

"I want," the Goonu at its zenith. "Can I stay with you, Ullumon?"

Ullumon clapped his hands, bright as a bell. "Datz a good boy. I tell you what, you stay with old Ullumon. We do more adventure. Den we can take you back. But only if you say." Ullumon sent away the birds, comforting the boy during his protests that he'd stay in the jungle forever.

"Where we going now?" The boy shouldered the bag Ullumon had given him.

"To da Nilosulans. Our peoples in da south."

✳

The jungles were still thick. Moving what Ullumon insisted in the dead of night was south bore them nearly impenetrable. All the stopping had worried the boy. He'd regained something of himself, though he discomforted still in seeing any old man cower and grimace under the burden of pain. Leebu, by a contrast grown expected, seemed to rejoice in the matter, strolling over and flicking his tail in the old man's face when he wheezed the greatest.

✳

"Sarge, look." A mailed hand reached down into a vat. At its still-warm bottom was discovered the head of a monkey. Orisulans were fond of impaling, and the hangman's noose. Beheading irked them.

The sergeant grumbled, walking from the doorway. "These jungle vermin, they should be round up and drowned."

The soldier plopped the head back in, afterward kicking the whole thing over. The handful of men tearing apart the hut paled in number to the company who tore down the snares and deadfalls outside. Every local finger had pointed toward the evil wizard, and the captain-turned-lunatic whom the sergeant served spared no expense at getting them promptly to the fabled hut.

Cots were flipped, cupboards cleared, sacks and bags run through then tossed onto a roaring bonfire. Religion and the soldierly came hand in hand, at least in Mulgara where civilizations beat metal into armor and not coconuts into annoying drums. Those inside were sickened by the obvious devilry; the nailed ears, unsettling smells, the ophidiarium under the man's dinner table.

"Sarge!" A tracker burst in. "We found tracks. A man *and a boy's.* They're leading away, seems to be following some path some leopard's on."

"Sarge!" came another voice.

The sergeant winced, then swung his eyes over. A soldier stood in the darkest, furthest corner of the godforsaken place, stammering until he squeaked, "You need to see this."

She was stuffed crudely into a wooden chest then covered by a zebra hide. Her wounds consistent with Suelan rebels. But nothing else fell under what the sergeant could call the norm. The boy's nanny's eyes had been cut out, carefully relocated into the clay jars tucked away under her exposed rump. Worse yet, causing one of the brawny men to run out and vomit, the angle of her sex exposed how easily its greater parts had been removed, their locations unknown, and would be forever. The Orisulans took pleasure watching the place swirl up then crash in cinders.

Somewhere before sunrise, the cat found a cave of ferns, tolerably moist, a place where the old man crawled in like a spider who'd been scorched by flames. The boy excited at the prospect of joining the cat. There was a hunt to be had, but his feet ached and his head swam.

What felt like an instant later, the boy was roused from a deep sleep. Wiping free from his face the leaf that had woke him, he grunted and squinted up into the canopy. Morning had come, and with it the grey and pink of a sky still determined to hide the sun. What pallor seeped through did so on the dreary camp. Leebu was sleeping directly above, on a sturdy branch, belly fattened by a kill whose uneaten remains hung nearby. The hooves reminded Conabitt of what he'd been yesterday. He managed to smile. Then he looked over at Ullumon.

It was as if the night had sucked him like a giant leech. His limbs, limp yet gnarled and root-like. His mouth, stuck in an awful expression. His skin, dried as a mummy's despite the humidity already beading on the boy's lip. He crouched down, relieved when he saw the slow up and down of Ullumon's ribs. He was old. Older than the boy had thought. At long last the man's wrinkled, brown lids cracked open.

"Are you okay?" Ullumon said nothing, but shifted a little in the sodden leaves. "Why not turn us into elephants? Then we could get where we're going."

"Now he is thinking, Leebu." The old man laughed. "The change. Too much pain for old bones. Help me up, dear boy."

And that was it. Conabitt thought he heard a hip pop, then they were off again. Leebu roused, savorless biscuits eaten, more vines and fern parted, and soon the three had reformed their file and trekked down what Leebu had said was a meat trail. With little deviation, the cleared-out sliver carried them southward, delivering upon them a second night of misery.

"Stop here." The old man had found a log, a less black shape mottled by fungus that bore a blueish glow. He looked like some demon, seated in contemplation.

"No good here," Leebu growled.

"Does not have to be a mansion, Leebu."

In the luminescence, the boy could see the cat was looking around. The cat said, "Your ears are failing you. We are—"

Then the boy heard. He got down and crawled over. "What are they?"

Similar to what he'd heard come out of Leebu during the quarrel over the sacks, growls were coming from somewhere beyond the trees. These growls, however, boomed and persisted. More than one cat was out there.

"Lions," Leebu said, to which the boy's eyes grew wide. "Heard of them, have you?" Conabitt listened, depicting as best he could them calling to one another.

"Are those their names?"

"We must reroute," Leebu said. "Come."

The boy followed, but not without hoisting Ullumon up and being the old man's second staff. Somewhere deep in the night the rains came again, as did another miserable shelter were the boy shivered until dawn.

Right as bug bites and the legacy of Ullumon's biscuits had convinced Conabitt they'd died and wandered into the hell Orisulan priests loved to warn him about, on this day, the second day since leaving Ullumon's dry hut and only three since being rescued, right as afternoon heat was giving way to the brief joy of evening, Leebu led them out from under the trees and onto the fringe of a Suelan village.

The cat accepted Ullumon's rope, pulled from his satchel and wrapped around its neck like a dog's leash. This pageant was the only way to prevent widespread panic, for as they made their way to whatever Ullumon had in store, they did so through the rickety fences of goat corrals. Never had the boy heard such barnyard mayhem. Suelans emerged from their huts. They were the same ebony as Ullumon, as the men who'd tried to abduct him, who had killed his nanny, the soldiers, the coachman. Yet with their dress, veiled only in ornate bone rings and the burgundy droop of tough loincloths, these Nilosulans presented an even wilder man.

Apprehension towards Ullumon and his plodding, cold-staring

cat lifted when the clear, big white eyes Conabitt saw took their turn to stare upon him. Conabitt hadn't noticed the lack of trees, the slight slope on which they walked down something like the main avenue. Only when they stopped at the pointy heads of canoes did he gaze upon the wide plain of water that ribboned around a bend.

"Da swamps be our friend," Ullumon said to him. "Village-burning whites be not coming here." Nilosulans had dropped their fish nets and now crowded around. Odd, but for all the monkeys and deer and cat talk, Conabitt scratched his head as a village elder begin speaking to Ullumon. The boy understood nothing.

Ullumon seemed to fair better, slowing the tongue they spoke to respond and point down to the water's edge.

As another night approached, a negotiation of sorts ended and the trio stepped inside a canoe. Accompanied by a local, this apt boatmen stood at the very rear of the canoe, pushing them along with a wooden pole.

In the last moments of evening, turns soft and sharp glided the boy past fields of grass. How far below their stalks went before rooting in murky bottoms he could not guess. It took only one look beyond the worn wooden lip, into the black mirror disrupted by their wake. The boy felt uneasy, passing a speckling of outstretched trees, the last of the islands, then they were swallowed by the delta.

The moon had been out early. Together, the moon and the boatman, they turned the watery grasslands that enclosed the three into sallow, rustling walls. At the walls' breaks, which were many, the boy soon recognized such blankness to be the openings of other channels. A maze was what they were in. Certainly safe from being found, at least by men. But the far black of island forests and the too-near lurkings under an ancient wetland hid every fear a boy could imagine. Sallow walls, when they squeezed in on them, the boy rightly perceived as the mark of a shallow bottom. In these moments the boatman, Boadu—as he'd replied to Ullumon's inquiry— softly guided the canoe so close to the grass that it rubbed against their arms. When the channels widened, Boadu repositioned them in the water's center.

"Why does he do this?" Conabitt whispered up to Ullumon, who in turn spoke to the boatman in the local, southern tongue.

"Says hippos," Ullumon translated. "Day be at da sides in deeper water."

Conabitt turned and scrutinized the strikes of Boadu's pole. They seemed gentle enough, enough not to enrage a submerged monster, at least. The paintings and rumors back at the colony were bad enough. Being out at night amongst those horrid water cows who chomped people and horses in two was—"Ullumon, I don't want to be here," the boy accidentally said in cat.

"Boy's right," Leebu said, stiffening the guide. The boatman heard only growls, the kind that came at moments where fishing ended and brutal fights against leopards often began. "No place to be, stuck out on a drifting log."

"Shut your jaws," Ullumon said from up front, causing the cat to growl deeper and the boatman to utter a string of chants. Leebu stood. The boy no longer saw the silhouette of the old man, only the leopard's side as the entire canoe rocked. "And sit," Ullumon whispered, "*down*." Ullumon repeated his command, but still the cat hung over the side, continuing to lap up water. "You wish to tip us?"

"Easy, Lathairboni," Leebu said, "don't go showing the boy how scared you get."

The old man cleared his throat. "Mock me," he said coolly. "In front of a pupil?"

"That's just the start!" Leebu made the boy jump and the boatman begin pleading. "The only reason we make it far enough to drift on miserable logs is because of *me*. Me! Otherwise you'd be lost, limping, or in the belly of a lion pride."

That was enough. Boadu the boatman saw the old man rise, turn, then belt the cat in the ribs with his staff. The cat clawed the air, hissed, and eventually retreated until on the very lap of the white boy.

Somewhere near midnight they poled through the waters at a renewed speed. Leebu, silent, saw them all. The boy saw only the ones whose glistening backs shined back the silver of the moon. Hippos had come on land. Conabitt squinted, counting fifteen before the nose of the canoe slid up onto the shells and mud of an island.

Ullumon groaned and moaned until once again upright, cursing the foul canoe for its hard seats. On land he took a worse tone with Boadu, who nodded and began carrying into the hinterland what meager supplies the village had provided. Switching to his broken Orisulan, Ullumon said to the boy, "See, Diamond? Do wish to live a life of such servitude? Scurrying about with a sack over your head?"

"Yeah," Conabitt brightened. "Let's move a little faster there, boat man."

"Ask him question. Go on."

The boy waited until the sweating figure reemerged from the shadows. "You, you like doing that?"

"Good, good," the Lathairboni laughed.

The boatman said nothing, but the moon revealed more than once a stare suggesting he well understood.

With the improvement of a scale-hide tent, the night came and went without the awfulness Conabitt concluded he was getting used to. In the morning the boatman was gone, and out into the expanse of a large island the three went.

Before long, the rolling grass and clumps of dense bush gave way. Beyond the hard dirt hummed another village. "Deez people even more remote," Ullumon said. The boy nodded, looking at what appeared to be some sort of primitive trash heap.

He'd always heard back at the dismal colony that Suelans lived as savages, yes, but ones at least in tune with their land. With the top of the nearest hut barely visible, skulls that looked to have once been owned by dragons lay strewn about, hacked and beaten—former owners of the scales. Scattered amongst the sun-scorched bones were fish heads and the rotting gore that accompanied them.

"Why are we here?" the boy asked.

"Da village? Oh, we not going in." Ullumon pointed at the heap. "Here good enough. Do you see?"

"Rats? Everywhere." And they were, sending a quick shiver down the boy. Rats in Orisula were for unsavory wards and ships that eventually sank.

The Lathairboni leaned into his staff and turned a lustful whisper. "Not da rats." Here he pointed that same bony finger, but at a bush near the wasteland's fringe. "Do you see?"

The bush was but a normal bush. The boy focused, intently, scratching his head and staring at nothing. A stick lying under the bush's dirt-powdered leaves, it began to move.

A large snake slithered, stopping at certain moments to regain its rhythm and place its dull yellow-brown stripes in blades of grass alongside a crushed skull.

One was wrapping itself around his leg! Conabitt screamed, sending the old man leaping, the boy leapt too, and the rats scurrying into every hole. Leebu unwrapped his tail and plodded up to Ullumon. "If the boy is to learn the way of the fang, I'll be his teacher."

Coming down and gripping his staff with both hands, Ullumon frothed. "Jokes and ruin. You, Leebu, *you*, great cat, ruin and now expect to teach?"

"Yes I do," the cat said, putting his eye on Conabitt. "You white humans love your plates, yeah? Our old man has told me. Made by others, caught by others, killed...by others." The boy didn't want to take his eyes off Ullumon. "Imagine, *boy*. Imagine that love, now add something sweeter than the cool drink of the springs. Sweeter even than a mother's love. Hunger, boy, filled."

"You're going to turn me into a snake."

The boy was talking to Ullumon, but it was Leebu who answered. "Patience. Ruthlessness."

"Are you done?" Ullumon said.

"The bliss of a well-placed strike."

When the golden powder rained down on Conabitt the boy had expected it, and the pain, contorting him as if crushed by hands into a stricken, convulsing rope. The old man's words sounded far away, then sound itself became something different. The site of Leebu caused Conabitt to do he knew not what. Coil? A pressed paw into the dirt *sounded* as if rolls of thunder. The Lathairboni may have instructed the boy, but he didn't need it. He was to experience lying in wait, to capture prey.

The boy slithered.

The boy didn't hear Ullumon say, "You hear the hyenas, Leebu? They must've crossed in the night. You wish to show *them* your knowledge of the fang?" Leebu's paws boomed off the earth as he leapt into the nearest tree. The boy heard nothing, but the earth screamed with an army of increasing trots.

"Hyenas," said a voice out of nowhere. It was in the native tongue, though, too, the boy could not hear. It cried, "Hyenas are not the only who've crossed the waters, Ullumon." Not from the village but out of bushes appeared a short and portly little man. The boy sensed a rut in the soil, where his prey would be.

"Chomcha," Ullumon groaned. "The *good* Lathairboni."

"All Lathairboni are good," said Chomcha, adjusting the scale-skin armor that covered his legs and chest. "Except *you*. Where is the white boy?"

"I have seen no white boy, kind and heroic Chomcha."

"My nephew Boadu says *you* have possession." Chomcha was without staff, but in one hand he waved an ornate and formidable wand. "Diabolic dog! Do you think of no one? They are more than looking for him. It's bringing ruin to people all over Suela, from the grasslands all the way down to the river edge." Chomcha began to cross the rat-infested ground. "*Where* is that boy?"

Ullumon slowly put his hand into his satchel. "Oh, he's slithering around here someplace."

The boy slithered forward, gaining speed.

He did not choose to become what he was, but he did choose to want it. *Want*…maybe not. Did his sister Dia want to be pretty? *Yes*, a snake's brain thought, like his sister Lia wants to fly, like their sister Mia wants to marry a prince. All just who and what they are. Put a boy in the jungle, and he won't be able to help it, he will become hungry.

Those sisters, they may live without beauty, they'll live without having cut clouds with bare hands or marrying, but the boy, he had no choice. It was oblivion or eat. He saw the short, fat man, his booming feet, but the boy cared not. Movement was in his eye, low to the ground as he was.

"And how dare you," the man called Chomcha cried, pointing his decorated stick at Ullumon, "threaten the village with plague if they didn't give to you what you ask."

"Watch where you point that thing, Chomcha."

The boy waited. One came out, briefly, then scurried out of sight and range when the ground's rumble gave way to Ullumon.

The old man had been smitten by Chomcha's wand. His curse of surprise ran through the boy, who, also stunned, watched as roots from under the soil burst up and seized Ullumon by the wrists, pulling him down, trying to pin him against the hard earth.

Ullumon slipped a hand free, flinging gold powder at Chomcha. The cloud, falling short, burst to life a cluster of fish heads. Their missed target jerked back as they writhed and moaned and hideously mutated into new, fouler forms. Mouths grown large crawled and clamored. Forcing his eyes away, Chomcha struck the air, calling forth a second volley of roots.

Ullumon, no longer free, crumpled as laughter stepped foot

onto their war. Both Lathairboni saw all the thick brown heads now. Chomcha dithered, dropping his wand, but Ullumon howled, eyes wild, wide—white—calling forth the slobbering pack.

The pack charged. Chomcha reclaimed his wand to thwart their attack. Teeth crashed into a globe that had instantaneously encased the man, flashing green wherever the beasts lunged before circling Chomcha in a thickening ring.

The villagers were long used to hyenas. A local clan foraged their broken crocodile heads and fish garbage and served as guardians against nosey male lions. Their tracks tattooed the soil, the trails leading away, their muzzles viewed for two generations as tools of use and protection. But these who surrounded Chomcha were Ullumon's.

Ullumon called upon two, who obeyed the human who knew their tongue, soon working with their teeth to free him from the roots.

For those who cast magic in an appointed village, or for those few Lathairboni who wandered the plains or dwelt in jungle twilight, there was no question: Chomcha was no match for the vile Ullumon. Ullumon cackled. Staggering upright, he raised his arms. Chomcha had no recourse. Ullumon then leveled them at Chomcha, popping his green globe like a boil.

The hyenas took note.

When the screaming became something nearer to silence, a youngster broke off to seize in its jaws the long body of a fleeing snake. Leebu had sought refuge in high branches and the tranquility of a rare moment alone, and had watched the skirmish with relative indifference. At the sight of the boy, the leopard flew down and pounced on the hyena's back.

Pulled from the display of carnage, Ullumon shrieked, baying the burdened hyena. Leebu swung to Ullumon's side, snarling at the pack, who, with loud commands and great somatic effort, Ullumon sent laughing and scampering back into the bush.

The two looked down at the broken snake. The tiny, fanged mouth opened. Leebu, unable to hear, spoke to the boy, but the boy could not understand. Ullumon looked at Leebu, then back down, over the boy, contorting his tongue and firing down the necessary reverberation. Conabitt heard the old man: "Why? The more violence, the greater the control; the greater the control, the easier the corruption. And when corruption seeps in, my dear boy, then appears the master for whom we work."

The boy, a dying cobra, driven by promptings from a borrowed guise, summoned the machinery of a long spine to plunge his fangs into his own side, not stopping until every drop of venom poured into unmeant places.

The human boy lay breathing, next to Chomcha, who wasn't.

✳

"Da hyenas did what lesson was meant for you." In his true form, Conabitt patted himself and found not a single bone broken. Not a scratch rendered. Observing the boy's astonishment, Ullumon came off his staff. "Did you feel da headache of an impala? No, Diamond, retrograde make all better."

The boy sickened when he saw what remained of the strange man. "Who is he?"

"Some wicked, wily Lathairboni. Meant to take you and Leebu away."

"Ullumon." The boy turned to the old man.

"Where," Leebu interrupted, back in his tree. "Where are you going to have us hide now?" He keened his eye at some point beyond the highest bush. "Smoke," the cat said, climbing back down. "It's near."

✳

The God's Broth was wearing off. Ullumon knew this, for he'd mastered the mixtures; the cauldron's load of blood, spring water, the incantation-covered herbs and the appropriate dust of once appropriated bones. Conabitt knew it because growls—plain and ordinary—were starting to come out of Leebu.

"How much longer will I be able to talk to him?"

They were in what the village had provided. Ullumon didn't just need rest, he needed to heal. The war he'd won, but it had cost him. That the villagers had hid behind every tree and hut's hard corner to watch the end of Chomcha the Lathairboni didn't surprise him, nor did their silence as the three had entered after, to be given a wide berth and a vacant hut.

The boy was wondering, if Ullumon died, whether the God's Broth would suddenly end. His thoughts faded when Ullumon sat up from a bed of rags. "Soon, Diamond. Want to talk to da animals forever, do you?" The old man cackled, calling the boy over to hoist him up and carry him to the open doorway. "Magic." The old man squinted and pointed at a patch of wild palms. "Magic be everywhere. Don't you worry. See da palms? Even day hold great, learned, ancient magic. *How are day magic?*—dear Diamond, day are da gatekeepers of da gods. First planted of all da plants. Of all da tall, day commune powers of man to da powers higher dan man. Day, dare leaves, day will wrap around born leaders, but only when da born leader be good an ready."

"Ready for what?"

The old man looked down, into him. "When ready to turn da white sands red."

The boy understood perfectly. When some warlord appeared, some great man, ready to take no orders but give them, then the palm trees would do something. Or he thought he understood— but such talk gave way to the settling in of evening and soon it seemed there was only silence.

Silence—except for the hyenas—out where the bush was thicker, out beyond the palms. The last event of the day had been a fight between the cat and his master so fierce that Conabitt thought one was going to bite the other bloody. Now a fire crackled. Ullumon and Leebu snored on opposing sides. The boy was back at that open doorway, listening. There was another noise out there. *Cries?* he thought. *Of men?* Not in the broken Orisulan as Suelans spoke, but in the plain, bald speech of his father's people.

Against good sense, he ventured out into the early twilight. The black of the village and the blue of the sky reminded him of the types of paintings one of his sisters liked to paint. Blocky, pointed shapes for men, though none strolled the dim ribbons of between-paths, and the warm dark night greeted him, as did the stars, twinkling high above a final scream.

"Hyena. Hyena. Hyenas," a frog croaked.

Perhaps it was the confidence he'd gained as a duelist impala, or a snake, broken on his hunt and repaired to normal by a black magician's strange powder. Perhaps it was that a fanged leopard had slept near him on consecutive nights. But whatever drove the young boy to skirt the edge of the palms and to tread into where now-gone hyenas had rampaged, he was most certainly driven.

Moonlight. This time brighter. Between he and it were the palms; tall Suelan trees that he could not tell if they'd grown wild or were planted. As he crept passed, the nearest, oddly, seemed to creak and sway, as if the dull-silver appendages of the great leaves were straining to reach out and forbid his progress.

Just beyond them lay slain men, white men, caught in the agony of their final moments. Some with swords still in hand, chunks of fur in the other. What feat these men had made, stabbing so deep into the Suelan delta they'd come within arrowshot. They had come so close. Gotten so close. A familiar badge sent Conabitt wailing.

They were the True Men, a crack reconnaissance outfit made from the colony's best trackers. Though small in number, the boy knew from harrowing tales that they went blow to blow with every adversary of the Suelan wild. Suffering the squishes under his bare feet, he welled into tears, seeing the unmarred face of one who'd let him once hold the great sword that he died swinging. A night cloud gave way, shining the moon fully upon the massacre. The way the skin had been ripped, the way muscle had been torn off the bone: all, by now, familiarities. They had been ravaged by Ullumon's pack.

There were dead hyenas, too. Many, one of which he kicked and slung sloppily a sword too big to bring it down on a devilish head. The True Men could have, would have, bested an ordinary pack.

"Ullumon," the boy uttered, letting go of the sword and looking back at the village. What conviction had driven these beasts? The old man was amazing, but the boy did not feel amazed. He wondered why he had frolicked in the wildest wood in all Mulgara. Long gone now was the last residual of the Goonu, popped free by the sight of supernatural murder. Unlike the joyous journey here, *here* the boy was a stranger, in a land that did not love him, herded by a stranger who saw to it that good men, men who were the lions of their own world, were mangled and eaten.

Conabitt began walking back to the hut. Fires behind doorways glowed. No noise came from the village, as if they too had been butchered by the mad man's schemes.

"Ullumon, sir." The boy stepped inside. Their own fire had burned low. Both were awake. "Did you know?"

"Know what, dear boy? Do not speak in riddle."

"The men. From the colony."

"What of dem?"

Sights too horrid for a boy to see had been seen and more. They had been felt, smelled, seared into a young impressionable brain. All at once, his nanny, dead beside him on a night that could have been a million years since, the dead guards and the sickening fate of that short, fat man, they all converged. The boy cried.

"What of da white men, Diamond?" Ullumon had risen off his rags, eyeing him.

"The True Men," Conabitt heaved, then pointed, "out there."

The Lathairboni reached for his staff, stumbling to his feet. "Where? Out dare!"

"You didn't know?"

"No, boy."

The old man hobbled over and addressed his crying, but in the way a coarse older boy may, having dared someone into accidently breaking a bone, and now worried of an adult hearing the wails and whimpers.

The boy looked at Leebu, hoping for something. But the cat only sniffed the air. "I want to go home," the boy sobbed.

"Yes, yes, you should." Ullumon renewed. "Splendid idea. Home shall you go." Ullumon hobbled over to his satchel, then triumphantly floured the boy in a new powder. The boy felt nothing, not even when the old man began chanting. "Dare," Ullumon smiled, "dare you go. Good as white man's iron shield. No harm now can befall you." Conabitt was being ushered out the door. "You don't need food, don't need water. Not for at least, um, six days! Six days to get back to white colony and never speak of old Ullumon again."

Conabitt Lotgard had impressed his tutors. They were obliged to clap and clamor, to show marked progress to his father lest be sacked, but they'd genuinely meant it, too. He was astute for his age—astute enough to once point out the clumsy timing in a story he parsed for a full day. All at once, the boy had pointed out, a master thief who'd been stricken blind was cured by the surprise benevolence of an appeared fairy, and on the same day another, unrelated fairy had dizzied a tyrant into casting away the fierce keepers of his famed treasury.

Such odd synchronicities were present this night, though the boy this time was unaware.

"Ullumon," the boy heard Leebu say in anger. What followed were only growls. The God's Broth was done. The boy understood the cat's admonishment of the foul Lathairboni no better than he did the old man's retorts. The God's Broth had worn off near the same instant the boy wished only for home. And Ullumon granted it.

But perhaps the stars were maligned, for this meant the boy was unable to hear:

"He won't live through the night!"

"Oh, the great cat shows tender, tender love. You worry about you, Leebu. Isn't that what you preach?"

"Then I'm going too."

"Going too! To guard the white boy? He'll grow to hunt you."

"No!" The cat sprang across the room, pinning the old man. "To be rid of *you*, Ullumon!"

What the boy saw next rivaled in its horror the battleground beyond the palms. It seemed the old man pulled from somewhere a shriveled, mummified eye. He pointed at it, then to the cat, who withdrew, hissing. The cat drew back, setting its might into its rear legs before leaping once more.

Conabitt fled the hut screaming. The old man and the cat screamed, too. Then only the cat.

The boy ran, being torn by branches or by animals he could not understand. Blinded he ran, right into a wall of metal.

"Corporal," a soldier said, absently touching his breastplate where the boy had bloodied his own nose. "Corporal!—we have 'im!"

"Where have you been, boy?" another Orisulan soldier appeared out of the blackness holding a sword. No sooner had he spoke than his sword became a ring of light, coming up just in time to drop an armed shadow.

More shadows were running towards them, revealing themselves as Nilosulans as they screamed and gathered. The True Men—Conabitt remembered—they always went ahead. What followed, now turning the night to orange, was a detachment of troops who'd lit the village on fire.

"No!" the boy cried, at the Orisulans who flung torches, at the villagers who'd taken arms against them. Searing light from an engulfed roof revealed that his nose hadn't been broken, but the man he'd collided into was the one who'd been bleeding. This man's face had become snow. His long hair sat silken wet. The one Conabitt guessed was the corporal grabbed him by the collar. The boy was released when a spear found the tall man's head.

"Rebellion" it would be called, if an Orisulan lived to tell it, and the villagers with a collective, honed hatred that splintered the troops. Those who were displaced were bludgeoned with clubs. Those who remained together fared better. But no place, no trampled patch of blood-soaked ground was safe from sword or spear. The refuge of the palms blazed light as day.

He crawled.

Wide trunks were useful against flying spears. Shadows made by fires were enough to seep down into and hug the earth. The fingers of the trees rubbed his back, *tickled* he felt the urge to think, as he heard footsteps. It only took one look to see the men who'd followed him. Their skin gleaming, their muscles taut from use of the spears that still dripped.

If Ullumon, if Leebu, if anyone were here. The men spoke at him in their tongue.

Crying, the boy shut his eyes and tried to run. They pounced on him, grabbing him with their hands and lifting him effortlessly into the air. When he didn't feel that unknowable certainty of a spear bursting through his belly, the boy opened his eyes. In the air, he was, yes. But, oddly, the two men now stood well under him. One was already chanting.

Palm leaves enshrouded, suspending him wickedly, caught in the light of blazing fires, a white angel of death and dominion. The chanting man fell to his knees, prompting the other to drop his weapon. Frozen by the sight, known in the villages, whispered in the plains, they were no match for the soldiers who snuck up behind.

Half blinded from the pain and the fighting, the Orisulans who hugged Conabitt had no interest in why he'd been in the trees. Before the palms had lowered him, Conabitt looked out over the raging flames and in the chaos saw the eye of a cat. Almost in the bush line, the orange ball gleamed, gleamed then seemed to wink, if cats do such things, then it was gone.

"Conabitt," a soldier later said, his own name now sounding foreign. Dawn awaited, as did the northbound ship the bandaged swordsmen assured him would take him and his family "out of this hell."

"Conabitt," the soldier said again, clearing his throat. This soldier, who'd been calling out orders to put on their knees the few remaining villagers, stood with the stature of a seasoned leader. "Young lord," the stout man said, pleasant enough, "you may wish to turn away. We have to deal with the rebels now."

"No," Conabitt said, earning him a surprised look. He was thinking about his brief, wild journey, who he'd made it with, what he'd learned, and how it somehow felt over before it had even truly begun. Wrapped in a new confidence, one as unusual for young boys as would be becoming animals or allowed to speak their speech, the boy salvaged from the ground the tattered remains of a soldier's cloak, turning it into a robe. "No, it's all right. May I give the order?"

ARIGOL AND THE
PARILGOTHEUM

In the city of Pelliul, mothers warn children not to venture toward homes or worn-down shops wobbling above the Parilgotheum. Beyond the threat of thieves or bludgeoning by loosened brick is the long-held worry that ghouls creep just below the cobblestones. It is said those dead-eaters vie for space with the inmates of the noted underground prison.

The Parilgotheum, said to have been named such after the epitaph on one of its pillars, existed long before Pelliul. Well, the ruins did—a city's worth, with no shortage of withered sarcophagi. Attempts to incorporate its porticos, crumbling tunnels, and what forth were abandoned when a sublevel, unknown to even the most ambitious archeologists, caved, pulling said lettered men down— along with the growing, top-level renovations—to an abyss since boarded and sealed.

A fresh block of city was laid out over the necropolis. Now, low-rent housing and sly shops carry on in their maledictions, distantly aware that iron cellar doors cap a dark world of roaming madmen and the various bones cluttered there throughout the settling of centuries.

It was above the Parilgotheum that the writer, Dandana Nix, arrived after following a trail of what magistrates called "clues." Desperate times called for desperate measures—one of the many clichés she tried earnestly to avoid penning into her work, though it perfectly applied these days to her daily life. Racking up tabs in breweries and winehouses did nothing to help her accounts, to say nothing of her productivity and ever-important health.

She needed new material. Nix had taken to writing crime dramas, starting with scrolls that sold in back rooms, and now up to the lofty height of leather-bounds that were driving her homeless. She needed another hit. Her work *The Embryonic Sorcerer* sold like wildfire, and like most wildfires was extinguished by an arbitrary change in the wind. Nothing left but wisps of smoke like fans who never bothered with the sequel.

That she'd paid a timid neophyte to further his putrescence in black magic until their petty crimes flamed up into his self-obliteration was a detail she omitted. Her readers fancied her a brilliant pensmith, inexplicably capable of diving down to the bottoms of the human condition. This was true, to an extent. Nix's spelunk into depravity had earned her a piquant, lower-level fame. The sort where fellow willows batted long eyelashes from behind the glass of immodest bookstores, or literate barbarians would sometimes embrace her as if she too were a sworder, one who'd shared in a vague but glorious conquest.

That she actually committed many of the crimes she wrote would remain a secret, her "magic," her vat of feculent ooze, her muse-like powers bursting from the constellations of her inkwell. To watch someone die just to take note of their struggled breath, the waxing gloss of eyes grown fearful, the terror when death herself grabbed them by the balls: it paid the bills. Bills that were growing right alongside the fear of getting caught.

Trying to address both at once, Nix decided to sheathe her dagger and pore over archives at a magistrate's office. Soon, wide-eyed and slack-jawed, the ambitious writer was walking, notes-scroll in hand, gathering one clue after the other.

Her first stop had been a ditch. This slump in the graveyard made its border walls above seem doomish and oppressive. The official report had read *the plot under the southwestern elm*. Staring up at where its trunk met the earth and accounting for new headstones erected since, the site of a "disturbed corpse crime" sat, as she would soon learned they all did, at a scene's lowest point.

She'd discovered a string of bizarre cases involving those who were already dead. Graveyards, low-earth morgues, public mausoleums flooded by rain. Unaffected victims, to say the least, but bereaved families howled when a son was dug up or a still-stinking matriarch was found flopped over her own tombstone, chest torn open and rotten brain missing. Visits to ever more nefarious places drummed up rumors. The mythic eaters of the dead. Those who worked in graveyards or meandered in the twilights where she huckstered her reads chorused ghouls were the culprit. Ghouls. Crime-committing ghouls. Who could ask for greater material? Not only drama, but fascination of the land's untarnished love for the gross and macabre.

Dandana Nix was a fictionalist, or, as she sometimes preferred, wasn't a non-fictionalist. Those preachers and prattlers, why with their treatises better spent putting people to sleep—she yearned to set them ablaze! If ghouls were real, then they were masters of secrecy. She wouldn't disrupt their doings. She merely wanted an interview. "The ultimate well," she said, departing lit streets to tread into the city's bilge. The ultimate well to bucket up inspiration. Hell, in a few years, if they spoke, she'd be penning ghoul stories right out of foul, fetid mouths.

The lowest cringle on the map in the lowest bowl between two of Pelliul's three great hills, there stagnates life above the penal necropolis. Onto a warehouse's cellar floor rolled moldering limbs she'd procured from a sympathetic mortician. While she squinted, while she held firm her lantern, moon-white claws ripped through the earth. She'd been right. A ghoul was coming!

Golbert Amphilliod refused to die in the gloomy subterranea. Prompted by forces he did not fully understand, underworld hues of gold and red had provided light during his exhausting journey, to a derelict path, one that was leading up. He'd already ascended the spiral protrusions of a crumbling staircase. Before doing so, stones had given way first, between dry earth at the floor of the necropolis and this dark soil on which the wide city waited. Crawling past clumps of rock, he threw them behind him. His heart had rejoiced at the sight of an undernourished root, splayed out from the ceiling of the tunnel which had brought him here. To his knowledge, he would be the first ever to escape the dread Parilgotheum, and the orange light pulling him forward like a current—wholesome, unbewitched light—up ahead waved and wiggled.

A busted gutter, perhaps a worn pipe from one of the city's unaccounted aqueducts: water had burrowed a claustrophobic tunnel. Only mud lay between him and freedom. So Golbert kept on, crawling through the thick paste, grunting, birthing himself until at last reaching out with his fingers into what could only be the World Above.

It was a mystery. What fueled the crystalline rocks? What still remained of the golds and reds that dizzied the underworld pressed against his cheek as a single crimson stud. Laying his head in the mud, he rested for a final burst up and out into hopefully a place near food and bereft of guards. His breathing calm, he couldn't help but think again of his brother, Aricow.

Brother, he thought. *Brotherhood.* Tragic. That Aricow had to depart—right when they were to learn how to escape this vile place. It was a cruelty just as it was cruel they both had somehow ended up down here together.

Their last adventure was still pulling at his thoughts.

Golbert was a veteran of the Suelan Suppression. Sticking around, he'd eventually been promoted to sergeant. Bursting the buttons of his once dapper uniform and rotting away by wine, he'd briefly manned the guard post that fronted the, then-brand-new Suelan Suppression Memorial Mausoleum.

Suppression—hah! While on the topic of cruelty. A merry dance of words—a lordship for you, you slimy, scroll-spinning bastard, you. To get *that* carved in stone, in stone on and in other mausoleums, gravestones elsewhere, and to the gods, the uncounted, uncountable native rotting graves back in Suela. Man had sought to conquer man, and did. Suppression, yes, Golbert was guilty, serving as he did, no better than a cog in a thunderous wheel. Suppression of only a doomed people's revolt to reclaim a stolen destiny. Suelan suppression now rang true, up there, in the World Above. Black-skinned slaves chopped wood and cleaned out slop and occasionally lost a foot.

But he had soldiered, and he had slaughtered. He had spent his most virile years serving a colony since abandoned. Worse— or equal, perhaps, he'd arrived at the age of his father when he'd groaned of growing back pain and ear hair. And Golbert had arrived there with no other skill. A life of military service it was, then, portly or otherwise.

Golbert commanded the ceremonial unveiling of the mausoleum's final addition: a statue depicting a masculine soldier stepping on the head of an equally ridiculous savage, ripping from the lower creature's hands a grateful Suelan baby. He got adorned in all the old kit that wouldn't fit, sang the songs he hadn't forgotten, and, as the sky brushed away its jeweled gloss for an evening's pallid splendor, he stepped inside the mausoleum to lock the front doors before bowing out a side exit. It was upon that stoop where he awoke, to his horror, for he reentered the darkness not only rubbing the phantom bump on his head, but sparked a torch to learn he stood center on a ghastly stage.

The next day he was formally accused. Defiling corpses was bad. Defiling the corpses of men of whom the public sang ballads of your bonds, worse. Those who'd long watched him sulk and slog were quick to assign his final descent into madness as the result of wartime duties. Whereas weight bolsters the constitution of some, it breaks the bones of others. Whatever the reason, Sergeant Amphilliod was stripped of his rank, his beard, and his freedom. His testimony in court only accelerated the iron door's opening, and their closing.

"And now we are done, and down here together, Golbie," Aricow had appeared and said, evoking the portmanteau they'd created as children when they'd banded together. "Ari—gollll. Arigol is back!" Fusing their names was an old strength, found again when the more able of the two mysteriously swirled in view. It had only been a few days—a week, at most, when he appeared. But down in the ancient ruins sealed below the city, those unlucky lawbreakers cursed to meander in near darkness did so with little use for time.

Golbert fell back on soldierly skills, killing fellow inmates with a voracity right out of that slut Nix's novel, which he'd once read while hungover on duty. Bumping into others was a universal cause for alarm, if not fevered panic, scrambling up slopes or clutching stones to bash a potential murderer. Those who made their way into the penal necropolis were few, but if their crimes were a population, and if those crimes' disturbing nature were somehow noise, then the Parilgotheum was nothing short of a bustling metropolis, and its tenants' last clinging thread of sanity bore them the preference to wander the underworld alone.

"But you aren't alone, little brother," Aricow said, his devilish sneer lit red and gold. "Let's find you a way out."

Aricow appeared very much like his brother, but commanded a superior frame of hulk and grace. Legs like trees. Arms like the learned pit fighter. Whatever unspoken crime had hurled the elder down to accompany Golbert, red-haired and unmarred by filth, Aricow wore a stately varnish, undiminished in the echoing hell.

Wiping some lunatic's blood from his fingers, Golbert followed as Aricow led them to the mossy shores of a languid pool. Light was good here, good enough to see the footprints leading to and away, the black bodies of idle fish, the shimmer of snails before they'd vanish in the grip of his brother's hands. Too compassionate for war, too smart for their recruiters, Golbert cheerfully watched as Aricow's back rose, becoming his chest and stomach and the fish and snails clutched against them. Aricow would insist Golbert eat, always joking of better holes or claiming pious quips of not being hungry.

One set of footprints had become familiar, not just around the pool but throughout. Maybe it was the narrow heel, or the way their owner seemed to skip about, not like a condemned man but some merry child, or how Edomax Ordrid always seemed to plant his feet where a reluctant and fearful Golbert had so recently brained a man. Aricow had known of him, back when they all had lived in the World Above. "Edomax," Aricow would say, "let's keep alive, Golbie. He may be of use to you."

The brothers, over a course of time that seeped and slimed like the nutritious slugs, established a cavern as the meeting place with the Ordrid. When he first shuffled out from the protection of shadow, Golbert thought they were being approached by a mal-formed, grinning goat.

Allowing for his hunchback's forward tilt and the man's pro-nounced, yellowed teeth, Edomax looked very much the Ordrid: keen-eyed and perhaps grown to full bloom of ghastly paleness, now deprived the daylight they so famously shunned.

For those he'd once given offence, or whatever kinsmen may have reddened at the thought that one of their own suffered his embarrassing peasant's plight, all energy was perfectly wasted. Edomax had to have been an unbridled madman of the lowest sort.

Low not in social stature, for Ordrids ruled like few other. But to be unprotected, cast out from that tribe suggested a lewd depravity not even his wicked kinsmen could conceal. The vile man, he roamed the necropolis, joyfully turning fellow inmates into the finalities of his varied derangements.

Aricow always hid in shadow and whispered to Golbert what negotiations were needed. Avoiding spells and curses, they accrued a larder of juicy rats, flint, and all for the meager barter of directing the Ordrid to Golbie's latest kill.

More tasty than plump rats, more invoking than chippable flint, Golbert wanted out. But Aricow had advised him against prying apart the Parilgotheum's impossible iron doors. Even their journey to find again the underworld's only entrance brought them peril. At the base of those stairs, familiar to all who'd been condemned, a band of misfits swarmed.

"Get behind me," Aricow said.

"*I'm* the warrior."

The unfolding combat didn't make sense. Not only his gallant brother's misguided, dangerous step forward, but that nearly a dozen men sped past Aricow and leapt on Golbert. Neither did it make sense that from the bottom of the pile, Golbert watched his brother's strikes go seemingly unnoticed. He could fell a man with one punch, yet these clawing biters clawed and bit with impunity.

"I can't help you," Aricow cried, crashing his fists into the neck of one raising high a sharpened stone.

Concentrating the entirety of his strength, an explosion of starved men became the air, some landing twisted on rocks or on the jagged, bottommost step of the stairs.

Free and on his feet, Golbert relieved the one of his crude knife, spilling his guts onto his feet before moving to another. Aricow cheered as he fought. Golbert, in turn, cheered now that his brother's strikes again found promise. Then it happened.

Aricow took a stalactite club to the chest, then the head.

His attacker was dispatched, but not before clubbing Golbert too.

Those who were dead lay still. Those who could scamper did. Aricow sounded as if he were fading, somewhere. Golbert couldn't tell whose knock made it so.

"Find that Edomax. You got enough corpses here to barter a spell out of here."

Summoned by his name or by the fresh flood of blood, the ghoulish Ordrid himself popped out from behind a rock.

"Good work, soldier boy!" For a slight man, his laugh boomed, growing in cadence with every corresponding cave or tunnel. "And all by yourself, too."

"Myself?" Golbert said, appalled, bending down to hoist up Aricow. Edomax watched this with keen interest, but said nothing. Aricow not only didn't speak but he now somehow felt weightless. "Show me and my brother a way out," he said. "Where this awful world and the one above meet."

"There's a price, such freedom. Freedom for you…and your brother."

The price wasn't just the dead strewn about, but helping chant a verse a million times, a million times a million.

Taking a break from prepping his spell, Edomax leisured up to Golbert. The burly killer squatted over his brother, reciting the incantation, the latter breathing wounded and mouthing nothing. Unmoved by such moments, Edomax demanded a perverse sex act as the final payment to initiate the spell being brewed. Relating the suction of a cave slug was more metaphor than needed.

"And would you want this of my brother, too?"

"No," the Ordrid snickered, as if remembering something. "No, you will do."

Golbert would have preferred seeing his brother off, over the words he had to mutter. He would have preferred shutting Aricow's eyes with his own worn fingers. But in the time he needed to pin the foul man to the wall and spit insanities that he'd "rather die!" Aricow, alone and on the cool earthen floor, beat him to it.

After a while, it was the Ordrid who spoke. Rubbing his throat, "Very well, soldier, I have you," adding as if obligated, "and your brother, the answer."

"If you knew a way, then why haven't *you* escaped?"

"I am in paradise. Prying lids and animating those who speak with now-dead tongues."

Golbert's question had come to him without form, but the man's answer brought him back to not only the prime reason for his wishing to leave, but why he'd been sentenced. "I didn't open coffins," he grumbled. "Didn't pry lids—to the gods, I wouldn't touch a corpse if it were flung at me."

"Pity."

Both men stood, looking at the bodies. Golbert had left him four, fresh and unstinking. Edomax asked and was granted a solemn touch. When he pressed against Golbert's brow, the sentenced soldier saw a way: the tunnels, the stairs, a route. Freedom.

"I'm taking him with me," Golbert said. "No way am I leaving him with your ways, sir." But Aricow was gone, vanished as if claimed by air. The Ordrid's laugh prompted Golbert on his way, and it continued for a long while, ringing in the tunnels and hollows and forgotten darkness.

※

And so Golbert lay in the mud in the tunnel, gathering his strength, weeping for his dead brother. When a frantic yelp rang out in the open space above, and his fingers at work gripped the cold flesh of a severed human leg, he merely flung it aside and kept climbing.

The deep exhaustion from birthing oneself out from a slippery tube fully revealed itself now. Golbert lay in bewilderment below the blazing light of a lantern.

"A ghoul," gasped a woman, tossing her ravened hair back in a way that could only derive from some wild, unhinged excitement.

Golbert wasn't out of the Parilgotheum, just occupying one of its cleaner upper rooms, with yet another mad—woman? How the gaping she-lunatic procured a lantern and untorn clothes were a mystery, but all solved by the revelation he was that much closer. Though the ground was less filthy here, it had been ornamented by not only a severed leg but a number of limbs, one of which this new lunatic lobbed his way as if she was trying to feed a dog.

"I'll rip you to pieces." Golbert rolled over to grasp the arm that had hit him and wiggle it furiously. To have come this far just to be stopped—for this woman surely would try. Blanketing rage came to a needle head, focusing Golbert on this backpedaling challenger. There would be no stopping him now.

Tackling the woman proved as hard as taking away her dagger, which had gleamed to life in a sudden flash. Golbert clawed his enemy's face. He bit at his enemy's neck, spinning the shrieking bitch into determined rants that a ghoul was upon her. He seized the dagger. But he fell backward, hard.

Golbert thought the unmanly scream had come from her. The throbbing eruption between his legs, and the instant, wicked glee on the face of this rogue persuaded him otherwise. Clutching his bits in one hand and her dagger with the other, Golbert kicked wildly at whatever he could send skyward. "*I'm* the warrior." That he'd said. His feet met nothing, but the flurry had given him the space to spring back onto his toes and point the confiscated blade tit-level.

"I'm the warrior!" he roared, or he thought he did. The stone that crashed between his eyes put him back on the ground.

Spinning in the blind explosion of pain, he felt the slip. Enough time on battlefields had left Golbert with a rare wisdom. He knew such was the first on a path to certain doom. Even acknowledgement could mean a man's death. He squirmed left, right, wherever a stone didn't crack. His brain had become pandemonium. Death by woman? Had Aricow truly died?

Worsening the confusion were oaths and shrill curses from his opponent, who'd traded small stones for a pregnant monster. "Die, ghoul!" Golbert's attempt to rise ended with his legs being swept and white lights dancing when his head smacked the ground. "No corpse for you to eat. Ungrateful graveyard worm."

His fall had broken the dagger's blade, and with it his spirit. The slip claimed him, wrapping him in its velvet fold. He still kicked, feebly. He still spat and challenged his doom to "do her worst," knowing full well she would. He'd seen the eyes of killers before, and no more determined a glaze had ever bore down on him as the one looking at him now. The lantern burned somewhere, lighting the rock that crushed his skull.

Pelliul had its share of normal jails. Those who knew Dandana Nix knew she'd briefly occupied a bunk or two in a drab block before. But such confinement was only for criminals of the most petty sort—that, or those awaiting the final go-ahead before a hanging. The Parilgotheum, by theatric contrast, was reserved for crimes that offended man's senses more than his written law. Surely the desecration of fellow veterans' remains was as exotic and perverse as the sentencing magistrate could have mustered from his own paltry imagination.

The corpse finally ceased its twitch. This mud-glazed, crazed inmate before Nix was no stranger. Well, not in the legal sense, she surmised, gawking to and fro from the reports she'd carried with her onto none other than Golbert fucking Amphilliod.

It was an accident, one on the part of a fearful writer—mistaking the dirty lunatic for a hungry, raving ghoul. Nix had seen fingers, seen their retreat, and when they emerged once more she'd been ready. Once dead, and wiped free of layers of mud, a faded tattoo of the Suela campaign rung clear as if shouted from a caller's horn: one of the very men Nix theorized took the fall for ghoul-mischief now lay lifeless as those stiffs who'd helped send him to hell.

Hell was right. Looking down into the hole, Nix noted her proximity to the penal underworld. "You were a fugitive," Nix kicked Golbert's foot. "Compelling."

The Parilgotheum lurked below. Nix salivated, double-checking the fuel in her lantern, entertaining a sudden paranoia that someone might stumble upon her find.

A brief excursion up the stairs bore news, though at first she knew not how to take it. A storm now raged, so unyielding that rain was going to make its way down to the cellar. Trickles and drips, before long, would be a waterfall. The deluge she noted, but it was the onset of lightning that persuaded her to do what her heart had been beating for.

Staying the night to work would be a nightmare for writers who penned the pomp of truth, justice, beauty. But a dream it was for those who penned nightmares. As Nix worked out this tangled arrangement of metaphor, she breathed deep and uncorked her ink. Such insane places only helped her work. No time better than now, with Parilgotheum prisoner brains all over the place.

Even if ghouls weren't real, who cared? The parade of nuts that might file out of that tunnel being carved further by rain; at least one might not be so bent on fighting. She'd already gotten a kill. A uniquely organic one, too. An interview now would be far, far better.

She wanted to be rid of it: the self-loathing she felt shuffling alongside other artists in places where every sort of failure proclaimed themselves the mistook owner of genius.

The charnel worm in her head shifted, burrowing. She was not a fraud! If such an unpleasant intruder were made of flesh, she would've scourged her brain to scramble both out with a sharp stick.

But alas her affliction, her whisperer of doubt, was no more than a figment of her intellect, an intellect she pulled back to the task at hand. She would write, and damn the gods, she would marvel the masses or slice her own wrist.

What tales were there to tell, from down there? Ignited in the moment, Nix needed not food nor drink, though she had brought enough to last verily a week. She only needed the portions of her scroll yet addressed, and her trusted inkpot and quill.

As was often the case, moments of pure vision, pure undisturbed creation, were disrupted by the imps only artists know. This one was an imp she'd grown accustomed. None of this, this encounter, meant ghouls *weren't* real.

Nix stopped mid-paragraph to consider the clues that had gotten her here. The lowness of the cellar. The proximity to graves just beyond the shadow of this rotting warehouse—where not one but *two* corpse meddlings had been reported. Escaped madmen could be to blame, yes, but her better sense still bode her a skeptic.

So, the lithe user of words and limbs redistributed the latter. Unsickened by their signs of continued decay, she completed her errand by dragging Golbert to a dark nook, hoping, if ghouls came forth, to lock in a deal by rolling out the larder at just the right moment.

Her writing went well enough, but her soul was nagged as if it were a new flounce pulled by a puppy. She'd converted this encounter with the hidden dead celebrity, but she disliked ever more the gaping hole before her, leading down, staring at her like a taunting, unblinking eye. Not for what might come soon shouldering out, but for what treasures it might hold. Could she really wait? Should she? She caught herself listening to the rush and gurgle of subsiding rainwater, sounding as if it too were singing her to everlasting despair.

Unable to ignore the itch, the writer put down her scroll and hovered over the mouth of the tunnel. If it would mean more violent encounters with deranged men, she at least could go forth with confidence many would not be former soldiers, nor would they possess what that poor fool must've to have made it out onto the cellar floor. Plus, having breasts rarely hurt.

Nix stowed her gear. She flung her useless dagger and made, as best she could, a bed on a slab cut from stone. A peal of thunder, late to the dying symphony, seemed to hasten her ambition. She'd soon regain her strength. Then, after her eyes were open and breakfast gnawed, she'd crawl down into what only madmen, and perhaps ghouls, knew.

※

"Pardon," the protagonist trotting around on Nix's scroll spoke. Sleep nothing, she'd tried, only to find herself working so deep it was as if a new character were with her. "My lady?"

Now that was strange. When worlds on both sides of her skull briefly converged, as they sometimes did, they were always dispelled by recognition. That one could persist? The writer swept her lantern through the blackness and across the stairs, almost dropping it when it revealed a man was standing at the top.

Nix squeaked a garble, uprooting herself to reach for her dagger in the now empty sheath.

"I'm sorry to bother you," the man at the top said. "This is going to sound awfully foolish of me, but I'm looking for my brother—" Nix then felt and saw and knew, felt again the words before they actually came. Then they arrived. "Golbert." Her head swam. "Golbert Amph—"

"Amphilliot...I mean amphibian. I study them. Did you know many such beasts proliferate down here? Frogs, mostly."

"I did not," the man said, tugging at his rusted beard. His eyes revealed a simplicity women like Nix could detect without effort.

Nix said, "What's your name, cutie?"

"Aricow."

"Yes. Yes, Aricow of the brothers Amphilliod. I've heard of

thee." Scrutinizing her notes to the point of pageantry, "Not only do I study frogs, cutie, but some have audaciously labeled me a journalist. Your brother, tell me, he was sent into the Parilgotheum?"

"Journal…yes, but how? You've heard of me?"

Nix hoisted her notes and flapped them in the air. "The courts—or the barbaric atrocity we refer to as such—they do surprisingly well when it comes to records. Says here…" Nix's undefined excitement made finding the correct page even more difficult than under the candlelight of a cluttered desk. When the dog-ears were at her nose, she called out as if they were in a ceremonial hall. "Says you petitioned the courts, stating your brother's 'postwar' insanity."

"He needed the asylum, not the tunnels. Yeah, I petitioned. And yes, he was mad. Talkin' to people who aren't there. Mother's batshittedness must've sludged down the cord."

"Roaring to life in both of their adulthoods" would've made a great follow-on, Nix thought. "Interesting."

Aricow, unarmed and about as fierce as a bloated tick, made his way off the steps and now padded closer. "I had the strangest dream. Why I'm here." This Aricow surprised Nix further by chuckling, slapping his own hip as if he'd heard a joke. "Maybe my days at the barrelhouse are over. Hell, maybe *I'm* mad."

"I don't think you are mad. Lucky, maybe. To your good fortune, cutie, I just so happen to also be a student of the brain." She furtively kicked out of sight a congealed glob of exactly that. "Interpreting dreams is a bit of a specialty, too." Nix found her notes scroll. She grabbed her quill. "Tell me more?"

Aricow studied Nix, from the toe of her smudged leather boot to the roots of her black hair. Deeming her, amongst other things, not a figment, Aricow took up a convenient stone and began. "It was the strangest. Last night. I saw this horrid little man, teeth like sticks of butter. It was like he whispered to me. Words became pictures. I saw the warehouse, this very cellar. And I saw those stairs." He stopped to stare quizzically at the woman. "I didn't see you."

Even for a starving lunatic, Golbert's inherent strength had been clear. As had his murderous skills. Nix shuttered at the thought of how her encounter may have fared if the dead man had been ready, and not nourished by fleas.

The same could not be said about his ho-hum brother. What beatings the dead one must have inflicted on the adolescence of this simple cooper. Asking Aricow why he hadn't joined the war that had reportedly sapped Golbert of his wits, the answer came as actors, which the writer now watched present themselves on a stage. Flat feet shuffled. Knees as knocked as a turned-reluctant voluptuary's. Only their wood-like deformities could take Nix's glare off the man's potted gut. Still, this made the sorry sight perfect bait.

It worried Nix that Aricow chose to wander beside the exit of his brother's tunnel. A skirmish Nix did not fear, but convincing Aricow to do what she was concocting would prove all the harder if the shuffling sloth found—"Brains? Is this blood?"

"I'm afraid so," Nix sighed. "It seems an animal was mauled there."

"The rats I saw comin' down looked big enough to take down a boar." Aricow moved directly over the hole, where he stopped and stared. "This was the last of it," Nix heard him say, "of the dream. He was talking to us about a way out."

"Us?" Nix asked, unleashing from Aricow a sublime rant that absolutely demanded transcription. She could hardly keep up. Shaking the cramp from her wrist, Nix, poised to scribble, was convinced more than ever ghoul magic was at work. "Way out for whom?"

"We had this thing, with our names," he continued, speaking as if to no one, blowing heavy air from his nostrils before swinging his eyes onto Nix. "My brother didn't just open lids and toss out bones. He defiled them, arranged 'em, gnawed on 'em. Mocked their remains. Or so the story goes."

"But you don't believe it." Nix was on her feet. "Cutie, it is true that I am a scholar of biology and the brain. Just as it's true your brother suffered for the deeds of other fiends. I didn't want to say anything. I figured you'd scoff at me as elitist men do when I try and point toward a menace in and under Pelliul."

Aricow stooped to pick up a piece of his brother's brain.

Nix said at his ear, "Ghouls, Aricow." It did not surprise Nix that the dimwit nodded, that his eyes lighted and mouth uttered an inaudible oath. Sailing upon this, Nix sidled closer. "I am but a girl, but I am the writer of things not accepted. The journaler of darkness the dimwitted need to hear. I am here to confirm the existence of ghouls, and to pin on them their vile deeds. Perhaps even your dea…imprisoned brother's. No, I have not seen your dear brother," answering his question.

"What happened to your face?"

"A romp with a feisty wench," she flung, smiling with clawed-on cheeks. "But this hole here, it was dug by someone. Was it not? And for a reason. The unfair Parilgotheum is just below. Together, we may stand a chance."

"I don't have food." To which Nix raised a loaf of bread and an apple. "I have no—"

"Water will be the least of our concerns." Nix followed a floating leaf as it disappeared into the abyss.

"Weapons?"

"Do you have one?" Nix asked. Aricow pulled a knife from his boot. "Yes, in front of me you should go. I'll deprive myself my lantern. To you it goes, as would all rations I can give."

"I saw him here," Aricow despaired.

"A dream. But the gods rarely give us gifts. Look at the freshness of that blood, the finger-holds in that mud. We, cutie, are standing atop such a gift. Madness it would be not to accept these divine allowances."

"…You want ghouls, and I want my brother."

Nix choked, not expecting the distillation. "Well, yes. Yes, I suppose so. Guard me?"

✳

Nix hugged the lantern to her breasts. She had to go first, but this had also been a valid reason to deprive Aricow his only weapon. With her teeth clamped around the knife, she dug the palm of her free hand into the wet, slipping mud. The tunnel's downgrade made a controlled descent difficult. All the more when she came to twists, slickened by quick rainwater, turning their journey into a chaotic slide better fit for burrowing lunatics.

Lantern light shook, mud gave way or clumped at edges. The two slithered over stones and lathered in filth. What may have been rocks intentionally placed by gods or men now sat obsolete, some sinking in softened earth. Able to stand at last, Nix stretched her back as behind her Aricow dumped onto the floor of an ancient staircase.

"What do we have here?" a voice said, sending Nix into a spin, costing her the grip of her lantern, losing its light in a sudden, floor-crashing crunch.

"That voice," Aricow seemed to say, finding one of Nix's legs and climbing up it like a rat. He squeaked, "Who's there?"

Nix repeated the question, remembering she held a knife whose blade was immune from darkness.

Aricow was frozen, and no more could a body stiffen than in the hollowness of an entombed staircase. The voice was humming, somewhere in the dark. Male, that much Nix was certain, but this underworlding's age and intent was decidedly obscure.

"Why don't you," the potential ghoul said, "why don't you both step into the light?"

"Don't say nothin'," Aricow whispered. "Don't provoke it."

Whoever this inmate was, he was surely insane, as all denizens down here were. "What light?" Nix snarled, taking a limp slash at the air. "Scum." The only light had been in the now busted lantern that sizzled at her feet.

What the voice said next sent Aricow shaking, though it should have Nix. "We have a fair maiden," it said, "one who belongs way, way, way down here…with us. What brings you to revel?"

Nix may have spoken. She may have responded, in normal circumstances perhaps even with something witty out of one of her manuscripts. But she was squinting, and in disbelief. A man came forth, black against a dilating bloom of light.

Aricow's yelp and the glowing contours of his face reassured her she wasn't suffering an illusion. "How?" Nix mustered. "There's light?" But the foul, bald lech was disinterested in speech.

The bent creature scrutinized Aricow, and Aricow, stricken queer, stared back at the man who stood laminated in glow. Not as in a barrelhouse, where torches burned their health at their heads, light down here showed Aricow and Edomax tinged by low teases of gold and rose.

"You," Edomax said. "I've *seen* you."

"I want to talk to a ghoul," Nix blurted, convinced that if she wasn't doing so already, this new character was connected to every foul string in this affair.

"Kill him," Edomax said leisurely, pointing his thumb. "Then I'll try. They are quite skittish, you know."

Aricow's knife was in his own neck before he could gasp. Fear had swollen the artery, serving Nix as the most convenient of land-marks. The second Amphilliod to die did so with a thump, taking his last breath on a stone floor pooling red.

Eventually, Edomax Ordrid received the sexual requisite for the use of his greater spells. In return, the necromancer promised to send a ghoul in the guise of Aricow, "once his heart and brains are supped, back up to your cellar air. Now shoo, girl. I want a crack at him first."

✳

These days an honest writer was forced to cheat. Nix spat again. Vandahl had already penned the great maxims, and other, less celebrated fable-flingers had filled Orisulan canon with the talking animals which the seven stories all derive. But perspective—*that* was the gold mine left. And perspective was coming! Not as bursts of inspiration, where silver wings fluttered onto the tip of a scribbling feather. Instead, an ascending ghoul would bare new eyes to skulk at the underbelly of her world.

Familiar walls of shadow greeted Nix again. From the storm that still raged above, not one but two waterfalls now poured down into the cellar.

She turned from the inundation to where she thought she'd stuffed Golbert. Surely the sweep of rain hadn't carried off a dead body. Just to be sure, she crawled into the crevice. Its stony walls had remained dry. Fanning out her fingers, blood dripped fresh and free each time she swept her hand across where a man she'd killed had lay. But the body was gone.

She was pulled from her agitation. The hole she had descended had matured into a whirlpool, but neither its roil or swirl was the noise that called her attention. She had watched Aricow die—more than watched. The voice—that voice, unmistakably Aricow's, gargled and choked against the downpour, making its way up the trafficked tunnel.

Dandana Nix's heart sped, taking her off her feet to rush at the rim of the swirl. A drenched head was emerging. "That weird little man did it. Here, let me help you."

A screaming fit popped through. "You killed me!" he screamed, over and over, rolling himself into defensive ball, until: "He—you…" All terror mudded away, replaced with gawking wonder. Aricow, as Nix had seen him but an hour before, stared up with eyes that did not burn with undead, waning grandeur, but were alive. "You—you stabbed my throat?"

"Surely and sweet," Nix sung.

Aricow, the ghoul's—the man's voice rediscovered panic. "Golbie, he was supposed to be here. Right here."

Nix waited out a feeble volley of feet. This must be a ghoul, a ghoul who'd subsumed dead Aricow and now was lost in its host's memories. *Confirmation*, Nix rejoiced. There was no wound in his neck, for its piping right then allowed: "Brother! Help me!"

Exposed to prolonged darkness, rank odor, mice, roaches, and rot, even the writer of dark works had been rattled. She'd remained forward-driven, yes, but her soul had been inevitably taxed by run-ins with those describable as the living damned. However, what lodged in her nightmares so firmly appeared so quick that she had to shake the brains in her skull and blink her eyes thrice before believing.

Aricow's pleas exhausted, the soaked and shivering man had laid his head on the wet stone beneath him. In that same instant, right before Nix was able to shoot up and spin around, Aricow had looked to the rear of the cellar, and he'd smiled.

Nix could only partway grasp who was the living figure before her. Golbert stood, healthy, better off than before his face had been crushed, a face now full and whole and looking right at her.

"Confluence," Nix heard herself say. Brother and brother, rains fall, streams flow, united, becoming the torrent. "Are you feeling well? Yes, come this way. Let us all speak. What a journey, um, you must've, both must've endured. You," Nix spoke to the one lifting up the other. "Or you. What craziness we endure. Down here together…in a mice-and-lice cellar. Soaked as a toad."

Dandana Nix could only stare at the look in Golbert's eyes, and how they matched the canine maliciousness that now twinkled darkly in Aricow's.

"No! No!" she pled with the hands of the larger, arisen

Amphilliod while Aricow watched sportively from the comfort of a slab. Renewed in strength, the trained limbs of Golbert pressed her down, down to a shallow pool, where she felt her nose and lips go under the water and then against the floor.

After a few encounters with drowning, it appeared to the writer that Aricow had found her notes-scroll and was now reading aloud all the first-draft deaths she'd concocted for various, ill-formed figures. "Then he or she held his or her face until the lungs burst, and he or she did so while breaking what rib or kidney the poor fool left exposed."

The stronger brother was equipped not only with brute force, but with guileful ears, and an apparent talent for converting words to action.

✳

Outfit in bodies who'd known and loved each other in life, the ghouls scampered up the stairs, where together they walked merrily onto a crowded street. Aricow and Golbert Amphilliod cursed out a bewildered foreman at a barrelhouse, then sold all Aricow's furnishings for wine, women, and emotional bets at the fighting pits. Impaired and soon hunted by lynch mobs prompted by growing rumors that a former Parilgotheum inmate had been seen carousing and caterwauling, the ghouls shed their guises and sealed the cellar dig.

The ghoul who'd assumed Golbert was especially eager to return, not only to the underworld below the prison, but to their kind. Insanity was a tough brain to ride, tougher to operate, even when Golbert's unhinged urges had them partaking in the ghoul's favorite pastime: defiling sanctimonious corpses.

A CONQUEROR'S TALE

By my Lord's twentieth year, he, once known as Conabitt Lotgard, had seen our land fractured and put in the gravest of peril.

What unity had wobbled and teetered came crashing down in thunderous fits when the Houses all decided to declare war on each other. Ouvarnias killing the House of Huell, Rogaires slaughtering a list of now insignificant lineage out east. Orisula had come apart at her seams. We were forced to abandon the war effort in Pelat, bringing an end to that failed colonization. Further south still, only my Lord's family, the House of Lotgard, retained any interest in Suela.

As warring progressed and more losers emerged, fracturing only intensified. Farms were burned, lyceums of esoteric import and astronomy were leveled in some tyrant of the day's transfer of one thrill to another. We were in free fall, heading back to an age where we tore meat from bones with loosened teeth and where symbols, as these I write now, were taken as heraldry of the demonic.

Sensing Orisula's vulnerability, Azad invaded through the Red Isthmus. What meager leadership remained banded together long enough to be denied help from Quinnari. Stating equal trade interest with Azad, that island's refusal officially opened the head panel of Orisula's casket. And it was my Lord, who emerged in his aforementioned year, who rose up to bat back the Azadi horde.

✳

Adding perhaps, in some small way, to the misfortune that has been put on my Lord, his land, and what bleak future it may see, I compose this volume while in fear for my life.

The Dead Kettle is a fitting district for solitary Pelats and the former scribes of mistreated rulers. This apartment is of little use. Rain is pissing in. Heat escapes like a banshee. But my stairs, old and beaten, creak and moan as if carefully fitted. For surely if one were tiptoeing, to slice my throat, my cohorts the planks would sound the alarm. Escape? No. No, I have no interest in running.

I write with some assurance, for this tale must be told, to vindicate my Lord. My last duty. And I'm afraid my days are numbered.

✳

There are two things contemporary historians quibble over: why our land was renamed and what prompted its unification to be done by way of stake after stake of screaming, impaled rebels.

There is an answer to the first, which I will come to in due course. I can assure you, though, it's not some woman's name, clung to the heart of my Lord, as some ridiculously insist.

Regarding the impalings, there had been questions over the style of the punishment, not the punishment itself. Pockets of territory were once wild and unruled. The farms and hill country clinging to our cities, though not wild and very much ruled, had the unfortunate habit of overlapping, spreading conflict between whichever great Houses were ready to spill blood over rocky outcroppings or a too-long twig. Eventually, many rebels required death; paling the quarrel of Houses by refusing all thought of a unified land. But why the noose and executioner's axe were stuffed into the closets remain a mystery.

Yet, scholastic men chronicling the past all seem to agree that when the boy once called Conabitt returned from Suela, his family never left again the comfort of the Morgeltine.

The same cannot be said of the young man, who reportedly immersed himself in hunting game off the speeding back of a courser. There is some debate here, but I am of the majority, inclined our prodigious leader did so to learn the lay of his land.

Later, he put away the bow to attend the University of Eight Chairs, earning a double licentiate in logic and law. A young officer in his sodded father's Nilghordian Defense Force, he broke away from his House by allying with Oxghorde Rogaires to deliver a swift kick in the gut of Azadi troops who'd approached unchallenged from the east. It worked, better than some say even he expected. Under the banner of an ambitious new leader, Orisulans trickled out of the hills to join his growing legions.

Over the next several years, he and a portion of his forces sailed to Pelat to deliver a crushing blow. It is important to distinguish the difference in this foreign campaign and the blasphemous one occurring now. This move was not to rape and pillage, but to beat the Pelats into an important alliance: offering them citizenship, even portions of the trade routes. The Pelats were ordered to fight Azad. They provided food for our ranks, supplies, and even the famous *Vendinao*, their regiment of striped, club-wielding troops.

Offering foreigners who eat snakes homes on our peninsula, and without seeking elder Lotgard council to do so, surprised the House of Rogaire, outraged Ouvarnia, and sparked an unusual interest in the House of Ordrid. All three were seen as ill omens. Combined, a threat that could not be ignored.

Dismayed by his son's brash defiance and worried the House of Ouvarnia would leverage the immigration to rally a fully-formed, anti-Lotgard front, his dying father, after Conabitt refused to submit, signed off on "Conabitt Lotgard" being stricken from the family roles. Learning this, my Lord renamed himself that epithet that will ring into the centuries.

Funny are the wheels of fate, for I had only been hired a month when I witnessed my first impaling. Law was the new way, slowly extending over the plains and forest of our land. That none were to speak his old name, nor to write it (I am only doing so now under the weighed deliberation that I am doing him the greatest of service) was best exemplified when a trusted member of the cabinet blurted out something other than "The Conqueror" in what, I attest, was a night of sword-won revelry. The brutal display I will never forget, as, it's reasonable to expect, none else have who witnessed it.

~~I believe~~ It is worth noting that I once overheard my Lord recollecting furtive colonial practices conducted in Suela, taught to them by local enforcement. I believe stakes were among them— perhaps solving the "mystery" of previous note.

Now formed, the Conqueror's army rooted out domestic resistance and pushed deep into the heart of Azad.

Chapwyn priests say only a fool thinks he'll escape his troubles by jumping from the Gahlerrion Bridge. An even greater species of fool, unwise by even secular metrics, spares themselves such dizzying heights and attracts crowds at the base of the Tower of the Waning Moon. There they wail and waylay and blather to all who'll stop and giggle.

No greater fool has ever taken that ill-famed stage than I.

Merely the rise-fall of a moon and sun, my rant. A day ago. Though it feels like an age has passed since. I am relieved, relieved I said what I did. Upon this parchment, the full account, including the things the bottle or my own shameful fear at the moment had robbed from me.

What happened to my Lord I could not bear, nor can I now,

though yesterday at the tower I was at my worst, most unbridled. The drunk explosion was not apocalyptic. My audience was given a respite from that long-held standard.

Fuming reappraisal of the past has been known to titillate, even earn the rare applause—as long as it be ancient. Raving about the recent, however, earned me grieve-stricken stares and a group of emerged scowlers who've haunted my tracks ever since.

✳

After the Conqueror's invasion, for the next twenty years the war in Azad groaned, bleeding one day into the next in a continued delirium. It got the desert rats out of our hair, though, allowing our domestic rebels to freely reveal themselves, signing their death warrants all the sooner. Orisula at last became unified, except for a single resister.

The House of Ordrid, foulest of the families, still claims their stronghold right here in Nilghorde. Perched nigh the House of Lotgard, it was the talk of the streets, when by falling of the inevitable stone the pond would usher ripples to waves, and those waves to bitter, inner-city war.

Despite the emotions their name could provoke, the Ordrids had remained quiet in the years leading up to the final battle. Ever since their warring with the Ouvarnias, the slinking madmen and witches preferred rather to swirl spells from the sidelines, manipulating moments to their own end.

But for all their magic, all their cunning, no spell nor chant nor lecherous cantrip could stop the marshalling of the mightiest army our land had ever seen. The campaign had rolled across the hills to Pelliul, up rugged mountains where men choked on thin air, southward to Oxghorde, to the very shores of the southern sea, and when the Conqueror cast his eyes north, toward home, his warhorses soon blew their steam on the black doors of the Ordrid keep.

I need not write what happened. The carnage, spewing forth from every door and gate burst open, brought the night of death, or as popularly ascribed: The Night of Death. From the passing of moonset to the first twinkle of dawn, more Orisulans were killed than in entire years already carved and speared into history. Steaming slop all over, I, Propagord Phern, had to desist my clerk duties to burn wiggling stumps in a ratty inn.

Many Ordrids there were. Females shot at us from balistraria or parapet with arrows dipped in every type of villainy. Their men led mercenaries from the hills and pirates from Quinnari, down to us: allies whom the world knew not trafficked alongside the House, promised inception into their powers, if not already versed.

These foul lines that broke over us like a wave at least bled and spit and feared as do normal, vile men. There were other fiends, though, in spiked armor sealed so no man could discern what brought down heavy sword or squealed in hateful pain as it was run through. Yet even these mysteries bled.

Both sides collided. Both suffered loss. Then, making stump duty obsolete, curses from a high window rolled over us like a bellowing disease. Here, I tell you, real as the rug beneath my feet rose the dead.

A lone Ordrid, hardly old enough to fill armor, had fallen in such a way that he crowned a lifeless pile. The red and gold of ours and the dead black of theirs, and above it all that lad, who began to move.

At first it was just a twitch, then a wiggle. His arm had been pulled to ribbons, yet that bloody mess seized a footman's flail and this corpse missing half its head rose to stare at the moon.

No, the moon merely sat by, voyeuristic beyond the bulked keep. It was that foul voice, calling him, calling them, for soon that entire pile stood erect.

No dead were spared. Men who cleaved one another right behind the veil were in one sickening swoosh sucked back, and now walked undivided. We, the living, were their enemy, which their mangled limbs and run-through hearts attacked in blindness.

They weren't fast. They were not able. But they were *dead*, and when we fell them for a second time it would be but a horrid moment before taxed, living hearts had to pump and burn to hack them again.

By the fourth resurrection, there were those who'd succumbed to exhaustion. Bitten and clawed, they arose members of the filth. By the sixth the sun was rising, and that evil hill crawled with more dead than living.

The barely dead rose, lustfully obeying the curser who loomed above us. But our army was not done. I believe at one point I even held a sword, to what good, I cannot say.

From the start, even before the first blade cut or first man fell, the battle was never between the banner I'd served and the mailed riffraff frothing from the keep. It was between the Conqueror and the Ordrid's grim tyrant, Maecidion. Killing the Lord's emissaries and sending back their remains in a way I will not describe, the offer of peace was rejected; Maecidion choosing to doom thousands rather than bow ~~his House~~ himself to a sovereign.

The night's unprecedented slaughter was outdone the next day. By the following, crows and other devourers came to the carrion dreaming. Not even the blackest of magic could keep count of the fallen, and slowly more of the dead stayed as such. Above the dead at dawn they awakened, the crows, and the ditch below the daily feast filled with the puss and bile and blood we slipped in on our way to victory.

Storming from the keep, Maecidion's sons led a mounted charge so fierce we were pushed all the way back to the Morgeltine. There, pinned against marble, the Conqueror concentrated his force on the heads of the snake, lopping off all three in turn.

Lower Ordrids and the polluted mercenaries in their clutch scrambled back up. The undead whose assault never vanquished were rounded up and hacked to bits.

Some of my Lord's top staff by then were Ouvarnia. Looking through the council notes, two lines of prominence: "Ouvarnian lore suggested burning all war dead. The Conqueror saw wisdom, gathering the dead (regardless of allegiance) and ordering them thrown into fires stoked at the bottom of the cobbled hill, sieged without relent."

Key to our victory was that order, for it ceased the resurrections and galvanized the men. Some would call it an error, citing the black forever of Ordrid vengeance. I will go to my grave defending its soundness. However the befuddlement of history chooses to view tossing Maecidion's sons' corpses in the flames, it was three fewer able to rise again.

"Bring your weapons," he said, "if you must." Doors sealed by tar and incantation had opened, revealing Morfil Ordrid with his arm in a sling.

The Conqueror removed his diamond-studded helmet; the first of the blond heads to bud a line of Lotgards, standing impatiently in dented armor. Morfil, his skin pale as his hair black and stringed, softened his leer, ushering in my Lord. Following in file was the entire cabinet: a cohort of distant cousin generals, Ouvarnian equestrians, me, and Rinmauld Rogaire. More on *that* scoundrel forthcoming.

We were led through a barbican, where from aphotic shadow emerged porters and pages to relieve us of our burdens. ~~Staring into the eyes of these living dead reminds one of a shark's, washed ashore.~~

"Record this," my Lord spoke unto me, and I have it here now: "The fortress of our last enemy, soon ally, be it bleak and stricken by wicked, wizened force, has initiated a parley unto which we humbly accept."

The sky hung above us, overcast and grim as all who ornamented the courtyard walls. Through some sort of garden we marched, confronted by another batch of undead; these though idle, arrayed in the regalia of their masters. Atop staircases and beyond the grip of "art" following you with painted eye, we were seated at a long table centering a plain room. Slaves attended sconces. I looked beyond the candlelight at the table's head.

To his left uprighted a canine so large its pointy ears could prick a man's throat. At his right went Morfil, understood to be second in their command. Morfil, who had been our escort and directed our seating, had also lamentably lacked the courage those three princes had, and had embarked for decades on every which way to pervert or weaponize the talents of frogs, worm, or bat. Yet what bookended Maecidion were but penumbras against a void. The void itself, concealed under prosaic blacks of coal and onyx, wore the visage of an old man, tightened by the skin of the tomb.

His face held the most single-minded concentrated look ever cast on a crowd, and his entire form seemed to pull the black from every corner of the floors to the high, unseen ceiling, to the needlepoint oblivion of his eyes.

My Lord, approaching forty, and the ~~old confusedly elder~~ septuagenarian sat across from the other. Cats in a contested alley could no better give a preamble for confrontation. I found a block of wall unfilled by burning sconces or on-duty undead, ready, as best I could, to transcribe what was to follow.

✳

A slave staggered with a tray. "That'll be enough," my Lord commanded, slapping away the chalice intended for him and soaking the corpse. "Enough with your breed of hospitality. You may chain that beast, Maecidion. You're safe."

"That I do know," Maecidion said, patting his creature.

"You know much," my Lord replied. "How to raise the dead and when best to surrender. Lovely home. But all this trouble to defend cobwebs?" Morfil grabbed for his own when my Lord unsheathed his sword. The cabinet laughed. "We can get rid of them too, if you like."

Maecidion joined the mirth, eking out a smile he perhaps believed would appear gay. "You must forgive Morfil," he said. "We perceive naked blades with intent."

"There is intent, ruler. Better it twirl in your candles than in any more necks of the...of our people."

"Oh, but the people who are mine, we are not inclined to share. Their heart beats affirmed, free blood, and my larking cubs, too, hear whispered truth of the gods."

"I know a truth as well, supreme Ordrid. Reap what is yours while you are fit to. Did your gods suggest yet ceasing this despicable resistance?"

Things went on like this for a while, a back and forth of cooling words and implied threats, until, at last, talk settled on a proposal of peace. Maecidion's lips grew white. "What are the terms?"

"Fully surrender. Rekill these abominations infesting your keep. Agree to inspections, thrice per year and—"

"Thrice," Maecidion said, and in a way that caused Morfil and that dog to both break their glares and watch his mouth as he spoke next: "That was the number. Three sons, I had. Sons you slew."

My Lord barmed at the interruption. "How many sons have you insisted die this week?"

"That was their number."

"Agree to inspections and you can—"

"It is not their death that troubles us, you know, but that

you burned them." Maecidion spoke, deeper: "We are unable to bring them back."

My Lord cleared his throat. "Who would want to be *brought back*," he pointed at the nearest slave, putting my eyes on its preternatural quietude, "like this?"

The Conqueror grabbed his chest. He pulled at his breastplate with one hand and white-knuckled the hilt of his damn sword with the other. His generals shed him free. We gazed in horror at the unarmored sight, gasping on the stone floor, eyes wider than the moon.

An Ouvarnia was the one who said it: "Look," swinging the cabinet's entire focus onto, "his hand."

What we saw, what that villain was doing, even I, trained recorder, ardent observer, am unable to describe with pure confidence. The best I can cobble is thus:

Maecidion sat on his throne, leaned forward. His hand was ~~holding~~ holding empty air; between his thumb and fingers the space of a human heart. He squeezed…nothing, yet my Lord agonized. My Lord writhed, and when that foul man balled his bony fist my Lord moved no longer.

"Seize him!" one general shouted, hiding behind the rest.

Dead servants did not unfix themselves, as for some reason I thought they would. Even when the necromancer called "One," then through a smirk Morfil sang "Two." Then, yes, that gargantuan canine barked three room-rattling barks, one for each time Maecidion animated my Lord—I still attest brought my Lord back to life, just to smite him back down.

Then, we saw the Conqueror burst into a lifeless flame, its heat so violent the chair he had fallen from withered to pitch.

✳

"Well done," Rinmauld Rogaire said. No figment of my imagination could his words have been either, for after my shock waned he said it again, aloud and across the perilous table.

✳

It's the unwritten parts of the deal which followed that I spewed out yesterday under the tower. How could I not—a great man's loyal subject, left to right the wrongs of a horrid lie?

Perhaps a week after this cataclysm, summoned and gathered were those who'd once sworn allegiance to the Conqueror, and were now ready to accept their Scepterhood. The House of Ordrid officially declared peace. The cunning cabinet wasting no time, they started the rumor and mandated its revelation to a crystalizing Chapwyn leadership: after a full victory, the benevolent Conqueror went into seclusion in his palace.

It took patience and an ear pressed against a door, but I affirm the Apex Scepters concocted the myth the Conqueror is immortal. Yet, I'm unsure if it can be traced, what source the secondary rumors sprouted from. Surely the Apexes, Rinmauld and some Lotgard who toes the family line, wouldn't have suggested Maecidion gifted the Conqueror with immortality. Our people believe this—even some Lotgards!—pelting one another with tepid regurgitations that the gesture was a victor's trophy, or, as some of the more rationally fooled insist, to show his forever-enemy the blessings of death.

Amusing, the contrast. Shaken by the display of that arisen, rearisen army, necromancy was formally outlawed.

Maecidion and his kind have been allowed to practice in private. As a confirming gesture, the House's hoods and witches were given the heap of battle-dead that had yet to be buried.

In return for his "cooperation," the foul House is to receive an imposing portion of the war spoils now that we've signed an agreement with Azad (under the guise my Lord, alive and well, orchestrated the plans). It was good to see those desert rats laid out and gutted on their own, awkward shields. At least some brightness belies what dark days surely lie ahead.

"Years of Peace" indeed—the new term being tossed around and carved on every gleaming balustrade. If my fears prove correct, just as the belying brightness above, at least I will be pardoned from hearing that insufferable term. Year zero, or one, or whatever, began the moment Maecidion the Virulent and a former war cabinet, turned Scepters with birth-gunk still in their ears, all walked out in a show of brain-numbing unity.

I learned the weight of the liquor bottle. Relegated to errand boy of a new Lotgard, I didn't last a year. Whispers observing where my allegiance still lay finally cast me out onto the street and into this hovel.

Before they did, though, I stood and scribbled when our land was renamed.

Petty I may very well be, for wishing this flippancy exposed, but pettier still are boys seated in thrones.

At first, it made sense if the necromancer gave us our new designation, as he brokered uncanny, fearful power. But Apex Scepter Lord Rinmauld Rogaire held power too. But the necromancer had just expressively destroyed my Lord. So both concocted the word.

The Virulent used the two letters beginning each of his dead son's names. Rinmauld capped it off "with a letter fit for Rogaires." Hideous. Thus, "Rehleia" was born, "Orisula" stuffed into scrolls on an unattended shelf.

What follows you need not a scribe or historian to tell. *Rehleia* is now unified under a central government. Connecting our cities, teeming with veterans of earlier wars, the Metropolitan Ward polices our streets.

Thus lumber the Years of Peace. The Conqueror has become "the Municipal One," perfectly fusing this contemporary era's incredible forgetfulness and the domestic saturation which it seems to hinge upon.

Having defeated Azad, our armies are now crushing harmless, helpless Serabandantilith. This avarice is speared and gouged and northwardly blazed with no consent of "the Municipal One," though the carnage is done under his name.

"Take what is yours while you are able," he declared, once even to me. And what was his, our precious Orisula, was all the great man ever sought to stitch whole. Conquer, indeed. It is I, his servant, who write in hope of ~~preserving~~ exposing this noble intent.

But I am fearful.

I am

If upon alien years such tales garner uncaused fascinate, I foresee my ending becoming the stuff of trend. I hear them. My stairs. Rain-sogged boots. One plea about the state of leadership has incited some, as I knew they would, to send their executives.

P

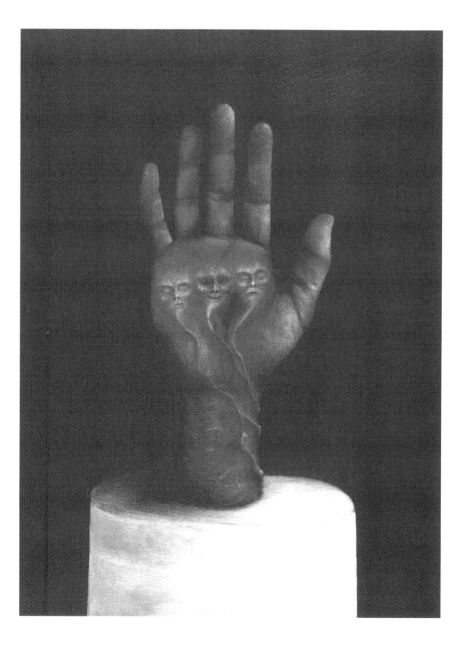

REVENGE!

"Lord Warden Rogaire,
Dumb as a bear,
But rich as a sly devil fox.
Stories be told,
And most have to do,
'Bout fate n' our big lordly ox."
—*Drinking Song of the Dungeon Guards*

I
The Final Meeting

So pleased was he with his latest proclamation, Lord Rinmauld Rogaire could only repeat himself: "Don't still my heart or turn *me* to ash." Lord Rogaire became grimmer, tapping his finger on the wood. "My donations are the only thing stopping those pestering priests from exciting a mob right outside your front door."

Maecidion Ordrid cast his eyes across his long black table. "Your seed will rue what you've done."

Lord Rinmauld Rogaire looked to his left, then to his right. The other Scepters sat in their seats, pale and stammering. But Lord Rogaire didn't scare so easily. "Your Virulence, please," he said, "our world has changed. Can't you see? *Rehleia* is a land of peace. Stability." He pulled from his tunic a gold coin, leering at it. "Wealth. Our people are sick of war, sick of thundering horses and our hacking swords."

Maecidion was still.

"I'll keep the gold from the Serabs. I'll keep the silk and the slaves and whatever else the very army you fought against brought back from Azad. In exchange—"

When Maecidion took to stroking his beard, several Scepters

leapt from their chairs and scurried under the table. In his own keep, no less, insults toward the world's worst necromancer were certain to bring down at least one curse.

"Get up! Get up, you fools." Lord Rogaire hoisted one by the hair. "In exchange, you may practice your foulness, and I'll continue muffling the baying of the many who wish to see this keep ground to pebbles. And they can do it, you know? Yes, you must. Even the great spell-weaver must fear the masses grown unified. Otherwise our first meet, with our dearly secluded Conqueror— well, that would have never been. Would it?"

Chair legs squeaked. The meeting finally over, the Scepters of Nilghorde began their exit. Slaves whose inhuman docility unnerved the brand-new rulers handed them their canes.

"It's not just a little money he's owed," one Scepter whispered to the next. "It's a damn ship's worth."

The other, ensuring neither Lord Rinmauld Rogaire nor Maecidion the Virulent were watching, whispered: "It's not just about a fortune now. Being hamstrung, humiliated, he'll never forget."

"Rinmauld," Maecidion spoke, rapping a whitened knuckle on his table, "your seed…and theirs."

II
THE MORTICIAN'S TALE

Part One

I enjoy my work, being a mortician, and how I ended up here is ultimately the story I wish to tell. It's an occupation I'm not surprised I ended up in, though it was not my original dream. But that's the case of all men who hold down honest wages.

I work at the Nilghorde Pauper Morgue, where endless droves of vagrants are flopped out of carts and off horse backs to land on my table. With me they all end. It's a brief inspection really, well that and some paperwork, as per a severely outdated policy that began in the Years of Peace, when the red, scale mail, sabers, and spears of the Conqueror's soldiers became the blue, chainmail, sabers, and clubs of the Metropolitan Ward.

After initial duties, the corpses are usually tossed down into the Pauper Vault, the mass grave of our fair city. My work is not limited to the homeless, of course, for there are many orphans, prostitutes, what have you. There is even the occasional victim of a crime of passion, one whose aggressor possessed the quick wit to pay off one of my bosses. I can safely say I've seen every level of our opulent society on my table at some point or another.

Now, as I toil among the dead, the statues of Do-Gooder's Row are finished, polished weekly by working parties sent from the Municipal Dungeon. Never one to forgo the juices of irony, tonight's assignment was brought to me from the vast confines of the Row. These poor sots killed each other over a damned mule cart. A mule cart! All five of them. Skewered and heads busted over life's wares and trinkets—though such wares and trinkets feed the desperate gullet, as I used to know all too well. Snier also knew this. I'll get to him later. He is, or, I've grown to worry, was one of the wiliest men ever to be met in Nilghorde—and that is no small feat, considering my home's rather well-deserved reputation for what I'd once heard coined "pleasant predation." I reckon that, if he would have slipped into this fiasco, Snier would have picked these dead men clean before the first horse hoof had echoed. But who knows where some end up, especially those prone to the ebb and flow like flotsam.

Ready for the table, all ten eyes have curiously found a way to look into one another. Flopped off a Ward cart to form a crude ring on my floor, Somyellia would have likely been able to summon some obedient demon straight up from its center.

And I must say, before embarking on this tale of magic and murder, I think this ring of dead men is fitting. An apt metaphor, if you will. Yes, morticians *can* be as lettered as they are solitary. Apt metaphor in that what lies ahead is more than just corpses on floors, but different people—characters on this grand macabre stage— different angles to be presented. Some would say it's the only way. Even time itself can become angular, for what is time to the dead? For this is the province we now call Rehleia, and most of us are inescapably linked, even if some will never know.

I can't impress that, this *linkage*, enough. Leading me, if you are one unfamiliar with our ways, to beg for what you may call some pre-tale forgiveness.

Rehleian tales are often told by a choir of orators. Some in your standard harmony; others, calculated step-overs as if competing for stardom and the license to history. These dead men here, my work tonight: The Ward did say there were others, the stronger ones, the ones with knife-skills and a wolf's temper, those who lived, and ran off with hands full as law enforcement rained down upon the dead and dying. Based on the tattooing, and choice of rags signifying to us locals what district they scoundrel'd out of, these men here were unacquainted, perhaps happenstance and hunger propelling their feet to the base of those standing tall on Do-Gooder's Row. Yet they would be so eternally connected. Please remember this, the web and how the spiders tell of it, as it is our way, in the city of Nilghorde, all of Rehleia, and I'd be willing to bet a coin or two throughout all Mulgara.

It is convenient last night's bloodbath allows me to mention Do-Gooder's Row. When its knees or eyes were chiseled free from the towering lines of dull white, these moments have served as time-keeping devices for us Rehleians. The chiseling began the day our Years of Peace were declared. And much like my own life, happenings and fortunes have often been remembered by what stage the statues were in when life gave us our surprises.

These days, champions like Zaderyn Fover, a citizen who dove into the Black Tongue only to be carried off by its currents while trying to save a drowning child, shine bright and polished. But much of my tale will pull us back, back when the statues were but ugly rectangles crowned with faces and shoulders tortured by tumors of marble.

✳

My name is Seasmil Oleugsby. Most would say I am a large man. I'd concur; made from the heavy lifting, but not solely due to. When I am handling the corpses, my hair is tied in a ponytail; black hair, though, like the many scars on my skin, it wasn't always that way.

I was named after my great-grandfather, who led a charge on a camp of cannibal pirates off the coast of Suela. His name grew to legendary status, despite a rather gruesome end. He and his company were roasted alive in suits of hardened clay. Apparently there is a holiday in that idol-worshipping land that still mimics all of this. A ragged sailor once told how the women rub their clitorises on the face of the still-screaming meal to be. I often wondered if my ancestor had suffered this intriguing punishment, and if he had felt a final delight before the world went dark. It was a neglected portrait that hung from a wall during my youth that told me from him I'd inherited the Oleugsby menace: flat forehead, deep-set eyes, and a square jaw.

I was born and raised in Nilghorde; in the Templeton District to be exact, designated for the martial servicemen and their families. We were on an edge of the city, where the farthest line of homes faced a great forest. Templeton was a sturdy square, once cut from the forest and sown on the Nilghorde quilt. Inside our heavily patrolled borders sat the steep-roofed stone houses surrounded by all you'd expect to see in the farmlands.

And I do mean heavily patrolled. Despite it being a district in Nilghorde, there was little crime. Most of the watchmen and the Metropolitan Ward lived there. They hadn't busted heads all over this land to allow swarms of riffraff to spill into their own domiciles. But in the earlier days, when the Conqueror was waging war and the future-wardsmen were his soldiers, Templeton was a place where fathers were gone most of the year, leaving children to be raised by elder siblings or their promiscuous mothers.

I was an only child, but that was just fine by me. From the beginning, I'd always fallen deep into the joys of solitude and imaginary friends. These playmates inhabited holes in trees and pawed the floor under my bed. By the time I was catching up to the height of my mother, I had shed any interest in sports or games played out in the streets.

That, though, wasn't from being alone too much—as Mother quibbled at times. I'd discovered the world of science. I begged Mother for an alchemy set. After much whining and mutinies at the dinner table, she caved and brought me a little wooden box. It wasn't just filled with mineral pouches, corked vials, and tiny cutting tools—it bore wonder. In my hands were the keys to the doors of the natural world.

The little box became my obsession. The few friends who still lingered about stopped knocking on our door. Mother's pleas to go outside and play eventually stopped too. Far less gratifying, imaginary friends turned to dust. One by one, faint screams, audible to my ears alone, and then there were only shadows. I particularly remember the elf in the old elm on the edge of Templeton Park. He sat crouching in the canopy, silent as always. His stare haunted me for a long time. Disapproving of me leaving the mists of fairyland for pragmatism was certainly understandable. But it also couldn't be stopped.

I eventually focused on the visceral endeavors and varied my experiments greatly, from futile attempts at tracking stars to more enjoyable branches dealing with the inner workings of anything I could either trap, scavenge, or lure with meat.

"Seasmil," I often have to tell myself. "If you are going to go into the backstory, be sure not to leave out the most important stuff." For backstory is merely useful for jutting us forward into that great, mysterious yonder. And I should know this, being I've spent more nights falling through book's pages than your average paid scholar. With this bit in mind, telling my tale would be a wide chasm from thorough if I failed to tell of my father, in his entirety, as is best known to me.

No, not some Ordrid—though you may have anticipated such a revelation due to, among other things, my habits and choice of work.

No, my father was Augnor Oleugsby, a cavalryman in the notorious regiment Swift Saber. The SS was a highly deployed unit under the Conqueror himself, and subsequently, I don't have any recollection of my father in the house amid my earliest years. Despite his absence, we did not struggle. Charges and pillages accumulated, bringing back chest upon chest of jewels and coin.

My father was a beast of a man, a stone golem with legs like unhewn trees, and a neck like an oxen in the farmlands where Mother had come out of.

The first memory I can muster was of him telling Mother a spirited story. With the smell of the saddle still lingering, he recounted riding through the farmlands of Serabandantilith and mowing the villagers down like grass. I didn't hear the whole tale, and time has a way of inflating and deflating the sanctity of memory, but I do remember a comparison of some people to the height of our kitchen cupboard. I was eye level with the cupboard myself back then and tried to make sense of how men were so small in other lands. As was her nature, or at least her developed one, Mother listened half-heartedly, trying multiple times in vain to clue Father in that I was listening, and do so without infuriating him.

Whether Father was riding the famed memory of his grandfather, or was an exemplary soldier, or a combination of the two, I do not know, but he'd embarked on a career in which he was being groomed for a lofty and prestigious rank. Chief Horseman perhaps, or maybe a lower seat in the Office of Scepters when his ruthlessness left the saber and moved to an inkwell. All I know is, wherever he was slotted to go came to a sudden and unmovable halt when I was about ten.

We never really knew where he was or when he'd be returning. There were the wives meetings, where the senior crone married to some military relic long overdue for retirement would disseminate the latest news through scroll and lecture. Mother hated those.

In one of her more humorous moments, she reenacted how catty they all were and how without delay the meetings would degrade to drunk clucking hens gossiping over which watchmen was the most endowed and notes on his availability.

So, it's no surprise to me now that one fateful winter, when Father was supposed to be on the forefront of some vague campaign, he was attending to the wife of a field grade commander in his SS.

We found out weeks after. Father had returned home a wretch, reluctantly telling Mother that he was done deploying due to "some arbitrary insubordination." For all the stolen gold in the Thunder Bustle, I couldn't fathom why Mother didn't tear the house apart and leave him emasculated after he had fallen asleep. She took it on the chin and seemed to recover back to her dismal role as housewife to the once-great warrior. You would have barely noticed anything at all, save the additional silence at the table and the lines in her face that had deepened. But hindsight is an unchained dragon, cruel but liberated. I know now why Mother remained in that house in Templeton.

Despite a heated debate among his superiors, Father was allowed to retain a paying position. As a man it occurred to me maybe it was his greatest detractors who gleefully fought for this altered retention. Demoted to a stable master for one of the SS garrisons, our once healthy stock of horses were sold off, their mountain of feed abandoned to mottle with the fungi that I examined and the vermin that I caught.

Most of the time, Father would bring his work home with him—we certainly had the room in the stables. Mother once whispered he was too embarrassed to be seen in his billet by his former brethren.

One of the few reasons he wasn't pulled apart by a departing pair of Saber warhorses was he'd saved the life of an esteemed officer. At the time Father's infidelities were being exposed, this officer had climbed to the seat of Vice Chief Horseman and had enough clout to muffle the baying of the scorned husband. Although the Vice Chief's influence spared my father, the same could not be said for his loose-ring-bearing mistress, whose corpse dangled on the Tower of the Waning Moon for a season of crows and maggots.

This Vice Chief's generosity bore our family other gifts too. Soon after the SS returned from the deployment where Father had saved his life, he came to our home one evening for a dinner. And not any ordinary dinner. Mother had banged around in the kitchen almost as frantic as she did over her wardrobe, ending it stuffed in a dress never to be seen again, and in front of a meal so large my boyish brain anticipated the Conqueror's entire army.

He was a noble-looker, the type whose gray feathered hair and blue eyes made you wonder why he'd ever signed on to shit next to men with blade wounds stitched by other lugs; squatting over the same trench, dug by men for whose wounds there was no fixing. He left us with a chest that *chunked* when it hit the floor, and he sang Father's praises until the night drew me weary. Right before he departed, he brought me from his carriage a baby lamb, black as midnight. My best guesses were it was either some custom of warrior etiquette—a gesture of giving life to the seed of the man who saved his—or a grand display of appreciation for Mother's cooking.

Though I was informed of every glorious detail, it was still hard not to wonder if Father had really dashed into that ambush to save him not for duty or for that brotherly love soldier-types love to go on about, but rather to quench a bloodlust. Truth is, that Vice Chief knew my father in a way I never did. I would be false to not say that a lifetime ago I wished to see this man, to sit on his knee and partake in his celebrations, to wear his giant helmet and be tossed in the air. Bruises simply meant I received something different.

My experiments on our neighbor's cat brought a particular

salvo, and the manner in which I returned the feline only heated the beating. Around that time, stable work lost a lot of its demand. To fill the gap, Father took an avid interest in denouncing my hopes and daily endeavors. That damn cat was all it took. The alchemy kit was pried from my hands, only to be shoved against my chest a moment later. I wept without restraint when I was ordered to break all the vials. Afterward I assumed the usual stance and held firewood above my head until my shoulders screamed. Somewhere in this memory I recited the piece of martial jingle I'd recite a thousand times: the SS creed. As an adult my mind has shunted all but two stanzas:

One rider, ten riders, or riders score
Through pain, through cold, through plain, through moor

I don't think he ever planned for me to be a warrior, and if he did, he surely changed his mind after his demotion. "Bunch of damn beggars in armor," he'd say. "Lousy mob whores praising the cowardly; worshipped those that pass out bread instead of the blade."

This, of course, worked to my benefit. The rank and file could march off our land's tallest cliff for all I cared. Like most children in Templeton, I enjoyed a comprehensive education, poring over sonnets and rattling an abacus with a series of tutors—maybe even more so, since no son of Augnor would wear armor in peacetime. My favorite subject was unsurprisingly biology, and it may have been boyish defiance, but Father's *soldier's disdain* for the arts and academia only strengthened my resolve to not only be a man of science but a medical doctor. So what if my tastes were a little unorthodox from the start?

With funding procured from Mother's undergarments drawer, which had been procured from Father's last heavy chest, I built an upgraded version of my laboratory—this time in the cobweb-infested cellar of our most vacated and dilapidated barn. Once I was sure the ogre who stalked my waking life was unaware of operational headquarters, I continued to explore the governing of all life-forms that I could drag through the candlelight.

Around the time when hair began to sprout in new places, I snuck out one night and penetrated deep into the city. I scurried through alleys. At the risk of abduction or worse, I finally found what I was searching for outside the back of a noisy brothel. It was soft, pink, and barely dead. I brought it home and down into the cellar. It was the first of its kind, but surely not the last.

"Leading minds say all this gods talk is nonsense," my old tutor used to say. "Tubes and muck are we."

One of many in a long line of educators that ran scream-ing from our home, this tutor had been a student himself. The Institute of Human Sciences, Rehleia's premier medical school, was placed on a Nilghorde hill like some jaded royalty. More than just eliminative materialism, I learned from this scholar that the Institute did all sorts of fascinating studies in its grand halls. The true tome of treasure came the day he brought me an old course book of his. I hid it deep in the cellar, behind a skull of a large dog and several jars of entrails from woodland fauna. The find-ings within the book were a stream of wonder. And soon a river.

I have been accused of being a callous man, solitary and apa-thetic to the plight of others, but I can say that if that is so, that I wasn't always. This tutor had been warned by Father, backed against a wall in our den, random sharp object to his neck, not to encour-age my peculiarness and stick to the curriculum. When a distant neighbor called upon our door to ask if we'd seen her dog, not only did I receive a staunch one, but the best teacher I ever had collected his last payment with the helpful removal of his front row of teeth.

Mother pleaded my innocence, even drumming up the courage to compare unfounded accusations made by the SS at Father's expense. In truth, part of that neighbor's pet hid my begifted course book. My guilt in that matter served no purpose to surface.

Now it must be understood, this lamb placed in my arms by the Vice Chief was also slotted for the operating table. I wanted to see if it could survive with a transfusion of my own blood. The experiment of course presented itself while I was reading one of the studies. The Institute had run a lengthy trial, placing vats of murderer blood from the Municipal Dungeon into orphans' arms. Most of the orphans died before transfusion, but a few strong specimens survived. The damn rainwater ruined the last several pages, but I imagined the spectacular transformation of these test subjects in their cages: street children screaming through the bars with eyes of predation, walking among the caged viewing areas while pumping the blood of cutthroats. I didn't have the resources needed for full replication, but a lamb wasn't bad.

I'd spent a week or so tactfully letting my blood, being sure to avoid the constant threat of discovery and cataclysmic reaction from my parents. Then the "Day of the Lamb," as I'd come to call it, finally arrived. Enough blood was stored, and Father was heavily asleep from a full day of the stable.

I laugh now at the ruthless ambition. Although cursedly naïve at the time, as we all must be, I am proud of who I was at such a young age. The story was already concocted: wolves stole the lamb. And I was going to use the blood I drained from it to make room for my own and paint a believable scene of carnage.

Down in the cellar, to optimize my sight, I placed candles in the shape of a triangle. In this triangle's center was a low table that I laid the lamb on. I tied down a front leg, but when I reached for the other, chaos erupted.

We fought like pit fighters. A mad chase around the table sent the transfusion gear into every nook and cranny. My jar became a half-congealed explosion. He stayed me with a rear kick to the jaw and when the lights went away I felt pure nausea.

At the end of it, we were covered in sappy blood, both panting. My heart beat harder at the thought that Father may have heard. Equally, I imagine, the lamb was terrified of some determined lad, with rope in hand at the opposite end of an unpleasant cellar.

It was then I looked into those black-jeweled eyes. Maybe I was being melodramatic then, and maybe I am a bit still, but this thing had the courage to fight off his attacker—like a drunken banshee— whereas I took my beatings without recourse. I'd killed hundreds of rats, snakes, cats, and dogs who put up less of a fight. It is hard for someone who dwells in the company of people and song to understand, but I felt a closeness with this creature that was beyond that of normal explanation. Up until then I hadn't named him, but right then he became Celly. A childish, campy, spondee of a name, sure, but it signified the cellar, where I met my best friend and where, I still believe, two spirits connected.

We emerged out onto the floor of the barn. Gigantic horses glared with an oppressive over-watch. We washed at the well, and I returned him to his corral. Sneaking back inside I breathed a sigh of relief, hearing snores that would humble a bear.

After that night, Celly and I were inseparable. He followed me on my long walks through the shores of the wood-line, where I showed him all the snares and pitfalls that I used to capture wide-eyed shriekers. I'd sneak him in the house sometimes, and he would sleep next to me in bed. His smell, long-lasting, I remedied with heavy incense and constantly cracked windows. He and I both grew in stature, and we spent many a summer night sitting on the floor of the cellar, one reading to the other.

A night in the late spring I heard strange noises from our kitchen. It was a faint rustling, followed by a sound that reminded me of the cracking of firewood. And after that nothing more.

At the time, a banishment to my bedroom for some shortcoming prohibited me from investigating any further. The next morning I awoke to Father screaming. That was nothing particularly unusual, except this time there rang a unique desperation. I ran out to see him on his knees, back toward me. He held Mother, dead as dead could be. The rope hung without motion, tied to a rafter where our kitchen met the den.

The thought of her watching over me in some a state of… *unbeing* the prior night sparked the hair on my arms.

Her face showed the full effects, and her neck I could not bear.

I must have let out a small yelp, because there was a moment where Father turned to me. He had the look of a painting made by a decadent and angry artist. He hadn't cried, or at least I hadn't heard him, but his eyes were red, and not the usual shade.

Mother was buried in the Ansul of Chapwyn Cemetery. We couldn't get one of their priests to do the service, due to some stipulation about suicide. This sent Father into a wailing rage, which deepened the sense of weight and sadness that only the family of a suicide can tell.

Father was able to convince a martial priest from the SS to come out. Formerly delegated to sprinkling incense on brand-new war dead, he waved his hands and saw her into the dirt. Word had passed through the ranks, and it was the only time I got to see a dressed array of some of my father's brothers-in-arms. I saw men whom I didn't know console him in ways I'd wished then that I was able.

We rode back home, me behind him on the notch of a one-man saddle. I put my arms around his abdomen, a place that was once as hard as mountain stone, now turned to gut. I retracted them and decided to take my chances with a slipping grip of the saddle blanket.

The times after Mother's characteristic exit were filled with an even greater silence. Well, silence between the remnants of the family more like—taking into account the tarts with more legs than years left on earth who frequented the house. Abysmal void at the dinner table followed by broken glasses, head-tilt feminine laughter, and sex made for a house better fit for a madman.

It took Father no effort to find these women, and I surmised that at least one of them contributed to my mother's suicide—maybe all of them. Years prior, I guess there would have been some hatred for my mother. Why couldn't she have informed me of her discovery, and why couldn't we have just left? But coin and shelter are not just given, and past the mere pragmatics, I also know how some are slaves to their own omissions, and I never pondered why there wasn't a note.

To separate myself from the clamor that had become home, I delved deeper into my projects and fought with all my might not to acknowledge my budding interest in Father's ill-gotten company. Many a time, a dissection was halted to ponder the contents under a silk black dress.

One evening a rotten carriage, pulled by a set of mares looking just as bad, brought three women to our door. When they stepped out I was dizzied by the heavy sway of the redheaded leader's breasts. The other two were quite young, close enough to my own age, but all were equally dressed for their trade.

There was a sickening wave of emotions for my father right then. Disgust—how could you disgrace your dead wife's bed with the juices of women whose names you wouldn't remember in the morrow? Envy—how utterly enthralling these women were, and then how I would have joined my cold mother for a chance just to feel their warm embrace.

I ran off to my cellar, seeing it as this ridiculous hiding place for bones. Weeping with my face in my hands helped; taking breaks only to—well. One night while spying on Father through a bedroom window, I saw two of his voluptuous companions do to him, one hand on top of the other, what I did furiously and frequently to break up the crying.

Hours must have passed before I emerged, for it was dark and the wind licked cold. As I walked up to our side door, it swung open, almost toppling me over. The three women filed out in their slightly rearranged attire. The night did not conceal the return of the redhead's jiggle, a sight that sent my soul wailing back into the cellar.

This time, however, before I could make my retreat, one of the young ones thwarted me. By the light of the moon and a street lamp I saw her: fair skinned, golden-eyed. Her hair was the color of dew on lilies, which she wore in braids that ended at the crack of a backside I already held visions of. Perky breasts exposed their contours under an evilly cut garment, and above them were eyelashes that batted at me.

"Hi," she said as if talking to someone capable of speech. "You're Augy's boy?"

"By blood," I managed to squeak out, utterly amazed at my own response.

I don't know if it was because we were both standing as still as Lirelet statues, or if it was because I was still mouthing *by blood* to myself in half-astonishment, but I didn't hear their ride pull up. It was her glance that notified me. Once pulled out of whatever jackassery I was surely swirling around in, I heard the full rattling of the carriage and smelled the low-burning lamps affixed to its mean wooden face.

"Time we're off, Somyellia," the endowed leader confirmed. The motherly tone wasn't lost on me—both in its oddity and its ability to soothe—as she and the other pranced down our wooden steps. This time I didn't stare at her tits. It was as if she never had them.

Somyellia, as she was called, looked at me, tilted her head, bit her bottom lip.

"I…I can take her home," I said.

"I don't know, young master," said the ranking mistress. "Come now, Morlia," Somyellia said to her. "Deny such a strapping youngling?"

"Silence, Morlia," wedged a croaking voice from the carriage. "You want her, it's twenty silver more. She'll be back by morning." The words ran up my spine like a dry tongue.

"I have it," I found myself saying.

"Somyellia," spoke the carriage, "come back with the money."

As the carriage departed, she looked more like a girl playing dress-up than one of *Augy's* whores. But she wasn't playing anything. She had cavorted and hiked her legs up in palaces and mansions all throughout Nilghorde—perhaps all Rehleia—perhaps beyond our watery borders. She'd bounced atop soldierly bodies. She'd escorted the unrepentantly wealthy, on her hands and knees above pits of decorated hunting cats and amid silk and gold. I was a whelp, and she had either found an appeal in my innocence or had much more devious plans in store.

Under a swollen moon I meandered. Her lip was bit again, and to my terror I'd once more lost my powers of speech. Pollen from nearby gardens filled our noses, and if it weren't for the decay on my clothes we would have looked like characters right out of the *Poems of the Classics*. Wind ran around our bodies, and the moon peered down upon its children.

"What is your name?" she said.

"Seasmil."

"That's an unusual name. What does it mean?"

"I—I don't really know." Beautiful *and* thought-provoking! "Never thought about it much. I was named after a relative. Does yours mean something?" While sunk in self-consciousness, I shifted my attention as best as I could from the ornaments adorning her to thoroughly digging a small hole in front of me with the toe of my boot.

"Of course," she popped. "All who are kin to Maecidion the Virulent possess names with direct meaning."

"What?"

"Mine means *daughter of the sleeping demon*," she said in the manner of a small child announcing their alignment with a favored pit fighter, flag in hand. She giggled, and her big gold eyes flashed. "Why are you covered in all that filth?"

"Oh, no I was—do you want to see something?"

Maybe it was because my dismal lab was the only thing I could claim in the whole world as my own. Or maybe it was because she had looked at me with the eyes of a woman who may have really bore the meaning of her name.

She nodded, and with her hand in mine, I escorted her to my dark cellar of experiments, where I hungered for an experiment of a different kind.

As with many men's first, I was in a state of euphoric confusion. Starting things off was a showing of human skulls. The stall tactic was excruciation itself, made only greater when they all found a way to tumble out of my fumbling arms. Aside from the stock insecurities of adolescence, the aroma of my lab—a thing I'd grown so accustomed to that my nose could almost omit decay—burst into my face as if it were the first time ever smelling a corpse. Surely, she would take flight up my stairs, this creature sitting on a table so covered in macabre. Most women would have stopped at the cellar door, yet she began to undress in the stench and shadow.

Never taking her eyes off of me, she undressed as she had so many times before.

Her buttocks rested on the edge of the table. Her dress was shed with the flick of a leg. Her arms were locked at the elbow, hands gripping the edge. Her mouth hung open, bee-stung lips moist and shining in the candlelight.

The candlelight itself; a thing between those shelves and pillars as familiar to me as portraits on a wall. On this night, though, the light gave birth to shapes that danced as if spectators to an enchantress…and me, standing awkwardly with a handful of skulls.

She curled a finger: *come hither*. I dropped the skulls again. My eyes were locked on a soft and sideways grimace. A faint patch of hair above it wanted to be smelled, and I walked closer, into the gap that her legs had made.

She gripped the back of my head with one hand and my small boyish buttocks with the other. "Show me you're your father's son," she said, showing her teeth. As she pulled me closer I felt like an animal caught in one of my snares—almost.

Our lips met, and she had my trousers off and my horned member grasped before I could even realize her perfume didn't overwhelm the odors that I'd momentarily forgotten. A cacophony of little pops and squishes erupted when I pressed her back against the table. I thought she was going to go berserk, but to my amazement, and to my delight, she smiled. We rolled off the table and onto the floor.

When our needs had been met, we stood up and looked at the other. She was still smiling; that girly side of hers having returned, save for the fact that she now looked like a recently feasted ghoul. I must have been a sight to see too, relishing the mixture of sex and death that was to become my adult life.

After we emerged, I took her to meet Celly, whom she endeared with petting and rubbed her face against with shut-eyed kisses. She soon informed me of the whereabouts of her unsavory quarters, and told me not to worry about the silver. I did not question her.

It was time to go.

Filled with the empowerment of sexual knowing, and drugged with the aroma of rot and her strong perfume, I stole one of my father's horses.

We sprung forth into the air. Wolves from the forest howled as we galloped out of the Templeton District, always on the lookout for a roving patrol. We were bound for the deformed, cobbled alleys that formed the crime-ridden Thunder Bustle District, where you were as likely to bump into a rotgut-riddled sorcerer weaving outlawed magic as you were to lose your purse.

As we rode, she clutched my waist, buildings and landmarks of the city flying by. Our route went from dirt to the *clickity-clack* of cobblestones. Eyes peered out, lurking behind glass windows that never opened. We avoided the shadowy figures that approached us when I paused at an intersection for Somyellia to get her bearings. The salt smell thickened. Except for the horse underneath us, we were the only living things for the last leg of our journey.

We arrived at the backside of an old warehouse busy leaning into the sea. It was a block of wet black, grayed at the edges by some source of light. At the door were the ugliest men I had ever seen. Armed with pikes, their scars came either from disastrous afflictions of acne or battling fierce beasts with dispositions for biting.

"This is it, Seasmil," Somyellia said with a calmness that had no place there. "Thank you for the ride."

She walked up a series of waterlogged steps to the guardsmen, and whispered something in one's ear that was met with a nod. Turning to face me, she looked like a thing of beauty who had chosen to give up beauty for darker delights, but whose attraction had yet to wither. Her hair now an unkempt mess of twists and shoots, she smiled and waved and disappeared through a doorway to a place that I wanted to follow at the expense of my very soul.

The brief introspection was cut short when a blood-wrenching scream erupted deep in the alleys, followed by a mob of hurried feet.

I was now again the boy from Templeton, on his father's stolen horse, without a weapon or a guide. I proceeded to fly through the wormy spaces, between buildings all appearing abandoned. Trying to remember the direction in which we had come, and later avoiding the shaking lanterns of surely pursuing sentries, I made it back to the barn before sunrise.

I tended to the horse and agonized over the minute details of the gear, mostly what side of any particular piece was facing the wall and what wasn't. But more than that, I agonized about *her*. Would I ever see her again?

Boys shedding their innocence for the more nefarious practices of adolescence is the source of ocean's worth of poetry. My towering escapade with Somyellia was no exception. Only such an encounter could intoxicate me enough to run off with one of Father's horses. Carrying out my clandestine venture undetected only provoked my sense of achievement. Although doing so far too young for the approval of the bland and proper, I had peeked into the vault of teeming secrets that no book or vial could contain or explain. I was hooked, and I found myself a terrible thirst in a raging storm.

At the expense of my bungling studies, I set my eyes on that dancing, warm flesh. An addled burrow of Nilghorde meant nothing. I was the second Seasmil; trapper of teethed mites, owner of skulls, avoider of the Ward, and one whose vigor listened not to the gray and cockless distracters of recourse or consequence.

Father had taken an even more nominal interest in my happenings. An increased workload and a growing penchant for the bottle carried him off into an advantageous solitude. I could stay in my lab for a full day and night, just to emerge for some wonted ramble of housework to be done. I was far past the days of subtle paternal want and hopes. Neglect was my ally. As long as my chores were done, my scholarly work fulfilled, and my changing face occasionally seen, I was free, and my loins would find their quenching, even if it meant the coming of terror.

And such quenching mandated that I did indeed see her again.

On the backs of stolen horses, Somyellia and I rode to new places to sow oats and memories alike, many lost now like rain in the sea. I became well versed in the ways of women. For she would on occasion nestle away one of her coworkers, and for my pleasant discovery they'd execute carefully rehearsed acts on my body, often tied down and blindfolded. Her expertise from her employment left me mesmerized and trembling, always outdoing herself with random accessories of opium, leather, or blood.

We chased moonlight, dancing wickedly behind tall graves before defiling them with human juices. She showed me the black arts of her Ordrid kind, explaining she'd shown promise in curses. I gave her animal hearts with Mother's few remaining jewels deep in the tough muscles.

I became somewhat of an expert in avoiding the black-drabbed ruffians en route to acquire her: a toss of silver here, a swift gallop over a rotten fence. I declare, I learned more about the Thunder Bustle, and remained uncut, than the most resourceful local. I became a most regular of irregular sights in front of that ogre-guarded door. Once she was wrapped around me, like the plague dressed in silk and wolf's fur, we would disappear into the smoke, shadow and brick maze to some predestined bungalow. Alone, we'd commence our carnal rites, and not the howling of the forest wolves or roaring of the sea could drown our ecstasy.

We both found a happiness that was all our own. When her work bid her away, I would pass the time with half-hearted dissections and long walks with Celly.

※

Celly grew into a beautiful hoofed beast. Our voyages through the forest were done in the contented silence that romance books always fawn on about. And maybe I'm guilty of wordy romancing too, as you may have already nocked that critic's arrow. But this silence was pristine, interrupted only by the occasional predator that met staff and stone, and a lone stumble into our land's reigning religion: a rural Chapwyn encampment.

I was lured one day by moans I believe belonged to a wounded deer in a tabernacle of young pine. The moans of such a deer struck by some woodland malady became a circle of men, no more than a handful, wrapped in the same filth-white garb as the tabernacle's roof. They were all kneeling, bent so far forward one fell over into the dirt. In the center stood a priest, in cleaner sheets and holding an unspooled scroll in one hand and an uprooted plant in the other. Both the scroll and plant lowered as he watched Celly, myself, and my fang-nicked staff descend the slope of bramble and ferns.

"He who walketh with Animal as Man is either thy steward of sentience or Animal himself." The Chapwyn priest wasn't reading from his dirty old scroll, but that didn't mean the obscure verse hadn't come right from the vellum. Lack of familiarity with this particular passage—any particular passage unsheathed at random— perhaps was the one thing I shared in common with the lay, scroll-thumping Chapwynite.

The verse lingered on the leader's face, emaciated and worn like ship wood, and the rest had either risen or turned to behold the object in question. I heard Celly's hooves, curious and cautious as they clopped down on wet leaves. Coming up against my thigh, my freehand found a good patch of his wool to grab and rest in. Animals that you don't kill can smile, I swear to you. Celly's made the warmer of the parishioners giggle.

"Didn't mean to interrupt," I said, eyeing the slosh of heavy-boot trails that led back to somewhere in Nilghorde. I was now close enough to this rustic communion to knock a kneeler over with the muddy end of my staff. Beyond them, wooden bowls made an inner ring around the priest's feet. In them were what appeared to be equal dispersings of water, bread, and hand axes. "Didn't know this was—"

"An intruder," the priest fired, "on Tersiona's faithful hath only strayed from his own wander and intruded on only that which hath been seen before he beeth born unto the world."

It may have been them rising in unison that backed me. My staff would've dispatched them with a few hard swings, but religious synchronization was a human convention new to me.

"He beeth no shepherd!" a voice shouted. "Beware those who giveth false witness, their…their sheep are black as their souls, those damned."

My foothold on the slope behind me ceased their advance. "Maenoch," sighed the priest. "Forty parthings and reread the blessed scripture: those who giveth false witness *for their souls are black and damn those sheep who stay their own vigilance.*"

Maenoch hiked up his rags and began the prescribed calisthenics. Long before the fortieth hop, he gave me a malicious look, one probably later seeing him fit for Ansul's True, the martial arm of their sprawling church, populated by the militant-chaste whose final initiation was rumored to be self-inflicted castration.

"Come see us again sometime," the priest solicited, reaffirming his grip on his accessories and sounding for the first time like a man born in my century. We both turned wearing our own versions of an awkward smile. Their practice recommenced and I climbed back toward Templeton. Before I went over the crest I overheard the gist of the sermon I'd interrupted: the intrinsic good of sharing.

What a coincidence, for I didn't mind sharing Somyellia—which may surprise you if you are from Oxghorde or won't bury a lady because she hung herself. But I found her profession a quaint enterprise that only made me want her more by the hour. I had only found discord with her livelihood on one occasion.

I'd watched the rotten carriage pull up one evening, expecting the usual gaggle of tarts to file out. To my horror I watched Somyellia exit. I saw her scan to see if I were around, and saw her relief when she perceived that I wasn't.

For reasons of sheer mercy my mind has precluded any re-hashing the events from that evening, but I recall being beside myself with the sharpest type of grief. Outside Father's window I stood, biting down deep into my fists.

Our favorite meeting place was an abandoned house. It was the last home in a row, all overlooking City Cemetery. While Nilghorde was peppered with quaint little graveyards, privately owned and surrounded by high flinty walls, the city held three major ones. Besides City Cemetery, there was Whisperer's Plain and the Ansul of Chapwyn Cemetery, that last one not only hold-ing my mother, but a virtual underground hive of the religious, the uppity, and the municipal who'd opted not to spend eternity near those who they'd ruled. City Cemetery, the colossus, stretched the farthest and the fullest. For the nights we'd float over its stones, I would leave alone the stealing of horses and make it on foot. Walking there was no short journey, and my legs after a time started taking the shape of my father's kind.

The abandoned house looked like a slight breeze would topple it. Only the cobwebs and rat shit glued the eaten frame together. Good thing those components were in such abundance. A witchy roof was still clad with a few shingles, all deeply warped from years of sun and bombarding rain. Crows made home the exposed rafters, and from a caved-in wall on the second floor, we would sit and view the silent resting place for many of the city's denizens whose families didn't possess the money to bury them with class.

We would stay the night, small fire lit in a bronze urn she'd plucked off a tomb. I loved the sort of mischievous unlife that came to shape below us, in the tiny hours of the morning where the world's shores seemed to rub against some other place. Holding Somyellia in my arms, fire to my back, I found myself longing for that place.

※

I awoke, grabbing for my knife. "Can't fool you," Somyellia larked. Years navigating the Bustle does bear fruit. She was on the edge of our mat with a bag on her lap. Her hair always took on a cooked straw effect in the morning, before mirrors and little pink jars and her ritual of locking herself in powder rooms. This game of hers, moving my knife while I slept, brought her more mirth than a seat at the front of a good theatre. She said she loved seeing the "whip and flash" of how I snatched it, and how I never missed, whether moved from our left side to our right, or stuck in the floor behind my head. For me it only brought a jolt to the heart and a lump in my throat, but it also woke me as absolute as Pelat coffee. Convincing myself this was the reason for her dropping loose boards or screaming in my ear helped me fight back a second reflex that sometimes came after I'd wrapped my fingers around the handle.

Rubbing the sleep from my eyes, the knife was tossed and I fell back into my sheets. "I better return all this leather," Somyellia said to herself with a yawn. Looking across my chest and between my feet, familiar portions of last night's ensemble were sticking out from her bag. There was a cool breeze, and angry crows squawked somewhere in the rafters. "Or have my hands dipped in oil."

"Would they even notice?" I said.

"I am *so* hungry. Do we have anything left?"

"No," I said, rolling onto my side.

"Oh. No bother, I'm going to pick up some things on the way."

"See you tonight?"

"Not tonight. There's some bachelor party for a Lotgard that starts at dusk and is going to last for three days."

"Yeah, I need to go home anyway," I said, having learned well to mask these mild disappointments.

"Well," she exhaled in a patronizing tone she'd come to perfect, "I promise to meet you here as soon as the festivities end," tickling my exposed side, "my beast."

We departed with a kiss. She turned to go back to her nest, as I began the long walk back.

The sun came out late but made up for its tardiness. By the time I stepped onto the first dirt road, I was sweating in the gleam. I rounded a bend that I had rounded many times before, viewing the red-topped roof of The Great Fuckity House of Oleugsby.

Now, when I tell you that I felt something was *off*, I don't mean that under the perfect reflection of memories retold. I don't mean to say that looking back I felt something was wrong merely by knowing what happened next. As I met the wooden fence that separated our yard from the road, there was a cold in my gut.

The cellar? He had found my lab! My first impulse was of him walking past its door. Maybe I had meant to close it, but some arbitrary piece of rubbish kept it open just enough? Maybe he had, for some uncharacteristic reason, developed a brief curiosity about where I spent most of my days? I snuck around the side of the house, constantly examining the windows, thief-like, for any signs of life. As I approached the back, I heard a faint monotonous ring coming from his favorite barn.

"Shoeing," I said, relieved. An image I had of him hovering over my cellar door began to dissolve.

I scurried there anyway. A quick inspection revealed that all was as I'd left it. I decided to go at least take a look at Father. Not for any reason one could readily ascribe, but I couldn't place a sensation that still lingered, and I now felt wrapped in some lurid investigation.

The farrier hammer, making the usual *tinks* and *tanks*, echoed from the other side of the barn. I approached in a timid walk. Talking to him wasn't something that happened all that often, and I was already formulating my rebuttal for his most probable, stern request for some laboring assistance.

Turning the corner, I stopped at the sight before me. In a pool of his own blood lay Celly. His coal black fur was so much darker than the white skull and pinkish brain.

A wave of emotions pummeled me. He wasn't dead…and I had enough tools to repair the wound. This creature, my friend, lay in torment unattended. Sickness, yes. Guilt, that too. I felt the world spin, and some chorus of nameless mocking things sang their pale and dead incantations as I tried to breathe.

Most of all, I felt hatred. A hatred that made the world turn cold.

I was not a young man who was naïve to the presence and yields of hate. I had dwelled in a sort of darkness my whole life, and wrestled with my disconnected family at an early age and left that hope abandoned, dead in some field. The hate upon the sight this day was a treachery. When I saw that the corral gate was ajar, I put together what happened.

Celly had managed to break out. With my increased time away, he had most likely made the mistake of wandering up to Father for something as simple as a head rub. Father, busy with his stable duties, turned out to be in no mood for such troublesome interruptions. He killed Celly with one hammer blow to the head.

Behind a stable wall, sounds of work resumed. I couldn't see him, but he was close. Tools hung about me.

I snatched a hefty pick and gripped its handle. I fought the urge to look over at Celly, knowing I'd weep uncontrollably if I did. I crept to the edge of the wall, then I could fight that urge no longer. My spine bent and jerked as I wept, vomiting violent and uncontrollable little meeps.

I felt again the oaken handle in my hands. I turned toward the hammer noises; face flushed with tears, jowls open and twitching as I squeezed it, wide-eyed and beyond all reason.

I walked the way a man may right before his own execution—before the concerns of the world have left the crude carriage of flesh and bone that vessels a spirit ready for voyage.

All it would take was one committed strike. His skull would split like firewood. All I needed was for his back to be turned and his pink brain attending the last shoe it would ever contemplate.

For all his conquests, he was to be ended at the hands of his son. He deserved this, and he could be buried next to Mother, as I would surely dance in their ashes.

I turned the corner and gazed upon his back.

His head was hunkered low. Behind him I, his son, wielded a farm tool like a frontline pikeman. I always picture this through the eyes of some nonexistent spectator. That tiny moment in time haunts me, the image of us.

Killing had been an obligation of my means of obtaining animals, and some of my more risky ventures into the city bore me witness to many faces of death.

But for reasons I didn't understand, my grip loosened. I was slipping from the midnight-garbed avenger to the terrified little boy.

I found myself filled with fear—worse, indecision. I begged for my rage to return to me, and with it the strength to carry out this monumental deed.

I wondered for years what my father's reaction was when he finally turned to see a lone pick laying behind him in the beaten grass.

Without as much as a sack of grain or change of clothes, I ran away from the barn, the house, the district, my life. I ran until the dirt turned to stones and wheezed as my heart burned from exhaustion. I finally stopped at the base of my and Somyellia's abandoned house. Molested by the sweat and grime of my flight, I laid myself on its doorstep. At some point I lifted myself and slugged up the stairwell, finally lying on our animal hides. The house creaked and the assorted city clamor carried me off.

I don't know how long I'd been out, only that when I awoke I was enshrouded in full darkness. My father still lived, probably having not yet risen a hair's suspicion over my absence. The mixture of grief and shame prohibited my rise. Sitting on the floor, I must have looked like a man after a fight lost outside a last-stop inn.

My eyes were adjusting to the black.

Peeking out from our blankets was a purse Somyellia had left behind.

An urge prompted that I crawl forward. Much to my hopes, I found inside this purse a small pouch of opium. I had partaken of it with her before. Small inhales here and there were enough to scramble the mind and titillate the senses, putting me in with sprites of the forest and pinprick demons that pranced and danced on and in me.

This time was to be different, though. On my hands and knees I crawled to a corner. I'd put together a bag in case some calamity required our egress; I had always imagined Somyellia, Celly, and I running off to some distant land, or maybe hacking a life out of a giving thicket somewhere deep in the magic-haunted wilderland. I sifted through loose silver, garments, candles, a corked vial, a loaf of bread which had molded horrendously, until at last I found what I'd been searching for: flint and steel.

With great care, I was able to burrow a hole in the side of the vial. With some additions found around the house, I built, as best I could, a vessel to billow my lungs.

A candle lit my back, facing the graves below, I commenced burning the remnants of my mistress's favored drug.

Once fully enveloped, I crawled to the edge of the collapsed wall and hovered over all the graves. Looking as if miles below, they glimmered with the glow of nearby street lamps and the few candles that burned in the land of the dead. Here, my soul was at zero.

I found what it was to possess utter rage. A rage that pulsated slowly and made all the world turn gray. I choked on dust and learned not to lament on the cliffs of lamentation. I remembered not to remember, and then the winds passed me. I ripped at my chest. I sat crouched, eyes staring into a ruined valley that I had never known. I gave myself to the gods of destruction, but they did not take me. I waited for my takers to claim me, but they did not come. No howling wind carrying my raiders from the shores of recallable time. No hordes of flesh and noise.

In what could have been ages later, Somyellia found me crouched in a damp corner on the bottom floor. The moldy loaf eaten, along with other things strewn about that neither of us could pinpoint by species or origin. I was naked, covered in dirt and parched with a horrible thirst. Even for a black-magic hooker from the Thunder Bustle, my ghoulish appearance stopped Somyellia in her high leather boots. Putting aside her carnal duties, with the care of a seasoned midwife, she nursed me back to health and to sanity. In a volley of screams and cradled flailing, I slowly began to let go of many things.

✳

The years that followed running away were so full of chaos and poverty that only a morbid collage of memories remains. For all the swirling turmoil of abuse and neglect, I had been a boy who was well-fed, regularly schooled, and had ample means of washing myself. All of that was gone.

I do recall the first few weeks as a vivid, sick sort of game. The Metropolitan Ward was summoned. Word found a way of trickling back to my ears that during their searches for me, many homes of former tutors and childhood friends whom I hadn't seen in years were ransacked as frustrations increased. My old laboratory had to eventually be discovered. I could too easily envision the laughing gaggle of mailed Wardsmen pilfering through it all.

As heavy hooves approached in brutish unison, I would scurry into the sewers or hide behind the wheel of a cart. With a crude sketch of me in hand, orphanages were scoured. I guess they thought a boy from Templeton would frighten after a night or two under the care of the Nilghorde streets. Little did they know me.

I was resolve, colder than rain on the mountain. I wasn't going back. Every time I eluded their patrols, it only bolstered my lost but freed heart.

Finally, after weeks of hide and seek, it all ended. The Prime Marshall had probably told Father in careful terms that I'd most likely been abducted and was already chained inside some galley far out at sea.

Other than a book I'd stowed and an armful of anatomy works procured from the rear door of an unaware bookstore, my youthful education had met its terminus. But this only, I'd told myself, was good reason to revisit my favorites. I read my third volume of *Poems of the Classics* so many times that its pages became frail with a sort of rot and rub. Reciting the voyage of Omiel the doomed Mariner and the poetry of Denom Vandahl were regular occurrences in my bleak obscurities.

For food, I started out by using my trapping skills. Hundreds of rats and several pigeons later, I took to joining those who haunted the crooked bricked jungle in search of money. If I wasn't able to find work—maybe a cheap laborer on some city project or sweeping the rubble left from all the statues being chiseled on Do-Gooder's Row—I learned through painful trial and error the grim arts of the street.

✳

Despite the battles with food deprivation that came with having run away, I grew well in frame. Shoulders stretched outward. My chest grew slabs of beef. I had limbs of vein and sinew, and my lower legs were as thick as my upper arms. A boyish face melted away. By the time the Do-Gooder's Row statues looked like men trying to free their lower halves out of blocks of stone, my summer-field hair had taken to looking like that of my late mother's, both in its darkness and its length. I fit well with the orgy of maliciousness that populated the haunts of Nilghorde, which I'd come to call home.

On occasion, I resorted to desperate acts of violence. Eating a plate of cabbage and rabbit with bloody hands was barely a step above the beasts of the forest. I had at first pitied my victims, but soon savored the taste of bursting cooked flesh or boiled mushrooms in spite of the screams necessary to acquire it all.

One night this led me to a scuffle right next to where Somyellia and I's abandoned house met the graves.

The man squirmed, no more than an innkeeper who took the wrong turn. But this was the way of the world.

"Thirty silver—she just walked, from the mantel to the seating—I—my—" I had long ago picked up on the patterns in such pleas, all silenced with the butt of my knife.

The night now quiet, graveyard birds soon choired their calls. They seemed as if all around, though no matter how hard I tried, their perches remained hidden. As I gripped the fought-for purse, a hand caressed the back of my neck.

Every hair on my arms stood. I wheeled around to deliver a hard fate to the innkeeper's brave friend, the same grizzly fate for so many of the brave and misguided. But when I turned fully, I gazed at a sight even more peculiar: a slender man wrapped in shining black. There was no outstretched hand, for both of this stranger's were clapped together, no different than one of the many statues ornamenting the graves. The moon broke through the fog to radiate on his silk.

"Good evening," the man said.

By some nighttime trickery, I couldn't rise. For I surely tried, but all I could muster were a baffling series of slips, falls, and curses while the back of my neck burned and froze all at once.

"No need for such…barbarity," the man said, unclasping

his hands and depriving me of my knife. The man straightened, looking at my blade, turning it this way and that. A milky light, brighter than the moon's clung to his cloak. "Do you always dispatch them?"

Odd, I know, but I felt whatever faculties had left me now making a slow return. The moment I was able, I rose to my feet and stood a clear head taller than this oddest of inquisitors. From this perspective, a far more familiar view, the stranger's regality lessened, and my knife in his grip looked more like a woman's hand fondling a Pelat machete.

"They call me Belot," the man said.

In my frenzy, better sense had escaped me. A few years around a woman like Somyellia had left me keen to know when black magic brewed. This man was a grave-walking necromancer. But threat of being turned into a toad wasn't my worry. In these queer years, dark practitioners were as liable to turn in lawbreakers at one of the many pavilions snapped together by confederacies made between the Ward and Ansul's True than sicking hexes on someone. Rumor had it that the cash reward could be handsome, especially if the misfit had violated both the laws of Man and Nature all at once. This stranger had seen my face, and though I'd only been caught violating the laws of Man, he—

"You don't speak?" he said.

"Bell-ought," I said, "split the purse and call it a night?"

"Do you always dispatch them?" he laughed, giving me back my knife. "Your holders of the *purse?*"

"No, never," I shot, jostling like I'd just discovered an itch, finishing with, "Well, not if they're smart about it." But this caused only more laughter. He looked over his shoulder at the abandoned house.

"Drab, rotted place. My own is but next door. Join me?" Before I could answer, he turned, taking no more than a step, "Bring him with us."

When I reached for the purse, I was ready for this bizarre courtship to come to an end. After all, that's what this Belot was after, for nobody disliked money. But this stranger responded to my grabbing in way that was uncharacteristic of a robber. He smiled. A smile that if placed on every man at once would put merchant's like Somyellia out of business. I hoisted the innkeeper on my shoulder and followed.

✳

"So *you* are the source of all that noise." Mr. Belot gestured toward Somyellia and I's house. "Thought I'd have to call upon the zoo so they could retrieve some tenants on the lam. Spirited girl." I had to put down my second glass to laugh bashfully and spill wine.

It turned out Mr. Belot shared both my old tutor's nihilism and my fondness for capitalizing on the deceased. Mr. Belot's eyes glowed, followed by full admission that he was nothing short of astonished; how a "large knifeman from the streets" could know every bone in the human body. Mr. Belot's interest in my ambitions had swept away the initial discomfort I'd felt. Soon we were gabbing like drunken military wives.

As the night stretched, I ogled at the skulls and bones and books. The prowess of scales and cauldrons were unlike anything I'd ever seen, and it filled me with a bizarre joy that Mr. Belot's collection of femurs was larger than the one I'd amassed in the old cellar. Then there was the wooden table. On it were leather straps, pulled and worn taut. At Mr. Belot's request, I had lifted the moaning innkeeper onto it, during which I saw bloodstains that had seeped deep into the wood. My timid inquiry into this man's looming fate was met with Belot's caress. I don't recall what his answer was, only that I was sated. It was as if I'd been charmed, though a necromancer practicing such things was pure and utter silliness.

A second bottle of Grest opened talks about more pressing

matters. To Mr. Belot, I would learn, the world was becoming harder for lovers of the dark and the courageous. "You see those silly statues, Seasmil?" he said. "Placating the masses; scared of their own shadows as good as a plague. Do-Gooder's Row is halfway built and Maecidion the Virulent is dying."

It was true, I supposed, at least to a degree. I'd seen the Chapwyn fliers swell in numbers and the pitchfork wielders soon follow. Although the poor and wretched had swollen even greater, a formidable army of limpers and squabbling hags, oaths to eradicate the world of wickedness seemed all that was necessary to satisfy the barking mob. But to people like me, such social ebb and flow meant about as much as what Lotgard shit last and where. I didn't want to tell Mr. Belot that those whose entire cosmos is the calling cookpot and alley didn't concern themselves with such prattle, especially dying royalty. But even I drank from the trickling stream of gossip— Maecidion, that lauded patriarch of Somyellia's, had indeed fallen ill.

Mr. Belot looked over the rim of his glass, "Times are changing, my hulking friend. There was a day those of us who poked and prodded at nature's rulebook could do so in plain sight. No longer."

I am no hero, nor am I the stuff of legend. No kraken to best. No dragon to slay. My war was painfully simple. I had to survive, and even amidst the brawls and illness and thievery, I still clung to the hope of one day, yes, climbing from such chipped blades and street grime to become a renowned man of medicine. It was perhaps my greatest fortune then that Mr. Belot and I's interests shared a component: bodies.

I left with a friend, a mentor, and most important of all, an employer. By the time Maecidion died, I was leading a pack of rogues. I would put intimidation to even better use, but Mr. Belot's thoughts on confrontation were even more prudent than my own. Most of the time, I would be working alone, and, at Mr. Belot's direction, digging up graves.

III
MAECIDION

As a young necromancer, Maecidion had climbed the House of Ordrid's ranks to perch on its highest seat. Yet, death finds us all, and the only man in history to force the Conqueror into negotiation now lay still as the men he'd sent to oblivion before him.

After a funeral where the Ordrids thronged in the ornate blacks of mourning, a gathering of mostly strangers had weathered the height of the rainy season, paraded under the half-finished statues of Do-Gooder's Row, and now sat and squirmed deep in the Ordrid keep.

Irion Ordrid was suffering this legal charade, administered by a barrister calling off names that made him grab and regrab the hilt of his dagger.

Irion's moon-pale scalp never took to growing hair, making it all the easier to wipe the sweat off his brow. The oppressive heat made what he was witnessing all the more unbearable. His House was in no shortage of enemies; but unlike the villainous House of Rogaire, too many had come to the will reading to now brush and breathe against him.

He thanked his eyes for being set back deep in his face, for in this gloom they were unable to give away who he razored.

Cackles erupted somewhere up front. A crone hobbled her way to the barrister's desk to be bequeathed the jabbering head of a dead Scepter. This was no ordinary head. Scepters, once elected, answered only to Apex Scepters, and the Apexes answered only to the Conqueror, the aforementioned recluse and ultimate ruler of Rehleia.

This head, whose mouth agonized moans out from grey brittle flesh, belonged to a legislative slug who in life garnered fame for helping outlaw necromancy. Now he caused great mirth, pleading with these users of the blackest arts to mercifully return him to death. Gleeful retorts made the thing weep dust for tears. While the world gazed upon his misleading tomb, he would be suffering long after even Do-Gooder's Row was complete.

Irion's amusement having been temporarily fondled, he was brought back to the day's ugliness. A jar of his great-uncle's Ghorlaxium went to the warlock sitting directly beside him. Blossoming only one day per year, its purple petals were unparalleled in their ability to hold an apparition in thrall. An assortment of books, scrolls, torture devices and various other clutter went to their new owners. Everyone but Irion.

But the mob would soon be joining him in his outrage.

Rumors that Maecidion Ordrid was dying had caused great unease. When he died, or so went the most common thread, demons would erupt from the earth and take Irion's great-uncle "back"—a charitable act as they could ever have hoped for, except that the demons were reportedly going to grab all the innocent souls they could before scampering back to Hell.

Those less inclined to listen to the holy dribble of Chapwyn priests were more worried that Rehleia—only a decade removed from total warfare—would re-splinter.

The Metropolitan Ward— dumb faces in even dumber uniforms charged with policing Rehleia and its three cities—they wouldn't be able to hold back *this* chaotic tide. Haggling farmers in the market tossed speculations of inevitable doom as hearty as heads of lettuce and copper coin. An Ordrid civil war was a top contender, how Irion's aunts and cousins would send the world to cinders by pulling in the various secular powers.

Perhaps more reasonably feared: if those powers who built roads instead of weaved magic became convinced that the House of Ordrid had sufficiently weakened. Ordrid annihilation had usually just been furtive Chapwyn church talk, or so the Ordrids had always been told. But trying to eliminate their entire House— the same House that once rose legions of the undead with wiggles of onyx-ringed fingers—the people feared it would merely provoke the notorious family into summoning more unnatural allies.

No, Irion waged, a good sheep of the new land would prefer if incorrigibles, strong or weak, would just die in jail, or maybe unclog their plumbing, and then vanish until needed again. And though Irion was from a lower branch, it boiled him that some referred to his kinsmen with the blissful condescension of one who's never had a knife to their neck. But it gave him some reprieve too, knowing wishful, anti-Ordrid fantasies resulted from outright fear.

Before attending the clandestine school the dead-raisers call the lyceum, as all men from prominent families must, Irion suffered the maps and history lessons of a primary education. But unlike the Ouvarnias perched in the flamboyant city of Pelliul, or the politician-churning House of Lotgard, Irion found such learning only useful to pinpoint his own family's prominence.

If Irion were obliged to give a geographical tour, it would probably ring as thus:

Rehleia is a knotted peninsula, like an afflicted fist stuck out on a withered arm. Pushing east and connecting Rehleia to the

Other Lands is the Red Isthmus—named so for the rivers of blood that had once flown from its narrow hinterland down into the sea.

At this east Rehleia meets the world of Azad, a desert kingdom littered with pit fires and bulb-topped minarets. Above Azad: Serabandantilith, raped by Azad and Rehleia once they figured out that ceasing their own war allowed for the pillaging of their weaker, northern neighbor. Azad took the land. Rehleia took the people and the gold. The former mixing with the dark Suelans, beefing up Rehleia's much-celebrated slave class.

A few years after the Years of Peace had officially commenced, trade began over the Red Isthmus, sweeping aside all the broken swords and lances.

And as far as Rehleia is concerned, the House of Ordrid's strong-hold is in Nilghorde. On a city hill above the brick wilderness, the family keep looks over the western sea. In this jagged crown, stowed in some charnel nook, the great Maecidion had taken his final breath.

It was long argued: when the most infamous of the city's celebrities actually discorporated. His form was kept together, Irion was told, but despite diplomatic transactions with the demonic, means of animation slowly seeped from the flesh as it rose from bone.

Most of the estate was already in the possession of Maecidion's most esoteric clutch: sisters Ophelia and Lialifer, cousins to Irion's mother, and Morfil Ordrid, whose entire life had been dutifully in the shadow of his Lord and pedagogue.

But that didn't stop the vile throng from attending today. All were in accord; given just a goblet by his wishes held the highest prestige in this society others dare called foul.

The air warm, like a kennel, sinking down around the attendees and settling on the stone floor. The room itself was but stone, that and shadow, both made known by a large ring of candle-light. In the center, attendants pulled chairs out from under the other, bites were delivered and tended to, and murmurs slithered amongst the bequeathings still to come.

The barrister—looking as if batting away thoughts of being skewered—readied himself and continued reading the last will and testament of Maecidion the Virulent.

✳

When Maecidion's familiar was read off to anyone other than an Ordrid, the only thing that brought Irion to a fuller froth was that it went to Denoreyph Belot. Belot!—a self-important narcissist who cared about such frivolities as charm spells. For pursuing a discipline outside necromancy, he was especially hated. His dimmer critics obsessed over this feat, and obsessed all the dimmer that those who didn't join them in their disgust had been in fact charmed themselves.

Irion joined them, joined them and then some. Arrogant, Belot's silk swayed as he strutted up and seized the imp in its cage.

Belot! That prancing girl, Irion thought, reeling back to spit. *Imp belongs in the family*. Irion watched him until he sat back down to preen his sash and cross his legs like an actor.

Irion hadn't received so much as a wall sconce. *One more carbuncled witch from the hills called up to lust over my family's property and I'll—* Irion checked his pockets. A bit of a secret pleasure, one he hid from the more established necromancers, was his love of caustic tricks. Irion's pockets usually ranged from such simplicities as malodorous vials to more severe components that helped build spells that could make one wish to see their mother couple with mountain trolls. A quick inventory proved he'd brought—

The room became noise itself. It was as if that Scepter's headless body had pushed up the doors of his tomb, stumbled through the streets, and then led a pod of the Metropolitan Ward to hack up the patrons. The uproar became awe, then it became envy. A statue had been placed on the barrister's desk.

Seen in the clasped hands of every portrait of Maecidion to ever cover a sullen wall, the statue, a hand itself, was made of pure lapis lazuli. The size of your average man's, strains of gold feathered and swirled in the deep blue of its outstretched fingers. In its palm, three faces made a row. The outer two left trails at its base near the wrist, thus completing a long-agreed-upon murmur that they resembled haunted tadpoles. And these both seemed poised to circle the central visage; caught in an eternal, devilish sneer.

Astonished grumbles carried "Morfil" and "…for who then?" Chair legs squeaked. Hopefuls rushed the desk. A fistfight erupted.

Irion didn't need to tear down the aisle or crawl over any cursed heads. He knew it well. This peculiar ornament had been in Maecidion's possession long before a single Suelan slave had been brought to Rehleian shores. It had also been previously owned by other powerful Ordrid leaders, long returned to oblivion.

What would it would mean if the Virulent left it to me? Irion leaned forward in his chair. This had to be it. *What misery would be deserving to anyone other than I?*

And while he'd been lost in such thoughts, fiddling in his pockets, a name had already been read.

When it was announced for a second time, the gathering boiled over from gasped vacuum to pure hysteria. Slugging his way forward, Gormorster Toadly, as surprised as his howling detractors, knew now the first announcement hadn't been a trick. With a rodent's face sitting on top of several glistening chins, the gormandizer smelling of sweat, sweets, and necrophilia looked to be the unlikeliest of all attendants to receive an invitation, let alone this choice artifact.

Irion was soon leading the mob, hurling insults and looking for an available chair not bolted to the floor. While an imp was highly sought after, this was an heirloom. It going to anyone outside the House was detestable, and all the more foul to the senses that a flatulent glutton-wretch like Toadly would now own it.

Irion had to wrestle down a misfit trying to rise from deep within him. Reappraising the genius of his deceased patriarch was by all accounts an ill strategy, even if he was dead.

Toadly gloated and giggled, showboating by a series of squinty-eyed sneers. He held the statue like a pageant winner, or a proud new father.

Irion burst open the doors and marched out into the lobby. *Last wishes be damned.* That inner-misfit was winning, and it was straight to the coat closest. He pilfered through the dampened garb. It didn't take long. There was the raven-feathered collar.

"Belot," Irion grumbled, "Still wearing lyceum monstrosities, of course." Irion opened the coal coat and rifled through it. A smile broke free across his face by the second or third pocket. Charm spells were one thing, but Belot loved a single practice above all else; raping the minds of the dying. It took the meeting of two special powders to enact such a spell—two powders Irion then swapped out with two other powders, ones you'd never wish to see conjoined.

When the crowd hobbled out from the hall, Irion melted back into the swarm. Some were angry, most disappointed, but those were more their ways than any. A few of the more brazen cursed Maecidion before catching themselves.

Before long the hall and the coat closet were all but empty. The fiends returned to their lairs to, as Chapwyn priests so ardently report, brew their irksome things; slither under the moonlight; and invoke, summon, and fondle the dead.

✳

From the lower branch indeed, Irion would one day be feared and exalted for this warpath that he'd undertook. Time was of the essence. It took days for an imp to submit to its new master, but once done there was no being undone. And Toadly, that degenerate, that blue hand may already be slotted for the nearest pawn shop.

Irion kicked the door open and pulled the clerk in by her hair. In a dark corner serving as a residence for spiders and scrolls, he uncupped his hand from her mouth and put a finger to his lips.

The Nilghorde Hall of Records was monstrous. The main doors towered royal green above and below midsections of ornate glass, but the deeper one journeyed into the hall's catacombs the more the place seemed to degrade. The central lobby had been a murmuring hive, irate merchants and disputing tenants slammed doors and stamped down stairs. Then packed corridors became dithering shadows and blocks of stone bouncing back distant calls. Further still, broom closets and boarded-up doors gave way to the lone room warehousing the thing which Irion sought.

He was at the Residency Office; used only by the Ward and magistrate's apprentices, and maybe that was why it was at the end of such a punitive tunnel. To his good fortune, only one clerk had toiled in lamplight behind the reception desk. To his bad fortune, he'd spent the last of his Ghorlaxium on the potion he'd made for her.

When boiled in small doses and cut with Leaves of Luka, Ghorlaxium makes the living spew out all they know. He knelt above the clerk in dual dismay. He needed another batch; if all went well, this woman who'd gulped the potion past the edge of his blade would lead him forward. But, more pressing, an overdose didn't kill—*that* would at least give him some options. If only Irion had the time. But rather than death, his miscalculation had resulted in a rolling blabber.

"Kornard kept coming on to me," she said, looking beyond him with her bulging eyes. "My sister couldn't pla…please him after having the baby. The baby that woulda been *ours* coulda never have been." He considered killing her. "Mother woulda never…" She trailed off into a string of inaudibles. Somewhere in this mess of boxes, scrolls, and wobbling towers of books there was a name, and with it an address. "Mother woulda killed all four of us!"

After an eternity, the abortion confession ceased.

"Are you scared?"

"Terrified." The clerk's voice was flat as her hair matting the floorboards, in a way that amused Irion. She lay like an open-casket funeral, even when he took his hands off her wrists.

"Are barristers designated by duty?" Her mouth opened but said nothing. "Here, in this office?" Irion added.

"Why...yes, by specialty you could say."

"Good," Irion said, petting her head. Then, spacing his words out to eliminate any more blunders, "Where can I find magistrates in charge of probate? In charge of wills?"

"I don't know."

Irion pressed down on her wrists. "Then *who* does?"

"Yodïor, my boss."

"And he comes?"

"Soon."

He'd heard of a trick back at the lyceum for keeping them quiet. "Make a noise now only if you've never lied."

It worked.

✳

To Irion's relief, not one larval lawyer or single member of the Ward approached the reception desk. Having deprived the clerk of her apron, he sat behind the slab and watched the lamp oil burn. He felt as silly as someone dressed for All Malevolent Masquerade. But he had to wait.

The lamp smoke grew thicker, his back ached, and then a silhouette appeared. A black dot approached, growing, soon emerging through the lamplight, having turned into a lumpy man whose glasses reflected the shifts of orange and yellow.

"You must be my supervisor," Irion said, putting down the sheet of parchment he'd picked up to pretend he was reading. "Yoddy, Yodi."

"Who—where is Loona?"

"That was her name, Loona. She went home, sick." The little man's face glistened with sweat he'd worked up while walking down the hall. But that wasn't the only reason he was sweating. Looks over his shoulder and nervous scratches to his crotch and ass told Irion everything. "I'm a temp."

"A temp? We don't—"

Irion leapt over the desk. The sheet of parchment balled and shoved in his mouth, Irion's blade to his chins, Yodïor kicked as he was lifted off the floor. The Residency Office door with swung open for a second time.

"No!" Yodïor screamed right before Irion kicked him in the gut. Gasping to regain his breath, he lay in Loona's blood, which by way of an unfortunate slip, Irion too felt: cooled and congealing. He'd slit her throat when the potion had worn off. A means to an end no driven man has time to worry over. Though she was on her stomach and this Yodïor lay on his back, Irion mused for but a moment how they lay locked in a stare, unifying two on opposing sides of the grave.

"As you wish to live," Irion crawled on top of him, "cease your whimpering and answer me." He nodded, emitting squeaks that sounded like a girl's. "Where can I find magistrates in charge of probate? In charge of wills?"

Given the vastness of the room, and of the rat shit, they'd be gnawed-on bones by the time anyone found them. But Irion's thoughts were elsewhere. The will reading was only a day old; Irion clutched the top half of a municipal parchment. The top was all he needed. The choices were an insult, almost arbitrary, as if the barrister had written the will the day of, just to see the crowd's reaction.

Irion found the barrister. In his bedchambers the lawman

frantically swore that he'd merely read the will as it had been written, a conviction that remained unwavering up to the last dagger slash.

✳

Ordrids are fond of the moon. Irion gazed upon her, the great beacon of his House. He'd thought he'd heard her call his name as he stumbled through the graves. Blossoming on the vines that grew on elder headstones, Orphedilias opened to vector in the gentle light. Poets and ninnies like Belot would have stopped to ogle at their shape perhaps.

He came to the graveyard's center, the Maedraderium. Irion halted and stood before the new obelisk. Black and gold, jutting out of a cluster of pediment tombs, this robust monument to his great-uncle now towered. His Virulence had worked in startling mystery at times, not issuing an immediate and savage revenge on the House of Rogaire was chief among Irion's confusions.

But now this. Of all the places to be buried.

The common man was at best a two-legged dog, and Maecidion had willed his obelisk in a graveyard hardly good enough for such a dog's dead fleas. What unfathomable nonsense! He could have been exalted a mile high; future generations of Ordrids and wide-eyed gawkers would have been straining their necks.

The prattling on about the Maedraderium being City Cemetery's wealthy centerpiece meant little to Irion. Most still just called this island of stones, more a small city of venerated dead, "Laugher's Lot." If it had any meaning at all, Irion guessed it derived from the morticians, mirthfully swelling the lot as their coffers filled.

Irion held in his hand a bottle of that corn liquor, Spiritual Oppressor. He took another pull. "I am sorry, dearest Lord," Irion said, "but I cannot see to it. See to it that I leave your wishes untouched." And why shouldn't he feel this way? The very man whose will he was rebelling against had once made such bold moves in his own time. Would he—could he—at least appreciate Irion's ambitions, providing the impetus to be so bold? The reading now three days old, it troubled Irion no less.

Swaying, emptied bottle in hand, he arched his back and stuck out his chest.

He hadn't come to talk to an obelisk; just a thoughtful gesture along the way. Irion tossed the Spiritual Oppressor and continued to a hamlet on the edge of the graves.

Irion crouched in the hedges like some sneak thief. But such humiliations were necessary. Toadly's tower wasn't so much a tower, more a farmer's silo, complete with thatched rotting top, giving the whole thing the appearance of a giant's refracting phallus that had caught Thina's Poxy. It loomed so close to City Cemetery that Irion couldn't tell if the neglected hedge, grown wild with weeds and brambers, belonged to Toadly or to Nilghorde.

He'd sobered quick enough, perhaps expedited by having suffered bouts of rain.

Shadows conjoined and shifted behind Toadly's windows. With-in, long bouts of silence would rip open in an instant with bellows of ignoramus mirth. Of all the nights for such a home to play host to the living. But as Irion adjusted a troublesome root for the third time, Toadly's door swung open and out poured the filth.

Though the departing gaggle was of several classes, they struck him as acquainted scoundrels, tarrying under a lone lamplight before finally leaving.

Irion froze. A pack of other men scrambled out from a hedge across from his own. The moment he began to rise he'd been put back down, reduced to peering out through leaves. The pack moved from one shadow to the next, then broke down Toadly's door.

Toadly had enemies like snakes have scales. It would have been amusing, Irion gleamed, if a brood of brothers with their stone-cutting father at the helm had burst in to avenge the lamentable state of one of the many concubines that had made Toadly famous. But the pack's look of intent villainy disallowed such fantasies. The thumps and sounds of breaking glass and feet pounding up and down stairwells were at the bidding of, he knew beyond a doubt, some other fiend who'd also attended the will reading.

"If it is gone—" the rest Irion hissed into his hand. A sudden headache needled his skull: Someone had beat him to it. He'd sat around, pitying himself with a liquor bottle, and it may have just cost him everything. He felt a shame that his conscious would not fully allow. An image of brewing tricks and potions on the lowest branch in all Necrodom faded, and the part of his mind where words were found refit itself. *The puma who slept through the deer migrating while dreaming of idle sheep.* Irion gripped his dagger's handle. Rain pooled on leaves and ran down his neck.

After some while, the thugs reentered the street, and with their reappearance the vice-clamp around his head loosened. On the ground, behind one of the larger men, was a mammoth bag, sowed tight and soaked with blood. He'd never quite experienced disappointment and elation at once, until just then.

One of the oldest Ordrids ever to be penned to a scroll, Prince Basofial had enjoyed a parade of carnage, yet was denied the blood dipping of his own morning star. Seeing Toadly dead and stuffed into a sack, Irion couldn't help but wonder if this is how the long-dead prince had felt when the droves of poor had killed the aristocracy over in Quinnari?

He was frozen again. The grunting shadows were dragging Toadly right toward him.

Grunts became words. Soon, shadows became scowls and leather gloves. Leading them, an over-muscled lug stowed a sev-ered petite arm into his belt. All it would take is one alley-grade wizard among them to route Irion out, one of the lugs then pulling him up by his neck like a chicken. His crouching became a curl, his dagger blade tight against his palm. If he were one of the Ordrids who prayed, Irion would have done so as legs burst open his hedge.

The trail of boot prints and a sweep like a crocodile's slide met the grass of City Cemetery. "Even split" and "not this rutterkin, ya pansy nob" became grunts once more, and soon, save for pats of rain, there was silence.

"It's been invaded by a pack of gorillas," Irion spit, having entered Toadly's trash heap. Knowing him, this parlor had always probably been a clogged artery of trinkets and spoiled meat. But whatever stage of slow explosion it had once been, it had burst like a zit. All was everywhere. Everything but the remaining army of candles; hung about on sconces, stuck into cracks, resting on frames of draperies that had somehow been spared.

The last Irion had seen of the invaders, they were making their way toward the other side of the cemetery. In front of him now were the remnants of their night's work: furniture upended, books torn to pieces, rather insignificant parts of the home mangled beyond repair. Irion would never be sure what a fire prodder, broken in three, could have ever hoped to contain.

Still, this mangling may mean that they never found what they were looking for.

He rushed up the first stairway. Near the top it was the swaying legs that he saw first, and behind them a large and well-lit room.

Without the command of their master, the female slaves exhibited all the fuller their state of unlife. Dull, lidless eyes, nestled in sallow faces, alive but not alive, dead but not dead, stared at him as Irion summited the stairs.

Passing between them was like walking through a forest where all the seeds had been planted in exact, nauseating little rows. Behind the last row of slaves was a giant bed. It was covered in blood; reflecting the halo of candles that hung above.

That he'd been killed right before one of his wretched orgies delighted Irion. From a new angle, Irion now saw that concubines closer to the bed had been sprayed by his blood. Their resemblance to a military formation suggested this was their position of maintenance when not bringing up a pot of cooked sea slugs or performing their sexual duties. Toadly's reputation for incessantly leering at the female backside was all the more confirmed, as the swaying columns faced away from where he'd slept and self-fondled.

Not a cauldron was left unturned. Irion shimmied up chimney shafts, settling for stretching a crawling arm up the ones that he couldn't inspect further. Irion ended up mimicking the prior stampede up and down the stairs in a fever. He turned the place end over end—thrice over what the goons had done—but Maecidion's lapis lazuli hand was gone.

After he'd found a surviving vase to shatter to dust, his fury cooled. Irion gave the undead slut who'd had most her arm hacked off a prompt smack on her ass. The leathery cheek gave in all the way to the bone. Irion was soon staring up at the candles. Their shafts were hardly shorter than when he'd entered. It hadn't been long.

Toadly's killers had been thorough in their search but careless in their escape. He followed their boot prints and spilled keepsakes all the way through the heart of City Cemetery. He was led right between Maecidion's obelisk and the bottle he'd tossed. Picking up the trinkets and smearing the mud and blood of heavy boot prints would keep the Ward out of this—in the rare chance an investigation into someone like Toadly's disappearance caught the fancy of an aspiring shift-lead. That concern, however weak or strong, evaporated when Irion saw where the boot tracks had ended.

※

"Theee revenge!" Toadly moaned from inside Belot's parlor. "I shall enact upon you." His curses didn't come so much from his mouth, but gurgled from the slash that ran across his throat. Blood and lung-froth spilled over and ran down to the table he was bound to.

Irion stood outside Belot's window, moon and graves to his back. It was a matter of convenience that Gormorster Toadly and Denoreyph Belot chose to live on opposing sides of City Cemetery. For those privy to such skirmishes, it created a sort of chess board between the two, rumored to have been encouraged by a committee of Scepters to maintain low property value in the surrounding areas. The demands of the dead had leveled entire city blocks to make way for new rows of headstones and cheap tombs. Yet these domiciles of the two corpse-diddlers remained: paragons of tradition.

Irion scanned the room. A place for poor work, surely; Belot stood at the foot of the table. Behind Belot, tall as a man, were shelves heavied by potions and jars. On the other side of this table, Belot faced the material he used when playing necromancer.

The stack of corpses appeared untampered, having died at ages from elder to infant, and now lay like decomposing firewood. And above everything, attached to a ceiling hook, watching from an iron birdcage, sat Irion's imp. Seemingly content to forever study the shelves; feet, arms, and nose poking out from the cage, the imp, Irion rejoiced, must have refused to imprint with Belot. Imprisoned until it assimilated to its new master, the little fiend was reduced to sit and watch.

Strapped down at his wrists and his ankles, purple with fresh death, Toadly could only squirm and weep. "Youuuu," slid off Toadly's swollen tongue as his eyes rolled upward against his will.

"Oh, silence now," Belot said, hands on his hips. "If you absolutely refuse to tell me where it is, I can't let you rest. You're doing this to yourself, you know."

Delight and intrigue fought within Irion. It was a delight to witness Toadly being tortured, and even more a delight to savor these moments right before Belot's big surprise. Irion knew what he was up to, for Belot, if anything, was consistent. Though Toadly's flesh was now dead, his mind again lived, one Belot had brought back, and now began to dominate.

Where it is? It struck Irion like lightning. Abducting Toadly had to be for good reason. *It*—Belot could only be referring to the hand! If Belot didn't already have it, then where did Toadly have it hidden? Irion glared through the window as he redeveloped his plan. He could usurp minds too.

Belot began to raise his arms. Toadly howled in accordance. Irion's luck had turned, for he couldn't have asked for more perfect timing.

Baying in protest, Toadly was feeling every thought he'd ever held suck toward his captor like warmed honey dripping from a wooden spoon. Belot, fueled by the frantic kicks and pleas for mercy through a slit throat, inched closer. He was putting Toadly in the state all necromancers feared most. For while what body one could occupy could change form, and the very boundaries of life and death could be hopped over like a naughty child hopping over a line deemed off-limits, the mind itself was the sole source of a being, to be preserved and unmolested at all cost. Belot's arms raised, he held the separate powders for his spell in each hand. Upon their union, Toadly would divulge all, and go forever to his grave defiled.

If Irion hadn't switched out the powders the day of the reading.

When Belot's hands met, he lit up as if made of lamp oil. A detonation erupted. Belot became ghastly whistles in a burgeoning gown of flames. Toadly, eyes wide and elated, showed even the undead savored comeuppance.

Irion kicked open the door. Toadly flopped his head toward the noise, just as soon recognizing Irion and returning to his panic. "That blue hand," Irion said, looming over the gluttonous wretch, "is in as many paintings in my home as pulseless whores are in yours." The pleasure of knowing he'd suck up every drop of Toadly's miserable mind was second only to the joy of hearing Belot's screams.

Perhaps Irion owed his late great-uncle an immediate and roaring "thank you". When Belot was bequeathed what he had been, it was the final spur in Irion's side to do the world a favor and rid it of him. That Irion would now own the imp, Toadly's mind for an hour, and, with the latter executed correctly, the family heirloom too: Irion breathed in the smoke as fires died on the charred meat at his boot toe.

How the zest for a meal is conquered by the desire to couple with a woman for the first time, and how retreating from a crumbling building would triumph over said coupling, his attention had been torn from Toadly to the burning of Belot. Now lamentably over, Irion was able to refocus.

Toadly lay motionless.

Irion shook his corpse. A sudden nervousness grew inside Irion, for this wasn't supposed to happen. The preparatory segment of the incantation had been broken, yes, but experience and experimentation suggested that reanimation waned at a much slower rate. Toadly was now fully dead, the normal dead, and secondary and tertiary reanimations were exponentially more difficult.

A sudden adjustment from the imp caused Irion to glance in the direction of not only its cage, but the bodies below it. Had that window above the corpse-stack always been ajar?

How much time had actually elapsed since Belot had been a crawling bonfire? But this wasn't the only pressing question. Toadly, though a low carcass in comparison to other practitioners that speckled the world, was not without his craft. There were tricks, hexes, and bedevilments accredited to his name. Irion was reduced to scratching his head and staring back at the imp.

After kicking Toadly one last time, Irion sat down to give it all a laugh. It was all he could do. "Irion Ordrid the Poor Planner" may one day be chiseled into his own obelisk, but he would at least enjoy this next improvisation. Belot would live again.

A few powders from his cabinet later, Irion had poured the appropriate line between himself and Belot. The invocations started, Belot's smoldering heap began to twitch.

The waiting was gruesome—not the visuals, but the agony of waiting for reanimation to fulfill. All people, bodies, and species were different, and in time-sensitive moments such as this, all Irion could do was pace about and kick convenient objects. It was when he looked up at his imp once more that from Belot there burst the grimmest consecution of cries. No less the sounds of Hell, in this was concentrated a hatred in life ripened one thousand fold through death, and by treacherous events of the trip to and back from those shores.

"What causes thee wakening of the Great Denoreyph Belot?" the grizzly skeleton wailed, rising to meatless feet.

"You were always so lousy with components," Irion said. Belot's skull cocked back. "Laying them about the room, labeling them in that thick gaudy ink, like a man going blind."

"For thissss, you summon me? To reminisce about dead lyceum days, and the women who juiced my bed next to your celibate cot?"

The skeleton, draped only in charred flesh, stepped closer, ribs stuck out and balled, bony fists cast back. In eyeless sockets, Irion saw an immaterial glimmer.

"Where is the blue hand?"

"That's no concern to me now," Belot hissed. "Let us ask our dear friend—Oh, Gormorster. Oh, look—he's dead, deader than I."

"If he still has it, I'll get it from him. We both know it," Irion said. "Professor Fryte did it with that stitched-up fuck she had locked up in her closet. We both were there. You remember. You may be," his smirk broadened, "excuse me, used to be an overrate, labeling your childish jars and cheating on tests, but you know how usurpation works."

Belot blew out a laugh that paralleled his recent cry in both volume and hysteria. "That may be. But I always remembered to close my windows." Everything in the parlor that could move stared at the lone open window. "My old freights looking a wee light there, Irion."

"What are you saying?"

Belot cackled. "Toadly is goooone, Irion."

No, Toadly was lying on the table. Yet as Irion listened to Belot hiss, practices that he'd heard of but had never seen himself began to encroach his mind. Casting one's essence into another form was a feat Toadly had been persecuted over and heralded for. It would have taken time to weave, but in Irion's savoring of the fire, he had given him such a vital commodity.

Irion looked once more at the stack of corpses. "Ah, yes, yesss. Good, Irion. Toadly is now," Irion heard Belot saying. There *had* been a body there, one that was there no longer. It had been— Belot's words then seeped into Irion's ear, finishing the dreadful thought: "a babe."

"You're going to help me find him!" Irion shouted. "Fire has seemed to have forgotten you the craft, Belot! This," Irion flapped his hand at Belot's hilarious state, "this is just the beginning. This living mind of yours, being used to mock and riddle as wasteful as done in life, it just came from me. Me!" He took a hard step forward. "We both know I can just as easily extract from it, as you were about to do to that fat lump of shit over there."

As best a skull with sporadic rigging can, Belot quivered. Irion opened his coat and withdrew a vial. Belot's bony hands made for his neck as Irion opened up the vial and drank down its contents.

The bitter syrup was exactly what Belot had drunk to own the mind of Toadly. Irion felt his will wrap around Belot's like a chain. The effect would not last forever, but maybe long enough.

Whether to pose a less startling silhouette, or maybe the damage of flame had made open night air feel like dancing razors, or maybe the vanity of Belot in life somehow held in his state of chattel-undead—for whatever reason, he draped himself in one of his black silken cloaks and followed his master out the door.

At the base of the open window Irion discovered a baby's footprints. They had scampered into the wet lawn of City Cemetery.

✳

They'd stalked clear across City Cemetery. The footprints cut through those of Belot's thugs, darted for Toadly's tower straight through the Maedraderium, but then surprised Irion by veering a sharp left. It led them through an embankment of streets and buildings that met a corner of the graveyard. They now lurked inside a large nursery, having found the final footprint at its lanterned door. Toadly, the clever little rat.

Toadly, the clever little rat, Belot ideated, reconfirming that Irion now owned his mind.

Absorbing themselves into the darkest corners of a nursery bay was easy enough. In the moonlit middle, a row of cribs cooed and stirred and kicked up little blankets.

The moon came through the bay's elongated windows, stretching shadows of the cribs long against a back wall.

Start at the far end, Irion thought at Belot.

Start at the far end, Belot ideated.

Belot moved off, drifting through the moonbeams and then out of Irion's sight. Irion began searching the nearer cribs. Toadly needed to be "alive," but Irion would certainly sever a fat little leg. Possessed bodies are impelled by stamina and dexterity far greater than the living. Irion knew it, as did Toadly.

He peered, cradle after cradle, looking to see if the miserable trickster had occupied an empty. After scanning the spaces underneath, he stood to keep an eye on Belot, slowly sailing through the rows.

What is that? Belot and Irion thought at the same time. Lamp-light approached, flat-footed plods coming right behind it. A narrow passageway that until then had remained hidden now bore an attendant.

Irion had Belot coil under his nearest crib. Irion pressed his back against the nearest wall.

A nursemaid, lamp cast out in front of her houndish nose, hobbled in.

Legs. Walking. Words Irion felt Belot think freely, almost whispering right over his teeth. From his obscure angle, it appeared the woman was passing the crib he hid under. *I'm on the ground*, Belot thought, making Irion's heart leap, for his dominion over him was already beginning to wane. Making matters more perilous, Belot must have said it aloud. The woman had stopped. The lantern shook.

If Belot was discovered under a crib like some hideous snake, the woman's shrieks would startle every babe and armed guard within a mile. Dagger honed, using each passing crib to conceal himself, Irion made his way to them.

"Smoked pork?" the woman said. A lone crib now from her back, Irion saw her shrug her shoulders then resume her rounds. He sheathed his dagger.

They continued searching, and they may have done so all night if it weren't for the imp flashing Irion a sudden vision.

Irion first elated, for this meant the imp knew it belonged to the House of Ordrid. The greatest of familiars, when one is joined with such a little fiend, it allows its master its cunning, to hear through its ears, and, Irion now gaped, the horrid sights seen through its eyes.

It showed him a scene unfold in an instant:

Toadly was climbing through the open window back at Belot's. His new hands he must have loathed, but they grasped the window superbly, as did his new legs, having bursting up from the ground below. His laughter while in his obese true form had sounded to Irion once like a creature being boiled alive. But now the infant, mottled and blue in decay, emitted its squeaks and giggles.

Irion had been tricked! He must have double backed as Irion made a fool of himself in the damn nursery. The giggles made their way into Belot's parlor as Toadly scaled down the stool and apron and jumped nimbly to the floor.

It gave Irion some reprieve to see that Toadly stood over his old body, lying there dead and humiliated. Irion was sure in some singular way he thanked him too. For Irion had given to Belot a fate that any captive would dream to see their captor suffer. But more than that, cringing at the laughter that had been aimed at him, by killing Belot Irion had freed Toadly's mind…and had given him time to escape.

Toadly walked around his body, his current head no higher than the plateau of the rack that held his former self.

Toadly stopped and picked up a chunk of blackened flesh. He then dropped it and sprang from the floor like a cricket, landing on his own bloated corpse.

Toadly was going to try to not only reanimate his old body, but reassume it! If so, and if he were able to seal himself off and repair his manglings to a semblance of function, Toadly half-alive and enraged could be worse than ten normal men.

Small arms were cast skyward. His baby mouth began to open. What would have been Toadly's booming moan was something quite different. The rites, though uttered perfectly, filled the room with that of a sprite's. The baby's head whipped down. Dollish eyes gazed. Then he cast his head back. Its eyes glossed pure white.

The imp flashed Irion this—its vision, sending him scrambling back toward Belot's.

Belot ran behind as if Irion were pulling him by a leash. The coming of morning bled.

That cauldron of shit couldn't have, Irion thought.

That cauldron couldn't, Belot ideated.

His control over Belot was weakening more each moment. With a surge, Irion willed him to stand guard at his open window, while Irion sweated against his door and caught his breath.

His worry was then confirmed. When he reentered the parlor, Irion pressed his back against the door, hung his head, and sighed.

The dismal worktable at the center of this dismal room was bare. Near his feet lay the baby, now limp and contorted, as if thrown.

Walking to the table, he stopped at the cage hanging above. The night was far from a loss. Irion had the imp, one who'd already done for him what it would never do for Belot. Plus, Irion had killed the Great—ornate—Denoreyph Belot, and even fulfilled an adolescent fantasy of commanding his corpse around. Toadly would be addressed later, once reorganized and a better plan made.

It was right then that Irion saw the imp's face change.

✳

When Irion came to, blasting pain flowed from a gash on the back of his head. He was face down, on the floor, in a pool of his own blood.

Belot stood above him.

Disenthralled from Irion's dominion, wielding one of his ornamental canes that had surely felled the Ordrid, meat and teeth sneered.

His sockets flashed.

Belot widened his stance. Regripping his weapon, "Not the fate for you I desired," he wailed, "but I haven't time!" He rose his cane to, Irion was sure, beat him to death in as many strikes as he could before oblivion claimed them both. But before the first one fell, Toadly came barreling out of nowhere. In Toadly's hands was a colossal iron spoon from one of Belot's cauldrons.

Though Irion had managed to roll over, he was still unable to stand. Separated only by Irion lying at their feet, the two then clashed like pit fighters.

When Irion rolled up onto his side, his head exploded in such pain he'd thought for a moment that the damned spoon had found him instead. He watched the melee as an emerged worm would. The skeleton was dodging the slow, skull-crushing swoops while hissing his curses. The fat man, almost a light green, gargled through the slice under his bottom-most chin, while his engorged stomach jostled with his violent wiggling. With a loping swing of the spoon, something fell out from between the glistened roles of Toadly's stomach.

Landing upright, as if placed by a servant, the lapis lazuli hand stood before Irion. Toadly's feet and Belot's bones danced as he clasped onto it.

He had it! It was done! Soon Belot would fade, and if Irion were lucky, while he waited on the floor unnoticed, maybe Belot would use that cane to break Toadly's fat head.

Confusion penetrated his euphoria, for right then the imp opened its cage.

Irion's eyes were pulled from the fight when the imp reached out and stuck its scorpion-stinger fingernail into the lock that had been—or so Irion had thought—preventing its flight.

Flew it did, to a shelf to latch its small hands around a small black jar. Little bat wings gliding, the imp flew over Belot, Toadly, and Irion, and dusted them with its contents.

It didn't take long.

The blue hand began to thrum. It began to burn Irion's fingers, but he only held it tighter. A moment later he had been pulled to his feet, but by what he could not say.

He was standing between both enemies. Belot's bones flew against him, sticking to his arms and chest as if attached by paste. Belot's teeth chattered in his ear while Toadly's head was slung back and a fountain of noise and bile erupted from the gash.

It was as if the three were standing still while the room spun at a terrible speed. Toadly was smaller now—his eyes glaring up at Irion while his arms hugged his leg. What looked like maggots squirmed where Belot's large bones had been just a moment before.

"No!" Irion cried as he heard Belot cry out the same. "Not this! Not him!" they cried.

Toadly, now a hideous tadpole, made a slow orbit as Irion felt the putrid itch of Toadly's fusion. Covered in the powder that started this, there was a sudden crowding in Irion's mind.

There was the collection of memory and thoughts that Irion identified as *Irion*. But there were others too. There was one: a maker of undead slaves and master of his craft. There was another: cruel, cunning, ever-working. Yet there seemed to be a looming fourth being, one who settled on them like a fog. Darker, this insidious force felt much older, and it was this one who Irion cried out to inexplicably in a dialect from times long ago, "What is thou which touches me?!"

Maecidion then felt the rebirth that few creatures can know. Without eyes he saw; without body he began to feel. "Worry not, young one," Maecidion said.

Pathetic whimpers and yelps in the periphery were all that was left of Gormorster Toadly and Denoreyph Belot. "I, I am sorry," that which was still Irion said. "Forgive me, my Lord. There was no way of knowing. I thought maybe, maybe in your final moments that you had gone mad."

Irion was sophomoric, but audacious and physically able. It was why he had been chosen, as both the other two had been chosen for their greatest endowments. Their poor qualities melting away, the synthesis was congealing as that which was still Irion pled, "Your Virulence, please—"

What was once Irion remained only a moment more, a fluttering of two memories: perusing a scroll under candlelight at the lyceum, and then the midnight garden in the family keep, playing with his cousins under the moon. As excited cries carried on the night wind, he ran from his hiding place. Finding his playmates, what was once Irion faded as if never existing at all.

Maecidion looked at his hands, then his feet. He breathed in the air of the splendid early morning, then extended an arm for his imp to perch.

The morning was the shade of gray that always brought rain. *Irion,* once again, stood at the giant obelisk of Maecidion the Virulent. Irion was mostly still garbed in Irion's black, adding to the new form one of Belot's cloaks. A satchel was slung about his shoulder; in it, choice mithridates and tinctures and philtres to help retackle the world. And his beautiful coiled imp. And his lapis lazuli hand.

He smiled at the obelisk. *His* obelisk. The world could see this testament to his departure. The more, the better. Times were changing; that part of *him* had been right. Even an ancient must adapt. The man the world had known as Maecidion was just an earlier vessel, and the predecessor before Maecidion the same. He could hardly contain his amusement; simply clearing out the clutter of a closet was enough to mask his plan. He cared nothing for the recipients at what he was sure was a riotous hearing, and prior to had laughed as he'd laid dying while Morfil penned their insignificant names.

Morfil had been a diligent and loyal subordinate, but he lacked Irion's intrepid nature. Besides, he was now obliged to the duties of the highest order, whereas Irion was practically a nomad from the lower. It was time for something new. Through Irion, he was free.

As the first rains splashed off his hood, he laughed as ghouls do. He was alive again, and the pitter-patter on his tongue was as sweet as bliss itself. It was time to pay his respects to the wondrous House of Rogaire. He marched toward the Thunder Bustle, through the flower-adorned precincts of the wealthier tombs.

IV
THE MORTICIAN'S TALE

Part Two

"And what are you two fine gentlemen gabbing about?" Somyellia larked at the base of our stoop. "How Maecidion is still rumored to rise again, even after these six years hence," adjusting the grocery basket from one hip to another, "or how that monument to stupidity over in Do-Gooder's is finally showing its figures below the knees?"

"Snier here," I replied, not done taunting my colleague, "*studied math*. Below the knees is, that's over eighty percent done, right? Right, Snier?"

"Oh, nothing, we're just talking about that time you tried to sneak him into your old place," Tymothus Snier said from the top step as I bounced up to lend Somyellia a hand.

"That one," she said. "Seasmil tell you how—"

"How the fiendish guards persuaded me to find shelter elsewhere. Yeah yeah."

"Well," said Snier, who had a fashion for clasping his hands more girlish than any third Somyellia'd ever brought over. "And shelter elsewhere you lovebirds did. Shall we?"

We all went inside, where, as per usual, Snier began his prattle about our "menagerie of skulls" and the "religious graffiti." My contributions, at least, were gradual preparations for the Institute, but even I had to concede how Somyellia's flare for gratuitous macabre had taken over our decorative tastes. But, though he was reluctant to admit it, our decorations were becoming as neighborly to Snier as we who owned them.

"Glad you'll suffer the market for us, baby," I said, tasked with a plum jar that Somyellia'd handed me. "They'd just come up with some new rule, say I violated it," the reluctant lid opened and spun, "and jail my ass."

Snier was quick to agree. "You are worse than what they got in the dungeon downtown," he said. "Sommy, let me tell you, having bumped into your menacing hunk here—while working his trade, no less—hell, *I* would have called the Ward. Bite marks, scars, clothing of nothing but black and questionable greens— well, let's just say that raven hair of yours, Seasmil, doesn't always look as charming."

I saw that the effeminate thief wasn't the only one looking me up and down. Work had taken Somyellia on the road for almost a week. I watched as she fondled our bone wind chimes.

Like most domiciles on the Avenue of Red Wolf, our place was coffin-like and smelled sour from an unfindable leak in the sewer pipes.

For me though, it was perfect. Although fewer than in my teen years, my dissections hadn't stopped. I'd made a pact with myself that I'd proudly kept: I never once took a human life in order to collect my materials. I came perilously close once, but two of my cohorts beat me to it. Their lust for inflicting pain and their general bristling nature, I had opted to view in quiet disdain, but that night I was grateful. Our assignment had tried to rise from his bed to cast some hex on us, and by the looks of his gaunt and soulless slaves, he was far too dangerous to be shown mercy. I'd left that night with one of his slave's arms tucked into my belt. Her limb had been meant to serve as a premiere piece to cut open and inspect, but its ceaseless twitching forced me to give up and throw it away.

This rule that I'd self-imposed may have been more difficult to honor if I hadn't been a grave robber. When taking my work home with me made a stack too high, our tiny but high-walled backyard took care of the surplus. Like jagged teeth, towering slums hung over our yard, appearing in opium-induced stirs as looming onlookers. In the queer hours of morning, I would bury all that was to be buried. Snier, like a good neighbor, admitted once that it lullabied him, the soft digs of the shovel.

The three of us reclaimed our stoop and I packed the pipe. The steps were still warm, but it would be night soon. Somyellia sidled onto my lap. It was easy to forget how fiercely she'd blossomed into full womanhood when she gave me her girlish smile. My gratitude had remained two-fold. This beauty wasn't just cause for erections all over Nilghorde, but because of her beauty our rent was still usually paid.

"The witch's bosom still gives milk, Snier." The cloud of smoke that burst from my mouth ate Somyellia like a wedding veil.

"Yeah," Snier said, sounding like he was already mulling over our night's work. "Pass it here so I can share such enlightenments."

One puff was all it ever took for Snier; not hard to imagine, being that he wasn't much bigger than one of my legs. The smoke tickled his lungs, then his brain, then shot out those blue eyes onto the beautiful filth of Nilghorde.

"How'd I get here," Snier said, "Nilghorde—*ugh*." He had a habit of doing this. We'd usually just sit and watch. I'd gape. Somyellia'd usually giggle. "Not sure where to start," he went on, "that's all. Too hard on yourself. Always have been. You abandoned the thought of it. Besides, looks fade—like your hairline. Too hard on yourself. Always have been. Robbery is—"

"Snier," Somyellia said, "kind sir, may we have our pipe back now?"

"Robbery is too dangerous. Street-thieving too competitive. Besides—here you go, Sommy—the margins are too low." Snier was still carrying on as we made our way back into our side of the duplex. "Oh well, every now and again we get a good load."

"We sure do," Somyellia said, grabbing my crotch then shutting our door with her heel.

Draped in a fresh intestinal track, Somyellia ground on top of me. Once spent, our pipe returned, cradled in her hands, the golden snake. Too stunned to go at it again, exalted visions came to me in patches, like a dreary giant who was blinking as he lumbered across the world.

"…You will be a doctor," I heard, coming to. My love was on her side, reading my latest batch of notes and sketches, bare, save the scrolls ribboned over her thigh. "We'll have droves of bodies to spin our wealth."

When I came to again, Somyellia was on the floor, dreamily covering our floorboards in the symbols of her craft with her red and white paints.

"I can buy a batch of girl slaves," Somyellia said, "and have a row of wiggling rumps waiting for you after a long day of curing washerwomen of their cough. Our garden will explode with all the illegal vines and bulbs. Finer arts demand it, you know. Many coffins will have to be dumped out for some of the advanced stuff. And I'll need close to constant petting too." I went for my work tools lying next to a jar of thumbs, a sight that would have made our landlord's head pop off if he ever gulped down the courage to come in. "But if my brute is too busy writing books and cutting out tumors," she blew me a kiss as I waved her off amiably, "then the boy slaves will just have to do."

※

"She really thinks I can get into the—"

"Institute of Human Sciences, never heard you talk about it," Snier said, rearranging the picks in his work-belt.

Copping to the sarcasm: "Just need the tuition."

We skirted a culvert and waded through a sliver of marsh. The night had come swiftly as I'd snored and drooled. During which, Snier reminded me, he'd paced all over our stoop until at last I emerged with our crowbar and short-handled shovels. My tools, of course, were now tucked away in my bag.

But the moon and stars this night were remarkably shy. Hiding our larger tools was probably as unnecessary as scaling the roots of an old oak to make our way through a hole in the cemetery fence.

Snier and I had met on a similar night. When Snier had fled to Nilghorde, his better judgment swayed him to put the sex trade on sabbatical. Snier had said his suspicions were confirmed when it trickled down that the Ward had ransacked every boy brothel. In fact, he'd told me a whole lot, which as we slinked past the first of several guardhouses, my amused mind replayed his grandest story yet:

Without a coin in his purse, Snier had said, one evening he'd sat and watched as a funeral procession went by. The clamor had been clad in jewels. Gold plates weren't sealed in some vault, but being banged by a parade of mourners.

Breaking into mausoleums was easy enough for a competent thief, and Snier surely was. But too many were in parts where antsy, spear-kneading watchmen marched about. Though it never ceased to make his skin crawl, the safer bet was the endless sea of graves.

Some graves are forgotten as soon as they are lowered, not even a shovel's load covers some of the more extreme cases. Others are in the outskirts of any given cemetery, usually the side where overgrowth seems bent on reclaiming the land for the wild.

One night, Snier wanted to try his luck in the Maedraderium. To him, as to most of us, the Maedraderium was a small city of twinkling lavish homes for those far beyond the ability to appreciate it all. Hoping to wash himself and bicker to no one about the heaviness of the coffin he'd given up on, he said he'd followed the gurgling of a nearby fountain. He went around one mausoleum wall just to slam face-first into another—his words. He wondered how a wall could have felt so warm on such a cool night. Then an arm pinned him flat to the ground.

His kicks pitter-pattered against not a wall, but a man's chest. Snier said his dagger was smacked away like a troublesome nat. Screaming may have alerted an eager watchman. Prison seemed like a dream by comparison, but his mouth was sealed shut by the man's large hand.

It was broken at the tip, but a thick knife flashed in caught starlight. As the knife rose higher, maybe it was his lust for beauty that pulled Snier to see the ornate casket behind the man on top of him. Yes, behind this man, this unrepenting fiend, a casket sat pulled out of the earth, and it sat unopened.

"Ikin owen it," Snier said against the palm covering his mouth, his eyes clinched like dungeon vises. After a moment Snier felt the hand lift off. "I can open it."

I let him up. The locks on that damn thing had cost me the tip of my knife, but with a little tooling, Tymothus Snier opened the griffin-emblazoned casket with a final *chunk*.

A year later, Snier finally believed me when I'd said that I had no plans on killing him that night, that and he had long since moved into the other half of our duplex. Alliances weren't just for the Ward and royal Houses. Nothing better than combining some muscle with a little coy lock work.

"Snier," I said, back in the present and entering a thicket of headstones, "remember the coffin that had that gold dildo inside?" Good ol' Sniery had seen such things before—in fact, he may have been the only person in all Mulgara to have encountered one in two different professions.

"Can we just get to it?"

We laid our tools on the grass, but I whipped out the opium. "Yeah," Snier soon giggled, "I sold it to a Chapwyn priest." Any watchman or fellow grave robber may have run screaming from our ghouls-feeding laughter. "Should have given it to Somyellia... sorry, no offense."

"Meh," I said, disenthralling myself from a comfortable headstone, "just her job. You wouldn't understand." Snier's stare tickled me. "Now *that* was a joke, little buddy. Let's get to work." I grabbed a shovel and got digging.

"We need to split the spoils the way you said you used to." Snier said. We'd hit a good one! A bloated noble stuffed in a coffin studded in bronze-lined jade. "And to think, he thought going the *in the ground* route would fool entrepreneurs like us, Mr. Oleugsby."

"Ansul's ass!" I let out. Quieting myself, I leaned in to stare at the plates and goblets. Disgracing the Chapwyn church father's name had just been upped from time in the pillory to a lopped-off head, and grave robbing had been a death sentence for years— whether at the executioner's axe or ripped limb from limb by the offended and turned-loose meek. Being killed twice over was a distilling notion, but the smiles on both our dirty faces gleamed still. I said without taking my eyes of our treasure, "The old arrangement was I'd keep the jewelry; he just wanted the body." I glanced over. Snier appeared to be listening, though steadfastly working a jeweled bracer off a leathery arm. "Still want it how I used to do it?"

"There," Snier exhaled. "Got her—I thought you were the one who only wanted the body?"

"No. It's a great way to collect material, sure," I explained. Snier handed me up the loot. Soft *tinks* and *tanks* sang as our bag swelled. "Materials is mostly why I do it now. That and bills. By the time I got back in business, I could hardly afford a bread crumb. But, such is your fate when a squadron of Ansul's True catches you slipping rings off lower clergy."

Snier chuckled while handing up a goblet. "That story made it all the way to Pelliul."

"You're kidding? Yeah, I'd probably have enough money for tuition by now if it weren't for that storm of torches and hymns. But, yeah, back when Mr. Belot hired me, it was simple: More bodies for him, more coin from him. I kept anything I found—which was usually nothing but worm shit—and he got first crack at the haul."

Jumping out of the hole, "And for that there was a wage?" "And a decent one," jumping down to cut off noble ears. "Of course, there was more to it."

"Not sure I want to know," Snier said. "It's a shame Belot's gone. Probably dead."

"Seaz, I got to finally ask it. What the hell does taking apart a few stiffs over and over have anything to do with becoming a doctor? Why not—"

—We were on their bellies. Out from nowhere a clamor of mounted watchmen had appeared. One said "Opium smell," thankfully riding right past us and then disappearing.

We slithered all the way back to the oak.

Once on the streets my heart pounded less erratically. I continued, "For practice. So, yeah, I worked for him about a year, then he just vanished. It was like he went up in smoke. Metaphorically apt, too. I found signs there'd been a fire where he usually worked. Somyellia thinks Belot disappeared because this one vile man he had me take care of may have had even viler friends."

"Fires. Vile friends. Somyellia hasn't pieced it all together yet for you? She's from folk not too far off from your Mr. Belot."

"Only folk of hers I've ever met is that onion-headed cousin, Irion. Always tasking her out with brews and broths. I ask her what for and she just clams up and tells me *family business.*"

We made it home and divided the spoil, as we always did. No fuss. No squabble. The haul put food in the gullet, but greater things called. Not long after, Snier broke the news to me that he'd had his fill of grave dirt. I'd made a friend. I'd cared for the little thief from Pelliul, but as is my fate, like Belot, he too would vanish.

V
THE MUNICIPAL DUNGEON

"Welcome home," the guard jeered, tossing Tymothus Snier in the cage. Tymothus was once again in the Rat's Nest, once again in the hay matting its floor, once again his back stinging and bloody from the lash.

Faces like staring monkeys from the Suelan paintings crowded the newcomer. But their wild eyes were not so wild. Rather, they looked down while he struggled to rise with the same interest as would a beast whose spirit had long been broken by the stifling monotony of the zoo. They hadn't crowded. There was no room.

The smell of men and globs of gruel rushed him as he wobbled to his feet. Unusually for him, he worried over what was going to happen when the rent was due, Seasmil and Somyellia not knowing where he was, the destinies of his possessions within that meager, gone-now home.

Gruel…for the rest of his life. He'd have to put in for trustee again.

"Snier?" a voice said, putting Tymothus onto its cracking, grinning face before it lightened. "What you do this time, pinch a priest ass?" Tymothus turned his back on the toothless pickpocket, resting his arms on the crossbars so he could stare out into the gloom.

A botched burglary.

A life sentence.

He'd started doing burglaries during the grave-robbing downtime. The split with Seasmil kept him out of the pauper lines, but Seasmil's strong interests in both the freshly dead and the poor made for easy access but meager returns.

The first dozen houses or so were a silken dream. Excelling seemed instantaneous; Tymothus considered himself an emerging natural. Then, on this same night when a choir of Chapwyn door-knockers did their civic duty and hung a poet who'd stirred crowds with lamentations of longing for pre-Years of Peace ways, Tymothus was caught and his life was over.

One of the many agonies of the Municipal Dungeon was the way it had been built. With long swaths of hallway without so much as torch or candle, with addition after addition leading up to new unnumbered cells or clever, rickety elevators squeaking down to the catacombs, a prisoner's inability to discern where they'd just been, night from day, or if the blackness staring back at them bore a wall—or, if the dungeon fever had reemerged, causing its loathsome hallucinations, if that black really went on forever.

It was fortunate perhaps that Tymothus was already familiar. The Rat's Nest took up the middle of a giant room. On all sides were the stone walls, caging in the cage by block and mortar. From the cage's front, in the light of the new torches, the corridors leading in and out of the room could almost be seen. A lone door in the wall faced them. Hanging over it was the ominous placard: *Special Concerns.*

Tymothus remained mostly up front, slinking against the bars, stomaching gruel, losing fast the track of days as his only connection with the outside world passed him in the form of working guards.

About when the slashes on his back stopped throbbing, the cage had transformed itself from the lulls and spits of lament and flare-ups to a congruent, startled hum. From the dungeon's belly to Rapist Wing, all the way to the shore of Crackpots Range, guards and prisoners alike were bouncing back and forth word that a convicted necromancer was coming in.

Sorcery, necromancy, crystal gawking—the whole arcana bundle that to Tymothus came with funny children who have more brains than blood—it all had been outlawed in Rehleia not long after The Conqueror and Maecidion the Virulent had struck some deal. The most common rumor was Maecidion's House could still furtively practice all the things Seasmil and Somyellia showed far too much interest in. The only clause was he had to barter new deals with new devils, the finer tuning of which was lost on the clerk or scribe, but it kept said devilry from stalking the streets and hills, having been common as cabbage in the elder days.

Despite the law, a convicted necromancer was something maybe seen once in living memory. The concoction necessary to discover, catch, try, and convict a man who for fun talks with the dead and realigns the fiber of natural order was something rarely accomplished. Since the offender often also specialized in the manipulation of the human mind, doubt turned to counter-investigations turned to lynch mobs decrying the inspector and prosecutor. Walls were slopped red, not only in court, but in the family rooms of the men misguided enough to spearhead such an uphill task.

When the sounds began, those in the cage who didn't shut their mouth immediately paid for it later. To some it was a black-smith, working in the near darkness on a metal door. Others noted the rhythm, how it changed, citing a new torture machine shifting with the needs of its first captive. Tymothus strained his eyes, ignoring the excited murmurs.

Then it happened. Out walked the first guard, then the second.

Behind the lugs and their shouldered halberds was a malevolent-looking fellow, barely able to move from all the chains. The culprit of the sound: the *chee-chunk cha-chunk* of the coil that had swallowed him ended when they reached the doorway for Special Concerns. There the guards stuffed the stranger inside, entering the room after him. Then they shut the door.

✳

"You know, it's not every day someone *wants* to be here."

Irion had learned their names during the walk. "Your esteemed warden is a hard man to have audience with, Moevelt. Can you think of a better way?"

"Yeah," Gunroe growled, taking a swig from a bottle then stuffing it back behind his breastplate. "Paint yerr face like a clown. That dummy'll come runnin'."

Moevelt laughed at his partner, listless and unamused. Irion was seated on a bare stool on one side of the interrogation table. On the other they stood, Gunroe unable to resist. "Watchu want to talk with the warden for?"

"To tell him to his face what a pompous piece of barnyard pig shit he is," Irion said, "of course."

Light in the Special Concerns room was better than outside with the whipped thieves. Moevelt and Gunroe could see Irion quite well; his bony knees in his black stockings, outcroppings from thighs holding up the mountain of chain. When they decided he was no daring trickster and that he actually needed to be hauled in, they'd given special attention to his hands. The exposed fingers could move, but not enough to keep dungeon guards wary of some prefabricated spell. It was the bald man's smirk they watched now.

"No, really. Why the request?" Moevelt asked. "What do you want with him?"

"I want with him what the world wants with him: to send his

gelatinous mass down to the void where he can join his mother and mother's mother in pleasuring devils with whichever hole presents itself the most urgent."

Whatever mirth was left in the sober of the two guards was now gone. "An Ordrid *would* say something like that. Put the hooch away, Gun." Placing his hands on the table, Moevelt leaned forward. "The warden doesn't give two high hells 'bout you. Who the hell you think you are?"

"Your warden will come to me," Irion said. "Loosen my chains."

Gunroe laughed. Moevelt didn't. "Dipshit, I guess you don't get it, do ya? You don't tell anyone shit in here."

At this, Irion points a finger. A lone finger that neither guard sees. It is shrouded by the weight and shadow of links of chain, but the finger is pointing. Irion's finger was pointing at Moevelt. "Kill him," Irion says, looking at Gunroe.

"Necromancer or not," Moevelt said, placing his halberd against the wall and cracking his knuckles, "you're gonna learn how we do things here, you—*Gun, what th*—"

The second slash did it. Gunroe's municipally appointed dagger sliced deep under Moevelt's armpit, blood spraying Gunroe and Moevelt screaming. Moevelt had never been afraid of Gunroe, or of any man. Gun being the smaller, little uppity brawlers always listened after a broken bone or six. But Moevelt didn't advance to start breaking.

"Gun," he heard himself say. "Put down the blade, brother." He stuck out his hands, like a diplomat, fanning his fingers, soon pulling back one missing a thumb for his trouble.

The entire Rat's Nest watched as the door flew open. They'd heard what sounded like screams, roaring to reality when one guard clutching his hand tore into the blackness of a corridor and the other chased after.

"Those two," chuckled a voice outside the bars. Snier jumped so suddenly he almost hit his head. The orange halos of torchlight made what shadows they couldn't reach all the blacker. Combined with what had just run out of sight, invisible had been this guard who'd come to distribute, of course, more gruel. The burly man called to another somewhere behind him, "Go shut that door, will ya?"

Warden Rogaire especially hated menial tasks. Trustees swept shit. His army of guards could damn well have the room better stocked with more and bigger candles. "Well?" was all he said, all he could say, lighting a few and staring at Irion Ordrid out of the corner of his eye.

"Do you know why I'm here?"

It wasn't characteristic of the big man to evade questioning. The warden lit another then walked to Moevelt's halberd, inexplicably left to lean against a wall. "No. Don't care either. Just wanted to come have a look at you. That's all."

"And," Irion let hang, curious what the warden saw as they eyed one another, "*you, prison master, are the bigger, dumber,* infinitesimally less interesting version of your dead father."

Warden Rogaire stared as he would a man who'd just shoved his head up his own ass. No one—in chains of all things, Ordrid or no—dared speak to him this way. "The hounds," he choked then repeated. "I'm thinkin' it'll be the hounds for you."

"Yes, torture, no doubt. May I show you? Free my hands."

"I'm the warden of the Municipal Dungeon…of Nilghorde." Irion didn't stir. He blinked and let out a theatric yawn. "Lord of the House of Rogaire!"

"That," Irion shot like a snake, "that, I know. Now release my hands." The warden stormed over and seized him by the throat. Irion's eyes were alight, every candle caught. Words flowed from his tongue like a sweetened air. "There, there we are."

✳

Making it all the way into Crackpots Range may have impressed the howling lunatics if they'd known, or understood, Moevelt's state. His side was wet, his uniform soaked by his sweat and the copper stickiness of his own blood. He could barely move his left arm, flopping it like a limp, dead animal to try and determine its gash's severity. Panic restruck him like an arrow. Recoiling his thumbless hand, he kept running.

Out of breath, he leaned against the nearest bars only to be propelled back by snarls and yelps from caged men. These men, residents of Crackpots Range, had long ceased their pitiful states and become agents of fear.

Footsteps struck the floor stones, fast and loud. It would be only a moment more then Gunroe would round the same bend he had, just brandishing that—

Moevelt drew his own dagger, thanking Tersiona his strong arm had been spared.

Reserved for the newest or laziest of guards, these crumbling tunnels and cages that heaped and fell into each other were always poorly lit. What good was light to those who fancied themselves a werewolf or an old worn boot? It was by either the best or worst of luck that Moevelt stood near a sun-bright torch. For he saw Gunroe's advance, and he saw the glazed but not drunk, depraved but aloof look he wore.

Moevelt bounced on the balls of his feet, finding his courage as some inmate who must've recognized him abusively hooted and hollered. He could skewer this menace with one well-aimed punch. Under the breastplate, where Gunroe's hooch-rot stomach held plenty of tubes and vein. Or directly above, Moevelt could punch the blade of his dagger through the base of his throat.

Moevelt had only one working arm, but he'd been down and out before. He stepped back, quick, giving himself the necessary reach when Gunroe lunged. His back pressed against cage bars, suddenly hostile as they exploded with the restraining bloom of dirt-matted hands.

Moevelt roared. He cut off a thumb, sliced wrists. He couldn't turn to see, for too many hands now pulled his belt, his beard, his hair. Ghoulish fingers, some mottled with pallor and disease, others chewed, pinned him against the pitiless iron. His right forearm was slammed against the cage. Hands squeezed and fingers crawled, all the way up until they reached his dagger.

"There we are," Irion said, pushing out a lustful hiss, tightened and distilled by Warden Rogaire's squeeze around the veins and piping of his taut neck.

If Warden Rogaire had been a more astute man, he may have observed the needling of Irion's pupils, the flash that for but a moment engulfed them. The big blond man let go and swung this way and that until finding a stool and sliding it under him. He looked at Irion with the dimwitted simplicity of an amused child, charmed by whatever whim was its fat little obsession.

"Did you ever hear of a man named Denoreyph Belot? Did such names ever cross your fine table? Such wonders, the right gestures, the appropriate philtres imbibed, the appropriate moment." Irion spoke as if no chains draped him. "The power of a human's touch."

"What do you want me to do?"

What fun was raising the dead if one never enchanted and marionetted the living. "Oh, dig up your father's grave and defile it with the rankest human juices. Set thy flesh afire and go whirling. Jump off a cliff—no, just release me from these ridiculous chains, then let me go. This was most fruitful, Lord Rogaire."

"…I'd have to mix up the roster a bit," the warden said.

The warden walked out of the room, shutting the door as

the cage of thieves fought for best position for peering inside. Tymothus watched as the supreme overlord of the Municipal Dungeon disappeared into a corridor, calling and booming for his lieutenants.

✳

After full bowls did not come because new guards did not deliver, what torches still flickered gave a wan ambience, just enough that Tymothus saw when the warden returned.

When he opened the Special Concerns door, the trapped light seemed eager to escape. The door shut. The Rat's Nest murmured and conjectured. The door reopened. Warden Rogaire and another man were making their exit. Having to be the same man formerly reduced to a walking metallic spool, the prisoner's bald head shined orange and white as the warden held him with a gentle pair of handcuffs.

Then they were gone, disappeared in the same direction those two guards had gone running, towards where Tymothus judged lead easiest to the cells of the dungeon's frontal layer.

It is possible that Tymothus Snier was the last prisoner to see the necromancer. His eyes were keen; his placement, irksomely pressed against the front-most bars.

Rumors would soon bounce back and forth, from the dungeon's belly to Rapist Wing, all the way to the shore of Crackpots Range that the confessed necromancer earned the warden's instantaneous ire and was broken on a rack somewhere deep in the catacombs. More rumors persisted he escaped, having bedeviled the guards and the warden too.

When prompted, Tymothus always stuck to which theory tested his credulity the least. In places like the Rat's Nest, though, experience taught him you don't always say how you really feel.

✳

In an instant when Gunroe leapt, the pinned man freed a leg and used it to send his attacker scrambling. The focused, bleeding guard locked his boot against a crossbar and pushed, pushed until his burning muscles tore and he began feeling his back press free of the cage and the ghastly, clawing fingers.

Moevelt had been deprived his dagger, a sinister tool to be fought over in such cages. He grabbed the torch from the wall with his good arm, waving it as he would a wooden club. Moevelt didn't hear the lunatic just behind him, hidden in shadow, using his dagger with an establishing authority on his peers. Gunroe was back on his feet, his blade gleaming in the burning light.

When they found the body, the dungeon summoned the condescension of inspectors from the Metropolitan Ward. A string of questions led back to Crackpots Range, where futile interviews with madman held a bizarre consistency.

That one guard had killed another was no strain on the imagination, to speak of nothing for the imaginations inside of men who work in dungeons. But, that after the victor had sliced the throat of his victim from one ear to the next, he'd abruptly shaken and wailed as if he'd woken from a dream— hardly. Hardly so, and any interview with the conscious-stricken assailant was now impossible. For the more articulate of the madmen repeated that after such entertainment had sadly ended, the killer pulled out a bottle from somewhere in his armor. After sucking down the liquor—verified by the investigation's discovery of said bottle and smelling its portents—he mistakenly leaned against their cage to cry and cry and cry. Here the testimonies got skittish. Fights erupted and an inspector was bitten.

Deep in the cage, the dead guard's dagger was found. It was licked clean, but it matched the one hundred and twenty-seven stab wounds on a murderer who now needed no cage of his own.

VI
ALL MALEVOLENT MASQUERADE

"And the loser is." The crowd fizzled to a murmur. Morlia adjusted her array of peacock feathers to better scrutinize the scroll. "Bennero!" she rejoiced. "Our dead poet."

They whole place rang with laughter, flinging wine-slimed spit on the faces of any would-be doubters. Morlia's entourage dressed in the pinks and purples of fairy, Rinlot's troops from the dungeon coated in the one-night black of the Suelan. All bellowed inane stanzas as Bennero ended the long walk to dither next to Morlia.

His first mistake had been dressing as Denom Vandahl. More Vandahls populated any given All Malevolent party than the red devils and demons, though these too were in no short supply.

His final, fatal error had been the costume itself. Vandahl: His pleasant girth was poorly concealed fluff, his auburn curls the painted wires of an old donkey tail. Most obvious, more even than the frayed ends of a soiled pillow, were his blatherings of acclaimed verse, proving the attendee's attempts were not mirthful mockeries but the worst costume in the lot, earning him, by way of tradition, the first sword to slice open the awaiting boar.

"And our *winner* is…" The lady of the house eyed her

parchment, pausing for effect. "Somyellia! The sexy lizard!" Cheers and lustful hoots. Somyellia was carried out from the dungeon guards who'd ringed her. Allowed to her feet and free from further groping, she stood at Morlia's other side.

The two women winked.

It was impossible not to feel the giddiness. Somyellia had enjoyed making her costume, parting with coins to conjugate straps of shamrock with her snug censors of seafoam green. Only the silk between her legs betrayed her monochromatic delivery, leaving paled husbands and reddening wives to stare at reptilian yellow.

Somyellia had hoped Rinlot would have been the one making the announcements. So had Morlia. That way the young witch would've accepted the second sword, touched the damned man, then begun concocting her best exit strategy.

But the lord of the home was still busy meandering, as he had all evening, disappearing to emerge at other corners of the loud mansion as if magically propelled by the fairies who dotted stairwells and danced drunkenly in the great hall.

Every time her moment approached, the Minotaur would hoof out of reach. But she'd just won best costume. Etiquette demanded the prison master come to congratulate her.

The lights were lowered for the sword-bearers as they sliced into the pig. Other than butcher's duty, the only requirement was passing the first cuts to the hosts. The lady, having no stomach for such things, excused Somyellia to break off from the clump and give Rinlot his due.

Due indeed, she thought, carrying the plate through the crowd, parting the partiers with her cattish strut. Rinlot Rogaire was one of the bigger men there, as big as Seasmil, though blockish and without the limber look that intimated her lover's athleticism. Keeping an eye on the oaf was made all their easier by his fashionable horns. They were breaking out of a pleasant tide of demons. Below such wooden foolery the man seemed to lock on her. He smiled and nodded, pointing to the obligation she held and gesturing a spoon to his mouth.

Here we go. She balanced the plate in one hand, extending the other for whatever form of handshake this impostering aristocrat was about to deem fit. *You're welcome, Irion—*

"You're the finest fuckin' thing I've seen in a long long time," spouted the toad, appearing in front of her as if she'd accidently summoned him out of a damned lamp. "Werlyle's the name."

"Thanks," she said. No, not a toad. The short drunk who blocked her way was an insult to such beasts. Toads were at least helpful components, or familiars.

Next, in one sweeping motion, a sequence unfolded. He relieved her of her dish, turned, gave it to Rinlot, spoke some familial trivia to that white-toothed grinner, then led her halfway out into the night before she'd realized, once again, her target had been diverted.

"No one—I mean someone," wrestling her arm free. She pressed against what little was there to prevent her breasts from baring themselves, ensuring he hadn't somehow diverted them, too. "I mean I came here with someone."

"Aw," the drunk gloated, "he oughta be keepin' a better eye on a lady like you."

It surprised her she'd let herself be escorted out a door and down the few steps. Now under the stars, it surprised her less that she allowed this kidnapping to continue. Outfitted most certainly for the macabre and lukewarm startles the holiday had become, a bar had been erected and manned amidst the obelisks of the Rogaire family graveyard.

She turned down his offer. A shot of Bleeding Anna sounded something euphoric right about now, but even the horniest dunce knew refusing a drink was a sign the shop wasn't open. One of his earlier advances was an attempted fondle that she smacked away.

Though forcibly remaining herself the dainty mooncalf, her eyes belied simmered annoyance. The awful power in her hand, the one she'd used to fasten back his fingers, if he only knew.

"What fun's a party then? No drink." His head had been painted, cartoonishly depicting his brains as having suffered full removal. Normally, she would've twisted and snarled, noting the perfect metaphor. But not even the *Worlds Smartest Ouvarnia* sign hung about his neck beckoned her mirth.

The spell was going to wear off. The hand resting on her hip was her own; that, at least, was a positive. The spell was going to wear off and she needed to get back inside. "You'll have to excuse me." Whatever else she'd said trickled out while she scanned the windows for any signs of a passing Minotaur.

"Here we are. Somethin' a bit more fittin' a woman of yerr beauty." The demon barkeep had left them with Sweet Victory.

Somyellia reluctantly accepted, sighing into the hand-blown glass and pretending to sip. Its translucent mouth ran rimmed with gold, the glass decorated with delicate and proud lilies. She observed such craftsmanship for it was a way to seem attentively absorbed in his newest onslaught of prattle. This time a grope landed.

"Enough." Her voice jarred the barkeep. "Lay one more finger on me, I promise you the first five who bring me your jelly-lathered ribs—man, woman, or child—they'll get me the way you're wishing."

What the hell is Morlia doing?

The somatics and subordinate incantations had been calculated, executed. The rites written, read, burned. The ashes used in the three ways only witches knew. The spell, the curse, the second act of three, it was loaded; crackling in her palms and ready to rip through the sorry carcass of Rinlot Rogaire. Morlia had told her she'd send her husband over if there were any complications. This wobbling blowhard was most certainly that. Opportunities were running thin. Moments left before the spell's depletion, even thinner.

No sooner had she sat down her glass than Rinlot came running. If a real bull had been unleashed into the parting crowd, their urgency may have only been slightly greater. Chatter and banter and the calling of night birds ended as Somyellia become the victim of the large man's sprint.

"Cousin," he cried, skidding to a halt just before the boot toe of the drunk who'd been pestering her. He breathed and billowed into the short man's face, panted and cussed out nonsense. And, as he was knocking her flat, he'd had his ribs squeezed by the unloading hands of Somyellia.

When she rose, she hid her face. Her knee scraped, her ensemble in tatters, the dirt clinging to a bare thigh was enough to distress any woman, or so the hoity partygoers would readily believe.

Satisfied she'd suppressed her grin, she stood tall. "A hex upon you," she said, following up with hummingbird-quick traces of the inverted triangle into the thin air between them.

After a time Rinlot blinked, confusedly. "Get this drunk whore outta here."

Not a moment more she was in custody. "Got a lively one," said one of Rinlot's men.

"Hot pepper," gleed the other, wrenching down on her arm. Their black paint rubbed and smudged against her, all the while her feinting a tantrum.

The lugs bellowed. The party began its resurrection. Rinlot squawked, unaware his pending doom. The lugs laughed the hardest when she tried to kick them.

Somyellia was being carried off by the guards, pretending she was screaming, but she was laughing. She was looking at the glass of Sweet Victory, noting its perfect metaphor.

VII
THE MORTICIAN'S TALE

Part Three

"A hidden grace
In this horrible place,
Come loping and leaping with breath.
The fugitive flowers
In the malefic bowers,
The captors of beauty and death."

—*Denom Vandahl, Poems of the Classics*

All Malevolent Masquerade was always our favorite holiday. She'd told me the party at the Rogaire mansion had gone off without a hitch, but I was still sour that I had to spend the night elsewhere. Duty came first, she'd said, but she'd also mused how she rather would have joined me on the one night a year the proper spilled into graveyards and disreputable bars, banging drums, running up tabs, puking on headstones, and cutting up roasted pigs while dressed as goblins and muskrats.

Somyellia lay in bed with her eyes shut. Some nighttime

clamor out on Red Wolf had distracted her, but she'd resumed one of her fonder pastimes. She dug her hand through the jar of severed tongues. Pulling a shriveled one out and giving it a good lick, "Thee neighborly would be less incorrigible if it weren't for those drat newcomers, by rights," said Somyellia. One more, swollen and still holding its redness, proved to be decidedly male. "Not that bonnet, woman! Makes you look a frumpish bar trout," she boomed, and then her voice returned to normal. "Lovely stuff."

I stood there, drying my hair. "So we're going to be swimming in silver soon for all this?"

"More to life than metal," lidding the jar, "one as keen for stomach tubes and finger bones as you should know this," Somyellia said. "Don't sound too Chapwyn on me." I tossed a severed hand that we used for intimate petting off the bed and flopped down beside her. "Mediocre in the many ways that he may be," Somyellia continued, "Irion easily dominated the Rogaire prison master. *Asking* for a guard change and an escort out of that lovely dungeon was no harder than robbing graves in a blind man's graveyard with a silent shovel."

As she came up on her hands and knees, the window above our bed held the night. She studied the angle of the moon. I studied the sleek dip of her back and bare buttocks. "It's almost time," she said, staying me and hopping toward her wardrobe.

"It's a wonder that termite box hasn't exploded," I said. Rummaging through the clutter, she swung out ribbons of dazzling green before tossing it in the trash. I snickered, "sexy lizard costume?"

"Ansul's ass, don't make me relive it."

"I still don't get it."

"Told you, my beast, I introduced Irion and Morlia years ago."

"Eight years ago."

"You *do* listen. And soon, as you know, after they'd met they agreed Morlia'd approach that dim prison master. Who knows, it could have been my tasking if Morlia hadn't been so insistent," giving the rummage a rest, her eyes sparkled, "but, of course, I would have tactfully explained I was already so uncompromisingly taken. But I knew it would work well. The weak charm Irion drenched her in probably wasn't even needed."

"Seduce the warden?"

"She is perfect for the prison master. Well," erupting in the laugh people do when ruminating on a joke's punch line, "perfect for both of them. Irion has really taken a liking to her."

This Morlia, the object of Irion's affection, had been Somyellia and I's third-lover many times in the earlier days. She'd stiffened me the first night I'd met the two of them as a teen in Templeton. Though I may have been overestimating Somyellia's sensitivity, I kept to myself my understanding of why men were so wrapped around Morlia's finger.

"The charm spell wasn't necessary," I said, trying to make it sound like a question.

"Hadn't seen Cousin Irion in ages," Somyellia said, perhaps wanting to shift the course of our conversation, "since playing in our family's gardens as children. Then there he is, rapping at the doors. Right after Maecidion died, actually. Funny how a death in the family can change people. Irion acted different. The way he moved. How he spoke. A lot like Maecidion used to, really. I think his death really straightened Irion out."

"That's fantastic—so listen, if he's so low in your branches or what have you, why the servant-girl role whenever he graces our stoop?"

"When you talk like that sometimes it makes me think I really should've entertained Morfil's advances," she said, successfully irritating me. I watched her as she pulled out what she'd been looking for: her dark robe covered in family regalia. She wore it only when practicing the type of witchcraft that demanded her utmost.

It didn't take living with a witch to know her work was

outlawed. Along with the parchment plague of new maxims about labor class virtue nailed everywhere, many false witches had been rounded up in plazas and burned to kick off the Years of Peace. Now all that remained seemed to be the real ones. Although there were those practicing black magic who stalked the periphery, Somyellia's House had, according to her, earned the trust of the evil gods. Such trust bestowed on the Ordrids the secrets of their trickery. But it came with a heavy price. When her family called, she said she had to listen. Noticing I was still waiting for an answer, she only said, "Tersiona weeps for a reason."

"I'll remember that. Who penned that lofty explanation for all life's quandaries, you or Vandahl?"

"We've been over this," she sighed. Somyellia knew I didn't care for Irion. He lived somewhere in the Bustle, and it was rare he appeared at our door, but when such rarities encroached, I always found a reason to slink on over to Snier's side.

"It's just I hear so many times," I said, launching my impersonation of her that made her blood boil, *"my beast—my beast, I can't do this or that or that and this*—but then he shows up and your schedule's wide open."

"Seasmil."

"Wide open."

"Seasmil," she said, culling a tone that started to bring me down out of webs in the rafters.

"Wide open as…like the Moliahenna River's mouth after a damn flood."

"Vandahl pen that?" she said, returning to bed.

"I'll let you get to witchery then," I said, climbing off her. Irion's most recent visit was to ask of Somyellia her major discipline. And she'd done her part. Somyellia had touched some warden who Morlia had somehow found a way to send barreling over to her.

The curse had been locked by waves of her hand that she told me was passed off as nothing more than churlish girl anger.

Somyellia was happy to help. The House of Rogaire had wronged the House of Ordrid, and Irion—in this newfound severity Somyellia occasionally mentioned—was just tidying up family business.

Even the common-most dung-scooper on the common-most street knew that when the Conqueror's campaign had swept over the peninsula that it had ended at the doorsteps of Maecidion's keep, and after enough death and chaos deals were eventually struck and the land was renamed.

Yet after enough talks from the bottom of our pillows, I myself could orate the finer points in her family's spiderweb of shifting powers and trickery.

The tale told within Ordrid confines was that after necromancy had been outlawed, and Maecidion and his kind were allowed to practice in secret, it didn't take long for the freshly outfitted Metropolitan Ward, and the people cheering them, to look for a new threat to their newfound tranquility.

Rinmauld Rogaire, father of the warden they all hated, was one of the chief legislators after the Conqueror turned to his unyielding seclusion. It turns out that law was the one magic blacker than necromancy. Extorting Maecidion had been both legal and lucrative. Keeping the House of Ordrid's share of agreed-upon war spoils was payment for Rinmauld not sicking on Somyellia and Maecidion's House the society that had as soon forgotten war as was quick to start a new one.

An Ordrid vendetta on the House of Rogaire had been talked about in their circles for decades. For reasons not entirely explained, her cousin Irion had picked up the proverbial hatchet on behalf of the late Maecidion, and now apparently planned on burying it into the heads of the Rogaires who remained.

Somyellia now had to conduct the final ritual and erupt the

curse they'd set. I personally didn't bother much with her duties in this arena, but I also hadn't in her leg-spreading one either. Our time together was all that mattered; however, even I had learned that all "great curses" required three parts. The victim must be touched by the curser or cursers, and she and Irion had. The curser or cursers must lock in their work with particular gestures, as she had done at the party. Now, the final act was being executed. It would take time, and the moon in the right position.

She began her work as I grabbed my shovel and crowbar to head out to do mine.

✳

When I returned home, my rather lackluster night amongst the graves felt noisy when compared to the silence that met me. I stepped inside.

Crimson and bone-white moons, half-moons, quarter-moons, and languages I never understood covered our floor. Near the middle, in the largest the red-white circle, Somyellia lay still.

Perfectly still.

Some of the red was reflecting the moonlight. Odd that it would, for her paints had to my mind always been ordinary. Odder still, her usual exactness had not been carried out; the shiny pools near her mouth and legs bled out and over and down what symbols had to be of her most importance.

I walked closer.

I called her name.

I stomped on a floorboard when she didn't stir.

The silly girl's morbid games would not get the best of me, even as I went to shower and later returned to the tomb-like silence that had become my apartment.

I am Seasmil, and Death has followed me from an early age. Mother and Celly had left the world in different ways, but stalked my dreams equally. Death was a part of life to me as was ink to a book.

Life owes us nothing.

She had died suddenly, without warning, at the hand of a ruthless venereal disease. Carried coolly by men but cursing the innards of females, I knew this from the blood that had let from all her orifices and pooled over the symbols she'd repainted. Although I had to be a carrier, she was most likely infected while working her trade.

In this moment she was terribly beautiful, her nose and mouth spilling forth blood as wicked as her ancestors that danced under the feminine moon. Those golden eyes stared at me as if to ask one final question. Her skin was still warm under the robe she sometimes wore when practicing her finer craft.

I lifted her off the floor. Her head hung far back and her hair waggled in her blood, like the fine tip of a large paintbrush. Hugging her was all one could do. Silence. I had never been in a place so quiet, not even the old cellar or the furthermost grave.

My own blood roared. I told myself she'd gone back to revel with her kind; wrought not of our world. And though this made me feel no better, after a moment the silence seemed broken by echoes from some far off place, a place I partly understood her to be. All of this could have been my own wishful thinking, of course; maybe the worms were the last to taste my sweet Somyellia.

I laid her on her side of the bed and went through her satchel. After, I went through our drawers and chests.

With a handful of silver, I laid beside her. She'd never once spoken about her burial wishes, an amazing feat considering the nature of our usual talks. She may have wanted a spiraling funeral pyre, an obsidian mausoleum, to be hacked to bits and fed to the night creatures she loved so dearly.

I kept her for days. Telling myself I was waiting on Irion worked for a little while. He was, after all, the only family member she'd ever introduced me to, and proper burial was I figured a family affair. But he never came, and as a day or two passed that reasoning melted away. Not being able to say goodbye stood firmly in its place.

To clean her meant moving her to the kitchen table. I walked around her studiously, solemnly; death had managed to steal many of the features we are so accustomed to.

An urge entered me as I circled the table. Pulling apart her legs, now heavy and cold, I positioned myself. In all the sexual voyages between us, all the desecration of graves, and juices spent, I'd never done this. How could I? She had on occasion teased me of my appetite, and joked I was capable of such "selfish indulgences."

As usual, she was right. I entered a place that was always so inviting and warm, now a rough tunnel. In the midst of my efforts I heard grunting. I believed for just a moment that I had thrusted her back to life. It was I who grunted, and the moment's realization came right as I did.

I wrapped her in a sheet and prepared to enter the streets. Much coaxing and the coins I'd scrounged up days earlier got me a mule to carry Somyellia to the Pauper Morgue.

Taking her to a place designated for the nameless and faceless forgotten made me ill to the core. Hooded, in midday, I took the laden mule down Red Wolf, over the little white bridges that ran through Nilghorde Commerce, past the Tower of the Waning Moon, and finally through winding roads that made the strange district called the The Dead Kettle.

Arriving at the front offices of the morgue, I tethered the mule and stared up at the fat man's nearby tower we'd once raided. Since then it had withered terribly, as if the ultimate perversions once contained within had howled free, leaving the rook beaten by decay beyond the normal brutality of the sun and rain.

I carried Somyellia through the doors of the Pauper Morgue. The transaction was as brief as one would expect. Then a pair of pale bald men took her.

Looking at these two, if you saw them you would find them

disgusting and queer, and not be ashamed of it. Stubby legs supported flab up to the neck, and pouty bottom lips held spittle ready to drip. It was too easy to see the types of men that had paid Somyellia over the years. Just as easily, to see them mongering over her body the moment my back was turned. Eventually letting go of my knife's handle, I helped them unwrap her from the sheet.

"What do you want on the tombstone?" the shorter one asked.

Throughout the years, I have read dozens of excerpts in poems and books, the ones loaded with saccharine romancing, and I wished I'd used a number of them. Particularly striking was a line out of *Songs in Regal Twilight*, authored by Vandahl five hundred years before I was born. At the time, though, all I could do was fight back a surge of tears and scribble out what was clawing:

SOMYELLIA ORDRID

CAPTOR OF MANY HEARTS, RULER OF ONE

A Black Lamb In Your Arms Do I Hope To Find You

"Good sir," the taller one said, the sending me spinning with about the last thing I expected to hear. "We are looking to replace an employee…very soon. The position requires the ability to read and write."

"Skills elusive to many willin' to work here," said the short one.

"We don't mean to ask you this without regard to the tragedies that befell you," the tall one said, brushing a hand over Somyellia, "but we need a strong back most urgently."

I don't know if I had death written on my face. Maybe these little trolls, so close to it on a daily basis, were able to see things others couldn't. This opportunity seemed to fall out of the sky and onto the lap of a man well-adjusted to life's apathy. This was so harmoniously ideal that my shift to excitement with the smell of Somyellia still on my skin pelted me with guilt.

Who was she really, though? Mocking her by remembering the version that suited me best held no love or honor. She was strong in life, and surely would laugh hideously at my weakened state. She would have nodded with that haunting nod, then "Do it, lover." Wherever she was, she had no need for my indecision.

Yes, this is how I got here. Where I speak to you now.

Telling them I accepted made them smile—sluggy, melted smiles—and when they told me the wages I almost danced on the ceiling. I wasn't going to rival the vaults of the ruling, but by my quick arithmetic, in a year I would be able to enroll at the Institute.

The former mortician was gone in no time. The first few days were shadowing the two waddling managers. My workspace was the morgue itself, vast and set back from the street. Inside, its walls made a stone honeycomb that contained bodies in all sizes and conditions. At its center, where I'd spend most of my time, was the table.

Above my station, the domed ceiling was a cap of painted glass. Hilarious in its irony, it depicted the poor and pious being whisked away by serene carriers to some orange and golden field. Waiting for them, Tersiona sat in a throne of wheat, surrounded by Ansul and a ring of lesser figures. By day, the ceiling provided a glowing vale of sunlight, and on the nights I chose not to go home, church icons holding books and teapots glared down on my solitude.

Following a downhill path, my designated cart was to be led to an iron door on the northern edge of the cemetery, an edge well known to me. This door was much like a cellar hatch, bolted on a granite frame leading to the Pauper Vault. The dead poor were dropped to reside forever with carrion, foulness, and things that scampered from the light. Even for me, the stench that belched up from that darkness didn't only offend the nostrils, but clawed at the skin and smothered.

Continuing downhill were the graves for those buried with just enough money to avoid the filling pit. And there was Somyellia.

At the end of my first day, I went down to see her. I sat at her graveside and stared across the sea of weathered stone teeth. Across the vast distance, through the gleaming spires of Laugher's Lot, I could make out our abandoned house, a speck that was once our grandest meeting place.

Pain exposes itself when it chooses to, and as most harden with the passing years it becomes an indistinguishable part of life. I leaned against her brand new stone and wept. It's like Vandahl wrote: *"Life is but wild flowers in the graveyard."*

A void in me was undeniably ripped open after Somyellia left. Perhaps that is why I fell into my work so. I enjoyed the sweating from the lifting, all legal for the first time.

It became a routine: inspect the day's load, tend the horse assigned to the morgue, attach her to the cart, throw a body on the table, report, hoist it into said cart, repeat. The short report was more gratifying than any bundle of obscure notes I'd made on my own. Cause of death—best guess sufficed, physical description, name (if known), a few other details, and then on to the next.

My bosses, I came to find out, were Qells; a once magnificent house that had long rotted away from lordship. They were pleased by my performance. So much so, in fact, that after only a month they never stepped foot in the morgue again. Their time was better spent in the front office, delving into the keepsakes of freshly brought bodies, dealings with cutthroats, and occasionally supporting the coup of some ambitious rising figure.

Though Snier and Somyellia were gone, I remained in my studio, or I should say my possessions did. The Pauper Morgue became my real home—as the commoners who pass out bread rather than the blade say, "It's where the heart lies." Sleeping on a mat of blankets in a favored corner, book in hand, and well-fed from lamplight was my only joy. Street murmurs crawled back to me that, not long after taking employment, an attentive group of urchins took me for evicted or dead. I laugh at the thought of them burgling only to run headlong into my ferine collections.

Some bodies at the morgue needed dissection to root out cause of death. In no time, I bore witness to the many malfunctions of our vulnerable flesh. Diseases that attached to organs, fiercely and without remorse, always made me miss her something awful.

The few bodies that were to accompany tombstones I'd separate early. Piling them like a stack of fingered and footed firewood reminded me a lot of Belot's place. Once filled, the cart would go to the mass grave and I'd play the game of trying to drop them in ways that would achieve the greatest cracks and thuds. Most memorable, I once invoked a peculiar squeal, after which I softly closed the door and backed away.

My bosses relished the tight-lipped approach. I was met with freedom, more coin, and ample food. My predecessor, I imagined, must have expressed some grievance with their dealings, and I wondered what hill of bones in that subterranean pit he occupied.

In time, I surmised they thought I killed Somyellia. In addition to being tolerant of murder, with my literary skills and build, they figured me the perfect subordinate. I never confirmed this, but a mind educated by both scholars and the streets cuts through inanity like a robber's knife.

Much like a child enamored in summer, I lost track of time. Weeks became months, and those too seemed to fly by with the wave of dead that gave me my livelihood.

You would have thought Nilghorde would have been desolate in a mere season. No matter the ebb and flow, the city remained as bustling and lively as ever. The occasional stroll to my studio would take me up Red Wolf, examining the living with new eyes. "I wonder when I'll be seeing you?" I'd sometimes say, a couple of times too loud.

My so-called experiments ceased entirely. Dreams of becoming a doctor were barely an afterthought. A bill on a dusty shelf.

Though dead, Somyellia had not left my heart nor my habits. Nights I would wake to see her gliding from a darkened corner of the morgue. It ended as soon as my mind took the step out of the world of dream and into the forever disappointing world we temporarily occupy. It exposed life's pallid and stagnant nature, a few punishing seasons of hot and cold. These visions were only a phase, possibly due to another phase of mine, one in which a young womanly corpse would be examined for far too long, though never treated to the carnal activities that had closed my one and only love.

My existence had met a livable rhythm. I'd never expected, or wanted, the sun-soaked slogging of many who claim to live the good life. I knew from an early age I was meant to dwell in other passions. I had money for the few things that interested me. I fought a small war with opium and won, resulting in an additional layer of meat on my hide. I read endlessly, making sure to visit libraries and vendors of the book and scroll. The dead had befriended me, and while sitting among the morgue's more comfortable nooks I often fell asleep leaned against their silent company.

On the anniversary of Somyellia's death, I abandoned my duties to sit beside her grave. The bouquet of roses and lilies I had laid were for the day. The wreath of coiled Orphedilias, for the coming night.

Staring at her stone, some lettered grooves had been corrupted by a year's mold. As I scraped the mold with my fingernails, I remembered. It's funny how the bereaved mind rushes back to the last time we've seen the dead when they were not. I was certainly no exception.

✳

Purpose tends to be a cruel morning, waking you sudden and thorough. My dour harmony, my focused aloneness, was to be disrupted once more, and once more it would come out of nowhere, as is its preference.

One day, we had a delivery. A giant man, killed by some disease, lay on my table bloated and blue. Normally I would have commenced to working, and the larger than normal corpse would have been in the cart and ready for transport.

But I walked around the table in the same fashion that I had done with Somyellia back on Red Wolf. This cold mound looked familiar, causing me without effort to mumble near-forgotten words.

Tension filled the room, was the room, making home places saved for the cobwebs and rodents grown fat on my forgetting to close the back door.

I knew who this reminded me of, with deathly certainty. I hadn't thought about him in ages, and he had been as dead to me as the inhabitants of the mass grave.

For a moment I wondered if it was him. But I was looking down on flabby jowls on top of a weak chin. His hair had been the same color, but coarse and curled. Just to be sure, and with some effort, I rolled the corpse onto his side. No, no giant scar on his back.

I had completely forgotten about it until using it as an identifier. My father had a deep swathe between his shoulders from a battle in the first campaign he'd ever embarked on.

He'd told of the ambushing Pelats and their crude, bony weapons. How they had skewered his horse and overwhelmed him. How he had one pinned to the ground, and how a moment before the fatal strike a sneaky Pelats opened up his back in the vain attempt to save his fellow savage.

Surviving the ordeal with a fresh trophy of tongues and charms, a field hospital repaired Father's back, and adorning citations followed in his recovery.

It may have been the thick neck, or some indescribable similarity, but I couldn't shake what I began to feel. An idea germinated in me, powerful and driven. Closure, something I had never known. It began to squeak and plea from the core of my being.

The rest of the day was spent in a hurried discontent.

After days of research in a back room at the Nilghorde Hall of Records, I learned that he was indeed still alive. He must have had squandered his war spoils. The house in Templeton had been sold long ago. Shoeing for a Ward substation, and likely led with a rabid taste for Black Monk, he took up residence in a small loft off Iron Belfry Boulevard. There, most roads and weaving allies remained nameless, and the view cast on a once thriving populace that hadn't progressed in the better part of a century.

When I took my covert observations on foot, for a fleeting moment I saw, silhouetted by firelight, a large figure limp past a window. Cloaked in a black hood, I moved like a rat. The few Metropolitan Ward who trotted by were oblivious. But I wanted to be sure my efforts would not be thwarted. I needed perfect concealment, and a moonless night was soon to arrive.

Then it came. Midafternoon in my mortician's cart, after a brief stop inside a blacksmith's, my horse and I rested under the massive Gahlerrion Bridge. Flowing under the bridge was the Moliahenna, or *Black Tongue*, cutting deep and swift through the heart of Nilghorde and spilling into the sea. At its shores, parked under an abutment, I watched the sunset and scowled at approaching beggars.

After the sun had completely died and the cold winds began, I reentered the streets. The clopping of the hooves and random squeaks of cart wheels echoed against the bricks of homes and shops. For some reason they all sounded too loud. Irksomely loud even. The glare of a Wardsmen and sideways glances from passing carriages sunk me in my seat. Eventually I passed under the Do-Gooder's Row statues, and began ascending narrow cobblestone.

If there had been a moon, around when it would have been at its zenith I crept the cart into the correct alley and cached it behind a withered hedge.

Hugging the veranda wall and unsheathing my knife, the time had come.

I was no Snier, but the poor man's lock before me was no match for the blade that wormed its way between iron and wood. When I felt the click and pressure release, I opened the door, painfully slow.

From what I had gathered, the bed was upstairs, and in his aged state it was reasonable to wager he'd be asleep. Although moonless, and candles out, I could see quite well. Maybe years spent in dark cellars or matching places had rendered me a brother to the night or the creatures therein. I was staring at a familiar parlor, though it felt a lifetime ago.

To my immediate right was the fanning display of sabers. Next to them, medals from the Far East, Pelat, and the massacres of Serabandantilith. To my left was a table in front of the very leather furnishings I'd once spilt milk on. My eyes passed closed doors to strain the exact shapes of stairs.

The distance between the front door and this stairwell was soon over taken. The muscles in my heart raced.

I had practiced on a particularly warped section of planks in the Pauper Morgue's office. Placing the tip of my boot on the first step, I pressed my weight onto the wood until assured I could plant myself without a crack or noise. Slowly, with a concentrated dexterity unfound in large bodies, I continued this method until I came to a turn in the stairwell. An arm's length more, a turn to the right, and I would be facing the final steps leading up to the bedroom.

Cough!

I nearly jumped out of my skin.

He had to be withered with age, battle wounds, and the heavy weight of the bottle. Moreover, I was no boy and had faced younger, more able men in the alleys of Nilghorde many times over. No matter how much one changes, I suppose, we'll never forget some things, and I came to this realization as I began the first of the last steps. My whole life as a man, I hadn't so much as considered him. Now I was in his home, knife in hand. I made the final climb.

He was asleep under the window. To my right, his dwindled fire still gave off enough light to expose how thoroughly his hair had grayed. The bedroom itself was a mess of chests and bottles. Preparing to wade through, I put away my knife and grabbed what I'd bought from the blacksmith. It was a special occasion, and, after all, I was a poet at heart. I pulled a farrier hammer out from underneath my cloak, then I stepped forward.

Without fail, a board moaned under my boot.

"In the doorway a figure in black, unknown to you, has come to claim you, old man. I have become strong. The menace is upon you. From the crumbling edges of life I have come for you. You taught me to never shut my eyes. You taught me discipline."

When I struck, Father flapped and batted at thin air. Above his eyes, blood escaped, violent and free. His hand gripped wildly for a weapon that wasn't there.

After a long while, after all the twitching had stopped and I dared to breathe, I opened the window. Like the nameless falling into the Pauper Vault, I dropped him out and refastened its locks. Walking down the stairs, I kept hearing Somyellia: "My beast, look at what you have done." Over and over, finally trailing off with that haunting laugh that could blot out life or breathe it in.

There was one more stop to make, and I needed to get the body prepared. The blanket, now wrapping Father, wasn't the only thing I had packed away. Once my preferred cove was found, I parked the cart and unpacked my cleavers.

In almost complete darkness, I dismantled Father and collected his parts into jars that I'd already labeled.

The scraps were stuffed down a drainage culvert, a feast for the rats I could hear gathering. In less than an hour, I had all the valuables packaged and ready.

Deep into the tiny-eyed hours of night I arrived at one of the reception doors at the Institute of Human Sciences. The groomed gentlemen peering out the viewing port refused to open the door. Holding up a freshly plucked liver, however, turned them around. I had pocketed a few coins this way before, but withered organs and mummified limbs were no longer in demand. Here I had fresh materials. The cart emptied as my purse filled. I called it justified compensation.

By early morning I was back at the Pauper Morgue. After the follow-on tasks were finished, I sprawled out on the floor to finger through the enrollment application the query-eyed doorman had handed me upon request.

At some point I fell asleep. There I dreamed of many things. When I finally woke, all I could recall was a thunderous storm, met with the charge of some unnamable legion.

Soon after, I applied to the Institute. With a successful attempt at their elect entry exam, much to the chagrin of my bosses, I resigned from my position at the morgue.

I signed up for the monastic dormitories and made its space home as best I could. It was strange I was told that I couldn't decorate the walls and shelves with my old tastes, considering where I was, and how it had always served as such esteemed motivation.

The scholarly swarm was quite younger than me, and during orientation I caught the ample look-aways from pubescent faces. Days at the Institute were long and tedious, overflowing with assignments and sapped inkwells far into the night.

Vast does not describe the vaults and exhibits that made the interior. Libraries towered up to ceilings so high their elaborate mosaics were but mere smudges of light and dark when viewed from the ground. There were the fabled viewing cages too. And, if you wanted to venture from the main arteries, you could easily lose yourself in the dungeon-like bleakness, where polished stairs became old wood and peculiar echoes.

The student body rivaled the Institute's vastness so that even I could sometimes get lost in the fray. To my shock, some students were hesitant to handle the muck and piping of our being. That was no issue with my studies, and I enjoyed anatomy class over the more daunting core requirements that left my head a scrambled bowl of confusion.

Dreams are a strange thing. Standing too close to the street performer may often lead one to see the flaws in his act and the streaks in his makeup.

I was passing the courses, though some with great struggle. But I noticed that I never read poetry anymore. My collection of works sat dusty and unused in a corner above all my research papers, scribbled in haste to make punitive deadlines. My muscles ached from inaction, and collapsing into a chair became a ritual after classes. Slowly I began to see my peers as spiritless larvae rather than prestigious scholars.

After a semester, it was clear my life was not in the clean walls of the Institute, or among the kind that never had to fight for their plate. I dropped out shortly after marks were posted. I was tired of feeling sucked dry and hung up in some closet apart from the world. I left numb. Nothing that was shown to me could raise the hairs on my neck or streak wide a smile across my face any longer.

Except for one.

In route from my dorm to my composition class, I would cut through the exhibits. In the Wing of Trauma, displaying hundreds of examples of life's hard edges, I walked past a familiar skull with a hole in its frontal plate.

I returned to the Pauper Morgue, where my return was met with great rejoice. They doubled my old salary, killed my replacement, and with a warm broth escorted me back to my old station, where, aside from a fresh batch of run-through workers who'd proved unsatisfactory to the House of Rogaire, laid many a fair corpse, nude and uninspected.

Such things, so beautiful yet so dead, went to their final resting places uncaressed. The post-mortem with Somyellia would remain unique. Call it loyalty, perhaps.

VIII
SNIER'S TALE

My name is Tymothus Snier. At least that is the name scribbled on the paperwork at the orphanage where I spent my childhood. I never knew my parents and have honestly given it little thought. A whore and a priest, an actress and a soldier; it all makes little difference to my plight. Having always been on my own, unknowable parents did little but cloud the mind.

The books that I dusted and rearranged had to be worth something. They better—fair compensation for suffering the House of Rogaire, and, in what was a growing likelihood in some peculiar way, the House of Ordrid too. The sand in the hour glass was running low. I was about the fuck out of this place. Things were always weird in the Rogaire mansion, but had recently gotten the kind of weird that brings with it screaming and pain.

The books: all that remained was finding an interested and well-funded collector. Verdigris-stained spines could be wiped clean, and with a little buffering, the leather covers could be restored back to their pre-Years of Peace glory.

Although the library was vast, its lack of occupancy was as if its towering double doors were seen by my eyes alone. But the volumes were just the beginning. Treasures hid in unlit rooms and behind cobweb draperies. A stout ladder would able me to chisel out ornate tiles covering the dome ceilings, and just a few of the paintings neglected in the great hall would feed a frugal mouth for years. In a mansion this size, the possibility of finding jewels, heirlooms garnished in guarded drawers, and glorious hidden vaults was worthy of a most thorough reconnaissance.

I hadn't always posed as a butler. I'd been a rent-boy. I'd waded foulness itself having briefly been a grave robber. But, I was always meant to be a burglar. There are essentially two challenges in my current profession. The first: acquisition of a worthwhile target. Worthwhile doesn't always mean the score.

I—

—wait, let me go at this from a slightly different angle.

Everybody squawks on about Do-Gooder's Row—its monstrous white inhabitants and what have you. If you are weary of hearing about them, I assure you your weariness pales in comparison to my own. But perhaps for different reasons. It seems I'm of the select few to take notice, but doers like Zaderyn the Poor Swimmer are in desperate short supply when it comes to finding heroes of the people in this vile city. While the Zaderyns populated the first few columns, the deeds and doers diminish as an admirer heads east, ending at the feet of heroes like the vigilante citizen who reported his overly masturbating neighbor to the nearest Chapwyn temple.

I reckon if you're around a Rehleian long enough you'll hear a peasant's calendar based off when this statue was being carved a necklace or that statue began showing its gauntlets. But perhaps I am no different—a Rehleian after all, and even a Nilghordian, though I admit that last part with the utmost reluctance. So you will have to pardon my provincial ways. It really is the best way moving forward, and, besides, not all of us were born and bred in Pelliul.

With this in mind, during a stint in the Rat's Nest, I shared straw with a couple of thieves. The Do-Gooder statues were all chiseled down to the knees; three-quarters built if you were fortunate enough to study mathematics. We were talking about target acquisition, and those two told me a tale that had with it an unorthodox but long-lasting moral.

At the time, I was rather preoccupied by my draconian arrest. How is it that the more laws made for the greater good, the greater the prisons swell? These two fops—their comical arguing and tragic story captured my interest.

Apparently they'd staked out what they thought was an appraisal loft. Under an assumption that the lavishly garbed old man was the owner, one night they made their entry. Much to their misfortune, the old man was guarded by a colossal dog. To add to their dilemma, the Metropolitan Ward was at the doorstep in a time unseen before by either crook. Naturally, once in the Ward's custody they received a volley of new bumps and bruises. Worst yet, they broke into a loft that wasn't meant to appraise coin and old silverware.

Any committed burglar would suffer a vicious dog to score a worthy prize, but as they took turns being mauled, they noticed no hanging scales or appraisal-loft displays of any kind. The poor fools—out-of-work botanists the moment our land cracked down on a growing list of herbs said to degrade the fiber of the working class—had broken into a bungalow of a Scepter, and the valuables they saw being carried in were gifts to congratulate him on his landslide victory over his mysteriously vanished competitor. In numerous portraits, their would-be victim loomed over them imperiously, or so they described when not choking one another.

Paying attention to the happenings of the city, getting in tune with Nilghorde's heartbeat, led to future successes. Failing to do so led to gallows and grain ships. When I confirmed who the old man was, reality washed over them. That was the reason why the

Ward had made it in record time—hell, for all we know, homing pigeons fly to their stations when men of monetary or political importance are in distress.

As I have said, the statues at Do-Gooder's Row back in those days were three-quarters built, which meant the Conqueror's macho quest, over somewhere closer to twenty. Once he'd declared peace in Rehleia, he was, and is, henceforth called The Municipal One.

The Municipal One brought about such wonderful things as new roads, new heroes, and a sea of graves as the goodhearted had a chicken in every pot. With all this came the new laws. Burglary soon came with a life sentence—said to serve as a deterrent, but around the Municipal Dungeon's twelfth or fifteenth grant for another sub-level, the deterrent speeches ceased in the public square. The two who loped into one of the many homes owned by a man such as Scepter Macudden…well, they didn't face a life sentence. They faced what was reserved for unrepentant blasphemers, murderers of the rich, and the rarity: a convicted necromancer.

I try to look for the good in all things. I was eventually released from prison, and in their story learned the valuable lesson of due diligence.

The second challenge of any burglary is dealing with the residents of the target itself. In the case of the Rogaire mansion, I had figured that out like the cleverest street performer. It had been years since I retired from duping spent clients or cleaning out their hotels. I found through careful study that homes were the most lucrative risk to take. The exhilarating joy of standing in an unoccupied dwelling surrounded by the fruits of your soon-to-be labor is mouthwatering. Besides, escalation is the sign of improvement.

I'd been staking out the Rogaire mansion for close to a year. I know you wonder: why wait so long? Why not just get the goods and scamper off? Many would follow your instincts, and there was a time I did as well. That jumpy impatience, however, only results in a minimal score—and, after all, it's the score we all do it for. I shiver at the thought of the money I left in unsearched nooks, mattresses unslit, and rooms behind mirrors. I reckon if I had the patience then that I have now, I would be long retired. Maybe buy a flock of young Suelan boys and live out my days in Pelliul, attending reenactments and theater.

Regardless, I had just about reconnoitered that behemoth place, more a small castle than a mansion. Still, there were locked doors and inconsistencies under floor planks yet to be pried. I had solved almost every riddle, save for the location of a few keys and a peculiar noise I'd regularly hear coming from outside my bedroom window. Besides, despite the high number of reasons that would make any sane person wish to leave, I wasn't leaving until I knew where the vault was, how to get in, and how to gallop off in un-pursued glee.

The denizens of that dreary house were as familiar with my face as they were the gargoyles that stare down from the cornice. It is impossible to repress a smile. Every day getting dressed in the mirror, fixing my bow tie and sash. I am not a big man, lean with shoulders that insist on a mild slouch. My hair, forever blond, now combed over a nagging bald spot. Yet despite such a modest frame and a face referred to as "birdish," I possess the bluest eyes in all Mulgara. Vain? Well, Dear Heart, in two of my careers it was a sad dog that didn't wag its own tail, or know when it could sleep next to the fireplace rather than in a gutter.

Dressed for duty, I tightened white gloves over learned hands and proceeded from my chambers.

"Tymothus, bring us the rabbit," Morlia said, sighing into the hand propping up her chin. Her breath fogged a jewel on her brooch the size of a ripe plum. "The venison has a salty flair."

"Yes, Mum." I went back, past her lounging armored goons, through the steam, and fetched the rabbits from anticipating cooks. By now our calendars revolved around the Big Three: Maecidion having been dead a decade, the one day a year the Lady approved of dinner, and the completion of Do-Gooder's Row. Yes, the dearest latter was only a widely rumored two weeks from being finished. I believe the final brilliance to extract from the marble were the bootless toes of some beggar who'd fallen into a puddle right before a Lotgard or Ouvarnian cart had to cake its polished wheels in Nilghordian street mud. As was the standard, the rabbits were in an array of poses, some caught in flight while others in cartoonish gestures of nobility.

For the life of me, I couldn't understand why that family insisted on using trenchers. They had the money to fund the forging of a hundred golden dinner plates without a care. It must have been the late Rinlot's doing, the former master of this ill place. He had been of the southern green hills. An Oxghordian. Those southern voices, with that hilarious booming accent, a continuous melodic blend of aristocracy and farmhand idiot. No matter how long ago a group relocated to the city, they maintained several imperishable southern traditions. He'd been a hunk of a man, the warden of the Municipal Dungeon. As large as a pit fighter, he embraced a regal masculinity in contrast to his rather simple mind.

The lady of the house, Morlia Rogaire—well, I can't recall the maiden name of that redheaded, bejeweled harpy—her family came from the quarter on the shores of the Thunder Bustle and was probably forgotten by her own decree. How those two ever met and married was the grandest of juxtapositions.

He was the one who filled their hidden vaults—wherever those infernal things were. The formidable and overpaid position of Warden didn't explain the wealth. I've seen crazier things in these lands. Although jewels jangled at the bottom of their pockets, they'd never been fully accepted by the Nilghorde elite. The few Ouvarnias who lived in Nilghorde barely acknowledged their existence, and the Lotgards had only invited them to one party.

She, on the other hand, was from the cannibal streets. She still wore her hair tied up for quick bathing and still wore her makeup with the gaudiness of an aging prostitute. A whore, that's my best guess anyway, and it would fit all the better that she sensed an opportunity to capitalize on male dimwittedness.

Once draped in the excesses of wealth, you'd have thought Morlia was an empress from some far-off land. Her knack for barking orders and her eternal dissatisfaction with everything led to miserable dinners and crucified slaves. Rinlot had been a southern boy turned middle-aged man, still hazardously trusting and gregarious. Her eyes carried a keen maliciousness, and her intentions seemed to mimic my own. Yes, she had to have been a prostitute; her cunning business approach to the prize of emerald-covered templets and ruby brooches was, in my best mood, admirable.

With Rinlot now dead, the mansion had only three residents. One was Morlia. Another was her and Rinlot's only child, that damned boy Rinmor, or as Morlia insisted for some blasted reason, "Morden." As spoiled as the meat that miraculously always found only the plate of the Lady; his incessant pranks were only dwarfed by his odd behavior. When not trying to trip me with string, I found him staring for hours at the moon.

Last and least, through some intertwining of two family tree's most low-hanging and moss-ridden branches, a cousin of Rinlot's crawled onto their steps years before I took employment and, to my humor, never left.

Werlyle Rogaire-Qell was a humble sight, even for a Qell. I recall from boarding school dreary parchments about their House.

Nearly a century had passed since the feud between the House of Qell and the House of Ouvarnia. The regal horse masters massacred the House of Qell, sending them scampering to every corner and down every hole in Rehleia. Most now huffed swamp air with the Rehtons down in Amden. A prolific drunk, only his high forehead resembled anything of his much fairer cousin, on the whole short and stubby and prone to a downward gaze. If he was indicative of the rest, I can at best give them credit for even mustering the gall to challenge anyone in armed conflict.

Werlyle's presence was like an indomitable itch under Morlia's girdle. Since Rinlot was no more, showering Werlyle with insults, often in front of company, had no response other than a few curses and spittle. Half in a bottle of Bleeding Anna most nights, his retorts while head down on the dining room table were their own lessons in hilarity. It took every fiber of my being to avoid dropping the tray of exotic slugs when he went into a slurred sonnet. Cobwebs on the chandelier was all the symbolism he required. That and twiddling his nubby finger at her, yelling "loins," and flicking his tongue at the guests who nearly fainted.

"Ah, this should do," Morlia said, as I presented the first batch of posing rabbits. The dinner guests were Morlia's usual entourage, a faceless lot of acquaintances with names I never bothered to remember. "Is there any of that wine left? What was the name of that one? Not that sickly brand from Quinnari; those people truly have no taste for such things."

"Yes, Mum, believe we ha—"

"I remember. That wine we had when—"

She continued her ramble as I thought out the night's rummaging. There was a room in the East Wing whose lock was giving me some real trouble. If the opportunity presented itself, I'd get into her master bedroom. That meant keys. Keys meant vaults. Vaults meant—

Maybe the bitch would pass out from the Grest she was

presently going on about. Better yet, one of those sycophants would bed her down in a corner for a few hours.

"Good butler, go find a bottle or two."

"Yes, Mum." I made my way to the wine cellar, chuckling as I heard the predictable foulness from Morlia to Werlyle, whom last I saw devouring his plate at the far end of the table.

When I returned with a bottle of Grest on a silver platter, both worth more than many denizens of Nilghorde made in a year, the fight was in full swing.

"—Leave me alone, you old bat."

"Old bat! That's what you call the woman gracious enough to allow you to stay in her home? You do nothing for us, unless you consider tugging your pecker a chore."

Some of the newer guests smiled through their discomfort, while those who'd grown accustomed to the exchange—perhaps even came to the dinners because of it—laughed loud and chimed in louder.

"No really, *cousin*," she insisted, "what do you do all day?" To her nearest cheering section, "You see what I have to deal with here? Wer-lie-all, such a prole name."

"Same as you, sit on my ass and squander someone else's fortune."

"He really is a boorish type," a man dressed like a poet said.

"You know what Rinlot said about you?" Morlia said.

"Leave me alone, bitch. You can entertain these opium heads and cocksuckers with a trip on your broom."

"Is something funny, butler?"

"No, Mum." I snapped to, like a soldier.

"I didn't think so," Morlia said. "I didn't think so because I know you are aware of the stakes in the outer bailey…and their purpose."

That damned Werlyle was going to get me killed. I had to find a reason to excuse myself, and quick. To my good fortune, Werlyle stunned us all.

"I doubt Rinlot had a chance to tell you much of anything," shoveling in his meal, "seein' as you killed him and all."

An air of silence became palpable, thick, ending when forks clattered as guests excused themselves.

I suppose I have gone into a good deal about the others in this tale, but perhaps too little about myself. You must excuse me, I am one who looks toward the future voraciously and views the past as burned leaves. Yes, but you are right, sometimes it is necessary to delve into the past. Not to paint the past in gold or fondle one's self with nostalgia, of course not, but rather to make understandable things that are not always apparent—in this case, the alleged interplay between Rinlot and the House of Ordrid, the unalleged interplay between Rinlot and me, and how I came to this wretched mansion.

As I have mentioned, I was an orphan. The orphanage I spent my early years in changed names so many times I've forgotten what to remember it by. Names mean and do little. You may not remember the name of someone or something, but you'll most certainly remember the contents of your interactions. The staff came and went in an ugly merry-go-round of snarls and abuse. A safe haven for just about every form of human depravity, it was also an academy for finding the vulnerable parts of the human body. When not being whipped by the disciplinarians, you had to contend with the older, stronger boys. I learned quickly the frailty of knees when engaged from the right angle, and the sensitivity of eyes when met with a twig.

No birthdays stick out, save one. The fog of early childhood memories unglue themselves. In the spaces between them are swish-swashes of disciplinarians disappearing to fight in the last stages of the wars in Rehleia, and armless and legless veterans hobbling in to replace them. Then came my seventh birthday, clear as summer. The Suelan cooks made me a muffin, shaped like a star with a little yellow candle.

Some of the other boys found it an atrocity they hadn't received a star muffin. After being pinned down, I watched the leader among them, already as big then as your average dockman, stroll up and devour my present.

I got to keep the candle, which I jammed in the eye of the boy who had held down my arm just a moment before. If you push hard enough and hold in place, you can feel a squish followed by a nauseating give. It became a specialty of mine, you could say.

This boy flailed on the ground next to me as the disciplinarians broke through the ring. A man that looked like a shaved carnival ape, known for his heavy-handedness, barreled through, a closing wake of silent children behind him.

I was sent to the cellar, and after his trip to the infirmary the other boy joined me. We were stripped of our clothing and had our hands bound above our heads. For what must have been hours we both just stood there on our toes like pigs at the butcher. He was sobbing into his bandage while I tried to free my hands from the binding leather. With no signs of success, I stopped my squirming as we heard the eminent footsteps echoing down the stairwell. The other boy must have already experienced the cellar. His fidgeting was only outdone by his pitiful squeaks.

I am a man who has never enjoyed coupling with a woman. Mutual exploration of inner folds is exhilarating. But after the whippings and before the march through the bay of eldest boys, I experienced for the first time by sheer agony what would later be an avid joy.

Slavers would come too. They'd pick the stoutest, giving us the added chore of balancing nutrition for self-defense and appearing just sickly enough to avoid being sold to a waiting oar-chain. The same boy who ate my star muffin left us wailing out from the iron bars of a carriage. I gave him a flouting wave, but I'd wager his tears prevented the full fruition of my passive-aggression.

Making it to adulthood and being released was a dim far light. Many ran away. It was my good sense that knew a runaway would just as easily suffer the fates on the streets that they fled from at the orphanage. This kept me there, but nothing else.

Several years later, a well-dressed man roostered in. He swung a cane and was outfitted like he'd just walked off a stage. All of us who were nearing manhood were lined up. He strolled up and down the file until at last coming to me. Clicking his heels when he halted, he inspected me from head to toe.

The boys in the line by that time had forged mighty friendships. It was our turn to exploit the dirt-faced youngsters and run amok throughout. I'll always remember those dearest friends, our savage rise and survival, the secret meetings followed by carnal expedition.

The Lord bought me. Lord Stanifer Voss, was of moderate wealth, but was so embedded in the spectrum of Pelliul exuberance that to many he was as envied as a king.

As he and I made our way in his carriage to Pelliul, I looked back at the frowning monster that had kept me swallowed for so long; I turned my head and uttered an oath.

With polished white woods adorned by golden leaves and seats of red velvet, his carriage was the most beautiful thing I had ever seen. Lord Voss loved my blue eyes. He told me many times. He loved much about me, in fact, and drawing the curtains he showed me the expectations of our arrangement. Although young, I think my developing zest for the endeavor surprised him. Or maybe he already knew.

No, acquiring another lover was not the reason that he had bought me, though it certainly became a perk.

Lord Voss was the quintessential Pelliuli. Arrayed in a dapper style, befitting the more welcoming climate, he would walk into an outhouse as if presenting the commode with an illustrious bequest. Pelliul, known for its festive and extravagant glow lamps, was a buzzing nest of artists, thespians, and narcissists. City of Lights, the lamps hung in every color. The place was not without its Nilghordesque features, of course. A throng of fighting pits, a locust plague of drug users, and the thunderous clamor of the Metropolitan Ward reminded any tourist that it was only part fairyland.

Lord Voss was in the business of entertaining the entertainment. In his gardens, what I would have called fields, he had a healthy stock of opium poppy. Those plants were permitted then as they are permitted now. Their special position in Chapwyn churches passes the law books, but most Scepters owning vast fields of it when The Municipal One and Maecidion penned their arrangements didn't hurt either.

More than the drugs, Lord Voss ran a professional catering service that was at every elite gallery or sold-out play. Most auspiciously, he ran a flock of rent-boys. That was where I fit in. And the stable of young men, under the grooming eye of Lord Voss, was no inane, filth-laden bevy, mind you. Plucked from orphanages throughout our province, he ran the tightest operation in the city and expelled a hefty sum of money toward our development.

At the orphanage, I was taught the basics in reading and writing. I guess literate slaves are worth more than drooling ones, and the headmaster had to do something with all that time on his hands. Regardless, I am grateful I left there with these tools, because after my purchase I was soon sent to a private boarding school. There I was molded into a makeshift gentleman, versed in etiquette, dancing, literature, and other arenas that had nothing to do with my mindless and naked chore. During my year there, I learned all that I know now about the Rehleian province, its families, loud whispers, and legalities therein.

It was also there where I learned of my greatest passion. Under the oblivious eye of instructors too busy recounting the stacks of tuition, I looted the place of all that could be buried and dug up later.

Upon returning to the Voss estate, I was immediately put to work. As you may imagine, I didn't mind the job. You may or may not be amazed at the different types of clients a rent-boy of value attracts. Politicians, droves of actors, and the occasional insatiable couple would render a chalice of flowing coin.

What a great financial opportunity too. Greed: the mere over-indulgence of self-interest. You may call me greedy and I will nod. When I started adding opium to my routine, the floundering orgy turned snoring nudists allowed for the greatest hauls.

I have mentioned the Municipal Dungeon, but theft was not the charge that landed me my first stay.

One morning, I was sunning myself at one of Voss's fountains when he approached me. He advised that I was to be taking a trip. We'd never done this before. The money had to be worth the hassle. Given the address, I was told nothing more than "be flexible." But how many possible meanings could that have in my line of work?

A carnival was wheeling out to Nilghorde that very day. It had been many years, but whatever it was that engulfed me in the back of one of those wagons took me quite a bit of talking to calm myself. Cold swished in my gut when we climbed a small hill, and Nilghorde's jagged fangs shot upward. A haze of smoke hid the summits, and in its grayness I saw what I'd climbed out of. The city smiled a sickness as I confirmed how bad I wanted to turn around. I knew I was *home* when I smelled the sea.

Wanting to accomplish my task without delay, I utilized a bath house and donned my attire. I'd forgotten how aesthetic Nilghorde was not. Back in Pelliul a young man in lavender jingling ornamental flare was as common as the scurrying rodents and cold stares that met me here.

I dodged one heckling clerk, two thugs, three snarling dogs, and a pack of good citizenry nailing fliers before running face-first into the gold-plated chest of a stout Chapwyn priest.

"Those carried by the winds of the flesh," the priest said, "are apteth for collision with more grounded things."

Sitting in the dust and dirt of the street and with my head swirling, I gathered my wits. For one agonizing semester I'd parsed the local religions. Some of the higher shelves in those orders were on Lord Voss's elite list. Of all their screeds and parables, a Chapwyn verse I was particularly fond of, from the same tome this looming clergyman had just spit down on me, had once been inked on a ribbon of parchment I used to unroll in moments of sizzling inspiration: *The rich man needeth not his golden foibles.*

But one I hadn't even realized I'd retained came out of my mouth as the flier-nailers gathered around the priest. "He who useth the Holy Word to mocketh the fallen be both a fool and a brigand."

The crowd spilled from the sides of the holy man and all but flanked me. A calloused hand, though I know not from whom, stopped me from rising. I couldn't help but postulate the sectarian nature of the fliers; some already ripped down the alleys, flapping in the wind. This was the peasantry, the loyal to good order, and some rebel using a priest's divinely inspired words against him was fuel for the burning stakes. A man in rags exposed the first half of a sword.

The priest's ring-laden hand halted the blade. "Offer thoust a tithing," he spoke, leaving a few of his plump fingers on his minion's scabbard. "From thee sinful wages, and be graciously spared thy just steel." The crowd nodded. Some mouthed the words.

Whatever was to come first—negotiations or the unleashing of the mob—was shattered by the Ward. Shooting through the crowd, spinning the priest, and toppling over men and woman alike, a boy emerged from nowhere and ran down the street. The Ward was right after him, a thundering blur of silver and blue, flattening the ragged man and sending his sword chittering over the cobblestones before breaking under pursuing hooves. The filthy youth dropped a loaf of stolen bread and scrambled over the nearest wall.

The gods weave openings in mystery, or so I believed the verse to go. I was on my feet and flying. Soon I was inside the Morgeltine District without a mugging or another near call with dismemberment.

The Morgeltine is the wealthiest district. The Rogaire mansion sits there, although at the farthest eastern sliver and butting up to a dark thicket. A bit of snooping shows the property is considered part of the Morgeltine by jurisdiction alone, and the mansion loomed on the crumbling edge of one of Nilghorde's original boundaries.

The Morgeltine's estates serve as a grand and shimmering moat, one encircling the keep of the Conqueror himself, or The Municipal One if you're the staying-in type. No place in Nilghorde parallels such wealth, and I knew my company for the night was likely to be a man of unquestionable prominence.

I have done so many house calls that I truly forget the mundane trivialities upon meeting at the doorstep. Also, I will spare you and myself from the details leading up to my arrest.

I never had contention with the woman's role; in fact, I made a living out of it. What I didn't predict was literally being ordered to dress up as one. In his bitter drunkenness this land owner, or banker, or Supreme Magistrate spit directives at me like I was one of his slaves. You gain experience, dealing with problem customers, so I tried to calm him and sway the happenings to a more controllable end. He'd have none of it. When I refused to put on the dress for a second time, a showering of threats followed.

Soon the Ward had me in custody. I assumed he pulled one aside and slipped him some gold, fabricated a story to incriminate me, or both. Only when I reached the Municipal Dungeon and was tossed in front of the reception desk did I learn about a new and fabulous Nilghordian ordinance. It was illegal for a prostitute to back out of a "business transaction" after verbal agreement. Since such agreements were impossible to verify, the legal victor was without exception the complainant.

What a vile city! First day back in almost eight years and I'd wound up in jail. Back east I wallowed in décor, mingled with and suckled the rich and famous. Nilghorde, however, seemed my place to be bereft of freedom.

My day in court was a farce. I gazed at the floor as a hot-blooded court room mercenary tore me to pieces on behalf of the absent plaintiff. His screed on the civil duty of merchants would have gotten him booed off a stage in Pelliul, but a stone victory in this urban coast.

For two long years I withered inside the belly of the Municipal Dungeon. I fell back on the learnings of a childhood spent in similar bondage. Steering clear of confrontation as best I could, and strategically inserting myself at opportunities, I made the role of trustee. Being that I could read and write better than most of the guards helped. I landed a position in the head offices—and this is where it all leads—to include the office of Warden Rogaire.

The first time I met him he came storming in while I was busy dusting. "Get the hell out!" Fair haired as I, but with golden brown skin, his hazel eyes made me avert my own as I made a hasty exit. Sweeping, carrying out trash, and taking notes for whomever, I opened my ears as I moused about. I soon learned, among so many trinkets, that Warden Rogaire—Rinlot—had just had a son.

It was like I'd returned to the backrooms of a Pelliul theatre. All the bustle and drama that the guard officers fussed on about was as catty as a group of drunken actresses, just provincial and gruff. One would leave the room to use the privy, and before he could sit down four others who had just sang about brotherly creeds were now gossiping at his expense.

It was in this gossip that I picked up the vital detail: the stinking richness of the Rogaires. Several shift supervisors couldn't get enough of it:

"…A deal with a pirate guild, about the Pelat spice routes."
"No, he goes into Crackpots Range—ever seen those skeletons missing their heads? He sells 'em to the Institute, he does."

"That there boy of his sure squirmed into the life. Probably a team of slaves to wipe then clap after a shat."

They shared my observations. Rinlot wasn't known for his exuberant salary or his keen intellect. What, did he trip in front of a toadstool-seated fairy eager to grant him wishes? It was said those still dwelled in the wildest glens and dales of the south, but I hardly took it as ostensible.

Upon my release, I bolted back to Pelliul. With some proper grooming, I'd be employable again in no time.

I could have kissed those streets. Cobbled beige and rusted ruby. On Lirelet Avenue the jasmine was in bloom, inhaled as jugglers and fire breathers lanced off the stained glass and gleaming lamp posts.

The portico of Lord Voss's home was as polished as ever. Rapping at the door summoned a housemaid whom I didn't recognize. When I advised that I was a former employee and specified my trade, she gave me the up-and-down then shut the doors in my face. Furious, I beat them until they cracked open once more.

"The lord will be with you shortly, sir," the housemaid said through the crease.

After I'd successfully kicked every dead leaf and piece of rubbish off the steps, and as I contemplated another salvo of rapping, the doors cracked once more, then they swung open. Out roostered Lord Voss. I danced on his steps.

He hammered me with the back of his hand. I was cut by a stupendous ring. I stood up only to take note that I'd fell.

"You dare come here now!" He rattled his cane. "I should gut you and donate those cum-bloated entrails of yours to the kitchen of that moldy orphanage where I plucked you from! Do you know what your little stunt cost me? The groveling," he became a parade of *grovelings* and high steps, "the groveling required to keep—the man you cheated—"

"Cheated?!"

"Ohh," dragging out his disdain, "don't you interrupt me. I am in *no* mood." He slapped me again. I fell down again. I curled up in a clump of dead leaves, forgotten by the gardener.

The sight of me crying only encouraged his rage. A furious assault of polished boots and an accurate cane had me soon screaming.

I wish I could have told him. I wish we could have sat down over wine. His grievances could certainly be unlearned, and after hearing my upsetting tale he would have surely shown pity. I wanted to stay in the enchanting light of the glow lamps and frolic among the dainty forever. But wishes only exist in the thoughtful shadows of regret. Reaching down into the dungeons of memory, I went cold and wrapped my hand around a strong twig.

✳

After a long while I dared to breathe. Voss's eye socket let out its last reserves of blood. I leaned over his flowerbed and vomited out every piece of me that I could.

The air was getting colder. The very leaves that swirled whispered an ill fate if I hesitated. Through my tears, I picked every ornament off of Lord Voss before fleeing into the night.

The doorwoman, the damned housemaid, she was the only one who saw my face. I never told her my name, and I believed no one saw the murder, but I learned fully the one-sidedness of our judicial system.

There were many things on my side. What, were the Inspectors going to chase down every blond man of minor stature to check the grade of blue in his eyes? "Are you a former gay prostitute who killed his pimp? No, be gone then, scum." How laughable. Yet, I couldn't know what Lord Voss may have told his housemaid or what company he'd excused himself from. If the housemaid had even a mediocre memory, a sketch of my likeness was going to be on every lamp post in the city.

I had to leave Pelliul—for a long time, maybe forever.

I was no woodsman and Oxghorde bordered swamp. The former would serve me up as food for wolves, the latter a crippling case of fen-lung. Against every fiber of my being I forced myself to consider my best and only option. There was only one place one could truly melt into the maelstrom. In a week's time I was back in Nilghorde.

Abject poverty alone. Cemeteries with a lunatic. And then finally, a mansion to burgle clean.

"Nice breeze tonight," Werlyle said, sounding uncharacteristically sober and approaching from my rear. There was a cool wind out, slipping through the black trees and caressing the balcony.

"Some dinner, aye? Don't know why she insisted on rabbit. Venison was excellent." Werlyle went on. "Those flimsy buzzards that circle her have to be from Pelliul." He sucked on his lip. "Where'd you say you were from again, Snier?"

"I'm from here," I said into my wine glass.

The party long over, I was waiting for the last slaves to retire from the brute chores a butler was thankfully spared—I was more a figurehead, after all, and had my own list of errands.

Werlyle and I talked when the deviations from my reconnaissance and his bottle both aligned. We'd developed a modest friend-ship, one could say. Mostly to share our disdain for Morlia, I would join him in his chambers for a game of dice or a few shots of a potent beverage. One night so potent I woke up half-horrified to learn I'd unwittingly cuddled up against him, having passed out on his bed.

"What a place," he said, leaning over the balcony as if he'd arrived that day. The outer bailey's wall faded into the floor of the black eastern forest. Squinting one's eyes under a waxing moon like tonight's, you could make out gardens turned wild thickets, neglected statues, and of course the stakes saved for the Lady's wrath.

Girdling the mansion was a wall separating the inner and outer baileys. Equipped with archer towers and weather-beaten merlons, the crenels from above looked to be once defendable, but now were crumbling with the breeze. In the inner bailey, or as Morlia referred to it if she remembered her nomenclature, the lower bailey, were the wells and a stable in front of the grazing ground. No horses lived in the stable anymore, just droves of rodents and the owl feasting on them.

Also in the "lower bailey" was the family graveyard. Staring at me from outside my chamber windows, the graveyard now lay somber below me as the night air weaved in and out of its vaulted obelisks. Werlyle was looking at them as well.

"A Rogaire male has sat in this house since it was built. You know, Snier, that this house is the farthest east in all the Morgeltine?"

"No, I didn't. How interesting."

"Many a marauder and beast used to live in those woods yonder." Tossing a nod toward the black. "Still some lurk in its bosom; it was the first Rogaires to settle in Nilghorde that were tasked with their confrontin'."

As I listened to Werlyle the Defeated carry on about mar-veled history and a homestead agreement with Nilghorde, my ears picked up a noise. I am in no regards easily spooked—choos-ing to live in that duplex on Red Wolf confirms that! Wind on the headstones, the rustle of faraway branches, the slave's distant chores: they were the cause of such noise. But scrapes and certain shuffles were not always so easy to dismiss.

"—so after generations, Snier, the Rogaires cleansed all the nightmares emergin'…right off the face of the world."

I paced about, nodding whenever he paused. I found a wind-blown sycamore writhing next to the base of the balcony, but it made no contact with the wall.

What fiends could have once thrived in the woods a strong arrow shot away? Few nights into my stay, when a full moon cast down from a cloudless sky, I'd seen the skulking and slinking of unaccountable shapes out on the lawns. A cold breeze caressed the balcony, and maybe that was what made me shiver.

"It's a shame. What you think, Snier?"

"Sir, it really isn't my place."

"Nonsense," he snorted, "a butler can answer a question when asked. You're no whipped slave putting away pots. You don't think it's an atrocity the Rogaire ruling this house is an evil brooch bag? One whose connection here, I might add, is by name only?" I looked at him for a moment and then back into my long-since-emptied glass. He was of the annihilated house of Qell, and his clinging to the name Rogaire was a desperate and powerful attempt to forget that.

"What of Rinmor? He will come of age soon enough."

Werlyle looked away and bent far over the edge. Scanning from left to right—did he hear noises too?

"Look, Snier, I am going to tell you somethin' you mustn't let get out." He belched into my ear. "Rinlot told me somethin' right before he died, and I honestly believe it led to it. That boy is not going to sit as head of this house. Not fer long. That big-boobed bitch and her melon-headed spawn are going to the bottom of the Black Tongue."

I sat my glass on the ledge.

"Snier, you never got to meet Rinlot. Looks nothing like Rinmor, or should we say *Morden*."

We? And I had surely seen Rinlot, not as much as I would have liked, but that little secret would have to stay with me.

He was right, though; Rinmor looked little like his father. Rinlot had a head like a statue of a Pelat god. Rinmor's was bulbous. The boy's frame was more like my own, and he didn't possess the healthy skin color.

That didn't really cause a big conundrum, though. Children can take after either mother or father; some display features that weren't seen since the days of their great-grandparents. Morlia's desolate beggared family could have worn any and all of the boy's features.

"Why does she call him that?" I asked, figuring if I was forced to talk about them at all I'd at least pull out a question that held some genuine interest.

"I'll get to that, but you should hear this in the order I did.

"Not terribly long before you got here, we had an All Malevolent Masquerade party. The place was crawlin' from top to bottom with fairies, demons, come-back-to-life celebrities. Morlia, get this, dressed up as a peacock." After a laugh, "I forgot what I wore— anyhow, I spent my night at the outdoor bar they'd set up with a pretty young thing, Sammi somethin', all dolled up like a lizard.

"Rinlot spent his night driftin' from one circle to the next. I remember watchin' a Minotaur with wooden horns goin' up and down the stairs all damn night. He had a lot of those men from the dungeon attendin'. Wonder if that lizard came with 'em?"

"What happened?"

"Well, you know the tradition: the boar was brought out to be cut up by the guests in the best and worst costume. You know. Right after, Rinlot came runnin' outside…to find me. I say, for just a smidge I thought a real Minotaur had bust in the party and was storming my way. He was furious. Barreled my sweet little company right over. Poor darlin' was so beside herself she did some hex before gettin' carried off by a few laughin' guards that were all painted like Suelans.

"He ripped his snout off and embraced me, Snier. I saw tears wellin' in his eyes. When he went looking for Morlia, about feast duties or what have you, Rinlot learned a thing or two."

"Let me guess, she was getting fucked."

"Close, Snier," he snickered, but there was no fading to his intensity. "She was tucked away in a nook with her flimsy buzzards. I can just see peacock feathers and crossdressers gigglin' in some damn corner. The spiked punch, opium, you name it, I guess it all allowed Rinlot to walk up unnoticed. You know that big statue on the second floor, the crane gulpin' the fish?"

"Yes, dusted it yesterday," I lied.

"He stood behind it and learned his boy isn't his."

"What?!" Looking about, I checked my volume. "Come on now, bunch of stoned drunks—"

"Morlia was braggin' about it." Rechecking his own voice. "She said she had met an Ordrid."

And there it was. The House of Ordrid, you've probably heard of them: fully known for their arcane practices, singularity, and madness. Not originally from Rehleia, they were commonly understood as delvers into the blackest of arts. Meeting an Ordrid meant meeting a necromancer, or a witch, and no other name I could think of mustered the same caliber of gossip. They peppered the landscape, their stronghold not far from this very mansion. Since Maecidion's death, however, that stronghold had become more a museum for scholars and macabre teenagers. A few coiled in Pelliul, but word had spread that most now nested deep in the Thunder Bustle.

Somyellia was one, though she had to be dismally low in that House to join me as a flesh peddler. Others were said to dwell in the woods outside Nilghorde and as far as the border that Rehleia shares with the desert wasteland known as Azad. Sailors from

Quinnari have told of a city of towers, across the sea and tucked away by a guardian forest. Allegedly, that is where the notorious clan had spewed forth.

But despite all the legends, someone claiming to have merely met an Ordrid was rather common. Hell, I had lived next door to one and robbed graves with her stud.

"Werlyle, are you saying Morlia had an affair with an Ordrid?"

"That's *exactly* what I'm sayin', what *Morlia* was sayin'. Rinlot must've listened for a bit; he told me more. She never said where she met him, but Rinlot and I knew she still had her connections in the Bustle. I still pick out the occasional dinner guest that's a sneak thief. Don't smile; I'm serious."

I knew what to look for, and the only person in the home with a penchant for that work, other than me, was Morlia herself. "Sorry, sir."

"So she meets this fellow and he throws a good fuck in her now and then. Don't know when, but how the hell could I? Poor Rinlot was at the dungeon most days, and he wasn't the assumin' type anyhow. So, she gets pregnant. Of course she tells Rinlot it's his, and of course he believes her."

"Wait, she said all this at a party, tucked in a corner passing around pipes?"

"You don't believe me, aye?"

I was foolish for letting go of my subservient front. His conviction was without doubt; he certainly believed himself. I really cared little one way or the other. I just wanted him to tire out so I could excuse myself.

Shrugs were all I could muster.

He sighed. "I don't know why I am tellin' you all this. Maybe it's just been bottled up fer too long."

"It's all right, sir," regaining my humility, "it's just a lot to take in." "Well, Snier, I will at least finish it since I started, and you be the judge.

"When Rinmor was born, Rinlot was runnin' all over singin' his praises, right? All the while Morlia was still sneakin' off. But somethin' happened to that Ordrid, 'cause the sly charmer ceased to see Morlia outright. Bitter, she starts to mock Rinlot. I tell you, Snier, there isn't a member at these little get-togethers that don't know what I am tellin' you now. She laughed behind his back and made fun of 'im, swingin' the boy around."

His tone had digressed. Amid the slurred curses I heard something behind me. I leaned over the balcony. The sycamore stared back and I heard a groan, or what had to have been a groan, from the graveyard. Completely deaf to Werlyle's words, I glared, the graves and sarcophagi glared back like the impeccant sycamore. What close-to-death creature had wandered in and now let out these ghasts? I needed to grab a torch, spear, and two slaves to carry them.

A hand placed itself on my shoulder, rendering me a paroxysm of yelps. "Snier, what the devil?"

"Nothing, sir—"

"Enough with the *sir* shit. I'm no royalty nor do I want to be a part. Again, all this is just kind of comin' out now. Don't mean to put you in an odd way."

"Werlyle, how about we call it a night? Let us continue this sometime soon. I feel there is more."

"There is." He paused, sliding his arm off my shoulder then giving it a squeeze. "There is and we will."

"Please call if you need anything, s—Werlyle." Then he slumped away.

Almost complete silence, save the night noises. Maybe the creature had died? I decided to go down to my room and grab my dagger and a hearty candle.

At my dressers, I realized what was bothering me so. It had been a bit of cosmic irony that I'd given up robbing graveyards just to be assigned quarters next to another one. Outside my windows, the outlines of white headstones and obelisks loomed, distorted by the texture of the glass.

For the longest I'd tried to track down a noise only heard when in my chambers. The sound itself shifted; sometimes a premonition of rats in the walls, the moaning of a crawlspace door yet to be discovered, drunken arm-wrestling goons, fucking slaves, or other times it unsettled my nerves due to its indescribability. But it was one of those things that happened with such regular irregularity that given long enough you tend to just go on without another strained thought tossed its way.

Tonight, however. A sound directly below the balcony meant that it was coming from right outside my window. I didn't wish to will my mind to actually speak it, but there was a chance the noise I'd heard many times was coming from the same place. No logical explanation appeared, the longer I sat on the edge of my bed. With a sturdy fire in the hearth and the dagger tucked under my pillow, I stared at the windows until dreariness took me. Sometime in the night I was awoken by what sounded like a labored grunt, but so faint that I could have imagined it.

※

The next few days were a blur. Things were getting too strange to stay much longer. Not least of my concerns, Morlia was not forgiving, and, as much as it pained me to admit, she had an iron memory. A few more insubordinations and I could easily see myself pleading I was no slave as her goons dragged me to the stakes. More than that, I'd located enough loot to rid myself of the servant cover.

The conflict within me howled. The fabled Rogaire treasury was here somewhere. Retirement was out of the question if I settled for leaving without it. Maybe I'd team up with Seasmil again, if I could find him. But an overgrown in dark garb was as common as cabbage in Nilghorde. Besides, a trek back to Red

Wolf showed that our old duplex had been leveled and covered in exorcising heraldry. I could keep working. A true professional—and that is what I was—can get out, move on, and let safety conquer hypothetical reward.

But most of all, as much as it nagged me to admit, was that confounded story of Werlyle's. The more time passed, the more his words seeped into my head.

I continued with my daily duties, high-stepping over the boy's string traps, all the while trying earnestly to remain focused on what to take and in what order.

Gold-lined torch-holders were—

Ugh, it was no use.

Regarding the boy, there was the creeping sensation that if I looked at him Werlyle's words would somehow become more and more true. They held at least some minimal plausibility; the impish gaggle, Morlia's taste for ruthless self-centeredness. All of which I could see rooted in a demented reality.

On more than one occasion, I had to pull the boy off a balcony for dinner. The result of breaking the seal betwixt his eyes and the moon was a baying and clawing from the little brat that I hadn't witnessed since the orphanage days. You would have thought he was being carried off to join a grain ship, when all that waited for him were tarts and pastries. Then there was this thing about his two names; what explained such strangeness? And yet looming over it all was the grandest quandary: how did this alleged affair contribute to Rinlot's death?

Rinlot had died when I was in the Municipal Dungeon. Sweeping the floor of a hall nearby, I learned he had succumbed to a gruesome ailment that viciously flung blood out of every hole. The guards who attended his funeral hooted and ranted for days about how awful he looked. Despite the undertaker's best efforts, the corpse put shivers down spines as the lid was sealed.

In fact, it was news of his death in conjunction with knowledge of his wealth that led to my current scheme. What I was shocked to learn, shortly before my harrowing prison escape, was that his widow was refusing to remarry—and, oh, how the brotherhood of guards left their wives to try and convince her otherwise. Popular gossip held that even the Rogaires of higher shelves had traveled from Oxghorde, calling upon Morlia at her doors in their polish and buttons. But she showed them all away. Before long, their outrage decayed to dismay, and finally to sagging departures.

I predicted the droves of suitors lining up to take Rinlot's place. The sight of them, larvae crawling on meat barely dead. What I didn't expect was his widow to show such fortitude. After all, isn't lack of humanity a prerequisite for maintaining wealth?

When I knocked on the mansion doors, my routine was ready. I was but a humble and out-of-work butler, famished from bandits capturing my employer's caravan. Taken to their hideout deep in the woods, I was bound to a tree and whipped for sport. Wouldn't you know my luck, I escaped. All the details were there: how I courageously led the Ward back to the encampment; the old fire pit, septic trench, and even my Lord's girl's dolls strewn about. Alas, it was abandoned. Applauded by the Ward, I was now just seeking humble employment and trying to forget the horrors of my past.

Such a tale would draw sympathy from the recently bereaved Morlia Rogaire, and in case she desired proof, lashes on my back were sure to draw tears. No Lady would question why they looked so old.

A sallow and sunken-cheeked slave answered the doors. After hearing my request to speak to the master of the house, he gave me what I later understood to be a weary look of warning.

After a wait befitting the smuggest of royalty, Morlia appeared. Dripping in jewels and adorned in a ball gown that was unsuccessfully concealing a bust like flour bags, she looked more like a doll than a mourner.

As I commenced with my bit, Morlia stood in complete silence, at some point crossing her arms.

"You have the bluest eyes," she said, interrupting the part where I defied the bandits to do their worst. Before I could continue, a hand was caressing my cheek.

On the way up to her chamber doors, my heart jumped about, not with lustful anticipation but with teeth-like questions burying themselves into me. This was definitely better than having the door shut in my face. Was I to be the next suitor? Did I somehow heal the fickle heart that was leading me up a flight of stairs and into the bed of a man who was still stinking? Was I to be used and then discarded afterward, and did she recognize me from my last profession if that was the case?

What cruel games the fates play. Rinlot had no desire for me, whereas his moll widow wrapped her rawboned legs around me on the first day of our meeting. Wretch. Moll. It is most fortunate I had experience with couples. I shut my eyes and pretended she was Illheador, on stage with muscles glistening as his trademark swagger carried him from scene to scene.

Before I knew it, it was over. As impressed in myself as I was for being able to perform, I don't believe Morlia felt the same. I was indeed given a butler position; apparently the other one had earned a place on the dripping stakes. In the beginning she referred to me as "the new butler that was tortured by pirates, or was it used to live in the woods with escaped slaves," and to my good luck never led me to her bed again.

This all reintroduced a reason to believe that Morlia had been unfaithful to Rinlot with every actor in passing or slave in the house.

But so what? Was it possible she'd fucked an Ordrid, snickered behind Rinlot's back, had the bastard, and was finally found out? Seemed humorously plausible as I put the pieces together. And maybe most jolting of all, though it didn't present as Werlyle said it: I'd spent All Malevolent Masquerade, my favorite holiday, locked away in the dungeon. And Rinlot had died soon after.

Curious, but even dungeons can feel drabber. With Rinlot gone and his foul replacement proving to be even dumber, my wheels began to turn. Soon after, curled up in the bottom of a prison wagon bound for the Institute of Human Sciences, I popped out of a pile of bones and regained my beloved freedom.

When I owned my own mansion, whether in the Morgeltine or elsewhere, I would have to gouge out the eyes of some slaves, and remove the tongues of others. You can't ambush a Pelat, you can't trick a trickster, and you can't steal from Tymothus Snier. Yet, at least in one way, I had been bested.

The fabled Rogaire vault! I'd gladly spend another year in the dungeon just to study this place's layout, learn its deepest secrets, and master its locks. So much would go unplundered, my heart lamented, but my better judgment was telling me that it was time to go.

Werlyle's proclamation that the Moliahenna River would be fed the bodies of Morlia and the boy was rooted in a hateful truth. I had seen the look in Werlyle's eyes, that same black intensity I'd seen worn on men's faces in the dungeon when bent to kill. The last thing I needed was the Ward investigating a missing rich kid. A burglary would be bad enough, a murder worse, but a wealthy person's murder the foulest.

The night's mission came back to me in a burst.

First, go to Nilghorde Commerce; rent the cart and mules. Done so many times at the service of the mansion, no goon or slave would give a second glance at the cart waiting in the inner bailey.

Second, handle the occupants. I had just the thing.

Third, to the library. With finite room, the books would lie on the cart's bed.

Fourth, the mid-weight items and sculptures, followed by the contents of the wine cellar.

Lastly, the fragile paintings, and if I was lucky…everything I could pillage from Morlia's room. I was going back in there; enough time had been wasted, and she would be drooling on some overpriced throw blanket.

My logical hope was that the way to all the stinking piles of gold started somewhere in her chambers. My one unfortunate trip into that maze had suggested one hundred doors could have been waiting behind all the hanging dresses and lip-kissed mirrors.

Werlyle and his contents were to remain untouched. Call me soft, but he'd been a friend in a certain light. Besides, living there seemed cruel enough of a fate.

Then I would be off.

Apochxal: the flower fermented in my vial. I couldn't remember where they grew, but somewhere far away.

I fiddled with the vial, imagining the side effects as a trapped air bubble responded to my fiddling. This was enough to sedate everyone in the mansion five times over, and the night's order for fetal-tiger soup was most opportune. Slaves and goons would surely finish off what the three would leave untouched.

For insurance, the backup dish was sabotaged with lamp oil. If summoned, the only casualty would be the cook's lives, but sometimes such ruthlessness is required, and every mouth would love soup tonight.

Many would tell you that moments before the actual plunder were like nails being driven past the skull and into the brain. Not me; other than wallowing in the aftermath, the tender moments before execution were my favorite. It was to be savored, looking at riches located, admired, appraised.

Walking past a mermaid statue of jade was like seeing someone whom you had a great appointment with later the same day. Envisioning the process helped steel the nerves: what would go where, how much it would sell for after. I paced myself, calmed myself, and fixed my cummerbund and bow tie to bloom in full radiance.

✳

"Good butler," Morlia said as if speaking to a housecat. "The chandelier needs dusting. I thought I told you."

She was referring to the chandelier in the south hall, not the one here. "Ah, yes, Mum. I tasked a slave to do it. Shall I have him beaten?"

"Well, the responsibility was yours, not some worn-out Serab too busy doing chores that would break the back of a man like you. You can beat yourself if you'd like. Later, perhaps."

"Yes, Mum," I said, slipping out of the dining hall and heading for the kitchen. That bitch was to see dust and webs on the cursed chandelier for a decade, or better yet two decades.

Emptying four vials into the vat was simple. After warning the culinary staff they'd better start with the backup preparations, they all scurried to the meat closet.

Soon after, the cooks filled three silver bowls full, placing them on a tray that was soon to find a new home. A line of Morlia's ruffians filed in for their share.

"Dinner is served. Baby Hunting Cat soup, with a touch of saffron. Would you be wanting some wine tonight, Mum?"

"No, my head hurts—and don't call it that—and wine with soup is like milk with beef stew."

"Yes, Mum. For you, sir?"

Werlyle looked up. Our eyes locked and it made me flinch.

Walks in the kitchen often met me with glances one would expect from the clump of enslaved men; Suelans, skin glistening shiny black from the steam of the cauldrons. They would occasionally fail to mask their discontent for one of the few free men working. This time, however, they all looked as if found in a bordello by their prudish grandmother, caught gulping the soup by the handful. My best impression of repugnance for their thievery got me down into the wine cellar. The smile afterward hurt my face.

Returning to the hall, Morlia was sucking her spoon. Werlyle stared at the table. He could make a meal into a night-spanning event. He of the Shaking Hand would take up his own spoon shortly. The boy, however, moaned and piddled, swirling the soup with his finger, scowling at me as I passed.

Then I heard it; the thud, clang, and swivel of a dropped bowl.

Maggot of Hell, curse that blasted boy! His bowl thrummed on the floor as he leered over it.

But Morlia was face down in hers.

"Mother?" the boy noticed too. His yellow eyes stared at me as I saved his mother from drowning in her own dinner.

"What the burnin' hell!" Werlyle yelled, startling me and the boy with perfect equality. "Leave her, Snier!"

Uprooting himself, red and bellowing, Werlyle careened through vacant chairs. As Uncle Werlyle approached, blind panic transfixed the boy. His eyes swung from Morlia to me, tender servant standing as I should. Would this be the dinner from Hell, young sir?

"Leave this one to me, Snier!"

I don't think I moved. As Werlyle pointed his finger at the boy, I wondered if his diatribe on the balcony had been some sort of an attempt at an alliance.

"Butler," the boy adjusted, desperately attempting at manners like a shield, "Butler, please stay Uncle."

I saw the ball of webs unraveling now. My best bet was to play it cool and hope that all the goon-guards had enjoyed their soup.

All my fine planning and this was how it turned out. Werlyle had the boy on his knees. Wind from far windows entered the dining hall. I turned away and acted the butler. Milling about the place, "Does anyone need anything? A butcher's knife here, or perhaps a hatchet?" The wind grew in strength, banging shutters at the last beautiful, regal, condescending, vile feast of the Rogaires.

"It's time, Snier! You and me! Told you there was more." Werlyle growled at my back, the boy pinned down by his boot. "I don't know how, but that bitch killed him." A furious squeak came up from below. "Once crossed—stop squirmin'—we resort back to older justice."

My nerves frayed like gossamer between departing horses. A descent of thuds and clanks was sure to come gooning into the hall. But none did. The plan began to reform. Werlyle had spiked the soup and had attacked the boy. I would cut out his tongue and assist in dragging him to the dungeon if I had to.

A terrible hiss came up from the floor.

"You dare, my father—" Werlyle reaffirmed his boot to the boy's throat, looking down at him with eyes that almost glowed.

For the briefest of moments, the squirming corpse in the guise of a living boy needed my help. A boy was being attacked by a man. For just a moment, I heard the jingle of orderly keys, but they were just a whisper in a dream. I found myself replacing Morlia into her final meal. A gurgle came out as tawdry make-up tainted the broth. I told myself it saved her from a more gruesome end. Perhaps I was right.

I walked out, not as a man ready to begin a mighty pillage, but sulking and unwound. The yelps and drunken curses behind me were penetrated by snores of sedated guardsmen.

What now? Kill Werlyle? If I didn't, he surely lacked the cunning to cover up a double murder. The dungeon, I knew all too well, had many innovative techniques (and overzealous technicians) that would easily get my name out of his toothless and spurting mouth. If I killed him, it would have to be by force, which would leave a wound. To the gods I wished Seasmil were here. Maybe I could get lucky, stab Werlyle in the gut, and make it look like a maniacal murder-suicide.

Why did the fool have to pick tonight to initiate this sloppy act of violence? What I guessed was a voice box getting crushed made a rubbery sound as my face sunk into my hands.

Wind howled through the windows. A good butler would have shut them. I began to rise.

※

"Well, what we do now, Snier, bury 'em?" Werlyle said, staring up at me.

Great—I was involved with murders in two provincial cities. I had returned to Nilghorde out of necessity. Now that I was quite capable of being put to death in both, was Pelliul the new old destination? I certainly wouldn't be the only criminal bouncing from one giant to the other. But my pragmatism won: Oxghorde and its addled silly midget of a neighbor, Amden, would have to do, fen-lung syndrome and all. But only if I figured out how to deal with Werlyle.

"The goons won't sleep forever," I sighed. "We are in this together now, whatever *this* is."

"That we are, Snier, that we are," Werlyle said, slugging to his feet over Rinmor. Werlyle wore the boy's struggle in the form of glistening scratches.

A furtive hand reassured my dagger was still tucked under my sash. If he demanded to sit on the mystic throne of the Nilghorde House of Rogaire, a confrontation was inevitable. He would deem the mansion, and all property therein, escheated to him. He likely thought I just hated Morlia, and it was enough that her body cooled with the soup that claimed her.

"Snier," my name lingered—not furtive enough—"what are you up to?"

"The servant role is over, old friend. Afraid we're about to have a bit of a disagreement."

"Don't know what you did to that soup, but I'm impressed.

Bitch deserved worse. I wouldn't have thought of that. Remember, though, *boy-o*, I'm not goin' to drown in some broth for you."

He stepped over the boy.

We must have looked like some pathetic interlude, ready to do our act for boos and drunken revelry before the main event in a fighting pit. The butler with a limp wrist and a dwarfed drunkard, battling with all his might to avoid swaying. At his next step forward, I drew my blade.

Werlyle turned and looked at Morlia. He walked not toward me, but to her. Sweat from my palm ran down my dagger as I watched him cradle one of her hands. A fight began to look less likely and a necrophobic bout of petting more probable. He slipped one of her rings off her finger.

"You know what this is, Snier? The matriarch ring of this House. A Rogaire Lady has worn it as long as this home has stood on the earth."

I flinched when he tossed me the ring. But I caught it too.

"Now," he said, pulling up his soggy trousers. "Times drainin'. Let's bleed this place of anythin' these miserable ghosts would care to haunt. Aye?"

"How long have you known?" I gaped. Watching his chuckles and ticks, his odd signature of laughter, I realized there were two snakes in this nest, and their tails were interwoven.

"I was working somethin' similar, drinkin' water out of a Bleeding Anna bottle most days. Long before you got here I came fer my own reasons. Rinlot up and died on me though, and that got me thinkin' a bit scandalous. I got to say, you really showed me a thing or two on patience. You're a planner, aye? I'll tell you what I am, Snier: a survivor. Figured you'd pull off whatever upstart you had cookin' before too long."

"But?"

He undulated like it stung, or tickled. "I saw you slitherin' about the place. 'Sides…you talk in your sleep."

Joining forces took little explaining, and perhaps I shouldn't have been surprised. Werlyle even added to the exploitation with a simple detail, so in front of my nose I almost smacked myself for not thinking of it on my own.

"I bet she has keys on her, Snier." My mind began to recalibrate. "We may not have enough time to get everythin'. What'd you put in the food? How long's it last?"

"That is absolutely no concern," I said. "Everyone in the house sucked it down and will be waking up this time tomorrow."

"Can't be too sure, though, aye? You think we need to take… further measures?" His eyes widened.

"Not necessary."

"But we can't be too sure, right? We don't want some thick-necked guard, happenin' to have a hearty constitution, chasin' us down or runnin' off to the Ward."

Rinmor turned out to be but a precursor. Werlyle ran as a man does when rotted by the bottle and owning stubby legs, around a corner and up the stairs. Finding the first of several sleeping goons, he relieved one of his sword and then dashed about slaughtering the lot.

Astonishment fails to grasp the feeling of watching the drunkard skewer a score of guards and slaves; not a ruthless swordsman, but more a pudgy child on a bright outing. The irksome noises of hacks and grunts, met with an occasional moan, echoed about the place as I did my best at staying focused. As he darted in and out of my sight, messier each time, I made my way to Morlia.

Her slumped state made my actions no less nauseous. Nothing was around her neck but a necklace lined with star sapphire. Removed and put in my pocket, I patted her all over, desperately wanting to feel something solid. After running my hands inside her girdle, I fingered through her wetted undergarments. Between her thighs, nestled snuggly against her pelvis, the ring I'd put on my finger came on a sudden *ting*. My fingers clasped around them. From that unholy perfumed trench I pulled out the keys. Two, one large and one small, dangled on a golden ring.

Dark, thick ribbons of blood trailed off Werlyle's arms as he reentered the dining hall. Panting, he was still taking excessive and bizarre routes in his search for additional victims. His gut protruded from his ever upward-crawling shirt as he exerted himself to a blissful exhaustion. The keys had found my pocket in a flash, but as I planned on explaining that no such keys existed, he exited to enter a dark nook where apparently someone still lived.

My excitement was incapable of restraint. What vaults those walls would surely contain. What we would pack into the cart together would be impressive, lucrative—quite, in fact—but it wasn't statues and paintings that had lured me.

"Snier," Werlyle said, emerging from the nook and brandishing his dripping sword. His boots emitted a mushy sound as he left a remarkable path of footprints. "Okay, think that's all of 'em." Restarting his ticks, "One cook wasn't fully out, drunk on whatever you did, and those big white eyes were so pink and hazy. He thought I was some ghost or god those spearmen worship. You seen those little wooden idols they have up in the kitchen?"

Werlyle had surely earned my attention. The toad, in plum and blood, fooled the eye. He was a plug of some visceral tissue that oozed out of a wound or woman's loins. But he also killed. As much as I had confidently calibrated him, and at some moments even pitied him, he had transformed before me into a man that was to be treated as a genuine maniac.

"Yeah," he continued, "I think he thought I was one of those. How he prayed—"

"Let us get to work," I said, hopefully appearing unmoved. "All right, all right. No rush as I see it, but I'm not the mastermind here. What shall we do now, sir?" He bowed low, like a butler.

Two hefty table covers later, we were in the library. All six volumes of *Poems of the Classics*, the legendary Denom Vandahl's *Transient State of Grace* and *Songs in Regal Twilight*, *The Embryonic Sorcerer* and many more I pulled from their shelves and dropped in Werlyle's blood-covered hands.

The sight of them made me have to consider: Was this come-to-fruition maniac done with his bloodlust? Was he even capable of splitting the loot and then merrily go about his affairs? Was I, Tymothus Snier, willing to do such splitting?

I knew from too much time in the dungeon who'd squeal. If he got caught—and with an array of bloody boot prints and his reckless blabber-mouthing, he would—it would only be a matter of time be-fore I was in some pre-disembowelment pillory. Equally troubling, he was possibly brewing a similar plan, trying to make my grizzly death look like a grand murder-suicide, swaying in his retelling to the Ward.

"How fuckin' heavy can a few books be?" Werlyle grunted as he toted an improvised satchel across his shoulder.

"You'll be surprised how much some of these will sell for. Besides, they're not that heavy." Hugging my smaller load, it was relieving to pretend I wasn't bothered. In time, my temperament began to follow suit.

I freed one hand long enough to open the door that led us out to the bailey. From over my stack of books, I saw the pale tops of the obelisks. The wind wasn't just strong, it was cold. I walked to the cart, Werlyle in trace. After placing one table cover at its base, Werlyle handed me the books and I made a solid bed of literature. I covered the second linen over them and hopped out.

Next were the sculptures, silverware, candleholders, decorative weaponry, vases, curtains, sconces, and a plethora of odds and ends, all packed into their waiting crates that I'd kept cached in the mansion's heap of undisposed garbage. Thieves in the night; Werlyle bellowed in mirth, impressed by my puzzle-piece packing. I stood atop the boxes, cold wind blowing my hair wild.

"Attaboy, Snier," Werlyle laughed. "Oh, did you check Morlia? Watch it. Careful, Snier, don't go droppin' boxes and lookin' all amateur on me."

But I didn't hear him. My heart pounded, my comfort annihilated, and I knew it wouldn't return. "She has to have keys on 'er." Werlyle said. "We find what we're both really lookin' fer—hey, how we goin' to fit it all? Make another trip?"

After a moment: "No, one trip is all we can afford, and no, I haven't checked."

Rinmor lay dead on his back, eyes wide as his mouth. Werlyle tossed Morlia about like a sailor emptying his duffle. The gown ripped, her red hair an unkempt mess dripping cold soup, her face placid, like a doll's. When he lifted her upside down, her head hit the floor stones. The sharp, crisp smack made my belly turn.

"Arhh," Werlyle roared, "they got to be here!"

"You're right," flapping in exasperation, "there's no other place they could be. Wait—some hiding place outside her door?" That corridor was so thin only one of us could check the tile or trim at a time, and I knew who should lead the file.

"Fuck!" Werlyle dropped Morlia like she had bit him. "I didn't come for books."

"Me either, friend. Let us at least concentrate on said books for the time being. Maybe our minds will re-stir. I have often found that—"

"What's next?"

Small crates of wine, along with dozens of Black Monk, Spiritual Oppressor, and Bleeding Anna fit snuggly in the wagon that was starting to creak from the weight.

A hellish moan came up from somewhere behind us.

Werlyle screamed and flapped, pelting me with congealed blood and dropping a crate of Grest.

"I don't know," I said to Werlyle as if he'd asked me what made such an awful noise. And I didn't know, not completely.

But I wasn't in complete denial either. The final result of my grim induction was that something stirred, and had stirred a long time, amid the tombstones. There wasn't even the luxury for conjecture; this time the noise continued.

Many may condescend from their comfortable parlors the actions we then took. No bother, there is no way to make rational what was occurring, nor make rational our response. Without a word, we walked side by side. We walked toward the noise. I unsheathed my dagger as Werlyle wiggled the bloody sword out from his belt. I knew the source far faster than my mind would officially admit. Our walk toward what was now a series of grunts and thuds ended at the foot of Rinlot's sarcophagus.

The wind had picked up to a near approaching storm. Thunder rolled in the distance. Lightning lit up the west. Maybe the weather was trying to mask our discovery. For the faintest of moments, I thought I saw a pale face between two obelisks, but before my eyes could strain further, Werlyle pulled me away.

"Snier, this is Ordrid work."

"Maybe, maybe—but maybe some animal burrowed in from the bottom," I said, trying to believe it.

"I have to open it."

"What!? Whatever's in there is better left *in there*. Remember why we're here. Grave robbing is *not* an interest, or important." My free hand clasped the keys in my pocket.

Werlyle placed his ear to the stone. "It ain't about robbin' it. They have a curse on him, don't you hear 'em," rolling his eyes up to land on me, "in there?"

No! I didn't! I heard some terrible moan, but it didn't have to be from where we stood. It was an awakened guard, not properly run through, clamoring out into the night while regaining his wits. I tried to convince Werlyle of this, but it was no use. Thuds burst up from within, and when they did even I finally conceded the most terrible of realities.

Sentiment comes at the oddest times, and certainly nothing odder than the moment before us. Despite all my current dilemmas, I began to wonder if maybe some form of white magic was available to help the thing that now pounded up against the inner stone. For a king's treasury the Chapwyn priests would maybe put down their incense-swingers and emasculation tools to evoke some assistance. I listened for words, something to discern that the pounder was in the realms relatable to the human experience. I strained, but nothing.

"Snier, I'm opening it."

"Wait—"

Of all my knee-jerk reactions that have surprised, I found myself pushing Werlyle aside to slide the lid myself. As my dagger's blade and fingers felt the stone separating, I held an image of Rinlot's somehow golden-brown skin next to mine, how grateful it was to be saved, and how forever in my debt it would pleasantly remain.

The stone was heavy, and I eased off to regain my strength. Taking in a breath, I looked up at the night sky. The gargoyles atop the corbels loomed down as they always did. Maybe it was just the darkness, the whirling of the leaves, or my severely jostled nerves, but they all seemed different. More *perched* rather than *placed*, as if waiting for some command unknowable to us to take flight. A little one I'd never noticed before, looking more like an imp from a bad fairytale, seemed to have eyes that moved.

The lid gave with a sucking sound. Through a sliver of blackness, fingers stretched out and into the open air.

Werlyle flailed back, shrieking and cursing. I possessed neither the ability nor the inclination to look back at him. The skin was brown, but to a leather. Fingers, their tips worn to the bone, appeared to be searching for something.

I had expected this abomination to toss the stone lid next, send it down in pieces, and emerge to wreak whatever havoc its unfathomable torment would see fit. Instead, the fingers vanished back into the sarcophagus. Without the pure stone to muffle them, all that emitted were sobs and moans of the lowest despair. There was rage possibly, but a rage of the rat in the trap, back broken.

The terror possessing me froze any ability to run. Aghast—the thought of me sleeping, while out the window tossed and turned this afflicted carcass. He—it—felt pain, or at least perceivably so from the noises he made. Rinlot, or whatever he was now, was unable to emerge from a confinement that even I was able to pry. Pity blocked my throat when I contemplated if an intelligence, some residue from his time among the living, lingered, him knowing full well what treachery put him there. Whatever emotion I may have felt next was destroyed as lightning struck the bailey.

When I awoke, the world swayed and pulsated as I found myself getting back on my feet. A pat-down gave me reason to believe the lightning hadn't struck me. With a wobble, I regained my senses.

I couldn't have been out long. The wagon was tearing out of the bailey, heading for wherever a pair of scared mules would decide.

That hideous hand had once more emerged from the open space, this time grabbing at thin air. My run for the wagon only sent me back to the ground. Rolling from my stomach and clutching my shin, I turned to see that the crate Werlyle dropped had bested me. Rain peppered my face as I stood once more.

My eyes then held the greatest of their disbeliefs.

Werlyle was on his knees, clutching his throat with both hands. His vocal tubing gave a rubbery squeak as the thin blade of a rapier returned to its scabbard. As Werlyle hit the ground, the boy stood over him.

In the open door, atop the small flight of its steps, stood Morlia and someone else. This second person, a man, I could have sworn I had known.

Maybe it was the moonlight, the lightning strike, or my blood rushing away from me, but her face, as the boy's, was not the same. Some form of unlife had replaced them, and its new demeanor I dared not guess. Their features were somehow more canine, their eyes beady.

Standing like figures claiming the summit of a nightmare wedding cake, I then knew with absolute certainty who the other person was.

"Morden," spoke the Ordrid. The boy ascended the stairs, coming to his father's side. Morden turned toward the graves. A pang of sheer terror erupted once more when they cast their eyes on me.

You'd think I would have run, but I didn't—couldn't. I stood as lifeless as a statue in that long-gone mule cart.

✳

The necromancer's disappearance from the dungeon surprised no one. Those with a penchant for gambling placed bets on the manner in which he would bust loose, while those prone to superstition debated what manner of ghost or beast would be summoned to assist in his freeing. All were wrong, and it was the nonchalant reaction of Warden Rogaire that now made sense.

Soon after the necromancer was paraded, in that most ridiculous presentation of chains, the warden had caught wind of the celebrity and insisted on a sit down.

The Ordrid's *escape* happened right after that meeting. In conjunction with a curious guard change that night, Warden Rogaire had his lower tiersmen come join in one of the dungeon's most famed spectator sports.

Prisoners who'd failed on debts to royal houses, or who particularly irritated the guards, would be tied to a stone altar. Naked as the day they were born, a guardsman would soak the flailing prisoner with bitch urine and then release a pack of deprived Imperial

Hounds. The fight to get to the scent was as brutal as the unsettling result. The honor to attend was normally reserved for only the ranking cadre and occasional whores that occupied the keyvaults in the not so quiet hours of roll call and gruel distribution.

Rinlot couldn't have known that the sorcerer, or necromancer, or whatever title best fit the man who came to him in chains before leaving at leisure, and who he foolishly bartered some deal with, was the very man who sired Morden.

Was imprisonment itself a part of the Ordrid's plan?

The Ordrid looked at me, or through me. I felt as if I would fall and never stand again.

Not through my own mind did I see what I say to you now, but through where my eyes may have been if I had been in league with the Ordrid and standing, fittingly, a bit to his rear:

I knew the place all too well. The gate of the Municipal Dungeon was built for giants. In front of its iron scales, each alone as large as a shield, two guards leaned on their halberds. In front of them, the Ordrid stood, clad in black leggings and a dark coat. His head was bald like an onion. His hands moved along with his plea, reassuring and coy.

The bewildered guards couldn't decide who to gape at longer, one another or this man, in the midst of a full confession he practiced outlawed magic. Some time must have passed between that image and the next, but the Ordrid—surely this fiend who rose Morlia and Morden—the Ordrid then turned to *me*.

He had wanted at Rinlot even more than I. For reasons I would never know, now he would have Rinlot's family, his wealth, and toast fine glasses to having caused such misery. The next thing I saw was he and Rinlot walking out of the front gate. Night had fallen. The two walked like friends, Rinlot gingerly swinging a pair of free handcuffs. I saw Rinlot's eyes, in some fashion glazed over beyond their usual simplicity, and then I see it. They shake hands. My mind's eye, or whoever's, locks in on these hands and does not move after.

✳

Wind was in the trees and rain pelted the gravestones. The three of them descended the stairs. I stayed like a cornered hare.

"Morlia. Sir, a great tragedy has befallen this house tonight. Your cousin, as you have readily identified as the perpetrator, has poisoned your slaves, your guards, and I thought you both as well. I caught him here beginning to loot our dear Rinlot's final resting place." I pushed out a grin, or it felt like one.

"Sir, I beg of you—" They had neared to an arm's distance, walking solemn and in unison. Morlia's eyes were two black stones above lips whose opening could have contained rows of fangs.

A hand grabbed my ankle, another my belt, ripping it off of me with tatters of my breeches coming with it. Breaking free of this terrible freeze at last, I felt for my dagger, but it must have lain somewhere amid the fallen leaves.

Stone slid with wet grittiness. I found myself looking up at the leering gargoyles. One of my hands pushed against Morlia's face, which appeared in an instant far less dead. My other hand was clasped around her keys in my pocket, and then they too were taken from me.

Epilogue

Tymothus kicked and screamed, bit and pled. Morlia slid open the lid as Morden and Irion stuffed him into the sarcophagus. The once summer-hued skin of Rinlot, turned coarse and loathsome, clung to the new inhabitant.

As the lid slid back, Irion Ordrid's grin grew as wide as his son's. Sons were a theme. It make have taken too many years and two bodies, but the Ordrid soul who Rinmauld had cheated finally avenged the Ordrid House, and sent Rinmauld's into tortured ashes, his dearest son moaning in this delightful little box.

Rinlot's hands found holds on Tymothus. Just before the lid was sealed, and what was left of the light of the moon would be conquered by forever black, Tymothus dared look beside him. Rinlot stared back, the agony of hell on his wry grimace.

Leaving a wake of bursting bottles, the runaway mules careened out of the Morgeltine. The last to see it in the district was a bloated Wardsman, watching in disbelief as a ghost-driven wagon wheeled past.

The beings that haunt the dark weren't limited to the Rogaire Mansion that night. As the wagon entered the celebrated Do-Gooder's Row, flowers and confetti and strands of human hair were kicked up by its wheels. The mules' hearts finally exhausted, the shadows stalking the nooks and miasma of Nilghorde began to envelope the cart.

Some would suggest more Ordrid magic was at work, but the mob was just the poor, the slowest five among them sent to the Pauper Morgue.

BOSGAARD AND BELLA

If I had to wear this sash and badge one more time, I would happily donate my corpse to the Wing of Trauma's next suicide exhibit. The sky's dreariness confirmed it was too early to crawl out of bed, let alone don the role of student-on-duty and wither away.

I slumped over my appointed desk and reminisced in the way of half-dreams. My brothers and I had just spent the better part of a month bagging each other's deer and concubines all over the green hills. Now I was back, at the illustrious Institute of Human Sciences, where, without end, professors and one-day doctors took apart their cadavers.

When I lifted my head, I saw him standing in front of the faculty mausoleum. He meandered back and forth as if looking for a way in.

I poked my head out just far enough to say, "May I help you?"

"They turned it into a fortress" he said, as if we'd known one another for years. "Don't suppose you have a key for all these locks?"

Those superfluous locks were, I guess one could say, *impressive*. With a new addition to the outer wall and a roof like a giant's shield, the mausoleum was buckling under its own burden. But no bronze dome nor fresh layer of granite had ever brought around any admiring tourists. I decided to extend my neck out of the duty hut a little further and make introductions.

"I am Legriel Lotgard. I am, you know, a student here at the illustrious—"

"At the IHS," he said. I'm sure I appeared most unlordly when he turned and looked at me. Gesturing at the mausoleum, he continued, "They aren't worried about a rival institute, are they?"

Though he was of only average height, his persistent scowl and shoulders like stones you'd see lobbed from a catapult gave him the appearance of one of the rare pit fighters who survive to middle age. More pleasant were the flowers he held, though their leaves had been bleached by the sun, petals withered by the pattering of a week's rain.

That he'd plucked the bouquet from someone's grave added to the impression that I was engaging with a rogue.

"No, they're afraid of ghouls," I answered at last. He stared at me, but said nothing. "You, you have a loved one in the mausoleum?"

"Yes," he said. "Bella."

I must have overlooked her when I'd perused the names of professors who'd joined their medium by way of entombment. "She was a professor," I said, exposing my skepticism, "for this institute?"

"Body snatcher."

Like all first-year students, I was made aware of our school's more nefarious histories. However, tales of warring medical factions under the light of the moon were something I regarded as a bit closer to myth. Even less convincing was his proclamation that a body snatcher had been placed in the IHS mausoleum, reserved only for the most revered contributors and reread faculty.

Emerging from the hut, the morning caressed me with the beginnings of rain. Standing under the plashing and patters, he stared at me as a man would if having no fancy for telling tall tales, or buying into them. He at least believed his words.

I had no idea which keys under my charge led to what locks, though we could kill the day trying.

I would later blame only curiosity, not inclement weather. Contrary to my nerves, I invited him to join me. "Out of the rain," I said, "for a bite and, hell, a sip of the hard stuff. Let's not get caught, though," I added, attempting levity. "A drink on duty'll land me in the Municipal Dungeon."

He smiled, though I wished he hadn't. He looked the way a madman may right before a euphoric killing. Thus convincing me I'd grown momentarily psychic, he said, "I was just released from there."

I would love to have seen my face. A child suddenly aware they're alone in the woods may have expressed less panic. I think I reached for the whistle about my neck. The institute provided one for all gate duties, but as I slipped and stumbled backward, I'd wished they'd given me a sword.

"Ghouls, you say?" the man echoed, patting the mausoleum's granite.

"Glibbmor Ghouls," I said, righting my spectacles and regaining my wits. I fell back on my father's preferred tactic, one he'd made a political career of: lambasting a greater buffoon if ever feeling one yourself. "The ghouls are tunneling in these parts more and more these days, or so the department heads would have us believe." I gave a good laugh. "All those years spent staring at bones and other maps of our cosmic indifference, yet when it comes to their own carcasses, they take a turn for the superstitious."

"Glibbmor," he said in a way I didn't like. "If you're inclined to…superstition, his clan is, or was, known for using the sewers. Hideous, that one. They called him Glibbmor the Infested."

"What do they call you?"

"Bosgaard."

My fear immediately returned—doubled. But, being the fool I am, I would have to endure it. Having accepted my offer, he followed me in.

✳

All student posts were a bore, an entire day dishing out directions to the lost and fighting valiantly not to fall asleep over your homework. This post overlooking the never-used side gate was widely known as the dullest. A dorm colleague I'd convinced to come help me stave off the day's appointments had gotten as far as the threshold, seen my company, then my face, then ran off in terror.

I began sipping on Bleeding Anna way too early. Soon, my fear began to wither, allowing me to bask: I was sitting next to a legend. There is something relieving about knowing a man can kill you but chooses not to. Bosgaard the Snatcher Slayer. He'd once been a snatcher himself, until, according to the most popular thread, he killed his whole team to greedily scamper off with the corpse of a holy man. He was caught on site, however, for the authorities had been tipped off by someone who matched him in treachery.

After devouring most of my breakfast, he asked, "Ever heard of Bileprine?"

Whatever myths may or may not have arisen, that the Bileprine Institute had once existed was a fact. A fact that now haunted our halls like a faint yet persistent ghost. The oldest of the academics, usually lost in a nostalgic trance and emboldened by strong drink, lisped and giggled at the expense of our institute's one and only and long-gone rival. "I have."

"Your schools proved the winner," he stated, making it clear he had once worked for the opposing team.

As the rain outside intensified, I noticed he no longer eyed the keys on the wall. It seemed he was now preparing to tell me a story. He'd spent my entire lifetime in a prison—what was another hour?

The youngest son in a long line, I had been shunted to the bile-soaked destiny of medical doctor. But as the notorious snatcher slayer took a pull and his eyes glazed, I was to learn how much worse a plight a man could be given.

"Winner in what game?" I asked, prompting what was to come.

"One with many players." That euphoric-killing look of his returning. "The institute here and the Bileprine, sure, but also all us snatchers who slinked and slithered and brained each other out in City Cemetery. Then there were all the damn ghouls."

I was the captor of intrigue, but in the same way I'd been when I'd silently waited in the cadaver repository, hoping to see a finger twitch or a leg rise.

I said I'd regret not hearing his tale, though later my only regret would be that I'd met him. He grabbed my bottle, and then he began.

No rustic campgrounds for me (Bosgaard said), at least not for long. As a boy, I was drawn in by Nilghorde. The clamor and whirl of her markets, the handsome laughter of her lively women. I knew I desired city life by the time I neared the height of my father.

Like most members in the Chapwyn flock, he was as strict as he was devoutly poor. I never shared his views, though I played scroll-beating zealot the same way other, more fortunate boys mimicked their own fathers as tiny lawmen or carpenters.

The only Chapwyn topic I enjoyed were the scriptures dealing with the undead. Though such ghasts and fiends were referred to as literal, they were treated by the religious as mythic and cautionary metaphors. My father viewed my poring over such pages not with pride, but with sideways glances and an off-put worry.

His problems, however, became far more tangible when our choiring camp fell stricken by disease. When petitions to the city churches became pleas, we received a short but pompous letter detailing how the priests wanted eagerly to help, prayed for us night and day, but were unable to provide medicine, labor, or money. Many bright faces withered. Death took my sisters and my mother, yet my father remained ever faithful, always sure to remind me that forces of good tend to work in mysterious ways.

I don't think I ever really believed him, and neither his rural maxims nor the city priest's abandonment of our parish dampened my desire to walk on cobblestone streets. It was no use scaring me with grim tales of abduction or murder either, though he and eventually the remaining congregation tried. The city wore its allure the way its whores wore perfumes and pearls, a metaphor I would've never dared speak aloud. When I was supposed to be learning the seven sojourns of Ansul, I was instead dreaming of days touched by trumpets, nights nestled in throngs above fabled fighting pits.

Like all young men, I viewed the world unrealistically. Reckless, I did what youth has always prescribed: pitied those who fed me, scoffed at how they were able to, and thought no more about it because one day, unlike them, I'd be famous and rich.

When Chapwyn children turn sixteen, they're given the option to renounce the religion. For most, it's a notional event, having already sewn the frocks and vestments to be worn until the rot of sweat and grime have reclaimed them for the earth. But my case, painfully then, obviously now, was one quite different. My decision left me without food or family, but it also left me free.

I'd hoped to become a celebrated juggler, or if that didn't pan out, perhaps pursue wider horizons and sign on for one of the Municipal One's ships. In my newfound freedom, I was free to learn that I was no juggler, nor was I the stuff of a future admiral.

I'd traded poverty in the woods for its meaner urban cousin. Coming of age, the need for money greeted me like air greets the lungs of a man chained to the bottom of a river. Many years later, our cell's most articulate inmate suggested that my widely-agreed-upon somberness was also an inherited trait. I'd always acknowledged just one. New to Nilghorde, starving and unskilled, I harnessed the one marketable attribute my father had given me: muscles under my rags like that of a shaved chimp.

I started working for Bileprine. By the looks you've given, I know you're aware snatchers were responsible for robbing graves. Well, not *all* the graves that got plucked were done by humans hoping to profit, or humans at all. But the dead hauled from coffins and tombs and dropped on examination tables, that was us.

Bileprine was new, thus an underdog, thus requiring tactics that snatchers hired by your institute didn't have to—or maybe didn't want to—employ. Our group was especially pernicious, headed by a man barely distinguishable from a lower devil. Though I hadn't participated, the Bileprine Boys also lured to their doom hungry drifters and hungrier orphans.

Having trouble one night out in Whisperer's Plain, I nearly jumped out of my skin when a female voice said from above, "I hope Bileprine isn't expecting her delivered whole."

I was down *in* a hole, one I'd dug and now standing on the edge of the casket I'd opened. Without the convenience of lamplight, my work was guided by the moon and stars, or, when unavailable, my hands. Moon and hands was the case this night, and I'd been caught trying to wrench free the corpse from an unseen entanglement.

"Here, use my lantern," the soft voice said: scouring me, the hole, the body, everything, in a blinding light. "And why no tarp?"

"Over the hole?" I grimaced.

"Well yes, silly. You could use lanterns or candles then, unless you see in the dark like a cat. *That*, however, is looking doubtful."

"I can't see anything now," I said, uncovering my face to a world of blinking dots.

"Poor thing. Such a sad fate."

I'd thought her words and the tone accompanying them were meant to jibe me, in the way inflicted and suffered by those typical of lurking about graveyards. Dark humor and hair cropped close to the head—this creature was most certainly a snatcher, yet most certainly not a boy. As I regained my vision, this slim silhouette sprawled on the grass to peer at my work, showing a fair face concerned over the corpse that I still held by the wrist.

Since her lantern was likely to get us both killed, it seemed wasteful not to take full advantage of it. The dead woman hadn't been dead long. This I knew, not only for the absence of repulsive odors, but because I'd watched them bury her. What I hadn't seen at dusk, I saw now.

"The neck glands are still swollen." the living of the two women said. My observations concurred, though I knew not what it meant, other than it made my skin crawl. The neck on this one, those glands, they were like lodged pears just plucked from a tree sunned by Hell's giving flames. "Did her family put any bouquets of Pavonia in her coffin? Or what about a wreath of onions around her feet?"

I looked. They had. Both. When I confirmed her prognosis, she did not elate as I'd thought she would. She only sulked.

"Just as I suspected."

She shook my filthy hand and said her name was Bella. The corpse that had brought us together had died of a disease whose name I'll spare you the annoyance and me the embarrassment of trying to remember—yes! That was it! *Tullbifita*.

Bella worked for your institute as a snatcher, but she wasn't evil, she wasn't even bent. Bella had worked at some rat-and-bandage infirmary in the southern sprawl of the Thunder Bustle. Full of compassion, she'd take the corpses of the unclaimed and the forgotten and bring them here. She did this to "better serve humanity" rather than see them "discarded like trash" in the Pauper Vault.

Though she refused to be called a specialist, she was. The contents of a vomit bucket, the size and demeanor of a particular tumor—that infirmary left her a reluctant expert in the signs of a cadaver's final killer. It must have been to provide for a sick mother, or maybe to keep off the streets and out of the whore-houses a brood of baby sisters, but for whatever reason, she joined the IHS Body Snatcher's Guild. We met on a night she'd been tasked out to find someone destroyed by *Tull-bifita*.

I gave her my body, though as I watched her supple backside strut off before disappearing behind an obelisk, I wished I could say that first part with an entirely different meaning. I felt the fool. A night's digging with nothing to show for it. Worse, I'd given a valued corpse to a competitor. Worse yet, I would never see that competitor again.

She disappointed me by proving me right. Night after night, restless birds become articulate, the winds whipping past head-stones seeming to call or to giggle. A week later perhaps, I'd perfected my foolishness by meandering near disease-riddled graves far too close to sunrise. Be it the Watchmen or the Ward who caught you, a trespasser with a severed foot in his pocket was met with far worse than irons.

My work was disrupted too. More than once, I'd toss my shovel and silently argue with no one why I hadn't been bold enough to kiss her. Would she have let me? Even in the faces of the fairer dead, I saw the woman who'd winked at me before scampering off the right side of the world.

Having convinced myself at last that she wasn't worth remem-bering, I'd just pried open a particularly rank coffin when she dropped down beside me. Three rags around my face had pre-vented decayed bowels from upending my stomach, but the sight of her bested me. Blaming the smell for why I'd puked, not flut-tering nerves, would end up being only the first lie I'd concoct because of her.

Like rat colonies rivaling over the same heap, snatchers were prohibited from interacting. The Institute of Human Sciences was the worst. If any of the IHS Body Snatcher's Guild were caught with Bileprine scum, it would result in immediate termination, a black mark on their underworld jacket, and, if the opportunity arose, the bone-mongers threatened to haul off to the nearest Ward station with a litany of allegations. True or untrue, on the head of a former hire, they were useful ways to rid themselves of a traitor.

But in that foulness, atop a coffin lid, she kissed me. I was good at it too, or so she said, prompting me to suffocate her with more.

This led to us meeting most nights. On the ones we weren't able to work alone, we'd slip away from our colleagues, even if only long enough to hug and pet like insane children. To our great advantage, both institutes back then demanded more stiffs than snatchers could unearth. With us all spread thin as mist, solitary assignments were the norm.

We picked graves together, bestowing the other with generosities. I handed her stillborn triplets. She let me take a man whose skin still gleamed so heartily under the stars that we couldn't help but entertain that a witch had buried her grown-obsolete plaything in radiant unlife. But for all the rings and brooches I furtively pocketed, she left the dead's ornaments in place, even refolding their arms back to their family's posture of choice after I'd slung them onto her cart.

After work, as the sun pinked the rim of the world, we'd skip off together. My hovel too often visited in those days by my fellow rogues, Bella and I would abscond to her quaint apartment instead, as pert with white lace and wholesome reds as I'd expect of a Lotgard Lady. No offense, of course. You understand.

One evening, the Bileprine Boys received word a member of the Ward had killed himself, so hulking he broke two branches on his garden tree before the third helped a noose send him to oblivion. The Bileprine slobbered their lust for this specimen. After an overdrawn ceremony, the Ward's color guard marched off under snapping standards, leaving the grave for every snatcher with a pocket to fill.

I don't remember much about that night itself, other than I had to work with my group and that the moon hung low and swollen. A strange thing about the Metropolitan Ward: for all their self-righteousness, they tend to bury their dead in the lowest bowls of a graveyard. This suicide being no exception, the tombstones surrounding our target served as concealers. We crept closer.

I made for the grave along with the rest, but as we advanced shadows met us from behind opposing sarcophagi. The first skirmish between the guilds: fists, teeth, and soon the clank and tear of crowbars meeting stubby swords. I had leveled one and was making my way to another. Then I saw her. Bella had come with her group. My vile leader had her pinned down, his dagger rising.

Without a breath, I beat him with my shovel until his brains were on and under and mixed with the mud as to not distinguish what was man's and what was the earth's. By the time I heard the smacks of horse armor, the frenzied tugs at my shoulder had vanished, along with their tugger.

I never blamed her leaving me. Bella knew what was at stake. Soon, I would too. I made it just over the cemetery wall before being detained and tossed in the Municipal Dungeon.

Funny how failing to drop a backpack can so drastically alter one's life. For the paltry charge of *possession of grave-robbing tools*, there I learned I could still long for the rugged comfort of the woods when opposed with iron bars and a stone floor. I ate when another man said to. I slept in hay turned foul and thanked my appearance more than once when I saw what happened to scrawny lads.

Bella, she wrote and wrote, about life and love and longing. The letters came until one day they didn't. I couldn't pull my heart from my throat. Was she hurt? Did she need my help? Had she found another? Deprived of the perfumed parchment that had connected me to the world, I experienced torment worse than any tainted gruel or bored guard could ever hope to inflict. After a year, I emerged from the dungeon to start again my work and find again my love.

Sucked back into the Bileprine Boys, slap-dashed with dug-up armor and outfitted with crude weaponry, I learned the IHS Body Snatcher's Guild had been blamed for the murder of our old leader. What had once been minor feuds had turned into an all-out war. My plight intensified, my hackles raised the higher. Upon my first battle, I learned from the enemy under my boot that Bella had gotten married.

Distraught, I did my shameful diligence. I found her in a merry little home nestled midblock off Burnt Beetle Lane. Several nights spent peeking through their windows showed me Bella, whose hair had remained short and sporty, though her kitchen apron gave her an appearance I couldn't readily describe.

Merry soon gave way. This husband, he not only doubled her age, tripled her in weight, he barked orders and made demanding gestures from their table to the washroom and back again. Cruel are the gods; I bore witness to her spread-leg serfdom for an IHS professor. I wanted to seize the first loose brick and kick open his door, but I held my impulses, for a year caged amongst thieves had taught me stealth. On the third or fourth night, I watched as his critique of her cooking escalated into physical abuse. Abandoning patience— I trust, young man, you'll keep this next part between drinking brethren—I stormed in and killed that troll with my bare hands.

After I was able to finally pry squealing euphoria itself off of me, I assured Bella we'd never be separated again and we took the corpse to Bileprine, where it was recognized and I lauded a hero for the second time in one night. "Let's work for both institutes," Bella suggested.

It was improvement at its finest. Not only would I rid myself of unpleasant company, but I'd gain the fairest. No longer pitted against each other, no longer imprisoned by the bar and the wall— or press-gang marriages, as Bella pled that I understand. We'd no longer be under the peering eyes of illiterate guards and husbands who trashed outgoing letters. We would fall off the face of the earth, only to emerge at night to loot the dead and, as she insisted, help the living. In no time, we sat under the spires of an obelisk near the wealthy Maedraderium, arguing over which bones would go to which institute and predicting which would bid the highest.

To our former colleagues, we were two more cases of snatchers being snatched. They'd warned us about working alone in such warring days, but we'd refused to listen, and our innards must've simply ended up fondled by larval doctors. Under this illusion, our purses swelled with coin, and later our new apartment with furnishing fit only for the most successful of lovers. With her knack for spotting a calamity's symptoms and my dungeon-forged ability to stand the firm negotiator, we rapped on all the doors we'd rapped on before, but now, sound the trumpets, not as face-less competitors from rival guilds, but as the formidable Bosgaard and Bella.

Success is a funny thing, in that what once drives us gives way to new concerns. We'd feasted on priced snails, fowl from Pelliul, gorged ourselves on Quinnarian wine, made love atop silk and under swaying braids of pearl and gold…and the prospect of losing it maddened me. Dreams of luxury were replaced with nightmares of pallid forests still calling my name.

She at first ignored my anxieties, then enhanced them with ever-worse versions of poverty when her frustrated attempts at consolation provided me no solace. I was able to eventually convince her we'd end up huddled in a shit-smeared corner of her infirmary if our ambition was to slacken so much as a flake chipped from a bar of gold. Higher risk meant greater reward.

"Can you believe it?" she said. "Another tunnel."

"Climb out of there."

I hoisted her off the coffin and out of the hole. Though we were in a work area not as heavily guarded as its Ansul of Chapwyn neighbor, City Cemetery was the most dangerous. There were the Ward-trekked thoroughfares, entire patches of graves lit like daybreak with the help of absent trees and the surprise of a smiling moon, and too, increasingly worrisome, was the discovery of more and more of these tunnels. Bella and I had made City Cemetery our permanent territory, but it seemed we weren't the only ones.

I had seen similar tunnels before. Digging down deep enough, hitting the *right* graves, long halls of packed earth had led to, or away. Though I told myself snatchers of a most ambitious nature had taken to the underworld, such a notion never gave me the gall to get on my hands and knees and see where the tunnels would take me.

As we lowered Bella's lantern, the broke-open, emptied coffin wasn't the only thing peculiar. The tunnel's collapsing narrowness and scrawled claw marks spoke not of the ones I'd thus far encountered. Who—or *what*—had dug those had done so with the tact and time suggesting reuse. The one before us was done in haste. Its architect new.

"If this is ghoul work, we're relocating to Whisperer's Plain."

"They won't hurt us," she said. "It's said they only attack each other, or set each other up for run-ins with sworders or to be killed by the sun."

A ghoul encounter wasn't what frightened me. For all the myths orbiting them, my upbringing had nailed firm that despite their brutish power and weapons-grade stench, ghouls were cowards. It may have also been a remnant of my upbringing, but the prospect of bumping into the undead didn't make me toss and turn in my sleep. Being poor again did.

In the few places where encounters with the underworld were

spoken of with the normalcy of farmers exchanging gabs about the weather, the murmurs were all the same: ghouls had always stirred under City Cemetery. Now, for reasons that were slowly becoming clear, they quarreled.

Still, Bella's observations had been correct. We couldn't afford to be ensnared in any of their schemes. Enraged men with blades were a threat to pickers of graves, man or ghoul.

✳

"Will you not at least consider it?" the flustered adjunct professor from Bileprine said. "They took a vote, twice. They'd want you to do it."

I can't remember his name, or if he'd even given it to me, but this messenger for the Bileprine always reminded me of a pigeon. Amongst his chalkboard-cleaning duties and scurrying under professors who were no longer worried by the threat of poverty, he had more nefarious obligations, like meeting Bella and I in a bleak bar where cemetery mud caked the floor.

"Look," he said, "we both know this will hurt business. While the rest of the world hopes ghouls do not exist, everyone unfortunate enough to sit at this table knows otherwise. This flare-up of theirs will pull eyes to the cemetery."

Bella joined me in my laughter, reddening further our company. Though he knew his message was a preposterous one, he was still commanded to convincingly deliver.

"Even if I could *sit down with them*," I said, "even if I could guard my hide from their boar-tusk fangs, ghouls have no more honor than their former, despicable human selves had—and, might I add, such forsaken lives are why those tallow-hearted, corpse-eating vermin exist at all. Being the broker of peace between two ghoul chieftains is literally the definition of time wasted."

"Then let us think beyond peace," he brightened, having walked me into a trap. "An alliance with Paltumorr."

Disbelief had once consumed me too, but Glibbmor wasn't the only ghoul to ever own a name. Glibbmor and Paltumorr, opposite as they were alike. Vile, stinking, just one a rock the other a spindly devil. Glibbmor, the rock one, led a pack that dug from graveyard to graveyard. From sources that not even I wished to know, word had risen that he'd wearied of roaming. This did not sit well with Paltumorr, leader of the ghoul clan that long reigned under City Cemetery.

"If they can't share corpses like nice boys and ghouls," the adjunct said, enraging Bella's snarls with that awful pun, "find us a way to side with Paltumorr. Things were fine before this Glibbmor invaded City Cemetery. You've heard the same things I have, Boz. Rumors of mausoleum doors being left wide open. The Ward clattering at the gates like hornets. It's bad for business."

It was true Paltumorr and I now shared common enemies. Ridding the earth and the burrows coursing beneath it of Glibbmor would return both our operations to normal. Normal for Bella and I meant continued payment, and not an increase in the chances that we'd lose the connection between our head and neck.

"But what am I to do," I said, "even if such a feat were possible? Confess to the Ward how I'm able to commune with ghouls and how I know of their tunnels?"

"You'd also be paid to figure such things out." The payment he proposed was good—very good.

Bella grew serious. "The IHS also approached us about the *ghoul problem.*"

"Yeah," I said, taking her cue and turning him into a stack of indignant snorts, "and they're offering double what you Bileprines are."

Ignoring Bella, the adjunct leaned in. "We want this...this ghoul civil war over and done with. You will want it over too, Boz." Then he staggered me with the sum we'd receive if we hauled in the body of "Bishop Vhulviel. The old brimstone thrower just died. And we want him."

✳

Walking in City Cemetery the next morning, our cover as mourners in route to a familiar headstone had perhaps been blown by our giggles and guffaws. We'd turned down Bileprine's offer. I had periodically said no to bolster our stance in future barters, but this last one I'd genuinely felt their absurdity. Besides, we'd said yes to the real task. Due to Chapwyn rituals, we had time to prepare. In one week, the church would place Bishop Vhulviel in an impenetrable tomb—made all the more impenetrable, we learned, by executing its master mason for the convenient discovery of his unforgivable sins.

As we'd expected, not only had the IHS become aware of ghoul conflicts, but they too wanted the bishop. If legends of his proximity to the supernatural were correct, theories would be tested regarding the housing of the soul in the heart and brain.

I remembered from the early days that those ascribed to the religion were never cremated. My own ancestors over in the Ansul graveyard were testament to that. Buried due to obscure and contradicting scriptures on resurrection, those hoping to be whisked away by Tersiona's winged messengers went into coffins, or luxurious tombs, to rot whole.

We had to employ our utmost caution and ingenuity. Bella's idea of hiring a skilled thief for the tomb's locks was high on our list. The bag of gold coming from this haul would require a cart and a strong ox to wheel off. We'd never have to snatch again. I never loved descending worsening layers of stench with a short-handled shovel. Bless religious charity, the bishop would allow me to apprentice as a silversmith, or maybe a juggler.

Bella did not join in my excitement. She recanted her

suggestion, and even began explaining that maybe we ought to respect the sanctity of the good bishop.

Our daylight sojourn had been rare, but for good reason. We had arrived at the vaulted mausoleum. We were here, despite Bella's bout of dithering, to conduct our reconnaissance.

"Look at that," I said.

"We'll never get in."

Almost as large as a mansion in the Morgeltine, the tomb's granite stairs led to iron doors bolted airtight against thick, siege-deflecting marble impartially reflecting the blue of morning. There were enough gables atop this mammoth to hide a score of arrow-ready guards.

"Maybe the sewers?"

"You think dead people need to use the privy, do you?" She joined me on a low sarcophagus to stare at a manhole cover in the cobblestone pathway.

The manhole gave me an idea, and perhaps the beginnings of a plan. From this entrance to the city's sewers, we were practically under the mausoleum already. Even if the church had considered infiltration from ghouls, the ghouls feared iron, which meant fortifications may not have included considerations for chisels or a hefty crowbar.

Lost in contemplation, I rambled as I sometimes do: "Did you know Chapwyns are called Chapwyns because they say that's the surname Tersiona gave Ansul?"

"What for?"

"Oh, he followed some instruction, pitied an orphan, kissed a leper."

Instructions, indeed. I'd seen what obeying such selfless commandments had done when sick Chapwyn families in the countryside called upon the aid of their gilded leaders. I drummed up dreams of what jewels I'd pry, what vestments encrusted with ruby and gold I'd stuff into my bag—compensation for too many years under the yoke that bled its most devout and best-intended the most dismally dry.

Bella gasped, stowing her protest for later. I'd scurried over and jammed my fingers under the manhole's rust-lined cover, lifting it.

"Someone may have seen you," she said, lancing me with one of those glances she did before giving me a bout of the silent treatment. "If so, this awful caper's over already."

"Nobody saw. There has to be a way in, Bell. If we—"

"Boz, I have a very bad feeling about this. Not only does it give me the creeps, but what about the charities these people've done? What about all the mouths fed and dreary days inspired because this man wished it so?" After a moment, she put the crown jewel on this rant of hers: "I'm thinking of joining their church."

Next her big bleeding heart would hearken pity for the ghouls. "Bella," I said, following her march out of the cemetery. "You don't mean that."

"Don't tell me what I do and do not mean."

"Bella. Stop."

"What?"

"We do this," I said, as if putting a saddle on a skittish mare, "it's the last one. No more robbing graves. With the money, we can build you a new infirmary. A better one."

Several pleas of a similar nature later, her face began to slacken. Her eyes lost most of their squint. Galvanized, I added: "We can make our own leper-kissing station."

I had become a juggler at last, though of words and promises. "And you'll be the one doing the kissing, good sir," she said, "if this goes awry."

We walked under the cemetery's arches and reentered the street. Bella hummed and skipped, in high spirits. Now it was I who worried.

Word reached us the next day, confirming a number of my fears. Watchmen not only caught some snatchers hours after we'd left, but bellowed how they'd been clued to such scandalous efforts by laughter that could have only come from the rasping jowls of ghouls. Much to the chagrin of Bileprine and the IHS, City Cemetery was swarmed.

I confirmed this when I braved another daylight trip. The stamping of Ward horses and the calls of their riders down to watchmen leaning on halberds, I lifted the manhole just long enough to slip into the sewer a small statue I'd torn off the nearest headstone. Then I was gone like a hare.

When I returned home, Bella had them laid across our bed. The Hall of Records held it all, including maps of the sewers and clerks who asked no questions to pretty girls. Nilghorde had suffered generations of fires, collapses, and rebuilds that could entomb a century. As a result, the squiggled lines all overlapped the other in a bewilderment of red and green.

Night meant little while underground, but it was crucial to anyone above, wishing to go down while living on a busy street. We entered the sewers with a goodbye to the stars, hoping to navigate by lantern and mark our way with sticks of chalk until at last coming upon the statue I'd dropped down.

I suppose years in our line of work had prepared us. The cramped spaces, the smell, the legions of scurrying rats. Shadows danced and flickered when we'd arrive at turns not shown on our maps or a sudden staircase leading to nowhere. After an eternity of backtracking, we discovered storm drains and avenues for run-off were our lines of green.

To our good fortune, we'd dropped in through a storm drain and, to my best guess, the piping that ran under the rim of the Chapwyn mausoleum was also for the weather. Though outdated, most city streets were reflected on the map as black lines. Sitting on a wagon wheel that had somehow fallen down and been forgotten, Bella and I double and triple-checked our own street. We at least knew where we'd started, and to get to City Cemetery, we had to utilize several junctions of red.

Comparing the smell of rotting flesh to rivers of shit is like weighing whether it's better to be eaten by a shark or a bear. Edges of teetering bricks and flimsy boards left by workers helped us avoid wading through waste, though it didn't help us find our way.

I was turning to announce my abandonment of our night's effort when it happened. It started when the brick she was balancing on gave. That give became a slide, and no grip nor ladder was there for Bella's flailing arms when she disappeared in an awful splash. When I found my footing and lifted her, flies that had been pulled down from the surface burst skyward while Bella cried and vomited and covered me in pure foulness.

Curse my soul, part of me wanted to laugh. I exhausted our waterskins trying to clean her. To no avail, I could only obey her frantic request, popping open the nearest manhole cover, keeping my concerns to myself when we emerged onto a trafficked avenue.

A new concern rattled me the following morning when I discovered Bella hadn't gotten out of bed.

"You're boiling," Though this was so, she shook as if lying on a block of ice.

"I'm going to die—that, or turn into a ghoul."

"Don't speak of such things." I retracted my hand from her forehead. Her paleness made it too easy for thoughts of either ill fate.

Her eyes glazed, her head jostled. "Have I been a good person, Boz? Am I now?" She said, "I saw her, Bosgaard. Her golden face."

"Saw who?"

"Tersiona."

Bella's spill had rendered her sick as anyone I'd ever envisioned her attending. Her fever had her seeing the Goddess of Good, and before long she engaged in protracted talks with similar hallucinations above our bed or dwelling inside the bowl of soup I'd made for her.

I had wanted to go over the night's route, a far better one that should send us over what appeared to be a pile of ruins. Then it was a straight shot to City Cemetery. But now I was unable. My offer to bring her to an infirmary only made her cuss and writhe, confirming my long-held belief that she knew what abject conditions she'd always toiled in. I sat beside her and clasped her fishy hand. She moaned incoherent fears about a cruel world, us fiddling with priests, fiddling with ghouls, death itself. After a while, she tired, leaving me able to pry myself from soaked sheets.

Her words did not leave me as I labored. Chalk sticks cinched in bags, both lanterns filled again with oil, both maps rolled and sealed in separate map cases made of bone. Redundancy calmed a nervous mind. I would be going below alone tonight, as I'd done most of my life. This time I would be leaving her to bake in her illness. The spike and plummet of her fits did not make this easy.

My hands shook when she wailed about dying and heaven and what might be crawling out from under our bed to take us there. Like a lever on a drawbridge, my breathing would slow and cool when she partially regained her senses.

Eventually, I fixed my thoughts on Bella pulling through. Even as I hiked my pack onto my shoulders and kissed her goodbye, I saw strong life still flickering. Her eyes no longer as crazed, my lips still pressed against clammy heat, but it wasn't the inferno I'd felt only hours before.

"You are leaving me?" she moaned, lifting a hand to point at the door.

"We can't afford not to get this route figured out. I can stay if you want."

"No. No, go. I could use the quiet."

Having moused about the place without so much as letting lanterns clank, I resented the remark, though given her condition it was easy to forgive. "You'll be better in no time," I said, "probably just a bad fever."

"You know nothing!" she snapped. "I don't tell you about lifting lids or shoving a shovel." The insults which followed were hard to ignore. I'd made soup for a turned-harpy. Wincing out the door, the last I heard of her was her trailing off a list of her own dreary symptoms.

✳

Back down in the sewer, I was immediately of a sounder mind. She was just sick, dreadfully so. In my own moments of irritated rage, I'd also unsheathed my share of harshness.

Amidst the arches, her words morphed into trinkets of their own charm. It bemused me, how she could be so soft, like a fairy, yet so full of hellfire. This was good for my morale, I suppose, for soon I was lost again.

Flustered, I followed the chalk marks I'd made until reaching my starting point. I kept failing to reach City Cemetery, but I was learning more with every failure.

To get my bearings, I carefully lifted a cover. My spirit joyed, not just at the night's refreshing coolness, but at all the tombstones that walled in my view. Though on the opposite end of my goal I had found the edge of the cemetery.

The walls here were thicker. Adjoining sewer-tunnels far less. These grounds housed the dead, and space had been made to accommodate. Despite fewer tunnels, I still managed to get hopelessly turned around. Perhaps the maps themselves were incorrect. I aimed to confirm this by lifting another cover. Doing so, I should have cheered, for my frustrated path had actually taken me closer to the Chapwyn mausoleum. Instead, the sight almost sent me scrambling down and backwards, staying my celebration.

After those snatchers had been caught, it was common for a time to see encampments of armed families or paid henchmen astride protected graves. One such mercenary was directly in front of the cover I'd raised, listlessly leaning against a tombstone, waiting for any reason to use his battle axe.

Having scampered back, I told Bella my discoveries, and my excitement doubled when her color began to return and malaise lift. Then she relapsed.

Her illness blew hot and cold, lasting for days. It also breathed new fire into why we needed to strike it rich. Bella knew her affliction, and the necessary syrups and serums I bought cost us a chariot.

Only two nights before Bishop Vhulviel was to be entombed, I slogged back down for another chalking session. Bella's last bout had turned into a cough and renewed contemplations. Her Chapwyn talk would not have twisted me so if it weren't for my disgruntled feelings over—well, by then I could tell you the street corners above which arch sweated grime and which sewer arch was dry and bare. What I could not do was arrive under the manhole next to the damn mausoleum.

I'd frontiered into a new tunnel somewhere under the Maedraderium and stewed in my frustration. My thoughts were on Bella, though I forced them back to my wretched navigation. There was no god, no gods either. And if there were, they must have enjoyed watching me suffer, for they gifted me nothing.

Then I tripped over a jewel-laden gauntlet.

I knew right then that I should have been plundering the dead differently. The wealth I'd left untouched while opting for convenience and cautiously avoiding the tombs of the rich. But where had this ornate piece of armor come from?

I covered my lantern. When I found no moonlight oozing in, I was unable to confirm my suspicions. In the world above, someone must have been murdered—a rich someone— afterward being thrown down so one of his gauntlets could somehow wiggle free and roll away.

I uncovered my lantern to gaze upon another delight. A necklace gleamed, its brilliant white reflecting off bricks lathered in slime.

I put the necklace in my pocket, and as I salivated over what I was sure to find next, I discovered I was facing the entrance to another tunnel. At the base of this new passage, the slabs that had been my walkway were covered with fresh dirt. Loose bricks, some broken, lain strewn about. Roots hung from its ceiling, a ceiling far lower than where I stood. Crude and malformed, it was like the tunnel Bella and I had seen leading from that coffin.

I crept to its edge. Blackness refused to give way until I was able to strain, far in the distance, yet another glimmer.

I entered to a worsening odor, one that made the sewer entirely less irksome. I'd thought at first the culprit had been found. At the toe of my boot, an arm lay ripped free from some corpse, one presumably missing a necklace. Maggots undulated and flexed, and amongst them were marks on the ripe forearm suggesting a once-tight gauntlet. I dropped that very thing, scrambling to wipe my hands, before picking the gauntlet back up and burying it deep in my bag.

I was no physician, but I had seen many effects of trauma. I lurched forward to stare at teeth marks near the armpit. This arm hadn't just been torn; it had been bitten. Every detail was there, right out of the pages. All that was needed were cackles and pointy ears. Ghouls—they were with me.

Turns out eaters of the dead care nothing for their meal's decorations. Despite my senses, I continued onward, picking up dropped pins and jewelry. It wasn't entirely insane. I'd listened a long while, waiting without so much as shifting my boot, straining into blackness to hear the digging of earth, the scratches of approaching claws. There'd been nothing.

But collecting more forsaken wealth was not the only reason I pushed on, nor even the main one. This ghoul path was leading directly across the cemetery and toward the mausoleum. If they'd broken the walls behind me, they may have done the same ahead.

The smell thickened. There were moments where I was required to crawl on my hands and knees, experiencing for the first time an earth that not only provided loose bones, but things that wriggled.

A sudden fall landed me on fetid bedrock, destroying my lantern in a light-blighting clatter. My nostrils seethed and singed. I'd face-planted into a pile of dung. I could try to describe it, how it was too large to be a man's and that I knew what decomposing shat I flung from my cheeks and chin while I puked more violent than murder. But it would do the nightmare no justice. Just know you can smell nothing worse, for I never had.

I scrambled for what I'd hoped was up and out of that foul pit. Doing so led me into another tunnel. Bereft of light, I crawled inside just deep enough to furiously apply my waterskins and begin fishing for my spare lantern.

It took only a moment to hear the echoes. Someone was talking.

My better judgment suggested that I remain without light. I held no desire to traverse that pit again, and my situation improved when I crawled forward, toward the voice, and found my hands patting the fluted grooves of a fallen pillar.

The map had indicated ruins, and I had found them. But any deliberations, any good plans revisited, any joys that I might have felt were obliterated when the voice returned.

A city sewer worker was an encounter I'd somewhat anticipated, though by the latter nights I was creeping about in places that appeared entirely abandoned. But where I crawled now was another ghoul tunnel. Not just for its characteristic stench or burrowed walls did I know this. When I peered over the pillar, I still saw nothing, but a voice not coming from a man's throat growled and gloated.

"You worm in here," it said, sounding like the scraping of rusted metal, "and think there won't be consequence! For such loitering?"

I was looking out over something like a miniature arena. It had survived the collapsing of pillars and walls that now lay toppled around the upper rim. I knew this because there was light here, though dim. As my eyes adjusted, from high up, a tiny window appeared in the dirt ceiling. Through it glowed the light of the moon.

I knew where I was. There is a massive headstone out in City Cemetery; though laid flat on the earth, its peculiar architect cut into its design a real window. Though thick and opaque, though I'm sure at first the headstone pushed against only harmless dirt, the ghouls had burrowed all the way up to its glass, and were now using it.

"Bring 'em out!"

What I saw both terrified and delighted. I wanted to run. I wanted to flee. I wanted to peer over farther and gaze upon these creatures. Human enough, the way you imagine them is probably close. Long arms. Sinewy legs. Bald heads sporting the ears of an elf. In the waning moonlight, their jaws reminded me of hyenas at a zoo, though these were fearfully unchained and from such jaws came shrieks of hideous laughter.

"Yes, yes," the tall one lusted, "bring them out so they can see mother moon one last time."

This tall one giving the orders must have been Paltumorr. A full head above the rest, his grey hide was lank and lean. His wretched, spider-like limbs all connected to a saggy torso, grown soft and bloated from centuries feasting on catered bits. His subordinates, ghouls of no less ugliness, dragged out other ghouls whose own limbs appeared to have been bitten off. Paltumorr's captives, I wagered, were Glibbmor Ghouls. This was confirmed when the wiggling wretches were dropped on the stone floor where the moonlight glowed the hardest.

"Use the sewers, do you?" Paltumorr said. "You Glibbmor scum invade my territory? Well, know *we*'re in *your* mannish tunnels now too. Enjoy the moon, boys. For the sun rises."

The Glibbmor Ghouls screeched. Paltumorr's chanted in a hoarse chorus: "Pal—too—more, Pal—too—mooore."

I backtracked. There was no way I could proceed further and expect to keep my life or sanity. So I backtracked, careful not to disturb a rock or loosen a gnawed-on bone from its fissure in the earthen wall. Able to avoid pits or worse, revisiting a chewed-off arm, I at last returned to the sewer, its familiar bricks the dearest of friends. I contemplated sealing the entrance, but with no mortar or time, I abandoned such thoughts and tied down my mind to continue in my original course.

Soon I found what I hoped with all my soul was the needed intersection. I turned right as the map had suggested. As dawn began to ache, the storm drains through which its light burned became spaced out by an encouraging cadence. At a slight bend to the left, I found myself staring at a statue lying amongst sodden leaves—a saintly woman, torn from a headstone. I had found it!

No water and no sleep made for a tough walk back. I followed my marks, giddy when I'd come upon a landmark now committed to memory. By noon, I made it back to the drain nearest our apartment, our starting point for the morrow's great task.

If there was ever a sign of our success, it was not fine dishes in our pantry, but that we could afford a place near Nilghorde's main Chapwyn temple. We lived close enough to their headquarters to be awoken four times a year by the banging of their gong. Coming from above, I recognized the hymns of an indoctrination ceremony.

For all its stupendousness, what I saw then I had a harder time believing as real than what I'd witnessed only hours. A "miracle"—though still wan, her hair marred by a sweaty pillow, Bella had risen from her bed, and from the concealment of the storm drain I watched her walk past and enter the church.

I waited for a break in traffic and climbed out onto the street.

Covered in grime, I fit well with the poorest of poor, taken to their knees. As I shouldered through, I watched Bella make her way to the front and get ushered up to the altar. Having been one of the very few humans to actually see, hear, and smell ghouls, I welcomed the confines of the church and its goers. Maybe I would even inform the Chapwyns of my discoveries, perhaps starting a ghoul-clearing campaign...but only after we'd cashed in on their bishop and rid ourselves of graveyards.

By his ornaments, the man who held Bella's hand was a high priest. He escorted her into a back room, infuriating me the moment the door closed. While I lingered, my discomfort was made all the more pathetic when I imagined every possible version of what could be transpiring behind that wall of golden leaves and white velvet.

She did not exit those private chambers to rejoin the mass, and the burning incense almost put me on the floor. I hadn't slept since I couldn't remember, but I took the long way home.

✳

I awoke from a deep sleep that bore disturbing dreams. I'd first wandered in the underworld before weaving into the second nightmare standing before me now, dressed in a Chapwyn surplice.

"What of their all-male clergy?" I asked, hoping to prod her from her musings on a fantasy world bent on egalitarianism.

But she wouldn't bother. "They must be quite gallant to women under their wing."

"Bella, that money-sucking cult is as ridiculous as you are! Are you going to tell me—" She held out her hand. In front of my nose, she dangled a large and archaic key. "...And that is?"

"Our way in, silly." I gaped. "Those priest's," she said, "their offices are as labeled as any shelf at Bileprine."

"He left you?" Knowing the answer: "To go grab oils, leaving you to read that infernal passage about rebirth and so on?"

She nodded. "There were maybe a dozen keys to that mausoleum. We won't be depriving them access—just one body from it." What had chained her to the bed had left us. Her spark having returned, she added, "Maybe priests are too busy, or maybe some interpret the scriptures differently, but, to me, we—you and me—we can be more Chapwyn-like here than in any other way. You were right, Boz, and their wealth will serve the world better in hands of those who still feel hunger."

"Take the decorations too?"

"As much as we can fit in our bags."

Sickness had boiled her a mastermind. We kissed and embraced like I had been plagued by fire, and only more kissing could help. After, we formally abandoned the notion of tunneling under to, maybe, get inside by the time we were displaying as many grey hairs as any corpse. Now we could simply sneak up and use a key.

The only consideration remaining was how to get there. Come nightfall, the cemetery would be crawling with watchful eyes and eager blades. Bella first cast me aside with disbelief, one that I remedied by giving her the necklace I'd found and retold my tale until she eventually grew quiet and shuddered. I now knew warring ghouls were maneuvering in the sewers. Yet their reluctance to pop out in front of men armed with sword and dagger, as I would be, left us willing to risk a final trek below.

✳

A brisk morning maligned then crawled through the red-hot hearth of afternoon. At sunset, we descended, following my chalk marks until peering out we beheld the mausoleum. The congregation had already begun to disperse, and as the first stars began to shimmer, the last of the church departed.

I popped the cover off, sliding it quietly aside as we climbed onto the cobblestones. In the still hours between moonset and the sun's first rays, we slinked to the door. The thrill of Bella's key working ran through me.

Soon I was to hear and feel the tumbles and click of the lock unlocking. But I experienced neither. In a discovery that almost sent me to the granite holding my sides, they'd forgotten to lock the door!

Burning lights greeted us as we slipped inside. Bright torches and bursting wreaths were held by hooks and sconces on walls of white marble. Bella shut the door, leaving but a sliver of air between iron and wall. Meanwhile, I inspected the walls themselves: cubbies for middle management.

In the center of this vast tomb were pillars of jade and sparkling emerald housing rows of ornate sarcophagi. It was clear where we needed to go. A castle of candles burned atop one in particular. A crowbar would do the trick.

I knelt to begin my work. So determined was I to collect our prize that I'd paid no attention to the jewels that the torches and candles reflected in, giving the place the effect of a grand ball.

Bella removed the candles. I began to feel the bishop's lid give but I was stopped by a unique foulness entering the tomb. It was so sudden, I'd thought we'd made a mistake and what awaited us under the lid was in its prime rot. Then I heard marble slabs sliding across the other. I'd suffered this smell before.

I knew a ghoul was near.

Bella gasped and latched onto me, costing me the immediate drawing of my sword. What we saw: It couldn't have been the head of a ghoul looking upon us like a sprouted cabbage. And it couldn't have been three—four—seven ghouls climbing out from a hole they'd made, having themselves tunneled under the mausoleum.

Paltumorr's pack was on us like flies. I flung Bella between me and the nearest pillar, slashing wildly at thin air. They snarled, they gnashed, they laughed at Bella's shrill screaming. They clawed with hands like spiked shovels, but for all their gestures their interest in us seemed at best mild. They s were surrounding not us, but the bishop's sarcophagus. It was to be contested, by me and brazen ghouls, until the door of the mausoleum swung wide.

Snatchers poured in, not just by way of the door—some had surmounted the outer walls and broke a high window I hadn't even known existed. With the falling glass, they too swung down into the bloodshed. Having once poked chipped swords and swung shovels at the other, the snatchers for the IHS and for Bileprine now toppled over sarcophagi wielding spears and war hammers. My disbelief clung to the ghouls. More than tunneling *had* been feasible, daring the world aboveground was an extraordinary act for ghouls—especially fighting armed men. They paid dearly for this. Some scampering off, holding their hacked-off limbs in their mouths or their trembling claws.

I had read how they can assume the guise of those whose heart and brains they devour. I saw with my own eyes a ghoul leap on a snatcher who I'd run through, then vanish entirely. That snatcher, nude and crackling with life, soon rejoined the fray. His was a futile gesture. Once risen, he was felled by Bella herself, having procured his old spear that had barely missed her.

Perhaps the disguised ghoul would have survived Bella's thrust, but another ghoul, confused by its cohort's act, attacked him, getting them both cleaved to bits.

I swept and I hacked. I tried to remain Bella's ever-parrying human shield. My swordsmanship was halted when a command-ing grumble erupted from the depths. Those that remained of Paltumorr's kind shrieked. Paltumorr, whom I recognized not only by height but by laughter as he deprived a snatcher of a much-needed arm, growled commands. Shields and blades lowered as the ghouls perked their ears and backed into a circle. Their own tunnel had been compromised.

Glibbmor had arrived.

Pouring onto the blood-smeared marble, the Glibbmor Ghouls attacked. Their leader was the last to emerge. Barking orders, compact like an afflicted gorilla, Glibbmor's red hairs bristled. Everyone, everything able to kill proceeded to. The ghouls' battle spilled in front of me and Bella. To make our escape, I hacked at two, busy rolling in a furious ball, biting the other.

Rushing to end the battle quickly, I suppose, then slipping in human blood, the one who ended up on the bottom was Glibbmor. I don't know why, but I looked far too long into the yellow globes of his eyes. I worked to slay the ghoul on top of him, who did not die easy but whirled in torrents of curses and teeth.

In such chaos, I didn't even know how I'd killed it, only that doing so had deprived me of my weapons, and my breath.

I was leaning against a pillar, gulping the intrusive night air, when a ghoul seized me from behind. It draped an arm over my shoulder then pressed the accompanying claws against my chest. With what I best guess was a fist, it then struck me squarely on the head.

Then I knew no more.

I awoke to find myself near Bella. She too lay on the marble, though no amount of shaking could rouse her. Someone had slit her throat. She lay amongst the knocked-down, stamped-on wreaths.

Screaming and stamping and clawing at my own eyes did no good. Howling at pillars and kicking fresh corpses gave me no solace, nor Bella any begged-for, pled for signs that life had returned. My pleas echoed off taunting, indifferent walls. I returned to her side. I tried to convince myself that her killing blow had at least been clean, her killer humane.

My grief swung back into rage. I would find her killer, somehow. Strewn about, I saw four other dead snatchers. I'd haul off with them all, for it was said that necromancers could raise the dead for a hefty payment. Maybe one had done the slicing, and if not, maybe one had seen who did.

Such thoughts carried me through until I at long last stumbled out from the sarcophagi. Not a single ghoul remained. Many had fallen, by iron and by their own kind, yet speaking I suppose higher of ghouls than of their human counterparts, their footprints led from pools of foul ghoul blood and ended at the mouth of their tunnel.

Bishop Vhulviel's sarcophagus had been knocked over and emptied. Who won, I didn't care. My entire body began to ache and sting, but dulled to dim thrums every time I dared to look at Bella.

I sat on a sullen block of marble. I could not move for I was as done with life as those bludgeoned and cut and strewn around me. My greed had cost me everything.

When Ansul's True marched in, I had no sword to fight with, nor inclination to find one.

I obeyed my first impulse, peering into all those grim faces for the statuesque disapproval of my father. Silence was broken by the squeaks of what I'd first thought was a corpse cart. They wheeled out from behind their ranks a decrepit priest. "Bishop Vhulviel," said his pusher, "your holiness, behold." The ancient buzzard sat in a wheelchair, a smirk running across his face, his skin the stuff of ratted parchment.

Turned over to the Metropolitan Ward, I'd later learn in the cold halls of high court how Bishop Vhulviel had a batch of criminals rounded up and strangled. Placed in a secret tomb, this cache of bodies was meant for Ansul's Call. Upon the great day of resurrection, the bishop, that relic of sanctimony, would triumphantly brandish to none other than Tersiona herself all the sinners he'd removed.

The announcement of his death, his funeral, leaving the damn door unlocked—all a decoy meant to rid the world of more incorrigibles in advance of his actual heavenly arrival. My father's wretched zealots possessed more trickery than feuding snatchers or tunneling ghouls. I'd hear even later, this time from the confines of a dungeon cell, that it was this colorful batch of sinners that had purportedly attracted the ghouls, appealing to their sportive whimsies. Both ghoul clans had hoped to eat the bishop, learn his treasure's whereabouts from his own vile mind, shed his flesh, then scamper off to assume such grand and notorious guises.

One by one, the cold, hard stares of my captors shifted to something behind me. Already seized and in irons, I turned my head and saw, hidden between dense shadow and overturned décor, one ghoul had been left behind.

I could hardly believe my eyes. Paltumorr had been the one attacking Glibbmor, and I had killed him. My sword was driven halfway to the hilt in Paltumorr's gut. My dagger was in his throat, the oaken handle clutched by talons.

This alone saved me the gallows and the preamble of soul-cleansing torture. I'd killed a ghoul, though Bishop Vhulviel lived just long enough to take all the credit.

Though robbing graves was technically a death sentence, killing their robbers wasn't. I was given five years per slain body snatcher, as our lives were not worth a pittance compared to a good citizen's. I was tossed every bribe by the Ward and Chapwyns alike. Five dead snatchers made for heartier bellows than four. Better food, my own cell—with a window even—the possibly of getting out before my skin had turned to spotty leather. But nothing worked. They had no choice but to accept my story: Bella had merely been a murder victim, hauled to that great site of slaughter that fateful morning by an unnamed snatcher hoping to cash in on two corpses.

So she was buried here, at the Institute of Human Sciences, in your honored place just yonder. Yes, I know. She must have meant enough to some here that they claimed her as their own. As difficult as that is to believe, if you'd have met her, you'd understand. I vowed one day to lay roses at her grave, though I would have preferred they be fresh, and my way not barred by so many locks.

Bosgaard's tale was over. Night had long since fallen, and so had the emptied bottle we'd shared. Another student would be slogging to the duty hut soon to relieve me. I sat up and scanned the keys in my charge before lifting from its hook the right one.

"What if she isn't in there?" I said, handing him his key.

"Rattle on church doors, I suppose. Find an old initiate who now wears the cassock of a priest. Find one who was there, beg and plead and tithe until her whereabouts are given to me. But," he said, looking instantly sober, "stories from the dungeon are rarely lore."

I remained at the desk when he left.

Only a few minutes passed before I could take it no longer. Could this woman be in there? I didn't want to intrude on Bosgaard's mourning, but strangely I felt the man might want me in there. After all, he had poured out to me his tale.

The door was open. Bosgaard was still lighting the menagerie of candles when I entered and immediately wished I hadn't. Without looking up, he asked that I shut the door, which I stupidly did, then leaned against it and trembled. I felt like I was in the tale I'd just heard, seeing cubbies for the dead lining the walls. At the outer reaches of candlelight, there was an opened one. The casket that belonged inside it had been pulled down onto to the floor…and opened?

Its contents were ghastly: a shrouded corpse, female and time-withered. Her chest and skull had been torn open.

"We have a guest," Bosgaard said. This guest, if she wasn't the woman he'd explained as his reason for entry, was no guest I wished to meet. He had been a madman all along, and I was about to suffer his unspeakable schemes. He lit the last candle and he looked up, but not at me.

"The sludge in these veins," an awful voice groaned, plastering me against the door, "no spineless dandy can move. He can stay."

"You haven't aged a day, Glibbmor," Bosgaard said. "I am ready."

I almost slipped right off the edge of sanity herself. On a sarcophagus, what I'd first took for a misshapen man sat and leered at me. Flashing his yellow eyes back to Bosgaard, he leaned back to assume a kingly posture. In his overgrown hands was his scepter—a hulking, gnawed-on femur. At his feet, broken tile and dirt had been kicked up from a newly dug tunnel, just as I'd envisioned in that Chapwyn mausoleum. The ghoul smiled a wide, greasy smile when an ill choir of snickers came up from underneath him.

The ghoul leaned forward and gibbered into the tunnel. Only Bosgaard's stoic demeanor shielded me from pure and utter madness, a shield that lifted when we both saw human hands begin to emerge.

What crawled up wore nothing. She covered her breasts with an arm. To conceal her more intimate parts, she reached into the open casket to tear free a piece of the shroud. When she looked upon the twenty-year-old corpse and its familiar dressings, she rose and stared blankly into the candles.

Her face was no less stricken than my own. Her mouth hung open as if preparing to scream, though not knowing to who, her confused eyes suggested, was all that restrained her.

Though frightened, she seemed to float, as if awakening from a dream. She turned and peered back down into the tunnel. What glowing eyes and hellish grins were looking up at her I tried not to imagine.

"They won't hurt you, Bella," Bosgaard said.

I wasn't the only one who heard the question in his tone. Glibbmor clicked his teeth together. "I learned long ago the benefit of keeping my word to men."

Bella's eyes squinted. Her hair, which I'd imagined short as a victim of lice, was unkempt, surely due to those days after death when our few features still grow. "Yes," Bosgaard said. "It's me, Bell."

"Boz?" She spoke, drifting through the candles' dance and flicker. She studied his face, with her eyes first, then her hands. He was older now, much older, for time had gnarled his frame. She examined his dungeon-paled cheeks, the wrinkles around his brightened eyes.

Of all the actors in this lunatic pageant, Glibbmor spoke. "I asked those of mine who were there that night. We didn't see who killed her."

"Killed who?" asked Bella.

"It's not important now," Bosgaard said, his eyes welling.

"Thanks are in order," Glibbmor stated. "Thanks, Bosgaard, for taking care of Paltumorr for me. It may have been my sorry carcass hauled off by those sorrier priests if you hadn't," he snickered, "so thank you, even if it wasn't to protect the glorious ghoul king before you."

"King or not," Bosgaard said, "you do have your messengers."

"Many," Glibbmor said. "And none much enjoyed their trips into the dungeon, but for you…"

Bosgaard took his eyes off Bella for the first time: "They told me it'd be quick."

"Indeed, mighty body snatcher," Glibbmor nodded. "As also promised, we'll give you a week to frolic. *You'll* believe you're you."

Bosgaard had told of Bella's shrill scream. Now I got to hear it. Bosgaard flashed a knife, slicing his own throat. But it was not her continued pitch that cost me my consciousness, nor was it watching Bosgaard fall to the floor amongst ribbons of red hot spray. It was Glibbmor, who unseated himself to begin tearing into Bosgaard's chest.

What I say to you in plain words I did not witness in plain belief. Yet I can tell such a tale only if I will myself to believe what my eyes could not have seen, what my heart could not have felt.

When I came to, I was on the floor. I was not the only one. Bosgaard lay nude on his back. There was a third. The *old* Bosgaard, torn open and head split like a melon, lay next to me too.

For whatever covetous nature was Bosgaard's, he had shed it by way of the most gruesome trial. Doing so, he was reunited with his Bella, who had not only calmed but rode the fresher version of her lover. They were still making love when I ran out screaming.

I abandoned my post as I abandoned my notions of life, my notions of death, and what rules had surrounded them. I ran. I ran past City Cemetery, where the tips of obelisks had me erupting in unhinged laughter, wondering if I would do so again or if I would collapse and cry the next time I heard talk of Bishop Vhulviel the Ghoul Slayer.

Roads became the polished stones of the Morgeltine District. I paused at times to retch against statues or lean into hedges. The world could never drop into my lap the calamities I'd listened to—or worse, the ones I'd seen. Had I ever known love, I could not tell, but if such ends greeted those enslaved to its pull, than perhaps I was better off without it. As I ran onto our street, I felt my life all the more deprived for not having something, someone, to burn my undeserved wealth and uncontested prospects over.

As the sky glowed morning's dawn, I collapsed at my father's doors. There I climbed to my feet, tearing off the IHS sash and badge then straightening my garments, ready to tell a tale that would never be believed. But if a rural son of a pious zealot could somehow barter deals with a ghoul king while in prison, maybe I could plead with my father for a new occupation.

THE ARCHER AND ADALINE

"We are Chapwyn, and we champion suffering."

"What?" I said. I was down on my knees and had to raise my head.

"I said we are Chapwyn," the priest repeated, fondling his censer, "and we give a Chapwyn offering?"

"Ah." I took to my feet, adjusting my sword and leaving the holy man to find another parishioner.

I walked out of the church and back onto the cobblestones of Lirelet Avenue. Glow-lamps and the waves of hanging tapestries almost hid from me the night. But soon I was under its early stars, lost again in thought.

The Azadi wars had been over for a decade, the "Years of Peace" ongoing for as long, yet I'd become conflict itself. Recent desperations had shown me it wasn't entirely uncomfortable, reverting back to ways of life I'd abandoned. The church, its smells, its rhythmic chanting—they gave me sanctuary when I needed to contemplate where things had gone so wrong.

I am a sex addict. That which is as simple as corking a bottle carries with it exhilarating heights and terrific depths of turbulent malice.

Let me explain.

All men carry a deep sense of love for tight, wet places. All men day dream about the tightening and slackening of cheeks that just walked past. It is solely men's insatiable drive to make love that has perpetuated our kind out of plagues, curses, and war. All men, from the time childhood ends to the grips of senility. This, however, does not make them like me.

Recently, I've attempted to open up about my *condition* to those who'd listen. I am assured all men feel as I do, often relating my obsession to a fat man's lust for his plate. Such a pity. When the urge comes at you from across the ocean yet you are still unable to dodge its wave, when the joyous trinkets of the day turn to rubble and ash—that's when you are beginning to understand enthrallment by an hourglass figure atop heart-crushing heels.

Most nights, I toss and turn in my bed. When the sun beat upon me in earlier days, I prowled about not much different than the mildly deranged predator. Any who prohibited me from sating my lust were thrown to the wayside, regardless of reprisal.

Understanding where I developed an addiction to women required enough soul-searching to waste two lifetimes.

I recall an original dislike for the fairer sex. Like the rest of the young scamps, I had once teased the girls who frolicked beside us. My interest only lay so far in lighting their hair on fire or proudly turning my back as they approached one of our scrape-kneed huddles.

My mother's parents had come from the southern fields. When they moved to Pelliul, they brought with them their Chapwyn credenda. That in mind, one night my family carried me off to attend the Garnishing of Spring. Barely old enough to lock in stern memory, the night seems now a fogged dance half-merged in fairy land. Yet, beyond the perfumes and spastic writhing, I remember clearly, under the glow of church lamps, the fair-hair thing watching me.

She tiptoed, avoiding all the chanting, flailing grown-ups, making her way eventually to the front my family's pew. I recall a sense of embarrassment when she handed me the nettielium.

While my family towered above us, roaring their agreements and oaths to the priest at the altar, I twisted the flower by its stalk, absently watching the spin of the petal's whites and yellow.

I laugh so hard remembering it that my stomach hurts. With a sudden pounce, I rained down punches on the poor little girl.

Her squeals became a world away when I was yanked skyward by my collar then marched out by my grandfather. As the rest of my family toppled over themselves apologizing to the girl's parents, the Zevon patriarch took me to a dark patch under the trees. As he died soon after, I remember little about him, other than the strength in his wood-cutting arms that had remained in his elder years.

"Arcus!" I'd later heard, screeched for what seemed its own eternity. I sat scolded in a corner, pout-faced and numb from the tirades of relatives, each taking their turn declaring the exact level of disgrace I'd brought on the house of Zevon. I didn't understand why I'd done what I had. My reaction to the damn flower, the squeamish fluttering of the unfamiliar. But I had done it.

A peculiar memory to retell, I know, and even now I do so in the vain attempt to persuade myself that my issues didn't originate from weakness, but sprang up from some form of primeval, manly aggression That singular event, though, I'm afraid, does nothing more than merely point to boyhood itself—just one of the many acts boys conjure up that lead to grey hair atop a parent's exacerbated brow. No, the first clear sign that my troubles were beginning came when boyish fantasies of dragon slaying gave way to new dreams—dreams of another kind.

I had a warrior soul from the beginning. The fistfights on the shores of Lake Oraga had once made the name "Arcus Zevon" synonymous with speckling the rich soil red. Days spent tackling cohorts in games of divitch ball and the bruised victories celebrated whilst limping home are fond memories still.

Lamentably, puberty had a different plan. As my pudgy friends became barrel-chested men, and the boys whose baby teeth I had once knocked out were beginning to sprout the preludes of beards, I remained in appearance that of a child. Before I could truly say why, my place in the hierarchy of maleness steadily diminished.

Eons later, after I had been forced to hide my hairless endowments from the eyes of my peers, I began to take shape, although not how I had hoped.

My mother was sure to tell me regularly how I was growing like a weed. In one way, she was right. In a summer I shot two full hands in the air, just without the benefit of a single added pound of flesh.

And that was my lingering fate: a skinny, twerpish lad. Worse yet, I still thrummed with my fighter's blood. Although a new anger had formed—that of being the target of jokes and bullies—rage alone is never enough to avoid being pinned and pummeled.

The school I attended was like many schools in Pelliul. Poorer children, destined to carry the spear and shovel, filtered past polished wagons dropping off their polished brats. I have been told other cities in the Rehleia follow the olden ways. The child of a bank clerk would never mingle with the jeweled child of that bank's owner. But Pelliul had long ago done away with sound segregations in exchange for a sense of progressive smug.

I mention school because, while I was supposed to be studying the beads of an abacus, I tortured myself, I suppose, by the relentless study of my shapely classmates. Pleasuring myself would spend my angst before school, and a shameful encore would commence shortly after I'd returned to fling down my books.

As often the case, in time most families sharing our neighborhood prospered or horrendously failed. The result: my cohorts were moved into shanties or homes of polished pink ivory, disappearing from my eyes as if they'd been zapped by a wizard into the ether.

One friend remained. Worse to my plight than any wizard, his sanctimonious parents, he eventually learned—and I was immediately told—practiced sexual liberties by way of some secret gathering. Although he said this gathering touted a "rule-free" existence, I abandoned my pleas to join when his interrogated father sheepishly confessed to their furtive joys and rolled out the cult's rigid requirements. A petitioner had to have not one but *four* sponsors. The only people I knew were the types who chanted hymns and tithed on the appointed day.

If my work in military reconnaissance had a telling prequel, surely then it was this night. After exhausting every ploy imaginable, after trailing behind their hastening pace to the flower-streamed doorway of the lair, I could only stare at a sullen wall, enviously fantasizing from the shadows what loin-frothed ecstasy transpired on the other side.

At one gathering, wouldn't you know, my friend was eventually inducted. This didn't help my jealousy any, making it so great in fact it soon blotted out all conscious thought.

Later I experienced a sigh of relief, then guilt for the joy that I had not been him. An eager member of Ansul's True had sabotaged the sex cult; the Chapwynite purposefully contracted Thina's Poxy, the street name of our province's most insidious venereal disease. After letting the pustules fade and the discharge ripen to prime lethality, in the company of duped sponsors, the bright-smiling zealot walked the same route I had, then through the flower-streamed doorway he penetrated into enemy grounds and shucked off his robe. Half a year later, most members had withered to gaunt mimics of their former selves. My friend being no exception.

Such tragedies are forgotten when the moral compelling them

is one we are too young or too weak to embrace. The last of my school days left me still yearning for the touch of women like the thirst of a marooned sailor.

At perhaps the most thirst-ridden, I was in route from one class to another when there appeared in front of me a girl whom I'd known from our days as children. Fate had transformed her lank, boyish frame into strutting eloquence. I walked behind this creature, one who long ago forgotten I'd existed. Dressed for fairer lads, her heels supported lean, long, muscular legs, olive from her deliberate appointments with the sun. Her skirt was cruelly short, her undergarments fit snug as shadows. I learned this latter torment as I walked straight into a wall.

My ego bruised, my nose bleeding, my soul crumpled, she sailed around the bend without so much as a glance at what dunce had just caused the mirthful riot. Looking around at those who clapped my back or roared in my face, I knew right then that what I desired most was to be gorged on by these other men.

Left me, the hope to learn the pleasures of women, but happiness, peace, fulfillment—all worthless when in the mind's eye of the smirking, hopeless addict. This, I must submit, is the chief similarity I've witnessed when braving talks with pipe-heads or an alley drunkard. For us, the addict, our need isn't merely *like* life itself, but *is* life itself; we who were made cosmically unwhole.

After too many memories of longing, after years had passed, my emptiness had grown teeth. In some dark place deep inside, an always open mouth screamed its hunger, its insatiability, and its demand to be fed.

No, I did not become a rapist, blast you, if that's where you thought I was going. No, chalk one up for Chapwyn upbringing— if nothing else, I feared hellfire in my moments of unspeakable contemplation. Religion, I am even prouder to say, was not what saved me, but my aforementioned fighter's blood. This I was soon to learn.

I was terrible with women.

I was a virgin.

But if I would die one, which was a likelihood, I was going to die in a blaze of glorious fire.

Desire to know women became desire to kill men—not odd if, all things considered, you give the metamorphosis its proper amount of scrutiny.

Unfortunately, the Pelati conflicts were over and the Conqueror's quest to unite our lands had successed into parleys projected to linger well into adulthood. But as my studies were ending, by the grace of Tersiona herself, flare-ups erupted with Azad. The desert people had marched over the Red Isthmus, and the Conqueror needed men.

I quickly found a replacement for all those lustful, futile day-dreams. I even found purpose herself. I didn't know why *we* had originally started fighting *them*, but I soon knew recruiters who'd soldiered under the Conqueror during our provincial warring, in the mangroves of Pelat, and in the sweltering heat of Azad during the first clash. These hard faces didn't scoff at my ambition the way my father had.

I will never forget the look in his eyes. Pure disbelief, holding my sister like the filling war wagons would sing her too to certain death. My grandmother, riddled with age, with help and demonstration, waved along at my departure. Finally there was Mother herself, who through a life of domesticated piety was left incapable of understanding why some men wish to spill other's blood. As our convoy to boot camp summited the first of many hills, she prayed, lamenting the death of my innocence.

It had been dead a long time.

I wasn't the only lad who jumped at the recruiter's trumpet. What is so damned laughable, though, is the finer details, the details I'm sure they, those other lads, omit from their barroom tellings. A boy from school who had the reputation of a fearsome brawler failed the entry-level crucibles. Another—an athlete cheered on by friends and family alike for being the future nemesis of all Azad—that coward scurried off to the first non-combat role available. Yet I, Arcus Zevon, rose like an iron sun.

Much of boot camp was like a stick in the stream that collects all the muck and the garbage. I could hardly believe my senses; able young men wailing their lament for faraway beds, intimidated by corporal punishment, or missing a girl. It was in this period I began to see a strength that had silently developed from my perceived inferiorities. I missed no one—no woman, no endearing touch, nothing. Pain was easy. No sleep, a dream. Being told I was nothing and that I was worthless—an average day in the looking glass. I was filled with pure glee, watching the same types of young men who'd once paraded and peacocked fail so miserably at military life while I so maniacally succeeded.

At the end of basic training, I was the target of much grovel and envy when I was awarded a say in which banner I was to bleed and die under.

I'd always been curious how units got their identifiers. This was true for their names and especially their symbols. All sorts of fierce creatures decorated the Conqueror's shields and guidons: wolves, bears, and the like. Dragons, rumored to still exist in the Other Lands, were a personal favorite.

I'd seen a goblin once in a performer's square when I was a boy. The rugged hill-men who'd captured the little abomination would use prodding sticks, whenever the crowd coughed up a coin, to make fangs clamp or claws rattle the bars of its cage. It was a hideous, smelly creature, leaving me terrified of the mountains for years. It made sense then, I suppose, for one of our larger infantry units to display such a face on their standard.

Like every recruit, I'd heard the clamor while tending my wounds in the barracks. An elite group had ceased the sharpening of their arrowheads to announce a tryout. I was told their name had come from the maritime raiders who'd once fought on the beaches of Suela. The White Sand, their snapping standard brandished an hourglass with its bone-colored sand waiting ominously all on the bottom: *Times up!* This unit, caked in blood and medals and the dirt of foreign wastes, had evolved from beach-stormers to covert spies and the deadliest of archers. Although trained extensively in the sword, and more arrogant than kings, their greatest source of pride was in their ability to remain unseen. Such was necessary for their greatest derivation of pleasure. A sudden arrow in an unsuspecting enemy heart was rumored to be the highest achievement attainable in their godlike ranks.

And to these ranks I auditioned.

It was sheer hate that got me through it all. From the first day in that beaten courtyard within the Martial Fortress to the indoctrination runs that began while the world slept and ended when the merchant sat for his lunch, hate got me through. And eventually, after I'd sweat and puked until my soul itself felt it had been beaten, I was a member, given sword, bow, and quiver after drinking the ceremonial quotient of pig's blood lit ablaze in liquor.

The vindicating misanthropy that came from watching men break ceased the moment I entered the White Sand. There, my cohorts were ferocious farm boys from the south, mountain children who'd buried their parents, Nilghorde-street types who'd killed long before military service.

Trumpet the heavens, my nights were not only filled with grueling hours at the archery range, but my obsessed unfamiliarity with the lithe female body was quickly ripped of its veil! My brothers understood my animal plight. Most, fairer-faced and well versed in subsequent charm, escorted many a maiden into our bay to be ravaged by a pack of hungry, hooting hounds.

Odd perhaps, perhaps not, but I'd felt an initial disappointment; the theatre I'd longed for wasn't so merry. The following day my eagerness was restored, heightened in some ways as I felt

I needed now desperately to attain some sense of satisfaction. Luckily, one generous wench had yet to shake off the night's drink and wobble home, allowing me a dozen more attempts from the confines of a latrine.

Having temporarily gluttoned my thirst for women, war was the next siren's call. The White Sand would again occupy pale dunes, this time in the Far East. Trained to live in concealment, we heavily laden ghosts haunted the desert kingdom.

What allowed me to remain an equal was not horse-like legs, nor a woodsman's shoulders; it wasn't innate leadership, and it damn sure wasn't my ability to enchant friends by the sheer voracity of my wit and charm. It was the irrefutable fact that every triumph, every brother I knocked out of the brawl pen back in the rear, every rock face I climbed with a combat load to find our enemy, every Azadi I shot to watch die, was another deathblow to the miserable wretch I'd once been.

Then, to my misfortune, the war had to end.

The church well behind me, Adaline Ouvarnia's art studio graced the north block of Lirelet. A boisterous rally point for many of Pelliul's elite, by day the mirror black glass out front was an amusing opposite to where I'd been instructed to wait. At the studio's back entrance I was staring at the bland chestnut door.

I almost knocked a second time, but her habit of leaving me banging until sunrise if I violated our rules persuaded me. I was to knock but once. I settled for pulling out her note and reading it again.

As always, my summons came not by call or by pigeon or by a courier whose face I might recognize. The note I'd found slipped under my door this morning was like all the rest, lustful caricatures of either the sun or the stars to indicate "when" and a whiff of her perfume indicating "why."

For all I knew, she lived in a mansion and crawled up each

night to her abode on the grinning moon. These five years that I'd worked for her, she'd maintained an unpierceable wall of mystery, revealing little more than her effortless ability to transform into the very traits of her tribe, majestic and cruel, every time I was summoned to where she'd have me.

It was ironically appropriate, then, that the back of her studio was covered in generations of Leaves of Luka. The crawling vines, if indelicately touched, would afflict their victim with a terrible itch. Awaiting the sounds of her descent, a casual observer might have watched me pace and jostle as if I'd wallowed in each and every one of them.

High heels struck stairs beyond the chestnut. The rhythmic gait against the wood drummed visions of an executioner, taunting their appointed victim while strutting to an ax. Or it would suggest my heart racing, as it now did, feeling for but an instant that it too stopped when the sound of her march ended at the other side of the door.

Those locks—three, five, maybe twenty…I couldn't know. The moment I heard the first, it was as if I was being lifted onto a cloud. The last deadbolt slammed back. The door finally opened. Eyes were on me.

Her courtly obligations were one reason our encounters were infrequent, making me howl in the lulls. However, her timing, as all else, was impeccable to the point you could easily believe she was able to read minds. Or at least mine. Though she was approaching the age when once-reckless girls become grandmothers, I gazed upon her toned equestrian body.

Other than heels, heavy and angular and black enough to win a bar fight, she wore nothing more than a Quinnarian ribbon pressing her breasts.

I was not human; I was meat. I followed her up her stairway, positioned to watch the sway of her hips and everything between them. When she turned to delight at my ogling, her hair more than shimmered. The stairwell was adorned in an alternating cadence of lamplight, transforming the silk blackness which hung to her shoulders into their red and blues as we continued.

By the time we emerged into her loft, I'd already been instructed to "lose the clothes." The same position was assumed, always: her in her red oval chair, me on my knees, face between her legs. Then I waited.

We stilled as candles burned and my knees ached against the wood of the floor. She then bit her bottom lip and seized me.

I swear to you—in all my experiences with women, nothing satisfied my appetite like attacking Adaline's own with flicks of my tongue and the soft rehearsed movements of my unworthy mouth. Not a row of wiggling bar whores could compare to such bliss, for I surely tried.

She ruled me. I was slapped. I returned to my duty with renewed fervor, filling the loft with echoes and howls.

She pushed me on my back and slithered off her red oval chair. Once she'd grasped my throbbing member in her hand, she lurched forward, leered, and opened her mouth. This was a reoccurring game: closest she would come to finally doing for me what normally I loved best. I was denied. Still I felt myself go stiff, then thrum, thrum then shake, shake then explode.

When I was finally able to control the shaking of my legs, I lifted my head to see that she still sat between them.

They're sometimes purchased from strong cages in our markets, and Adaline's languid alertness was no different than one of them, the great hunting cats of Suela. And I never hated or loved anything more.

Given the season, most of Pelliul had been overpowered by all the raging jasmine. Still, I lounged on the couch and took in from an open window a closing flower market and the oil from a fire guild's final act.

Adaline had holed up in that maze of mirrors she called a bathroom. Our time after spending each other to puddles was usually quiet. Alone, I was left to reflect.

Her loft overlooked the belly of her studio in a way that always reminded me of the balcony in my family's church. One just held sculptures and paintings in various arrangements of display or purchase; the other, sad people, including, of course, my mother. Having been the only one to rebel from Tersiona's grace and abandon the Chapwyn faith, whenever my recent and foolish attempts at deliberation persuaded me a church was the best place to do so, I was forced to slink in and kneel at night, lest I risk running into them and revitalize her desperate hope I'd rediscovered religion.

I leaned out of the window and took in a good whiff. It all seemed so foreign somehow, now, the cobblestones of a small square, the pickpocket alleys all leading away. The streets, what a relationship we'd once had.

When I'd gotten out of the army, I was on, then off, then on them again, separated mainly by long bouts at the bar. My ill-fated relationship with society wasted no time returning. I tried, the whole light-hearted have-fun attempts that all aborted and buried themselves. The musical festivals were the worst, departing the city in overloaded wagons. I would stand in the swarm, at varying states of discomfort, stranded, drinking, and ultimately wishing I had brought my own horse.

These were also the days where I bounced from job to job, usually kicking myself for having not reenlisted. The sheer number of changes that have passed my eyes makes it hard to believe that I didn't hang up my White Sand quiver a hundred years ago. The Years of Peace began. Our land went from "Orisula" to "Rehleia." The Conqueror was suddenly the "Municipal One"…and a year and a few loose coins later, while I was a stable boy picking up horse shit, we allied with those fig-eaters and marched north to war it out with Serabandantilith.

Do you know what the definition of useless is? I do. It's also the definition of frustration and the occasionally pathetic. It's when a former member of an elite fighting unit realizes he has no other skills. Better judgement had me soon toss the broom and bucket—nay, throw the bucket into splinters and break the broom over a knee. I walked into the recruiters' ready to sign my life away, this time with the desperation one can only reach having stared warless life in the face and much preferred war. Yet I was to be subjected to another disappointment, perhaps the greatest of them all. The White Sand, most beloved of the Conqueror's men and the Scourge of Azad, had been disbanded forever. No need for reconnaissance when the entire Serab campaign was a one-sided carnival of burned huts and dripping swords.

As the Years of Peace's two-year anniversary commenced in the street, I was patching leaky roofs. One year later, I was the sourest recruit in the entire Metropolitan Ward. The people surrounding me changed from armed men ensuring their unit's lethal pride, to befattened louts shamelessly preening themselves in front of an audience who'd all grown tired of their harrowing tales about braining pickpockets. Two years more, I was being fired.

"Hand it over, Zevon!" Sarge hammered at me. "You know-everything, know-nothin' prick." My one and only shift sergeant wasn't a bad man, just terribly impatient. That I was sluggishly returning my sabre only fueled his wrath.

He may have been the occasional target of my discontent, but Sarge had also fought in Pelat. Eventually he had possession of all my gear, allowing the walrus to calm. "You don't follow rules," he said. "Ya don't do what you're told. I don't know how you survived in the army—hot shot or not. Maybe you need to use that big bouncin' brain of yours, Zevon, and attend some damn school somewhere."

Sarge didn't nod when I unloaded on him that I still needed *adventure*. Sure, some of the weapons were the same, but the jobs just too damn different. He just fiddled his mustache. His one-liner that followed about duty set me on high.

"These jackals!" I burst. "On the streets—most need to be run through. Like we did in Azad. Hell, Sarge, like I heard you all did plenty down in Pelat." At the time, I lived in festering housing near the entrance to the Parilgotheum. I calmed myself too. "I think I liked Azadis more than the people outside my apartment." He nodded this time, also showing me the door.

The fruit of night's spent kneeling in churches is this getting-fired memory remains so unusually clear because it's when I was confronted with a sobering fact. Some veterans could adapt back to civilian life. I couldn't.

Begrudgingly, I chewed on the old walrus's advice.

School, though, was as attractive as rolling in the nearest gutter. Schools attended by adults were for tuition-paying men who swung scythes by day and by night hoped to, one day, do all the land owning. Instead, I invested elsewhere. Handing all my departure pay to a doorman at the Pulsing Plum Baths, I attended the school of the drug-fueled orgy.

It may have been my movement. It may have been my body, still chiseled by the sharpened edge of White Sand days. Knowing what I know now, I believe it was something else: infinite want, even in infinite abundance. Amidst the swaying flesh, there Adaline saw me. I was whispered to. All I had to do was promise to give her my all, at all times. The dreariness of life fell to the marble along with her robe. It was an easy promise to make.

Adaline emerged from the bathroom. "The wagon's all set," she said, drying her hair. "Mostly sculptures from Nilghorde."

That I was destined for another trip to Azad in the morning was nothing new. I'd made at least a hundred trips back there since working for her. It was also nothing new that she'd come join me now and lay in a robe determined to stay open. What was unusual was her recent outbursts. It was as if she was arguing with someone else living in her head.

It was understandable my boss and mistress would be acting a little strange since returning from her last trip. After that fateful orgy, Adaline had hired me as security for her convoys. A "muscled pet" to "protect her investments" sounded like a dream. Putting murderous skills once more to good use, my knowledge of customs and terrain served an even more apt purpose, as she'd stricken deals with seemingly every sultan and mullah in Azad. But she sometimes made the trek too, to ensure lofty contracts maybe, or, I cringed to think, to ravage the mind of some other man. Maybe a score of them.

Her company had three convoys going at all times. If I were there, on that last one, I would have taken scalps, surely. Those damn Azadis—bandits had chased her wagon right of a cliff. No paintings to steal if pulverized on a rocky bottom. No Rehleian bodies to triumphantly mangle if done so already by a stupendous fall. What a waste. According to her, she'd jumped off the runaway wagon and hid until a convoy bound for Rehleia eventually happened by. No food, no water, that scorching heat—only a woman like Adaline could tell me she toughed it out and have me believe it.

"Wagon's all set," I repeated, in the way I usually did, like I was back in the army and she my stalwart commander. When she put my head in her lap, I knew she wanted to talk. I'd fought there; if anyone could understand her traumas, surely it was I.

"When you were in Azad, Arcus, did you learn anything about ghouls?"

"…A little." She detected my amused confusion. "Why?"

"Oh, I don't know. I just find them fascinating. These desert creatures…are they dead, are they alive? Do those delightful children of the night even care?"

Of the night, sure, but *delightful*—that was a most generous description leveled against beings who purportedly lived near graves and ate rotting corpses. "I know they're supposed to have originated in Azad," I said.

"Anything else?

"That's about it," I lied, hoping to steer the conversation back to normalcy.

"All that time there, shooting arrows and hauling that big dick around, and you mean to tell me you never learned anything more?"

"Well—"

"I've learned loads of things. One of my favorites is there's an especially cunning and contemptuous female ghoul they call Ghila—get out of my body!"

She did it again. My rise was met by her palm, pressing down, insisting that I remain. "Adaline, I—"

"Yes, that's who I am, not this," her face angered, "not this ghou—good grace of Tersiona, there's a chill coming in." Her expression was back to normal now, making me almost more concerned. "Should we shut the window?"

A woman who'd always been the paragon of poise acting like this. My best judgment compelled me to just keep her talking, though I didn't care much for the subject matter. "You know this girl ghoul's name?"

"And her lover's," she said, almost bragged, suppressing another twitch that rallied for an instant then was gone. "Gorial is *his* name. Her burly accomplice. Legends say they cause all sorts of mischief throughout the dunes—when not coupling like wild beasts, of course."

She began fiddling with my hair, instantly sapping me of my consciousness. "Do you know what romance is, Arcus?" I don't know what I answered. I trailed off, only noticing at some point her strokes had grown rough, like a distracted owner preening a goat. "Filling that ever-ripping rent, most enjoyably. Defiling the world together. Gorial and Ghila. That, my useful chunk of meat, that is romance."

✳

As our horses plodded merrily in morning's rays, Adaline's shipment continued eastbound. The last of the Red Isthmus's Rehleian land, this midsection of the world filled me brimming with nostalgia, a sensation that admittedly cooled as I'd come to recognize the various thatched huts and windmills. These hardy installments preferred wolves and raiding parties over losing the sustainable rhythm of rural life, often reminding me of my own grandparents, how they must've lived, and how dismally ruled I was by plumbing and money.

A protocol that had saved Adaline whole chests of the latter mandated I ride first to the summit of any approaching hill. Doing so, I soon waved the wagon and its teamsters on. The route was banditless, giving me time to adjust myself in accordance with weeks in the saddle.

Azad: a sun-brushed schizophrenia of flat desert then beshrubbed rolling hills, both littered with towering minarets, the twinkles of pit fires flickering, and then all the fortresses, their bulbous tops many and multicolored, their bodies built low, hugging blistering sand.

Able to feel my ass once more, I executed my enduring ritual of spitting at Azad's westernmost minaret.

The tower was a white shard on the horizon. By nightfall, the road had taken our convoy under and past her.

Beginnings of desert nights are blue with enchantment. I trotted well ahead of the wagon. In my loneness, surrounded by waking stars, I breathed in the hills. What orders had I carried out on that one? On that other, had I ever been?

At the heart of all adventurers is a core of loneliness, for warriorhood is a lonely world. On the cusp of battle, standing armed with men whom you know better than your family, whom you can identify by belch or break of wind, you are still alone.

When Azad attempted to take over the Red Isthmus, there was great concern our entire peninsula would be invaded soon after. For a time the Conqueror's army fought both rebels in our land and pushed aggressively into Azad's. Before we won our domestic war and were unified, the Conqueror hadn't the formidability to negotiate with the six sultans and their sixty battalions of scimitar and spear. With a new and centralized "Rehleia," the Azadi Agreement was signed, allowing peace and stability.

I had fought in these lands, when there was fighting to be done, giving perhaps the best of me in the process. I'd spied on troop movement, or watched from the observation posts we'd dug the charge of the mighty Swift Saber into outmatched enemy hordes. The Conqueror had tasked us with the disruption of supply routes, giving me my most harrowing encounter when I laid three guards to waste after their armor clunked down right next to my burrow.

The wagon caught up. I'd stopped at the fork, and even my horse seemed hesitant. We had to take the southerly path.

"Is there no other way?" protested the accountant. He knew there wasn't, and his rhetoric annoyed me. A minor debate ensued, going needlessly over alternate routes that would not serve us. After talk boiled over from my assurances to the moon's gleam off my sword's withdrawn blade, he stowed any further points of argument and the coachman guided the wagon wheels onto the uneven stone.

The road from Pelliul to Azad was more or less a straight line. However, once deeper into the quicksand and pan shrubs, the road broke into a spider web of follow-on routes, some better and more traveled than their fellows. What we embarked down now was one that we took the least. It was less developed and hard on the horses, but the Azadi prince waiting at its end was paying Adaline a small fortune.

The three of us clinking along did share at least one agreement. Despite handsome payments, we still thought it strange our employer would send us this way, and so soon after what had happened. But Adaline Ouvarnia was as extreme in her persistence as she was all else, and we abided on.

As we now bobbled down the very road Adaline had almost died on but a month ago, my unnerved colleagues had petitioned we wait until daylight. If reminding them the extra bags of silver for returning early hadn't worked, the sword certainly did. I had to admit, though, it would stay loose in the scabbard.

Treks like these were tours through the dead. Graveyard after graveyard—mostly slain Azadi fighters, but such plots were also broken up by burial sites older than the dunes.

Passing the first of these, I was reminded of Adaline's odd talk—well, oddity in general, but in particular her romantic talk of ghouls. I didn't want to encourage her, but I'd heard a thing or two myself about those creatures.

More than just wars, the barren kingdom was riddled with legend and witchery. At the top of this list was the colonization of ghouls. Spoken about by our prisoners as if as real as the hair on my arm, they were said to have originated in the desert's cool burrows.

Many nights us White Sand would mock their rumors. Men who knew no life but the one thundering in their chests or dripping off preferred weaponry pissed on graves and stamped the ground. "Come, you," a brother had drunkenly challenged, "lurking fucks. Taste somethin' foreign!"

We were told they delighted in roaming the dunes and the outskirts of villages in the guise of wild dogs, much to the lament of whatever mutt came across our arrow's range. Also, and I still remember my team leader's exact words before an especially dangerous mission: "Well, Zevon, if we do get overrun, let's hope those ghouls eat us." Causing endless jest was a myth that ghouls could eat certain parts of a corpse, surprising widows and toppling weeping kin out of their chairs, reassuming the role of that very corpse amongst the living.

Our path took us under the lee of a jagged hill. More stone in this area, all three of our horses glided a bit easier as we followed a long curve leading us by yet another patch of graves. Embedded in a plateau on the slope of the hill, on our left sat a cemetery, neglected and leering. I was hugging my saddle all the harder. The drop-off to our immediate right—there were few cliffs in Azad, but we had been bottlenecked by one of her highest.

We rode closer in parts like this, the wagon's horses nearly breathing down my neck.

"What was that?" the accountant whispered.

"Probably just the wind. Relax." I hadn't heard anything.

"There it is again. Arcus, you don't hear that?"

"Hear what?" I turned to the coachman, pulling his eyes from our left-hand side. "Don't let the coin-counter rile you. Keep moving."

But there was something now, there was, coming from up on the slope.

The moon had risen to shine the world into hues of black and grey. Rocks had been dislodged, and their sounds and shadows were rolling down to greet us.

"Ghouls be lurkin' here," the coachman said.

"Shut…" I stopped to listen. "…shut your mouth." Jackals were prevalent in these parts. "Jackals are prevalent in these—"

An arrow whizzed by my head.

The wagon stopped. The horses reared as cries descended upon us.

"Shit!" I freed my bow and nocking an arrow, recognizing the clank of shoddy armor immediately: primitive Azadis, riffraff who'd either missed out on old battles or been raped by them. Now the guerrillas waged a personal war, one they'd insure would never be over.

The wagon careened past me. When I was able to see again, what may have been four or five men was now a charging dozen. They had ran out from behind headstones to become shaking blades in the moonlight. I dropped two of them with as many arrows, then put two more in another before he had the chance to cough on me his blood.

I had thought for an instant some night creature had arrested my horse. She kicked and whinnied perilously as the first arrow plunged into her. Even in the ball of dust, I could see something had stopped the wagon ahead. Abandoning my horse as she fell, pin-cushioned, I ran toward my only cover. From the protection of the wagon, I could perhaps mount a defense. I'd encountered such men in recent years, but never this many.

It is likely my colleagues were dead before I could climb up. I would not know, for when I was at arm's length from our wagon, I was beset by a turban with two swords. Both swung wildly, providing me a pocket for my own blade to pierce his foul heart and send him sprawling.

Another took his place, better, and I was growing tired. I knew admitting such a reality was the road to doom. I swung. He swung. I whirled my sword as if the world itself encroached upon me. They withdrew, then I howled in pain. One of their blades had found me.

Sometime later, uncouth tones loomed above me. It was as if I were lying on my back, staring up at them from the bottom of a deep well. They, these shadows, grinned and snickered, then they began to fade.

It was meant to happen this way. All the far lands fought…I now see the grand vista. For out of my heart, I have always been free. One with no need, alone, and combat-wretched and wild.

✳

I awoke to the desert twilight, cold and blue. The moon peered down on its...its what? Its child? Yes.

The wide eye watchful, I shivered from the winds coming down the slope to lick me clean on their way southward. I was alone, and I was nude. Furthering my surprise, one horse remained, still half-bridled to our capsized wagon.

How had I survived that injury? I patted my bare sides, at first frantically, half hoping to find where a scimitar had cleaved me. As I found nothing, my franticness turned to lunatic joy. I had survived. I had...imagined my own death?

Seeing the state of our wagon, I surmised I had suffered not a cut but a blighting knock to the head. They must've thought I was dead. That at least explained why I'd been spared as they stripped me of my clothes. These bandits and guerillas were known for fighting a buzzard for the meat off a bone. Odd, then, that they'd leave the contents of our haul. Statues and paintings littered the ground.

A second thought on the matter, and it all made sense. These fig-eaters who'd cost Adaline yet another shipment were easily spooked, known to jump sky high at the bark of a dog or the hoot of a desert owl. Something perceived to be more menacing than three Rehleian men must have scared them off.

But what I could not explain was how, when I came back to my senses, to sense itself, I'd done so not on my belly, nor on my back, but on my feet, as if I'd walked up to this mangled corpse in the hopes of learning his name.

I stood above one of my ill-fated companions, too badly marred to discern. Someone—something—had torn open his chest and removed his heart. I felt my stomach churn when I removed the painting that was covering his head.

His face had been ripped apart like a melon. Whiter than moon-lit tombs, the inner skull still held chunks that globbed and glistened. The brain had been attended to by claws, larger than a panther's, and had been removed greedily before whatever was brandishing such weapons scampered off.

Or had it? I went for my sword, remembering then that it was no longer at my side. Rather, furthering my vexation to the point where my head felt as if it too had been split, my sword laid at the side of this unidentified corpse.

My team hadn't gotten far. The accountant took one to the skull. The coachman, a less charitable fate. Whatever had mauled this third man—who I surmised now could only be the Azadi who deprived me of my clothes—whatever it was it only had time for one mauling. I was forced to entertain a question: if it too had fled, had an even greater threat scared *it*?

A moment's work got me wrapped in rags and on the remaining horse, with little food and less water. A saddle I would have to do without. Retrieving my sword strengthened my heart, but I would not carry on here for all the gold in the Morgeltine.

I headed west.

Days into my return journey, I began to feel strange. Hungry, yes, parched with thirst, that too, but also the sensation that I was not who I once had been.

There is a small river in the western parts of the Red Isthmus. Some say it's the true border between our lands. At its edge, I stooped to lap like a wild dog. Filling my waterskins, I stared at my face for the first time in days. Appalled by the leathery look my skin had taken, I hurried through my chore. I noticed then a throbbing gnaw—not in my mind, as you would say, but something like it. A voice that spoke under my thoughts. I shook the annoyance. Remounted, I continued west, swearing an oath I was done with the desert and its peculiar persuasion.

My condition worsened with each passing day. "Desire to travel is unusual for ghouls," I found myself saying, "especially couples. That two ghouls could even be called a couple is more unusual yet, as their lot generally attacks and offers holes to whomever gets there first. But Gorial and Ghila…" Such inanities continued.

When I would arrive home, I would visit every priest who would have me. Something had happened that night in the desert. Something I could not grasp, though I felt it strengthen with each plod of the horse's hoof.

Upon seeing the far-off lamps of my Pelliul—

—"Gorial is back, world!" I howled from the disgusting back of this horse. I felt Arcus fighting for control. "Nope," I chortled. "Nope, great warrior. You're just going to have to learn to live with it. Slump down in that subconscious of yours—I mean *ours*—take a few years off."

I, Gorial, couldn't go with Ghila when she ate that tasty bitch, Adaline. Those brown-skins had proven useful: kill, take the rubbish, leave the rest. But Tasty Bitch's caravan went off the damn cliff, taking her moon-skins right along with it. I was left without a body to jump in, no fancy caravan to hide from the sun in.

"Shut up, great warrior!" Grief pop my carbuncles—this human here, Arcus, he has some stones. Took me days to wrestle him down. So anyhow, with her suddenly a moon-skinned woman, Ghila developed our little plan. She was always the brains of our operation. I just crack the coffins and pummel her hole. That cra—

"I'll kill us both then, foul ghoul!" Arcus screamed, toppling off the horse. "If it means a million years in Hell!"

After what appeared to the owls and other night creatures to be a man banging himself helplessly against a tree, I felt the struggle come to an end.

"That crazy bitch pulled it off!" I said, getting back on Arcus's foul horse, cracking my knuckles and giving my new back a good stretch. I knew from the beginning that Ghila—excuse me—Adaline, she'd masterminded our biggest caper yet. This rowdy soldier boy she'd sent me was perfect. Tortured and driven to use this cock of his all the time. Healthy and strong—and conflicted, no more. There'd be no holding back, no tears to weep, not with me stepping into his sins grease easy.

I howled at the moon—and this damn human still trying to resist. "There's only room for one of us, warrior. Oh, don't worry, you'll get used to my laugh. Gorial is in the land of the moon-skinned now. I was so sick of the fuckin' desert anyway."

I had to stop one more time to slap my brand new thigh. "I can't believe it. That bitch actually pulled it off. Be seein' you soon, baby."

A HERO, EMERGED

"Long has our land suffered," Irion Ordrid intoned. In front of the congregation he stood, gazing down upon the kneeling, illiterate flock; one that had primped and groomed itself to near-cleanliness. He stood at the altar, encircled in a ring of braziers whose flames danced solemnly off the white walls and their golden leaves. He looked up. Nilghorde's main Chapwyn temple was so vaulted that the embossed icons of piety could hardly be seen.

"Yes!" a voice in the crowd cried. "Tell us what is now being done." Earning like-minded shouts and joyous proclamations throughout the throng: "We are with you!"

Irion held out his hand. "And I with you, brothers and sisters. And I with you." He looked straight ahead, over the stilled congregation, to savor this moment as the sun set outside the church's open doors. "I know my House has not always had the best reputation, but today is a new day. A day where we together bring forth a new era. A new era not only of peace, and of safety, and of mutual prosperity, but a renewal of our greatest virtues. A society must soon wither if consumed by such improprieties as—as *this*."

To his left and to his right stood tall church fathers, politicians, and his well-dressed son. But none cut a figure as entirely enthralling, none pulled the severe focus of every eye, as the book which Irion lifted up off the altar.

"Vandahl," he declared, tossing it into a brazier. "Today we pen the outlawing of such base, senseless trash."

Unable to contain himself, a bishop shucked his sectarian bearing. Irion shook the excited bishop's hand. "But," Irion continued as the roar subsided, "as Ansul himself said in the blessed scriptures; *one is but the start*." This time the crowd roared so unrestrained there was no way to deliver any word further. But, as Irion had planned, the end of his speech had garnered upheaval. Rubbing elbows with not only bishops but an attending Scepter, the new darling of the mob, Irion Ordrid bowed low, handing the Scepter the official quill.

And so the great Denom Vandahl, in one fell signature, became illegal to read or reprint. Members in the crowd ushered forward, dropping their copies into the flames. As the book fires raged, Morden Ordrid stood by his father, watching through the velvet wafts of incense with a bored indifference.

A priest embraced the young Ordrid. "Rinmor, your stepfather, he is without doubt the single greatest thing to happen to this vile city in many a year."

Morden remembered his snarl, and his dagger, hiding both with his ceremonial garb and a painful smile. "Let go of my hand."

"I…I am sorry, young sir."

"Priest Masairee!" Irion purred, eyeing his son, then taking the gone-limp hand of the priest and shaking it vigorously. "Thank you for this wonderful opportunity, but my stepson and I must be going. We have another ceremony which we unfortunately are unable to miss."

※

At the doors of the old Ordrid keep, Morfil had greeted the new incarnation of his former lord. All had been arranged. The overseer of the old hierarchy then hobbled on his cane, leading them through halls Morden was laying eyes on for the very first time.

Life was different in the mansion, where his father told him amongst lit banquets and merriment the ways and manner of the family keep. Morden was not disappointed. Halls, gloomier than bliss. High windows cut and carved with consideration of the movements of the moon. Through such wonders, Morfil's grey head led them to the event Morden had been preparing over for the better part of a week.

In an amber room of candle and stone, gifts were stacked upon themselves: bows, boxes, ornate ribbons wrapped round silver chests and baskets of sweets. Irion and Morfil left Morden there, climbing a short flight of stairs to join the others who'd been waiting on the observation deck. There they sat and watched.

The young Ordrid paced about, his attention not on the gifts. He walked and he stared, scrutinizing the fabled brazier that menaced the room's center.

Irion accepted his wine from Morfil. "Whenever you are ready, my son."

Morden clasped his hands, going over the rites one more time. He walked to the low brazier, reaching down and retrieving from inside the tiny golden bell. When he rung it, directly below the crowded observation deck opened a tiny door. Out crawled a startled orphan. Though marred by dirt and grime, the child's face brightened when he saw the stunning array.

Morden bent down. "Do you like sweets? Yes? Good. All these nice shiny presents, they are all for you." Morden moved over to the display, setting down the bell and picking out a morsel. The child was handed chocolate and figs, scarfing it all down and soon asking for water. Morden asked him to pick out a box and unwrap it. The boy skipped past, and when he did, Morden upended the little brat, grasping in both hands a skinny bare leg. The most prominent of the House of Ordrid watched from their perch as the newest to become a man ignited from the brazier a roaring, violet flame. Kicking and squealing, into it the orphan went, vaporized in one last squeal before Irion rose.

Morfil held on his lap scroll cases made of solid gold. All were sealed, but one. Morfil placed a scroll in Irion's hand.

Irion looked down, a shadow against the violet fire. "For eighteen years, Morden, you have walked this world. These gifts we hope you enjoy. Yet, let us acknowledge the greatest gift of all, one you have given yourself. For on this day, the day of your birth, by rites and rituals bestowed on and to our great House, you have become a man, my son."

Panting, eyes wild with the lust of completion, Morden stood as Irion unfolded the scroll and began to read:

"There are many gods. Of those included, Oedrus and her dark majesty Analeera. There are gods who are good and those who stink of the perfume of evil. In eons past, the gods were presented to Man in their true form. Soon, ogling at the kicking babe and blooming flower were trampled by the sturdy sword, the inveterate taker who swung it." Irion gave the scroll back to Morfil. Morfil rolled it, slid it back into its case, sealed the golden cap, and then handed his master the second:

"Behold!" Irion read. "That gone great epoch of the rulers, men seated in the highest power. Tyranny in full bloom. But then, the seed of Man, long starved, its taproot one day plunged, its soft shell slowly hardened. In time, the masses rose, overthrowing the great rulers of old, and in so doing defiled and dethroned the evil god's work."

"But then, the evil gods conspired and tricked the gods of good. And once tricked, Man, that orderly wanting creature, began smelting the insidious powers of law. And with this the good gods disappeared, their whereabouts known only to them. Except one—Tersiona: Goddess of Peace. Pitying Man's ignorance to what was to come, Tersiona let herself be enslaved, cursed to be forever mocked and prodded. She works among our evil gods even now."

"Our gods and weeping Tersiona guide the inkwells of Man. Law is driven by the purest bliss of greed. But useful Tersiona, she weaves her power. Law provides peace. How hard she weeps, and how joyous do sing the evil gods and the unaware Man. We, the Ordrids, at the highest echelon, we know, and we pass to our own, the true nature of the world." Irion and Morfil exchanged another.

"Just as our immortal, exalted, reigning Conqueror is but a phantom, wouldn't you say? So too dwells nothing of love in what prompts Man's ultimate order." The top Ordrids all laughed. Irion cleared his throat and began reading the next:

"Until the foundations of the earth crack and shutter. Until the seas retreat and sizzle, or the heavens are hung in an ever-lackluster grey. Shall there be a seeking, marching Ordrid, fed the true state of the world by gods of unrepentant evil. Chosen for his line's unrepentant desires. For no better a man, in this world or another."

"Who salivates to obliterate all natural order. The lust for quiet rooms, toiling, unweaving the inglorious rainbows of life and death. In all manner they defile: the joys of sex over the binding apertures of love. Power over grace. The warm bath of starless nights, where a different wisdom reigns, rather the paltry crop-feeding of a bland and burning sun. Tyrants and tormenters of old held blades to the neck of poets, convincing the world, and themselves, in vain, that they were the morally righteous."

"But we, the venerable House of Ordrid, who at its highest ranks, at its noblest blood, run not from dank and moral evil. *Evil*, penned by the trembling hand of Man, is not uprighting a world inverted. A cosmos ponderously viewed by eyes afflicted upside down. We, of the most honest House, know Good is merely a tool of and for the greater power."

Morfil then gave the final scroll. Rites of the oldest, most potent filled the room. Irion called to the dark gods of above and below, paying homage to the noblest vehicles of passion and power. Irion's words turned the flame white, backing Morden into his birthday gifts before the fire extinguished in a sudden wisp of colorless smoke.

The room was black. As their eyes adjusted to the lowness of torches, Irion, for he knew the rest, rolled up the parchment. "Envy," he said. "Dominion. Betrayal. Murder. Vengeance. Avarice. Lust. Corruption." Sealing Morfil's golden case, "Do as you will. For inside Good's gilded halls, hide, my son, the scrolls of sin."

✳

After the second ceremony in one evening, Irion and Morden trotted down midnight streets to hand off their horses to waiting slaves at the Ordrid mansion. No moon this night blackening the obelisks of the bailey as they entered. Inside the main parlor, a rippling pool of harlots was about to burst.

Morden plunged headfirst into the orgy. The cast-back locks and breasts perking beyond dropped robes was, after all, all for his most lauded celebration. The father, who had primed and arranged such bliss, took it upon himself only to grab a chair and to watch.

Sex up in the master bedroom had spiraled to a dismal halt soon after Irion and Morlia had been officially married. Sure, a resurrected woman's loins could still juice and, though her revival had not been as immaculate as their son's, her desires still burned with the same carnal greed as before. Yet, how could Irion ever truly respect such a double-dealing whore? Finishing what that Werlyle had started was swift, clean, and little loss to his ruthless, awkward son. Besides, becoming full proprietor to all this wealth was that much more savory without the old ball and chain around.

Irion urged his entertainment on. He suggested one man be switched out with another. He called for his most impressive slaves, slapping bare black buttocks and stroking the auburn hair of his favorite Serab before adding them to this pile or to that.

Morden wallowed among them, licking and smacking, nibbling and pinching, accepting only the finest touches from the fairest, warmest flesh. He smacked and he nibbled, but these slaves and the trull atop him, they'd all been had before. Like the gifts back at the keep: it was their wonder that enticed the young Ordrid, not what lay inside. And wonder had surely gripped him, stronger than the trull's hand now encouraging his most-important limb.

Ever restless, Gorial and Ghila had moved their guises to Nilghorde. Using her social prominence, "Arcus and Adaline" had quickly been absorbed in the branch of the city's elite who delved in such depravity. Both Morden and his father had noted with marked curiosity this couple. A member of a royal House accompanied by a wolfish brute, striking all the more when they'd shed their clothes before even the drunkest voluptuary had undone her button. As the orgiastic mass broke off into pockets, Morden staggered forward, grabbing his wine and his robe, introducing himself to this inspiring duo.

"I am so sorry, birthday boy." Adaline soon said, "But we don't do that."

Aroused indignity was a new sensation. Though she was an aging beauty, this thing under an unkempt ponytail of sweat-soaked hair was a beauty nonetheless. *Besides*, Morden mused, not hiding his smile, he was getting older too. His examination ran down her body, ending at a pair of heels supporting lean, long, muscular legs, pale white as the moon.

He lifted his eyes, restating his demand: "I wish to play with you, alone."

Her smirk was not the kind he was used to. "I'm sorry—"

"What?" Morden fired. "Come to my orgy just to turn Chapwyn? Your *man* here." Arcus had been standing alongside Adaline, fully nude and silent, but as Morden eyed him as a barracks sergeant would his feeble recruit, Arcus's mouth begin to open. Morden continued: "He doesn't mind. Does he?"

"Young lord." Arcus placed a hand on Adaline's hip. "We embody liberation, yes. But even liberation has its rules. As the lady said, we don't do that."

"Prudish," Morden snarled. "Pious hypocrites."

"Young lord," Adaline said, "you are still most welcome to *join* us."

The crowd had ceased its thrusting to gather round, all soon whispering this pair had to be mad. Who else would argue with Morden? The crowd's vexation exploded when Arcus begin arguing with thin air. "Oh, let the Ordrid have his way, Arcus—shut up, you foul ghou—sire!" Arcus's face thrust forward, toward Morden's confused frown, then seemed to shift, appearing for an instant to look almost like a dog's. "Sire, spare this idiot, I mean me, he doesn't—Gorial," Arcus grunted, his face now normal, then, stamping out his words, "Get. Back. Down!"

From his seat Irion had watched this curious display. Aware of powers and creatures his son was not, he laughed and called out: "I don't think you want to stick anything in *that* dead meat, Morden."

One of the worst duties as an armed guard in the mansion was having to stand rigid as even slaves humped and moaned. Irion waving them into blocking positions was a welcome respite. Cracking the head of a troublesome partygoer could vent even the most ardent jealousy.

Their armor clanked as Morden missed his father's point. "Yes," he vowed, tossing his wine and tying tight his robe. "Dead meat they are."

Arcus and Adaline had heard the grim patriarch's words. As

had then, truly, Gorial and Ghila. The disguised ghouls divided their efforts. Adaline's regal voice pled to Irion that her lover had been afflicted by legacies of the war. Arcus, hoping to assuage, took a step toward Morden.

"We don't want any trouble," Arcus said.

"You presume to negotiate with *me*? After humiliating me—in my own home—in front of my father, on my birthday?"

Arcus had suppressed Gorial, who very well may have waded them through far better. The soldier uttered blunder after blunder until Morden reeled back and swung for his head. Arcus ducked, without thought balling his fist and putting the squealing lord on his back.

"Guards!" the young tyrant cried. But Irion held up his hand. Though the soul who peered out from Irion's eyes was another, the first Irion had been fifteen during the war with the Conqueror. Not yet a man, he'd taken up arms against those who'd aimed to smite his House. Morden, by contrast, would flail a slave's back to tatters but shivered at the thought of combat.

"No, son." Irion's words seemed not only to echo but grow. "This fight is your own."

Morden scampered to his feet, running to his clothes and retrieving his dagger.

"My lord," Adaline pled, crawling on all fours to take Irion's hand and kiss it. "Show him mercy. This is one big misunderstandin—"

"Show mercy on him?" Irion gazed down upon this creature. "Don't you mean *us*, foul eater of the dead?" Adaline reeled back, plopping her haunches on the cool marble. "Look at what my son wields. Look! Yes, you see. It is true your kind fears iron."

He knew the answer, as did she, as did Gorial screaming deep inside Arcus as Morden charged. Slashing wildly, Morden cut the backs and forearms of patrons, slave and free man alike. Arcus's steps chose a tactical retreat, all the way to the main door before his back met the mailed chest of a guard. Arcus was pushed forward, almost losing his footing before ducking once more, avoiding the wet blade before lunging forward. Tackling his pursuer, he climbed atop, as he'd done to an Azadi once when he'd been out of arrows. He disarmed Morden easier than disarming his own woman from her playful whips.

"No!" Arcus heard his enemy's father scream. Or he thought he had. A stench was overpowering the room, oppressing all save Arcus. He hadn't raised the dagger, though the thought was crossing both minds in his brain, surging with or shunting its blood. With one hand he pinned Morden by his throat, turning then to see the screamer.

Adaline was gone. In her place was his sportive Ghila. Irion held her by her talons, saying nothing, staring menacingly, and at him.

Only the guards held their places as the hall now laid eyes on the ghoul. Tables flipped, chairs were kicked over and garments flew as partygoers scrambled and slaves were driven briefly by thoughts all their own.

Irion said, "Now shed your guise, warrior. Let us see you."

"This is done," Arcus said, human as the next, taking his weight off Morden and handing him back his dagger. "Great lord," he turned to Irion, "may our inconvenience to you end. We came only to—"

Arcus screamed. Morden was clutching his most intimate parts, wrenching them so that a bright pain shot through Arcus as if he were about to be dismembered. Suddenly Arcus was clutching something too: the hilt of the dagger that had been plunged deep in his thigh.

"Hold your positions!" Irion ordered his guards. "Or be turned into something fouler than this graveyard bitch here!" The guards stepped backwards to their posts, though even their lord's command could not make them sheath their swords. They stood, dutiful, mouths hanging to the marble as ghoul breasts swung and her human lover pulled free Morden's dagger then used it to open the boy's throat.

Every eye that was left in the place, even Ghila's, turned then to Irion. The face of the grand architect had turned a paler shade of white, though his head never moved nor lips gave the faintest quiver. After a moment he released the ghoul, waving his men toward their murderous guest of honor. "I want him alive."

Romance never held much sway in the mansion. Certainly ghouls were not to be spared. Arcus was beaten to a quivering pulp. Through the guard's legs he saw Ghila make her escape. He couldn't blame her.

The slaves who'd sought refuge near the stables suffered a new terror at what barreled out of the house and past them. Last they saw, as was reported fervently to their master, was a grey, bristly rump scaling the outermost wall, then it was gone.

"You like that?" a guard growled, tightening the collar around Arcus's throat. "Ghoul-lovin' scum." The torch-lit sublevel they were in, once reserved for slothful slaves and recalcitrant solicitors, housed many a torture device. None better than the preferred garroting chair. The guard eased the chair's crank back a notch, allowing Arcus to gasp as he fought against the clamps pinning his limbs.

Through the past few hours, enough sweat had pooled under Arcus to send preoccupied guards slipping to the stones. One did right then, perhaps taken out of his concentration by the sounds of footsteps now descending the stairs. Quickly recovering, the guard burned another blotch into the prisoner with the tip of his red-hot sword.

"My lord," the burner said. "He be good an' primed, just as you ordered."

Irion stepped beyond the threshold of the stairwell, wiping his hands dry of some pungent oil before tossing a rag into the blazing stove. The coals turned green for an instant. "Thank you, Moath," Irion said, then asked for the guard's sword. Swinging it to the praise of his men, he whipped it upright and examined its blade.

For the moment able to use his throat, Arcus collected his hate, and his courage. "Chances are," he croaked. "You'll be able to do a bit better with a weapon than your son."

One of the guards was marching over to deliver a mailed slap but was halted. "My son," Irion said, drawing closer. "Yes. It is fortunate that we're not up where you insisted on killing him. The sun is rising." The guards all looked at one another. Irion turned and said: "Leave us."

As a sundering of boots and armor filed up the stairs, Irion closed within a breath of Arcus. He held one hand over Arcus's bare chest, clenching his fingers as if gripping his heart. Then he whispered a word.

Arcus melted away, replaced by an expansion that burst the ropes around his stomach and strained each and every clamp with an excruciating metallic whine. Gorial's roar sent the guards clattering, not down but up, leaving, as their lord had wished, Irion alone with the huffing, puffing ghoul.

Irion had not seen such a creature since taking his new form. Eyes that had never witnessed the foul metamorphosis glanced up and down the grey skin, sleek as a shark's though mottled and roughened in places by the rot of a fungal white. Irion admired the square, set jaw. He caressed with the tip of a finger the boar-like tusks protruding through exhales of steam. Gorial rolled his big yellow eyes, following Irion as the iron-wielder moved to his side.

"You wish to speak?"

If his massive hands had been free, Gorial would have clasped them together. "Please!" the ghoul replied. "Have mercy, dark lord. I could not overpower that pesky human, as you have. His spirit was strong, too strong." The bound ghoul begin to cry. "Too strong for poor, pitiful Gorial—but you know what?" The ghoul brightened, exposing a grinning cavern of fangs and broken teeth. "I have crawled his mind as a tunnel. He has family, alive. With your blessing I may visit them. Wreak on them the sorrows your family has this night suffere—"

"I am listening."

The ghoul elated. "Yes, yes, you let me go—if you let me go. I'll bring back, to you, to you, lord, the entire pack. Peasants and Chapwyns, food for the slaughter."

"But I am now a Chapwyn, dearest ghoul. You did not know?"

Gorial looked at him a long while before answering. A Chapwyn? Certainly the iron he swung heedlessly gave him the appearance of those holy hunters who occasionally descended to become martyrs in their burrows. "Well, lord, be that as it may, I—"

"You know my favorite line in their blubbering scriptures? I think I shall tell you." Irion bent lower, sniffing rot-ridden hair before whispering in the ghoul's pointy ear. "Vengeance is mine."

"But, my lord—"

"Guards!" Irion yelled up the stairs. "Prepare a cage!"

Irion often told his House that Chapwyns were good only at providing torture with their ludicrous laws. But this hot morning, he laughed aloud at the thought of how wrong he'd been. Still going after a night without rest, he'd ridden ahead of his men. He hid a yawn as the on-duty priest hammered home his weariness worse than wine.

"And you are sure this will do?" the young priest asked.

"You get good sunlight here, correct?"

"Oh, quite. This courtyard was built for no other reason than to pay homage to the sun." A flat stone altar middled the place; once brimming with allegedly Ansul's favorite flower, now reserved mainly for penitent floggings when theology students forgot their verses or dozed off in the choir.

"Excellent. We will provide the chains." Irion looked at the three walls and the open gate in the fourth. "I assume some of your brethren will wish to attend?"

"Absolutely—once their scriptorium duties are satisfied, of course." The priest took note of his own excitement and hung his head.

"There should be room," Irion said. "I alerted one of the other churches on my way here."

"Splendid. Actually, I think I hear them now."

It would take a lot longer to mobilize a brood of groveling priests. The morning's prayers weren't over yet. But the priest was not deaf: wagon wheels squeaked and clacked on the cobblestones just before the courtyard.

"Oh," the priest said. "Your men, I see."

The other priests soon came. They'd spent the better part of their collective morning calming their startled flock over rumors a ghoul had been seen running about the city. The clergy was soon holding their noses. All but the oldest, most seasoned leaned forward. The few veteran priests who knew what waited under the blanket prepared for their young brethren's excited repulsion—which raged the moment a turned-showman guard dramatically uncovered the cage, exposing a naked, muzzled monster. Amidst cheers and prayers and one running for a puke bucket, the consensus emerged; it was a sign from Tersiona herself that such a creature was being chained to the stone altar, though they were unaware that muzzling the ghoul had cost Irion's guard force two of its finest.

By noon, word had weaved through every church in Nilghorde. A body of priests and seminarians jammed the courtyard or joined Irion's men atop the wagon and its empty cage.

Those who'd hoped to keep the righteous cleansing a private one were prompted to slither through the crowd and return with loaded censers. On its back, covered in chains, the burned and prodded terror rotted before their very eyes. As the day burned on, incense and prayers could not keep the smell of the thing inside the hollow square.

"I swear," the on-duty priest said at Irion's side. "It's starting to look human. Is this right?"

Through the steam Irion also saw the returning of ordinary bones, the curled darkened hair of an ancient Azadi male. Tapping the priest's censer, he said, "Don't tell me you'd pray it stay a beast."

Irion's men had been properly instructed. As accustomed as anyone to witnessing the bizarre, they tightened down the chains as the body shrank. But nothing could be done about the muzzle, too small now to prevent those in the courtyard and all beyond to shutter at the ghoul's dying wails. Gorial, who amongst his pack had not only been daring but a hotheaded rebel when parley no longer held promise, gnashed at the air, yelling, "I'll eat your mother! Come back as your inbred fathers and fill those praying mouths with that pathetic piece of flesh that brought you into this miserable fucking world!"

Irion's men, looking to their lord for approval, followed suit, smiling without laughing until their faces hurt. Not sharing their mirth were the clergymen. Some stood shocked, others covered their ears. The rest descended on the changing ghoul, attacking him, first verbally, then with censers swung like footman flails.

Unnoticed by the enraged holy mob, the ghoul began arguing with itself. Of the guards who still watched Irion, they all witnessed his demeanor change. So much so they stowed their good mood and begin exaggerating the postures of their duty. The moment Irion heard the ghoul scream "Arcus," the Ordrid held up his hand.

The captain of his guards boomed. Every Chapwyn in the courtyard, from the most distraught student right down to the frothing fist-beaters, all ceased their doings and turned their eyes.

"Noble and pious," Irion spoke to them calmly. "It has come to my attention this creature still needs more cleansing, a cleansing that is beyond the powers of the sun. I beg of you, let me take this child of the night back, to private chambers, where I am better suited to rid us this particular breed of fiend."

Entire tomes were written on how to deal with ghouls. Chapwyns had practically patented cleansing by a full day's exposure. But the newest friend of the growing church had a power the priests truly envied. If they spoke with the subtle command that this dark-garbed saint did, they'd belong to a church made entirely of beatific bishops.

"Very well," the on-duty priest said. "Just please, take this man—I mean ghoul away."

That evening, three Ordrids, selected by Morfil and sent from the keep, chanted over Morden. The corpse had been brought down on a bier without wheels and matted by leaves and minerals from Irion's securest vault. As the ghoul was originally being toyed with in the garrotting chair, Irion had personally prepped the body, bathing it in a preserving oil that reeked of amniotic fluid and semen. The chanters continued their monastic tones as Irion, showing now his weariness, prepared to invoke a second resurrection.

From the chair Arcus watched Irion practice concentrated movements of the hand. The warrior's back ached and burns still seethed on his chest, though the sun had gone and moon had clearly risen. He fought the familiar wrist clamps as Gorial blathered in his skull.

"You got us into this—fuck you!—no, fuck *you!* If it were me, I'd just of rather died in Azad."

"Impressive, *Arcus*," Irion said through the ring of guards. "That you've held onto those bones—or should I say, latched onto them then refused to let go? That flesh isn't yours after all, is it? Certain, then, you were a warrior. This means you were the one who killed my son, not the ghoul who ate you. Which…" Irion's shift in tone alerted the guard manning the chair. The guard moved into position, tightening the collar a notch as his lord continued. "Which is why you are back in that chair."

"Look, it wasn't up to me—yes, it was. Sire, it was Arcus. He—" Another tightened notch ended the afflicted rabble.

Irion stared down at Morden's loins and throat, both covered in ribbons of silk, adorned in the most potent heraldry. "I shall let him cut out your stout heart," he said to Arcus.

Performed by the right necromancer, the dead could in fact be resurrected a second time. It was only the very real chance of the corpse's exponential degrade that discouraged such work. But Nilghorde knew Morden as his stepson, never mind the odd coincidence whispered by many how they looked alike.

Years ago, he'd sensed the death no one can escape. So he did what he'd done before: select and synthesize. In so doing he now lived, and in suitable form. He had usurped the Rogaire wealth, punished that House, and Morlia had easily seduced and married Rinmauld's blockheaded heir. She'd bore Irion a son and Rinmauld's was sent slowly to oblivion pawing and munching on some screaming, troublesome rogue.

It was just such a type of rogue, Irion worried, looking over again at the garroting chair, that he may have been forced to suffer yet again.

A decade had passed since he'd stepped into the shock and awe of a converted society, assuming the role of stepfather while being handed the keys to the marvelous Rogaire treasury. During Morden's earliest years, Irion had good reason to lay tucked away in the Thunder Bustle. There were mighty webs still to weave, plus, he'd wanted Morlia's highly talked-over remarrying to not appear too soon. Rogues had forced his hand. Two thieves had done something he hadn't predicted and now fate seemed intent on sinking her conspiring fangs into his hide once more.

"I must say I don't care for surprises." Irion walked about the cramped stone room, gathering his strength. When he finally spoke again, Arcus and his guards watched as Irion's own chant blasted out the light of every torch.

A guard, privy to the ritual, had been assigned the flint and steel. In the darkness Arcus heard the man's armor clunk and creak as he moved to relight the torches as Irion's voice grew louder.

"If it were *my* eyes, we could see." Arcus, tight against the chair as wire, ground his teeth and whispered, "Shut your mouth."

One torchlight, two torchlight, three; the pale shape of Irion clung to the paler shape on the bier. Irion's hands hovered over Morden's eyes and heart, and then Morden sat up and puked.

Two guards fainted. All three choiring Ordrids chortled dark cheers, hugging one another. But Irion did not share their merriment.

Blabbering and belching, flopping and farting, the only heir of the made-powerful Irion was an ongoing display of jabbering-limbed meat.

Irion hung his head. And then he called for a guard's sharpest dagger.

Irion had long debated if Morden's weakness was a remnant of his first death, but after years of balking most forms of study, he came to the sad conclusion his son, no matter the tutoring, took after influences of the old Irion's blood.

The slice was swift and clean, flowing free from Morden's throat a blood that was still reviving from the cold of the dead. The guard lit the last torch and then none in the room dared move.

"We're in for it now," someone in Arcus said. He then saw the hammer levitating, moving from near the cold iron stove towards the ring of guards. Arcus's eyes bounced from the hammer to the guards, from Irion to the heavy hammer he floated down into a guard's hands.

"Only after his bones are splinters," Irion said, heading for the stairs.

"And after, my lord?" asked the guard.

"Get them out of my sight. Both of them."

"Begging your pardon, but where, my lord?"

Irion turned once more to look upon the abysmal scene. "A place fitting such lowness."

And so happened Arcus Zevon was thoroughly beaten. When he could scream no longer, he was choked to death in the garroting chair.

✳

Ghouls always came back once their borrowed guise was slain, but few came back in such excruciating pain as Gorial now did. Standing was useless. His legs, thick and sinewy as the roots that burrowed through graveyard earth, were shot through with bolts of lightning. They'd been smashed so that not even the retrograde back, usually a moment of pleasure, could mend the cruel human doings. One of his arms hung limp and broken. A grinding tore through him as he sucked in the hot air. His arches, once high as grasshoppers, were now smashed flat.

"What an awful dream," he said to the pure blackness that surrounded him. With his working arm he reached, clasping his talons around nothing.

In the long nightmare he'd suffered, a willful meal had beat him into a realm of helplessness like a shovel patting down a troublesome patch of mud. It was no trick of the mind, he soon realized, though it was surely, yes, a nightmare. He couldn't remember the man he'd eaten, more now a dim apparition in a fitful dream. Strange he couldn't remember, he mused as he grimaced, trying in vain to upright himself onto his haunches. Whatever end he—they'd—incurred must have been an inexplicably bad.

But he remembered Irion.

An anger so wrenching it bristled his hair was vanquished by another bolt of pain. Still, Gorial tried to unseat the object that had been poking him in the back. Most retrogrades, he'd come to on war-made piles or once on a cart for the wounded. But, even moonless nights bore stars. Here—*down here*—there were none.

"I am underground," the ghoul affirmed, sniffing the wondrous decay about him. "A bit of good news, yes."

Although his growls echoed off earthen walls, his ears knew he now sat in something more like a cavern. Had his last host been slain in a cave? No, he thought, reaching behind him. There may have been plenty of bandits and baiters, but caves near the city of Nilghorde had to be rare.

The ghoul gripped the protruding nuisance behind him and dislodged it. "A bone?" he wondered, squinting down at its white human brightness. "A bone," he said, forgetting for a moment his pain to suck in with his returning senses the rotting hills before him.

Though it hurt his neck, Gorial looked up at what was no sky. Cracks in the vault door's frame, no matter how well carved, struck even a starved, battered ghoul as crude. Light from a day burning above filtered down to not only illumine the cracked femur in his grasp, but a larder so grand the sudden shift in emotion almost toppled him down a heap of maggot-crazed flesh that he perched on like a king.

He laughed. He cried. He screamed in pain as he tossed into the vault's fly-swarmed air a delightful skull after he kissed its beautiful grinning teeth.

"The Pauper Vault!" Every ghoul from the fishy docks of Nilghorde to the dry sands of Azad had heard the legends, laid their ear as they suckled as yellow-eyed pups to lustful tales of paradise. Newer ghouls had set out on pilgrimages, never to be heard from again. "And I'm not leaving either," he whispered.

Gorial listened. He heard the rustle of his own breath, returning in a fit of pain so fierce he could only squint. Entrances to tunnels could be seen as he slowly reopened his eyes. Ghouls knew of this place, many of them. His solitary kingdom would be short-lived, destined forever to crawl and rip scraps as the more able of his unsympathetic lot watched on with glee.

Irion. That moon-headed Ordrid; he'd done this. The cause of his sorrows probably sat somewhere in the brutal brightness of the Upper World right now, laughing at his expense, sucking down that awful thing they called wine.

This time the ghoul's cries shared no joy. Ironic, the humor of fate. Here he sat atop the fabled vault, but here he would dine a broken, ruined creature. Sucking up his tears, he decided to dig into his first meal and hope his spirits would revive.

Doing so, he saw he'd come alongside a fresh one. Carrion was just starting to strut and preen on the unmangled limbs. He flipped it on its back, gasping at the hilarity. Irony, yes. Humor beyond measure. Fate? Just perhaps. He salivated and licked his lips, staring down for a long while at the amazingly familiar corpse.

That horrible Ordrid had known much of ghouls. Had he really been so careless? "Seems so," Gorial said, running a long talon down Morden's cheek.

It made for difficult work, cracking open the chest with only one hand. Once the ribs were wide and breast bone a flung, forgotten dream, Gorial pried the tough heart from its tubing. Each bite he savored, until it was gone and the forehead of the flavorful Ordrid sparkled with the wings of flies. He waved the little bastards away. This next part was to be more than special. Plans—big plans—teemed in Gorial's brain. "On that very note," he snickered, then bent down to clamp his jaws around Morden's skull.

Depending on mood and if others of his kind were gibbering within earshot, Gorial would use his teeth to saw off the top of a corpse's head as clean as humans did a jar. But only now, stooped over so, did the ghoul learn yet another of his many wounds. Some bone in his neck had been cracked. "All the more reason," he uttered, doubling in his efforts and forgoing artistry. He began to scoop out clods of the Ordrid's brain and gobble them down.

It tasted so good that he—

"Gods of Below!" Morden suddenly shrieked, toppling down the putrefied heap to scream: "Help! Help! Help me!"

"Get back down," Gorial said, surmounting the hill. "And stay there, weakling." The decomposition was glorious. "Now *this* is a resurrection!"

Gorial now remembered more. He looked down at the emptied body of his newest host. *Host*—he snorted, dancing a jig with working legs so reckless he himself toppled down the hill. This was no host. "A human easily overpowered!" he yelled, staring with inferior eyes into the blackness echoing his triumph.

Morden ascended the rotting heap to peer up at the slivers of the sun. When he would eventually tire of the Upper World, this feast, forever restocked, would be right here waiting. There were considerations to make. His bare foot pressed upon a decayed face. He hardly noticed the rot-crazed flies swarming about his new and sensitive flesh. He'd hardly felt the rats nibbling, scrutinizing if his feet, indeed, belonged to the living.

Yes, the ghoul procures the memories of who it devours, but never before had he wandered so blissfully in the enchantment of a nemesis's kin. In this mind, *his mind*, one easier to subsume than prying open a water-rotted coffin with two good hands, in this weak and spiteful mind spun dead deeds more beautiful than a swirling museum. Gorial parsed Morden, looking for anything to use against Irion. His waded through tedious sightings: the smell of sweets and a mother's fawning praise; the unspooling of string to trip a slim and slinking butler; an agony of pain as a throat is crushed, a sudden reawakening and the hilt of someone's sword gripped tightly in a trembling hand.

Recent years fared more interesting. Entire clumps of Irion's teenage life came to full pageantry. Sailing beyond the mausoleum of imaged evenings spent self-stimulating, Gorial watched on with wrathful hope as the fondler's father begin appearing more and more.

A long while the ghoul sat, and a long while he punched his human body, as the damn boy had continuously paid no heed to family secrets. Then, distracting himself with an elbow caught in a sunray and needing to be gnawed, a new memory began to take hold. Flies flew. Rats scampered. Stranger things clinging to the walls beat their wings or slowly coiled. For what he witnessed made the ghoul howl through human cords in pure, bone-shaking glee.

✳

Gorial got sick of being Morden fast. Riding that cheerless self-centeredness was like breaking open coffin after coffin just to find nothing but hot, stuffy air. Once committing Morden's secrets to his own enduring memory, Gorial shucked the young Ordrid to gorge himself on new corpses.

And so he fed, until his broken limbs could hardly support the paunch that rubbed helplessly against the cadavers he crawled over. His kind returned to the vault in droves, tired of their capers and eager to dine—delighting in their newfound oddity. He slithered and supped and he cursed his fate as the laughingstock of the fitter ghouls, until, one day, while he was alone once more, a little girl happened to skip by the vault's opened door.

As he'd been informed by those he ate, Nilghorde had suffered a minor rebellion. There was some lofty bard, so long dead that dreams of his consumption were pointless. He'd been banned up there. A fortunate event for the ghouls. Inveterate poets formed en masse to protest, sucking in others, resulting in a glorious stampede by the Metropolitan Ward.

Now, day and night, the aftermath was still being hurled down into the catacombs, so much so the iron door above had been deemed too troublesome to shut.

Gorial picked a piece of grizzle from his teeth, happy he was tucked under a roof of limbs and guts still letting out their stenches. Hugged by the arms of a poet whose skull had been crushed by a horse, the ghoul was now so close to the square of sky, another minor rebellion and he'd be free—to do what, he could not say.

Those who dumped the bodies mumbled their logistical concerns, one even praising "ghouls be about" to soften the growing mountain. Gorial's snicker ended with a row of heads peering down. The sun, forever cruel, made black smudges of those it burned beyond. Gorial's edible roof served him, though in the places where concealment faltered sharp rays had slipped past backs and swollen tongues to scorch him to blisters. Worth it, it was. For the best and juiciest crowned the pile.

A beggar's blouse tied around his eyes had allowed him glimpses up into the daylit world. He tightened its knot, moving slow as worms not to alert the lone smudge staring down at him now.

Strange that a human child would delight in walking amongst the graves. Ghouls knew the human fear of death and their never-ending superstitions. Her humming leveled in one moment all Gorial thought he'd known of children. She did not lean over the granite frame of the Pauper Vault to weep a mournful ballad. She whistled and sang, her hair blowing in the bright wind below the sun. She was happier than any single memory in Morden Ordrid's entire sour life.

"Oh," she called down. "How I wish just one of you could talk. I do think I would have things to ask. Like…" The little wonder leaned harder against the frame. Even through the tattered blouse of a trampled beggar Gorial could see her arch her neck and look up at the clouds. "Hmm," she said, calling upon their inspiration. "I know: what does Tersiona look like? Oh, and do we eat and drink after we die?"

Gorial surveyed the larder, quickly picking a bagwoman whose head and breasts were within reach. With the utmost subtlety, as the child swirled her dress and sang one question down after another, he cracked the woman open.

"Oh, yes, and after we die, can we fly?"

"But of course, deary," an old crone croaked up from the depths. "Fly and eat and more."

With eyes better suited for the sun, Gorial saw: her hair was black as a raven, how it became a stiffened blur as she, about half the height of a full-grown human, bolted from the edge at such panicked speed he couldn't help but cackle. And with the old bagwoman's eyes Gorial saw the child return.

Peeking over the rim, the child asked: "Are you okay? How did you get down there?"

"A poor old woman," he said, crawling out from under the others. "A poor old woman," he said, standing upright, so close now the old woman's matted grey head nearly protruded out into the light. "A poor old woman should be advised not to fall asleep on certain stoops. Took me for dead, they did. Dear girl, might I ask you, is there anyone else up there?"

"No—wait!" the child cried, having shifted in one instant from fleeing terror to ardent help. "I can go get my dad. I will get him now—wait right there."

"Just a moment, deary." *Why am I doing this?* Gorial thought as he waved her back. Whim, of course, for little else drives a ghoul's sportive nature. The child had tickled his curiosity. If the child summoned an adult, the game they'd just begun would vanish, and possibly priests and sworders emerge.

But there was something else, a stronger more immediate reason he wanted the child to stay. He didn't like to admit it. He'd spent centuries with Ghila, cavorting and clamoring under the soil of graves or the light of a good moon. Ghila, now gone and, he dared hope, maybe, possibly searching for him now; her absence: he now truly felt the emptiness the lack of her company had imparted him with. It was perhaps this reason above all else he desired to banter with the quirky little human girl, but, if he were a fiend prone to superstition, he may have soon believed her to be an instrument of fate.

"Well, okay," the girl said, turning from where she'd intended to run to stare back down into the vault. "What is your name?"

"Oh, Ghila. Ghila is my name. Thank you for asking, sweet girl. And yours? What might yours be?"

"Niera. Niera Oleugsby."

If he'd been in his true form, his yellow eyes would have keened right then to a predatory glimmer. The old woman's face creased for a moment, then the mirth was gone. But her eyes, hungry and livid, gleamed like blazing coals.

"O-lee-ogz-bee?"

"Yes, ma'am. My father's Seasmil."

He couldn't believe it. "Seasmil Oleugsby, you say? Are you sure?"

"Why *of course* I'm sure," she larked. "He's in charge of this place…do you know him?"

"Oh, plump and so sweet you are." Gorial called upon the flesh to rear what he hoped was a bright smile. "Lean closer, Niera. Good, that's good. The fates are kind to an old woman. Oh, Niera. How I have a little tale for you."

It had been many years since Seasmil had killed his bosses and took over the Pauper Morgue. The place looked the same, the glass dome above his worktable still filtered down orange and wholesome the day's Nilghorde sun, but each year that passed the bodies undoubtedly felt heavier and heavier.

Unusually attentive to the day's load, he surmised his self-aware attention to tumors and stab wounds was driven by the circus that had been ongoing down the path. The city had hired a gang of miscreants to rid the affected streets of the prior night's explosion over Vandahl. As he worked he mused how if he would have been ten or fifteen years younger—if not so much grey streaked his hair and he didn't own a gut that hung over his belt—that he, the greatest lover of Vandahl to recite a drunken teary sonnet, would have gladly met his end last night with those braver souls.

Having a kid also put a wet blanket on such ambitions. As if summoned by his thoughts, the door swung open and Niera ran in.

"Daddy! Daddy! I met an old woman."

"You did?" He would have covered his work with a sheet if in any way his daughter would have been bothered by it. But, settling in Seasmil an unmovable plaque of discomfort, Niera was far too much as he was, or at least had been. She breezed past a festering stack and leaped into his arms.

"Yes," she said, "and she said I have the most beautiful name ever."

"That you do, the name my own mother once wore. Now what is this about an old woman?"

"She's down in the vault!" Niera pushed herself off his chest, scrutinizing him with her dark eyes. "Daddy, who was Sumeelia?"

Staid—that idiot. He'd promised shortly after their marriage he'd never mention Somyellia again. It pained him to do so, but not such a pain as his wife, he conceded, must have felt when his ramblings led to troublesome waters. "Why is your mother telling you about her?"

"Mommy didn't say it! The woman down in the vault did."

"Honey," he said, moving her to his other knee. "You remember what I said? Make believe makes the world go round…but not when talking to Mommy and Daddy. That's lying."

"But I'm *not* lying. The old woman said you two used to love each other like you and Mommy do, and her cousin's name is." Seasmil watched as she searched, nearly dropping her when she announced: "Irion!" He asked her to repeat it. She did. "Is he like an uncle to me?"

Niera held imagination in no short supply. Her adventures in City Cemetery often brought back tales of friendly ghosts, bones that moved, smiling fairies that hid behind thoroughly searched tombstones. But no such childish grandeur had ever produced a name he had never told her. Seasmil had never even told his wife about Irion. No reason to: just an apparition in an epoch he'd decidedly put behind him.

Unable to decide how to think or feel, he asked his daughter to tell him her tale.

"Well, Daddy. The old woman—who we must rescue—she said to tell you that Irion did something bad to Sumeelia." Her face took a turn for the serious. "Something really bad, Daddy. And that you should know."

"Know what, honey?" She stared down at the floor as if searching for the right clod of dirt to jar her memory. After a moment she cried, "I can't remember."

"I don't like you running around the graveyard." He put her on her feet.

"You said *you* used to."

He cleared his throat and glanced her a wry one. "If I go look for this old woman, she will be there?"

"She has to be. Someone threw her down the vault."

Seasmil took off his smock and grabbed, certain he was a fool, a length of rope. "Let's not mention this to your mother."

※

As he'd expected, no woman was there. Niera wailed and pled, pled and wailed, pointing to the "exact spot" where a dirty smiling witch had told her things that caused Seasmil to scratch his head and console his girl that yes, of course he still believed her.

What he hadn't expected was for Niera's tale to burrow so firmly in his chest.

Next morning, after Staidilia's usual breakfast, he told his women he'd be gone until sometime in the evening. "What for?" Staidilia asked, but he felt disinclined to answer.

It was a long walk to the skirts of the Morgeltine, but he could use the fresh air and exercise. It had been ages since he'd sojourned the city. He marveled at all the new buildings, the cleanliness of the streets, the unpuked-on cobblestones devoid of the type of society who still found itself almost daily onto his worktable.

By noon his legs ached. The highest obelisk in Laugher's Lot was long hidden by steep roofs and smoking chimneys, and now the untamed luxury of mansions shined and mixed with the sweat in his eyes. *Maybe I did need a walking stick*, he thought, mirthfully shaking off his breathing. No matter, the forest at the city's edge now in view, a few more palaces to his back and he'd be in the shadow of the old Rogaire place.

After what felt a hundred miles more, he was standing in front of a guard. "What's your business," the thug said, clacking to life to place his shield and armor in Seasmil's way.

Seasmil looked beyond the helmet and the frowning face staring out from underneath. Somyellia had told him the grounds were vast. Growing up in Templeton, he couldn't exactly agree; lawns of higher Wardsmen there had been that of small fields. But, through the guarded side gate and beyond the bailey wall, sun-whitened tips of, of course, more obelisks seemed to stretch out in an expanse fitting a district of such wealth and territory.

"Do you have an appointment? You don't look like a tradesman."

"I'm not a damned carpenter," Seasmil said, hearing now the

rhythmic beating of hammers. "Your boss and I, we have, we know some of the same people."

The guard rubbed his beard. It perhaps served Seasmil his hair was long and dark, matching the clothing he now deemed unfit for such a journey under a scorching day. "Begging your pardon, sir, but if you are an Ordrid please say so."

"I am no Ordrid."

"And no tradesmen either. I dare say, you strike me a lurker. Perhaps looking for another purse to plunge." The interrogator removed his hand from the pommel of his sword to grab the whistle hanging about his neck.

"Would a thief come and strike up a lovely chat with an armed guard, midday, and have you ever seen one so damned out of shape? I'd die before besting the first open window. Now tell Irion that Seasmil Oleugsby is here. I need to speak with him on, about family matters."

At length the guard unglued his eyes and chirped out a cadence from his whistle. Another soon appeared, receiving orders and disappearing once more behind the wall. And there Seasmil waited, being baked by the sun while the smirking guard drank theatrically from his jug. What an idiot Seasmil felt. Word had reached him years ago of her cousin's maneuvering into this very mansion. Whomever Irion had become, the dour little Ordrid was sure to have no interest in entertaining the question if he knew of a pit-trotting wench.

"Oh, to hell with it." He threw his hands up and took the first step home, already contemplating the extent of his foolishness and the workload that had surely piled.

"Seasmil," a cool voice said. "Is that truly you?"

He turned to see Irion standing at the gate. Age had landed on Irion too, though graciously so. As we all do, Seasmil took in the wiser features: the familiar cheekbones, a more sunned skin, the subtle creases sowed into the corners of eyes that stared at him.

"Tis I," Seasmil said, embarrassed. "It's been a long time—"

"Come in, come in," Irion burst. Only the guard's oft-tested bearing prevented ogling at his lord's current demeanor. "Come in, Seasmil. Let us speak."

Time as an aristocrat must've rubbed off. Irion led Seasmil by the hand, speaking pleasantries until they were both seated in the graveyard. "It's too loud in there," Irion said, waving a hand at the wall of his glittering mansion. And indeed it was. Irion explained the pounding hammers and saws that were grinding were all for renovations. Two girls emerged, each bearing a glass of wine. The black one, carved and velvety beyond much anything Seasmil had ever seen, handed him his glass. The auburn Serab, looking almost Rehleian, served her master where after they both simply bowed and marched back into the cacophony. "Salt and pepper," Irion winked, then referred to the chambers underway. "For the newest batch of slaves. A man needs joy after the untimely departure of his love. You of all can understand this." Irion nodded at someplace beyond his guest's shoulder. Seasmil turned to see a weathered headstone: Morlia Ordrid.

"No obelisk?"

"Another?" Irion said, finishing his wine. "Werlyle! You maggot!"

Seasmil hadn't even taken a sip, and didn't plan to. No sooner had Irion barked than, stumbling out from where the slave girls had vanished, the most unsightly creature appeared holding a laden tray.

For a moment Seasmil thought one of his old bosses had risen from the dead to serve drinks to the living. "Ah, Werlyle," Irion said in a way that reminded Seasmil of the man he'd used to know. "My favorite slave."

What waddled out to sate his master's thirst was short and fat and bereft of eyes that signified even the slightest sentience. The foul slave's preternatural silence was not undone by a mouth that hung permanently open. In it Irion worked the base of his empty glass, causing the bailey to come alive with chuckles from the watching guards. Irion patted his slave on the head, sending him off.

"You're not drinking." Irion said.

"A bit early for me."

Irion sidled closer on the sarcophagus. "Tell me, what's on your mind."

After a self-conscious delay, Seasmil did. It was true he never particularly cared for Irion, but coming to a man's home to try and explain Niera swore she'd met an old woman who'd had tales to tell—he could hardly believe his words.

In contrast to Seasmil's expectations, Irion did not smirk or sick on him his guards. He listened attentively. "The Pauper Vault, you say?" Without a trace of judgment the Ordrid nodded his head and showed only the friendliest curiosity.

Seasmil went one deeper: "If this woman wasn't real, how could my kid have made this up?"

"Dear Seasmil, the world is nothing if not noise. Why, the very sarcophagus we now perch on once rattled with nonsense. Now it's as quiet as peace herself, as your daughter's glorious imagination will one day be."

Seasmil took in these words, careful not to lay out any accusation when he explained Niera had relayed that the old woman had said Irion somehow wronged Somyellia.

"Seasmil, many people know of me, and of Somyellia. And I suppose of you too. More importantly, this old woman, as you say, she wasn't there when you searched for her?"

"Likely never was."

"I see. Well, black magic is everywhere, especially these days." Irion sat on his next thought. "With your permission, I'd like to look into this a little further. My House, as you know, has its fair share of enemies. Curious that this…information is being put into the ears of little girls."

"Very."

"Thank you for stopping by, Seasmil." Irion stood. "Though," he added as they walked, "I am not pleased to have to revisit the demise of my cousin, it pleases me all the same to see you. Again, after all these years." Seasmil prepared for the long walk, no less confused and now owning a head swimming with wine. At the gate Irion said goodbye. "You shall return? Perhaps next time with the new missus and that little storyteller of yours."

✳

According to the city of Nilghorde, Gormorster Toadly had simply vanished. This humorous fiction complicated Seasmil's ambition when he petitioned to buy Toadly's home. Close to work, a top-floor view of the cemetery's white-green sprawl; it would've been foolish not to purchase the old tower. The waiting period slogged and agonized to where, at one point, shortly before being handed the deed and a new set of keys, Seasmil considered testifying that good old-fashioned homicide had rid the city of the tower's previous ruler.

Now the Oleugsbys lived there. Staidilia's tastes had swept and polished a rotting cadaver into a flowered conquest of the domestic. Where undead slaves had once been made now hummed and steamed the work of a warm kitchen. A built-in shelf had recently become a repository for a number of Niera's dolls. An office at the top of the tower, however, had stayed very much the same. In its gloom, that same evening, Seasmil sat down to write.

Work at the morgue still paid the bills, but he'd long ago lost his necrotic zeal. Writing—the immortal written word! The greatest, truest way to explore life's ephemeral nature. And there was that, too: *life*. That sunray which had entered his dark cosmos on the day of Niera's birth. Now he held new inspiration.

But his thoughts this evening were blockading him even worse than usual. The odd, fruitless talk with Irion had been replaced by an even greater despair. Vandahl: if this was the direction of the market, his hen scratch would now surely never see print. Sunk in his chair, surrounded by bookshelves broken by the window lighting his desk, he stared solemnly at his collection. He chuckled. They hadn't had a reason in quite some time to throw him in the dungeon. He slid all his Vandahl under a shelf, infuriating his dreariness by then picking up his own work.

I lie here, awake, on a hard made bed
Where branches and moonlight scrape a window
Nights are cold and old arc the shadows
Busy raping a day's familiar room.

Awake I gape at milky moonlight
Traversing a course— sly and majestic
These weary years begat worn wasted tears
Until morning peeks then off to work I go.

He crumpled the poem he'd penned in an idle hour and tossed it into the wastebasket where it belonged. If Vandahl was base and pornographic, his own attempts to depict life in its truth were downright villainous. He let out a sigh and moved on to his manuscript.

What a beast. What monument to confusion. What a hulking once-tree, unfinished and bogged down to a penultimate screed with likely no ending worthy of all the sore wrists. *The Hero* ~~*Fails*~~ ~~*Comes*~~ *Returns*—no title worked. Nothing encapsulated what he was trying to say, and perhaps, he brooded, it was simply because he himself didn't know.

He set the pages down and made anguishing gestures at his inkwell until becoming thirsty. Seasmil headed over to the bottle, but before he could get to its shelf his eyes caught something orange glowing outside his window.

Down below, a crowd of men stood, stoking a fire. In his tenure he'd seen one or two cremations. Yet the black smoke that billowed out from the vault was not the inferno of a corpse, but of hundreds.

"They must really hate protesters," he said, pouring himself his drink. The vault was technically his duty, but zealots burning down the population only made his work easier. He'd even asked the city to do the same, once. And now they did, burning the protesters who'd possessed more spine than he, those he watched fly up into the evening to greet the heavens as one torrid smog. His glass broke against the wooden floor when Niera screamed.

That wasn't an ordinary one: the thought shot through Seasmil as he leapt down the stairs and ran out the front door. Her cry had been desperate, shrill, and too close to those flames.

A ruckus had ringed the vault. Its iron door open, members of Ansul's True were looking down into the fire, holding tight their torches and swords. Their presence meant little, but what caused Seasmil confusion and concern were the black-sash ruffians mixed in with the holy warriors. Guards from the Ordrid mansion were there, pouring jugs of oil into the roaring flames.

"Is this one yours?" one of Irion's guards demanded. Niera was flailing in the man's grasp, bawling, pounding her little fists against a mailed thigh, crying on and on about a poor old woman.

"She is." Seasmil eyed the curious mix of men. "What are you doing here?"

"Thank the gods," the guard said, shoving Niera toward Seasmil in way he did not like.

"It's okay, honey."

"But the lady, Daddy. She'll—"

"Niera." Seasmil bent down, straightening her dress and making her look at him. "I want you to go home. Right now."

After a teary protest she did, running up the trail until all that was left was her father and a crowd of armed men lighting fire to his vault.

"This vault is my responsibility. Church or not—"

"We have responsibilities too," a Chapwyn crusader wiggled his torch and said.

"Weren't we supposed to," a guard pointed at Seasmil, turning to his cohorts, "if we saw him—"

"Silence," another guard said, emerging from the rear. Seasmil immediately recognized the beard.

"You were at the gate," Seasmil said. "This morning." Seasmil eyed all the naked swords, the balled fists. He'd seen worse. "Why are you here?"

"*You* sure ask a lotta questions," the leader said. "Too many. Now get outta here!"

But Seasmil didn't. The guards became indignant. Seasmil made things worse when he asked if the Chapwynites had castrated them too. A fight ensued. Ansul's True stood over the dogpile, sanctimoniously holding their torches while Seasmil, despite his best efforts, definitely got the worst of it.

※

Next morning, Irion sat at his desk, petting his imp. The little fiend was hidden from their esteemed guest. Coiled in its master's lap like a kitten, it pawed at the underbelly of the desk's walnut apron.

Over the sound of hammers finishing up somewhere below, Archbishop Drot said, "Is it true, Irion, that the ghoul originated from here?" The portly leader of the church frowned at all that covered Irion's desk: books sealed by heavy locks, a vial full of squiggling worms, and one clean, white, grinning skull.

"I am afraid it is so," Irion said. "You must remember my House comes with much baggage. Poor girl must have been banished from her clan. Must've been seeking old refuges, and," nodding out his window at the mansion's graveyard, "perhaps an untapped larder." Irion fed his imp a fat worm.

The archbishop had arrived and took off his ornate chasuble, spinning through a preliminary of small talk. He was still looking out the window at all the dead Rogaires when he turned and said, "Well, at any rate, reports are that a she-ghoul barreled over watchman, eventually turning eastward, taking out every picket fence along the way."

"It didn't smell like a Rehleian ghoul."

"How do you know such things? It seems—"

"It seems it probably scampered back to Azad. Allowing, of course, it found sufficient shade along the way."

Archbishop Drot furrowed his brow, immediately dropping another question before clasping his hands. "At any rate," he rejoiced, "dear friend, that undead horror we owe a great deal of gratitude. We've worked all month and now it's being carried over by the Ward to be signed by the Scepters this very minute."

"Oh?"

"Because of this most unusual sighting, the church was able to pass this morning a more profitable charge for funeral costs—to laden coffins with slivers of iron and vials of blessed water—to prevent the deceased from becoming themselves such a stinking horror, through digestion or otherwise. The people won't like the new prices—those who can avoid Grandmother from going into that Pauper Vault, anyhow. But they like the thought of ghouls even less. The coffers will swell. I must ask, did you plan this?"

"Yes," Irion lied.

The archbishop retrieved his chasuble from a coat hook, smiling. "Then we owe you a worthy percentage."

※

That same morning, as the head of the Chapwyn church departed Irion's graces in an armed carriage, Seasmil entered for the first time in many years the dirt and grime of the Thunder Bustle.

"I wish you didn't look like a raccoon." Niera took her eyes off her father's face. It brightened her spirits a bit he was taking her on this adventure. New streets. Tall buildings. People who peeked through windows like elves. Seasmil held her tight by the hand, touching the bruises around his eyes as she asked him again: "Where are we going?"

"To see a man."

Despite his injuries and mission, Seasmil couldn't take his mind off the brothel they'd passed right before officially stepping foot into the district. Niera's mother was far from amused when he'd announced the day's itinerary. Her silence would have been all the more painful if she'd known about his many sojourns to that whorehouse.

Staid had her passions. A favorite was rubbing Seasmil's back. He would lay still, his mind not. The secret hurt him. He didn't want to betray Staidilia, but he also didn't want to feel the nothingness he so often did. He hated keeping his private arrangements the caustic, painful, hidden note that would crush his wife. But he also hated that he became relieved whenever she'd leave the room, or their dreary home. More, Seasmil had found that stronger than love is the desire to be loved. Faces change, names are replaced, and, in the end, regardless, the need is met.

"Daddy, are you daydreaming?"

Seasmil stared at the blank wall of a dead-end alley. "Sorry, honey." He led them out, back onto the road toward Little Pelat.

"Dreaming about what?"

"Grown-up stuff. Excited to see Little Pelat?"

Indeed she was. Her father had spent the better part of breakfast explaining how the little people from faraway islands had made a veritable village. There was no way last night was a coincidence. What he omitted from the day's outing was word at the brothel had shed a potentially useful light. There was a magic user among the Pelats, one not connected in any way to the House of Ordrid. Irion had sent those men to the vault, for whatever reason, and Irion would not know Seasmil's newest move.

"What kind of man?" Niera asked as she skipped.

One who can show me what that old hag said to you. "You believe in magic?"

"Of course I do, Daddy. It's all around."

"Someone who knows how to use it, love."

Due to the incessant harassment from longtime locals, Little Pelat had erected walls and palisades, allowing these days but one clear way in and out. Just before this entrance, a stone's toss from the first row of Pelati shops, milling about a stoop, stared a group of foul-faced men, barring Seasmil's way.

Where once he'd walked with impunity, he instead now took full consideration of his delicate cargo. No doubt he still appeared menacing. Despite walking with an attentive sprite in a frilled yellow dress, his scowl kept the miscreants at bay. Except, of course, for an especially drunk one.

"Looks like she gave you a wallopin'," the snarly, short drunkard said. Seasmil counted five, but that didn't take into account those who may have been watching from the concealment of near-noon shade.

"He don't look to be from around here," spoke another.

"On the contrary," Seasmil said after swallowing with some success the coal burning in his throat. "Used to live right here in the Bustle."

"Is that so," the drunkard said, dislodging himself from the stoop. "And then what, Your Grace? Struck it rich and moved to the Morgeltine? Come back to show the kiddy what humble starts ya rose from?"

"Daddy?" Niera tugged at his arm.

"It's all right, sweetheart—fellahs, it's busy day for us." He'd seen kidnappers before. He'd once alluded them in times that, to his daughter, he would never tell. These men looked to be of the sort, lounging after a night's work. They'd be fools to try anything in the light of day, but fools were abundant. He reaffirmed his grip. "Excuse us, please."

"So that be it," one said. None moved. "Make a little visit to the little brownies takin' our jobs, cloggin' our streets with their smell and squealin' damn pigs."

"Come on then," the drunk said, wheeling his fists, scanning his audience for approval. "You're a big lad. Best me an pass. All in Nilghordian fun."

Seasmil sighed. "I'd rather not," he said, envisioning his dagger.

"Porpho," said another, seeing Seasmil's eyes. "Maybe put down the punchers and let 'em pass. It's early for—"

"Shut up, coward!" cried swaying Porpho. Enraged by his colleague's gutlessness, Porpho sent forward a glob of spit.

Seasmil saw the knives. He saw the one in the back unspooling a rope. He wiped the phlegm from his cheek and broke the drunkard's jaw.

"Get 'em!" a voice yelled, prompting a flimsy ring. Niera stood like an ivory statue; her hand vanished from Seasmil's grasp as he slammed an assailant to the stones.

"Stop that!" A strange voice burned through the crowd.

Seasmil had unsheathed his dagger, causing Niera to let out an ear-ripping wail.

"Stop that!" the voice said again, this time much nearer. "Stupid Rehleians."

A tiny man jumped into the melee. Swinging the bulbous end of his club, the Pelat opened up the ring. One slow-mover took a thud in the stomach, met after with the sharp smack of wood meeting a weak arm bone. The Pelat looked up and past Seasmil.

As quickly as he'd joined the fight, like a brown spider, the little man jumped out of the crowd and hid his club behind his back.

"What goes on here?" yet another voice now said, this one condescending upon the whole lot.

Seasmil tried to catch his breath. As he tried to calm Niera's explosion, he couldn't help but notice the nerved murmuring that was still spreading amongst his attackers. Spackled in Porpho's blood, Seasmil turned to see he was eye-level with the black nostrils of an armored horse. He continued his eyes up. The clean-shaven Wardsman leaned forward, overtly thumbing the hilt of his primary sword.

Seasmil sheathed his blade, but it was the Pelat who spoke. "They fight all time, sir. Bat for business." Seasmil and Niera both watched as he pointed his club at the first of the Pelati shops just beyond the ruffian's precious stoop.

"I see," said the Wardsman. "Quite a mess we have." He paused to scan the crowd. "Porpho!" he delighted. "You wish to go on another ride with me?"

But Porpho couldn't respond—could hardly walk. The slug mumbled as best he could his rebellious obscenities as his men lifted him onto his feet.

"What we have here," declared the Wardsman, "is a clear case of civil disobedience."

"Daddy, is he a good guy or bad?"

The lone member of the Metropolitan Ward swung a whistle around his finger. "One blast. Just one and the wagons, they will come."

The scene dispersed after every single man, including Seasmil and the Pelat, lined up to move a coin from their pocket to a municipal saddlebag.

The Pelat waved his club and yelled curses in a foreign tongue at the departing, laughing rider.

"I sorry," said the Pelat as Seasmil ducked to enter his shop.

The shop was as Seasmil heard it would be: an unclean floor below primal cuts of hung pork. The butcher went in and out of a backroom, cursing and grumbling.

"Don't touch," Seasmil laughed, slapping Niera's hand when she tried to finger the lips of a shrunken human head.

Several shrunken heads later, the Pelat reappeared. "Here you are," he said, handing Seasmil a piece of vellum. Seasmil looked at the directions written on it. "Sorry took so long, couldn't find ink—you want to buy some meat? Maybe precious loin chops for you precious girl?"

Seasmil had asked for information. Word was a defrocked priest, a Chapwyn deserter, had sought protection amongst the Pelats. "No thank you," he said kindly, parting with another coin he'd intended for this mysterious religious rogue.

Soon Seasmil and Niera were again treading the streets of the Thunder Bustle. He hadn't been exposed much to the ways of Nilghorde's newest citizens, but as the two followed the butcher's landmarks and scribbled lefts and rights, he walked a bit easier. Compulsion to hold onto Niera like a chest among pirates lessened as they parted the sweet smokes of the sidewalk fires, skirted around colorful stations, and bopped past throngs of ever-singing chimes. The onset of a headache had moved from his black eyes to the base of his skull. All the walking. All the damn fighting. That butcher had every reason to think he'd saved a potential customer from a righteous beating.

"I'm getting old," Seasmil grieved after they'd stopped to buy Niera a Pelati doll. The seller bowed graciously, confirming by her gestures that they were indeed very close. From there they took the final right and soon, surrounded by high walls of buildings the Pelats were busy gutting, he stood outside the locked door of a derelict shack.

"Is this someone's *house?*" Niera asked, running her palm over her doll's pig hair.

When Seasmil knocked, a man paler than he emerged.

"Hi," said Niera.

Glancing at the child before lifting his eyes to scrutinize Seasmil, the man, dressed in a filthy robe that had once matched his complexion, softly placed his hands on his hips. "I must say," he said, "those eyes are a bandit's mask of sorts, one could say. But if you are an assassin, I doubt you'd have brought your daughter."

What followed was a talk, a petition, no less uncomfortable to Seasmil than his earlier chat with Irion. It was a blessing Niera was there. He hadn't considered the disarming power a six-year-old could bring to a cold introduction. She was there for other reasons. Nevertheless, before long they were invited into a candlelit room.

"Priest Bonaveere," the man said, shutting and relocking the door. "At least that was my name. They just call me Bone around here." He smiled. "Here, sweetheart," he then said, guiding Niera to the only stool. When she was seated he turned squarely to her father and said, "This is a most unusual request."

"I, I'm sorry. I don't know where else to turn. If you have something that can help, this pouch is yours." Seasmil of course was referring to the pouch of coins he'd brought, now three light, which he jingled in a way that made Bone roll his eyes.

"I am no petty soothsayer," the once-priest said. "But," studying the silver Seasmil insisted on spreading out onto a bare table, "you say Ansul's True took part?"

Seasmil placed a hand on Niera's shoulder. "Honey, what did those other men look like?"

"They were in white—and had swords. I don't think they were very nice."

"That's them, all right," Bone chuckled, crossing his arms. He then took a breath and finished explaining his plight. He had been in hiding ever since his vocal condemnation over the church's move toward irreligious tyranny. There was a price on his head, though the church was keeping the manhunt under wraps as best their haughty declarations had been able.

"I'm not sure what your old church is up to, but they're rubbing elbows with some shady folk."

"And *that*," Bone said, sliding the coins off the table into a pouch of his own, "is why I think I shall help you, Seasmil. Please, sit down."

Soon the esoteric works of the church were on full display. Coming out of sacks were odd garments, components, and a large bronze bowl. Seasmil had no issue leaving Niera in the shack when he'd been asked to fetch a bucket of water from a nearby well. Niera had taken a delight in the setup, distracting its architect with excited questions about spirits and the afterlife.

When Seasmil returned, an acrid odor was filling the room. Bone sat over the bowl, tending to a small flame that burned within. He ushered Seasmil over, who then carefully poured the water, resulting instantly in a tongued flume of white smoke.

A strand of Niera's hair, a pearl ground to powder, smaller bowls of crushed this and that, the feathers of an owl—all went into the broth at their prescribed times as the severe man repeated a chant that reminded Seasmil of the ones Somyellia used to sing. Before long, the smoke engulfed the once-priest so that not even the bright blue biretta he'd capped his head with could be seen as he spoke into the pops and gurgles.

Bone waved the smoke away. "It's time."

At his directive, Seasmil sat Niera beside him. "Just do as the man says."

Bone first spoke to Niera much like Seasmil did, referring to her pretty dress and pretty new doll. Then Seasmil watched his words change. Sounds of a secret sect put his child into something like a trance. Her head swayed. Her eyes drearily shut. Then they reopened, her neck stiff. She looked not *at* but *through* Bone. He looked up at Seasmil, who gave him a nod.

He slipped one of Niera's hands down into the bowl, making sure her fingers sank below the calmed surface. Her other hand he placed in his own, and here he said a final word.

All at once the bowl became a glistening mirror. In it, from vague hues, were emerging the forms and borders of a familiar scene. Having witnessed Somyellia's work, Seasmil still almost toppled over with dizziness when words wisped up from the figures in the broth:

"Lean closer, Niera." An old woman—the old woman—said to his daughter from down in the vault. Niera, dressed as she'd been, did as the wicked woman said. "Good, that's good. The fates are kind to an old woman. Oh, Niera. How I have a little tale for you."

"Is it a happy story?"

"Oh, I am afraid not, dear thing. The best stories are usually sad. You must promise me, little girl, that you will run home and tell your father this tale."

"Yes, and he will get a rope."

"Yes, quite. Now, there was once a cruel, wicked man—a man named Irion. Have you ever heard of him? No? Well, this cruel and wicked man had a cruel and wicked son. And to this son he once said: *Somyellia, a loose and low Ordrid whom you never had to meet, she sacrificed her life for our House. Though she didn't know it. A means to an end, Morden. Weaved us a mighty curse, she did. One that cost her her very life. This is why you must take serious your studies, be you the hammer or a useful nail. Perhaps if she'd proven better she'd still be with us. No bother. May her sulking, hulking lover—what was his name?—Seasmil. Seasmil of the House of Oleugsby. A face you wouldn't soon forget. A real madman, that one. May he shed a tear for the rest of us over our dearest departed. One who didn't take serious her studies. Now get back to your tinctures.*"

✳

"And now," Archbishop Drot said to his gleaming audience. "We officiate the brand-new Ansul of Chapwyn Home for Orphans." The crowd cheered. The archbishop handed Irion the ceremonial shears; who then cut the ribbon hanging across the orphanage's polished doors.

"As the sun shines above us," said Irion, calming the packed gathering of parishioners and parents eager to sign away their obligations. "So do shine the good graces of the church."

As the people cried and cheered, one face did not smile. Shouldering through the crowd, Seasmil kept his eyes on his target. Like a zealot marching toward martyrdom, he made his way past priest and parishioner and armed members of the Metropolitan Ward. He hated his concentration being disrupted, but thoughts of the past few hours still plagued him.

He had no reason not to trust that defrocked priest. Bone's eyes had worn the concern of a man watching another learn of ill and unwanted news. More, he had drawn Seasmil a new set of directions: the route he himself slithered when needing to avoid the Porphos of the world and breathe beyond the confines of Little Pelat. This had gotten them home, and in the wee hours, after his daughter—who remembered nothing—and her mother—who demanded to know everything—had both gone to bed, he'd made up his mind that something had to be done.

"Where do you think you're goin', black eyes?" one of the black-sashed guards said, putting a hand on Seasmil's chest, stopping that something in its tracks.

"To pay homage."

"Then do so at the tithing box, like the rest."

Seasmil sent the man to the ground without a thought in his helmet. At first only an old codger had seen, but his shriek at the sight of the second hewn guard sent the place into a whirl.

"Get him!" someone cried. Seasmil shot forward, taking a

swing at Irion with a closed fist. Irion ducked, far faster than Seasmil had seen men do.

"You," Irion sneered.

Seasmil cocked back to try another, but the archbishop had already bellowed. The attending Ward had snapped out of their complacency, and the crowd now descended.

Seasmil gritted his teeth, pushing and shoving and tripping and knocking senseless the shocked mob. Heads were cracked and a third mansion guard got a mangling under his boot before the Ward broke through the thickening ring.

Seasmil had brought his dagger, but he had, perhaps foolishly, hoped for something other than murder. Now a member of the Ward buried a blade into Seasmil's hide. His scream alone parted the crowd.

He had no way of knowing, in the moments after, who he attacked or what damage he'd done. Blinded by blood and pain, he burst through and was once again free. He had escaped, though, once home and tending an egregious but non-lethal wound, he could only surmise he was now a wanted man.

Nothing is avenged
My despair a raven
One who perches laughingly
On wearisome shoulder
While I wither slow to dirt
And dust in despair
Coming last heartbeat
However it pumps
Nothing amended
No sunny conclusion

It only continues
The rotten daylight
Nothing sought rectified
Sorry I to her
Oh Hell bring me blackness
Your moon it burns me
Nothing sought rectified
Sorry I to her
Oh how it dances
On a very beating heart

Seasmil laid in his tower, on his bed, alone, wounded and healing, the pages of his poem sticking to the sweat beading off his chest. It had been days since he'd scrambled home. The sight of him had sent Niera into tears and his wife up into the rafters to finally come down demanding answers. His women bandaged him, washed his new bruises, bathed his aching body, and now toiled downstairs as if he were a ghost.

Despite his worry, no one had come to put him in shackles. Staidilia still mourned the fact that angry groups were stopping by to hurl feces and rotten fruit at their door, but the extent of Seasmil's heresy hadn't seemed to have inspired much else. Whenever he limped to his window, there were still those who guarded the vault. That group had dwindled, leaving but two of Irion's and one member of Ansul's True to wait, day and night, for some sign of whom Bone had advised must have been a cloaked and mischievous ghoul.

Work was impossible. Hiring Pelats to attend the morgue had allowed his seclusion. The thought of filing past the three manning the vault had only intensified his despair. They may have been camped around the granite, but they often scowled at the tower.

Niera was ordered not to leave home. A storm was brewing, one he could not afford to break on the head of his charge.

Seasmil peeled the poem from his chest and reached for a bottle of Bleeding Anna. His lips were denied when he heard Staidilia burst through the door. At first it was slamming, then screaming, then feet pounding up the steps until she appeared over him, the basket she'd taken to the market dangling empty in her hand. "I can't take this!" Her hair, brown as a dying leaf, was covered in filth. She'd dodged spit and accusations, only to "run to my own doorway while strangers threw their garbage. Make them stop, Seasmil! Or I'm going to." She suddenly scanned the bedroom. "Where is Niera? She was supposed to—"

He sat up. "What do you mean *where*? She's not downstairs?"

"No!" Her basket hit the floor. "You don't think—"

They were down in a flash. They yelled her name, opened and rummaged through each of her hiding spots. While his wife broke into tears, Seasmil stood for a moment with the knob of their door in his hand. Niera was gone.

To their good fortune, no hecklers barred his way as he ran down to the vault to question Irion's dogs. Oddly, only the holy warrior was there. He greeted Seasmil with a cautious stare.

No matter how many times he'd told her, Niera, so loyal to her own blood, had to disobey her father. And in so doing she hadn't returned. The lone Ansul's True begrudgingly told him: Irion's men had taken her.

✳

The night was cool for Nilghorde. Early enough for the last of the grain carts; their axles squeaked as their wheels clacked over stones, staying on thoroughfares whose lamps were still being lit by workmen. Such convoys had once inspired a different reaction from the poor who swept their stoops and prepared to batten down their windows.

The newest law had been passed. A good citizen should have at least one pound of flour per child per household. This passed due to fiery proclamations that, if not, the city's most dear, most vulnerable may still suffer. The Metropolitan Ward now had sweeping authority to inspect homes to confirm stores. Reasonable suspicion surmised: searches had thus far been triumphantly conducted in the outskirts of districts where coin was hard to come by. Offenders were being swept into the Municipal Dungeon, leaving their children hungry, thus proving the wisdom of both the law and the opening of the newest orphanage.

The Thunder Bustle had yet to be raided. Too large. Too violent. Still too clinging onto a dark past that some whispered had been preferable. Little Pelat, wedged as it was in the black heart of the self-polishing metropolis, crawled with the low street fires and the sullen faces that attended them. A foreign silence hung over the encampment, interrupted by a hard knock on Bone's locked door.

"Mr. Oleugsby?" He peered out, opening his door and inviting Seasmil in.

Seasmil remained in the shadows outside. "I need your help," he said, wasting no time explaining Niera was gone and who had taken her. He'd made up his mind before the long, thoughtless walk had consumed him. Bone had been recklessly noble; enough to desert power and position for this decrepit hovel and constant looks over the shoulder. He might be willing. "Ordrid black magic," Seasmil heard himself saying. "There will be plenty of it where I'm going. A little white magic may go a long way."

"Seasmil," Bone pled, offering again he come inside. "Call upon the Ward. Go home to your wife. No good will come of this."

"My wife is at her mother's, and right now our home is in flames."

"What?!"

"It'll be burned to the ground. One final act of the people on Irion's behalf."

"Seasmil, there is little I can do. You will have to pardon my terseness, but if I wanted to attack Ordrids I would have already done so." Seasmil was a black statue as Bone explained that even if he did come, his presence meant nothing. He could not divine Seasmil's daughter's whereabouts, could not hypnotize another to tell. And certainly, in these sad times, the sight of a former priest would hold no sway. "I'd *still* be in this rotten position."

"A way out of your rotten position then?" Outside the door, Seasmil crossed his arms. Bone had not been able to see his face, but his tone undeniably changed. "Let's talk of a way how."

"Seasmil, your home is apparently burning. Your child is missing. Now is not the time to set up schemes."

"*Now* is *exactly* the time. What do you need?"

"Other than prove the entire clergy's corruption to a regrettably complacent flock?" The man threw up his arms, casting their long shadows through candlelight against his far wall. "Well, let's just say a miracle." He declined Seasmil's request. "I am dreadfully sorry," he said. "About your daughter. I will pray, though, I must confess, I am no longer sure who listens."

Though none could see, Seasmil set his jaw. The muscles in his neck pulled taut as burdened rope. "Fine," he growled, turning from the open doorway. "The fucking archbishop," he blurted, "he opens a fucking orphanage with an Ordrid. If that can't convince your flock he's as corrupt as a worm-eaten apple I don't know what will. Have a good night, Bo—"

"Wait," Bone whispered. "Wait! Come back. Drot is working with the House of Ordrid?"

"Get out of your shack, chaste one. Orphanages. Law. Those two are attached at the purse."

For a moment it seemed Bone was only speaking to himself: "If I can witness…" He scratched his chin, then shot his eyes at

Seasmil. "Or have *you* witness church leadership conspiring with blatant Ordrid devilry—" He pointed to the mirroring bowl still centered on the floor. "Do you think bad Chapwyns will be at that mansion?"

The whole time Seasmil had stood in the darkness. Now he ducked his head and emerged through Bone's candlelight. Bone didn't feel his own mouth fall open. On Seasmil's arms, his black garments, his face that pinned Bone to the wall, were the streaks and flakes of a lathered browning red. "Bad Chapwyns will be there," he promised. "I'm wearing one of them now." Bone's eyes followed Seasmil's hand. In it were a pair of eyes that would guard the Pauper Vault no longer.

Bone drained pale. He knocked over his table and other sticks as he fell, covering his mouth. After a time, he regained his composure, standing, turning to Seasmil with a face made of stone. "I vowed to vanquish evil. Do you have me a sword?"

✳

Seasmil and Bone walked together on Bone's path out of the Bustle. Taking alleyways that scraped their ribs and skirting an imperfect palisade, they moved beyond the fires of Little Pelat, past the last crumbling edges until, seeing the waning inferno of Toadly's old tower, they disappeared inside the Pauper Morgue.

Close to a lifetime of dealing with the dead had bequeathed Seasmil an exploding chest of overlooked items. A murder here, a bar brawl there; given enough time there'd been left unplundered coin and boot and clothing enough to outfit a low-rent merchant. There were three swords.

Picking up one of the finer two, Seasmil bounced its blade in the torchlight. "What a cumbersome weapon." He turned to Bone, who was holding his own as if he'd never seen one before. "I much prefer knives."

"Well," Bone said, taking a clunky swing at the air. "Bring both. Sounds like we'll need them."

And those were the last words spoken. Bone had received much praise in former years. Rarely had merely a priest tapped so deeply into the well of the arcane. He'd learned quick, fumbling and stumbling only to master the crafts necessary to do the greatest good. As he watched Seasmil practice with this hulking sword, long-gone praises refilled his ear. He now saw what his brethren had seen in him. Where a moment before Seasmil swung sloppily, the blood-covered man sliced through the vacuum of the morgue no less proficient than an ancient, gore-mad raider.

Bone watched as Seasmil prepared the morgue's horse. Nothing but an overgrown nag, though as Seasmil hopped on, straddling the beast and seizing its reins in one hand, the mortician appeared a great and mighty warrior.

"Ever been on one?" Seasmil asked.

"Not as often as you."

"Hop on. I'll let you off where we agreed."

✳

On his horse, alone, Seasmil came upon the side gate of the mansion.

His hair, wetted by a feathering of rain, hung over his face as he approached. His sword was drawn, hanging low by his side.

Three guards were ready. Idle stomps from the unarmored nag echoed as one guard detached himself from his post. He walked without words, slowly acknowledging Seasmil by reaching for the horse's reins while the others held steady the points of their spears. The horse blew steam as Seasmil looked up to a lone lit window. In that window, high above the bailey, the district, the world, Irion would be.

Seasmil jammed his heels. His horse reared up, whinnying, kicking the foremost guard square in the face. Amid the shouting, another guard leapt over his twitching cohort to put his spear into the horse's heart. Seasmil went onto the cobblestones, springing to his feet, paying no heed to injury as he whirled his sword upward. Cutting through the guard's armor, he lodged the blade in the dead man's ribs before sliding it out and charging the third. Seasmil slipped past the last spear seamless as a thief, punching the frantic man so hard with the hilt of his sword a mess of enemy teeth went flying. He pulled out his dagger. He followed the guard to the ground to puncture down through a useless breastplate. Then there was silence.

"…Ansul's ass." Bone came out of hiding along the wall to gaze at the carnage. He held his own sword with one hand, using the other to guide him to the blood-covered stones to kneel and pray. As he did, Seasmil rummaged through one of the guard's belts.

"Let's go," Seasmil said, jingling a ring of keys.

When the entered the bailey, the space was empty. "No guards," Bone said, more a question than a sigh of relief.

"They're around."

Together they moved across the dark space. Closer now to the windows, the lower floor had been lit by what appeared through the glass to be an army of candles. The glow flickered against the graves, giving them the hue of being under a low and leering moon. The light had also put on full display the stone and shadow of the side door. Seasmil and Bone climbed its steps, Bone nearly jumping out of his skin when what they'd thought was a statue vibrated to life.

"Dearest," Bone gasped. "It is not alive." Werlyle shuffled forward, silent, covered in the night's leafs, holding out a laden tray. On the tray stood a glass of wine and, splayed out in front of it, Niera's Pelati doll.

Seasmil snatched the toy, bringing it to his chest. Bone reached out to the poor creature and placed his hand on the slave's cold head. With a word the sack of dead bones collapsed, sending the tray clattering against the stairs.

"This place is an abomination."

Seasmil opened his eyes, stuffing the doll in his belt. "Come." Seasmil attempted the first key, then a second. By the third, the two were looking at an unlocked door.

A clanking of armor somewhere out in the darkness marched over the pitter-patter of rain. The returning weather brought with it a howl, sounding all the louder when Seasmil flung wide the door. The massive room before them sat with an oppressive quiet; nothing moved, save for the burning sconces. Bone clutched his sword, fighting an impulse to run down the steps, out of the bailey, and back to his knowable shack. He found courage in Seasmil's determination as he walked solemnly through the doorway.

Determined, yes. Able to be reasoned with, no. Bone's accomplice was beyond the scope of normal retribution. Knowing this, Bone followed, wiping the wet from his brow and squeezing a harder grip on his sword. Bone had assumed he'd follow the killer up a stairway they'd inevitably discover, but that established itself impossible. The sconces hadn't died—they had suddenly, perfectly vanished. The room was lit, but not by candle nor torch nor earthly hearth. They'd entered a realm of great dread, one even a defrocked priest could see.

The floor beneath him felt nothing like wood or stone. He poked where he stood with the tip of his sword. The blade cut into a compliant texture. Mixing with the soft steps of Seasmil, he heard a wail or weep come up from the injured floor. Seasmil turned and took a knee where Bone had struck, running his fingers over the cut before looking up. "This place *is* alive."

And indeed it was. Bone turned his head to where they'd entered, no more than ten paces, and his heart bawled as he saw there was no longer a door. In its stead stretched and wiggled the encroaching wall. He placed one hand on Seasmil's shoulder as they continued through emptiness, stepping on a floor that gave way under their boots. All about them pools of acidic ooze bubbled up to fume the hot, moist air as they struggled to breathe. A wall was before them, pink and glistening. Dead sconces and décor dissolved as the mansion's guts became exactly that. They trudged their way up the beginning of an incline.

A sharp swooshing sound, interspersed with high-pitched growls, forced Bone's attention off of Seasmil's back and into the air. Bat-like creatures flew. Some dove to flutter their fleshy wings before disappearing in the dank void. Pink as the walls, they went up in a collective whirl and then crashed down on them like a wave.

Bone scrambled for the prayers and defensives he'd preloaded, but no holy incantation had anything for the wild swings of Seasmil's sword. As Seasmil would cleave a random flyer, sending it to shadows in pieces, above them loomed a dark figure, darker than all else, a figure Bone was sure, as he faltered his first rite, was the watching lord of this fetid house. Bone took a heroic swing at an approaching bat, missing and lodging his sword permanently into the bleeding wall. Letting go of the hilt, remembering finally a useful string, he yelled out an incantation, slowing the winged beings, bringing them into the full power of Seasmil's blade.

Prompted by instinct, they pursued their exit by climbing up what had shown the last angles of dissolving stairs. "Look!" Bone pointed. "There's a light at the end of the tunnel." As they climbed a stretched breathless throat, stalactites and stalagmites were all that existed between them and the ordinary light of an ordinary room. They dug their boots deep, surpassing the giant fangs by way of walking on a carpet only recognizable as a moist and motionless tongue.

After their nightmare, Bone had never beheld a sight more decent than the well-lit office before them, never sucked in an air more honeyed than the vile station of Irion Ordrid.

"Where is Niera?" Seasmil demanded.

"Just walk on in." Irion said.

Bone couldn't help but spin around, seeing nothing but the opened double doors of the office, a long red carpet, and the sconce-lit stairs it descended down.

Archbishop Drot had jumped at the sight of them, taking a step backward before regaining his bearing. At his side a young priest tried not to stare at the imp that perched on Irion's desk. And, dressed in his most potent robe, Irion was not posing lordly as Seasmil had half-expected. Seasmil's foe sat coolly on his cluttered desk, petting his leering familiar.

"Where's Niera?" Seasmil again demanded, this time taking a hard step into the room.

Irion's feet rested on a large locked chest, which he thumped with a heel. "Somewhere safe."

The young, stupid, insignificant priest held a bag of: "Gold!" Bone cried. "That, Drot, is what you sell our church for?"

Irion looked at Seasmil's belt. "I see you saw Werlyle."

Bone waited for the evil archbishop to speak. Getting nothing, he dared turn to Irion. "That," he said, "undead abomination out there speaks to all our church fought against. Drot, how can you allow such—"

"I must say, Seasmil." Irion waved limply at Bone. "I hadn't anticipated a priest. A real one."

Drot furrowed his brow, deciding wisely not to speak. "You allow such foulness?" Bone cried to the archbishop.

"Is she alive?" Seasmil snarled.

Drot then spoke, addressing his critic. "My dear Bonaveere, how we have searched for you so."

"She most certainly is," Irion answered. "Asleep like a lamb. Don't you worry. There was just much to extract, that's all—a lot in that little head of hers, as *you* well know."

Archbishop Drot extended his soft white hands.

"Bonaveere—*Priest* Bonaveere, think soundly. Do not let your zeal blind you. There is still hope. All can be corrected."

When Seasmil turned to Bone, the warm bath of lies Bone was being soaked in evaporated. "Do you see?" Seasmil said. "The House of Ordrid is in bed with your priests."

"You mean these priests?" Irion said like a song, jumping off his desk to point a straightened finger at the archbishop. The archbishop clutched his throat.

"Oleugsby!" Bone grabbed Seasmil, commanding he not let go of his hand. As Drot went down to flail and gasp on the floor, Bone frantically chanted. Seasmil knew he was being enveloped in some crackling buffer. Through the amassing force Seasmil watched to some degree of glee as the wretched archbishop's face went purple as blood poured from his nose. Irion next pointed his finger at the archbishop's terrified assistant. The young priest clutched his heart, falling on top of the gold he spilled to the floor.

A forceful wave reverberated all about them. Bone opened his eyes, ecstatic his attempt had worked but sent to his knees to vomit upon the sight of Archbishop Drot and his dead, swollen tongue.

"All the better," Irion said, acknowledging the irksome white magic, sending his imp up into the air. He sneered and kicked the chest. "I think I shall make her a slave."

A muffled cry came from the locked wood, in one instant transforming Seasmil's hate into white-hot action. He took a better grip on his sword.

"Stand tall, Irion! Stand tall and die!" he screamed. "You took my daughter. You killed Somyellia, and now blood from a House of war will spill yours clean!"

Charging forward, lifting his sword and drawing his dagger, he brought down the larger blade in a thunderous chop, hewing deep into the desk as Irion rolled over and behind it. Bone yelled out a continuous prayer, stricken by a weariness that buckled his knees. Seasmil swung. Irion touched him in return. The great blade missed, and Irion continued his attack. Soon Irion had punished Seasmil, slipping around and beneath his attempts with deviant quickness, blasting dark energy into his stomach and chest with each slap of his hand.

The grinning skull on the desk shot across the room, but it was the heavy jar that the imp dropped on Bone's head that sent the praying man to the floor. Seasmil did not see the torches and candles all flicker and dim. He swung and stabbed futilely, turning in a flash to swat the approaching imp with the side of his sword. The little fiend squealed, flying out the nearest window as Bone staggered to his feet, praying louder.

"She knew the curse could kill her," Irion hissed, keeping the desk between them. "She *knew* the risk—the cost. It's what one does for family. What would *you*, grime-fly, ever know of such things?"

A fearful noise seized Seasmil. "Bone!" Seasmil yelled, not taking his eye off the neck he aimed to cut. Bone's words ended as he ran to the door, working its iron locks as the rest of Irion's guard force charged up the stairs. Bone leaned against the doors, breathing heavily as swords and axes hacked against the other side. The sounds just beyond a closet door that Irion now pointed at were worse. Hellish moans and bedlam slapped against its wood. Monsters were coming.

"You are trapped, great avenger," Irion said. "And now you'll join who you wished to avenge."

"Wish this," Seasmil wheezed, leaping over the desk with legs that had been stricken more than numb. More a fall than a tackle, he pinned Irion to the wall, suffering the strongest sucking blast yet from his foe's foul hand.

Bone roared over the bursting of the closet door. His frantic prayer did not slow the creep of slimy tentacles, the blinking glitter of fire-swirled eyes, or the sickening paw that reached slowly out of the blackness. Seasmil drove his dagger deep into Irion's gut, wrenching it upward with a hard pull. At the same moment every flame flickered, went out, then burst anew. In the sun-like light, Irion stumbled away, the dagger still in him as he fell back against his desk. He held his arms up to the sky, signifying his surrender. Seasmil watched as he mumbled.

"Speak up," Seasmil commanded, drawing near. "Let me hear your plea."

"What? Yes—yes, Seasmil. Spare me." Irion shut his eyes, bleeding from his wound.

Seasmil felt himself falter. He was unforgiving: remorseless to life and those early in it who'd wronged him. Streets had been painted a darker lacquer of black through his deeds. Flawed and directionless, he'd wandered under indifference, to what good it sickened him to consider. But he'd had a child, prying his eyes to be washed by a light he had been otherwise blind. But some transgressions must remain unforgiven. He gripped his sword with both hands. "There are things more powerful than magic."

"No!" Bone shrieked. "Oleugsby, no! Better a prison. Let us show we—"

Seasmil brought down his sword, driving its blade right through Irion's skull, sending the great Ordrid to the stones in a spew of brains and gore.

Bone hesitated for a moment before dashing to the open closet door to see not a thing crawling forward. "It's empty," he gasped to Seasmil. A very human moan then sent Bone running over to the young priest still sprawled out over the loosened sack of gold. "He's alive!"

But Seasmil was not listening. He stumbled over to the locked chest, severing its lock. Inside lay Niera, bound, gagged, drugged by some potent filth, but joyously alive. He lifted her from her prison, tearing free her binds so she could cry into his neck.

Seasmil felt the stings of Irion's hand fading. He dropped

his sword and looked at his own. "The power of perseverance," he said to his friend, flexing his fingers. "You," he laughed, drunk with pain. "You are far more powerful than that church of yours thought."

But Bone was not listening. He grabbed the young priest by his garments, pulling the battered man upright. The young priest coughed, then puked, then loudly spoke.

"I hated that vile Ordrid—and hated worse," he cried, "that awful archbishop."

"Then why, why did you go along with such devilry?" Bone shook him.

"Because," the man stuttered, still unable to stand. "Like so many, I lived in fear. Fear of black magic. Fear of speaking out. Oh, forgive me brother," he cried into Bone's chest, hugging him with trembling arms until suddenly pulling back with a startling joy. "But now," he said, placing an adoring hand on Bone's cheek. "But now a true hero of the church has emerged."

"That's not a bad idea, Bone," Seasmil said, noticing for the first time the cacophony outside had ceased. He turned and nodded over to where the archbishop lay. "They kind of need of a new leader."

"Yes, yes," the young priest said, not only rising to his feet but helping lift Bone. "I can say Drot wished it so, right before this disgusting Ordrid killed him. The effects of black magic," he forced his eyes away from the ornamented corpse, "they are clear and they will convince all who may doubt us."

Petting his daughter's head, soothing her whimpers, Seasmil could not help but feel a twisted form of amusement. Would Bone—this beauty of humility—accept such a call? Bone walked over and removed from the dead archbishop the official chasuble, placing the bloodied rag over his own shoulders, taking up in that instant the mantel of whatever was left of his church.

"I swear I will testify Irion killed Drot," the young priest reaffirmed, then dropped to his knees to rejoice in his newfound allegiance.

Though the supernatural clatter that had half worked its way out of Irion's closest had permanently ended, the same could not be said for the natural noise of his guard force. Right then, the dozen or so men who'd abandoned their efforts to procure a battering ram used it to burst open the doors and spilled into the room. The sweating wild-eyed men dropped the ram and drew their swords.

"Daddy?" Niera whispered sleepily.

"Take these—look at me," Bone commanded. "Take both of these bodies over to the main Chapwyn temple, now."

The guards stood as if stricken by a spell. "Yes," the young priest jumped in, drawing attention to what Bone now wore. "Yes—you heard the new archbishop. Now get out of our way."

"It's gonna be all right, honey," Seasmil said.

The guards argued amongst themselves, and were still arguing when Seasmil parted their ranks and descended the stairs.

✳

Out on the Nilghorde docks, the sun burned and seagulls mewed. Up into the day's brightness Seasmil watched as the birds wheeled above the great mast of the outbound ship.

Bone had asked he attend, and for that reason alone he suffered the jubilant crowd. Two ceremonies were to go off in a moment where trumpets would sound and confetti would fly. The idea had been not to hold another commencement in Do-Gooder's Row, but out in the salted air of the bustling docks, where, lighter hearts insisted, icons of the virtuous workmen still lived and breathed.

"And there he goes," Archbishop Bonaveere said, climbing down from the platform still being decorated by wreaths of nettielium.

"There he goes," Seasmil said as together they watched the

young priest who'd aided them, not only in his testimony but in an even more recent survey of all things damning in the now-for-sale Ordrid mansion. At the young man's insistence, the new archbishop graciously caved. Now he rode upon the back of a fair horse, up the gangplank of the ship.

"Departing for unknown lands," Bonaveere said with a smile. "To spread the good word."

"Well let's just hope wherever they land is a better place than here. I'm not sure Nilghorde will ever be—hey!" Seasmil said to Staidilia, who'd appeared with Niera on her hip.

"Daddy!" the munchkin squealed, reaching out for him with one hand and in the other holding tight her hideous Pelati doll.

"Hey, handsome," Staidilia said, as if it were the first time he'd heard her, perhaps ever. He looked at his wife, her tested smile, her brown hair shining in the sun like a river.

"Hey there, beautiful."

"Seasmil Oleugsby?" a gruff voice then said. The crowd made room for the approaching Ward. The leader unrolled a lengthy scroll. "You are under arrest for—"

Archbishop Bonaveere, who still had legal powers no man of the cloth should ever wield, used for the first and only time his sway before its banishing by his own hand. "This man," he said, slapping a ringless hand onto Seasmil's broad shoulder, "is hereby pardoned."

"But, Your Grace," stuttered the Wardsmen.

"But nothing, gentlemen. Now enjoy the ceremony. After all, it is you who we must thank for ensuring such gatherings go unmolested."

At that the lawmen dispersed, some floating on a cloud in the light of such flattery as the crowd reabsorbed the Oleugsbys. The new archbishop then winked and pulled out from under his nearly bloodless chasuble a hefty pouch and plopped it in Seasmil's hand. Inside was more gold than he'd seen in a decade of donations to the Institute. "I believe you left this at the mansion," Bonaveere whispered, then winked again. "For a better tower."

"You know," Seasmil said to Staidilia as they watched the archbishop take the steps up to join a throng of bishops doing their best not to appear irate. "I think I know how I can finish my book."

Soon Seasmil's wife and daughter watched as the new church leader nullified a number of church orders amidst a throng of cheers. As the ship set sail, the young priest climbed off his steed and handed the reins to a bowing sailor. He then extended his arm, onto which, floating down from the brood of seagulls, a sickly creature swooped low and perched.

The young priest looked across the water and to Seasmil he smiled. Slung over his shoulder was a black satchel, which he then opened to briefly expose the cool blue of lapis lazuli hand. Then he put his imp deep inside and cinched it down.